PRAISE FOR LAUREN B[...]
ZOMBIE A[...]

"I loved every hilarious moment of this delightfully unique mash-up of *Downton Abbey* meets *The Walking Dead*."

— **Alyson Noël, #1 *New York Times* bestselling author**

"Highbrow British aristocracy meets *The Walking Dead* in this tongue-in-cheek tale, a historical and modern mash-up."

— **Wendy Higgins, *New York Times* bestselling author of *Sweet Evil***

"More scandalous fun than *Downton Abbey*, *Zombie Abbey* is a glorious and zany romp with the undead."

— **Tasha Alexander, *New York Times* bestselling author of *The Counterfeit Heiress***

"Funny and captivating, romantic and horrifying, Baratz-Logsted's fast-paced story will leave readers clamoring for more exciting adventures from their new favorite foursome."

— **Karen Dionne, author of *The Marsh King's Daughter***

ZOMBIE ABBEY

LAUREN
BARATZ-LOGSTED

WITHDRAWN

Entangled Publishing, LLC
2614 South Timberline Road
Suite 105, PMB 159
Fort Collins, CO 80525

Entangled Teen is an imprint of Entangled Publishing, LLC.

Visit our website at www.entangledpublishing.com.

Edited by Stacy Abrams
Cover design by Fiona Jayde
Interior design by Toni Kerr

ISBN: 978-1-63375-911-4
Ebook ISBN: 978-1-63375-912-1

Manufactured in the United States of America

First Edition April 2018

10 9 8 7 6 5 4 3 2 1

For Stacy Abrams: Without you, there is no Zombie Abbey
(plus, you're a lot of fun!)

PROLOGUE

Since the Anglo-Saxon settlement in the fifth and sixth centuries, in the many hundreds of years of its existence, many attacks had been made upon England. Those assaults had come from without, in the form of many wars, and from within, like the Black Plague. No matter how large or severe the threat, however, people still said that the sun would never set upon the British Empire.

But the people who said *that* had never seen anything like *this*.

CHAPTER ONE

Lady Katherine Clarke, Kate to those who were fond of her, just seventeen years old and the eldest of three daughters born to Lord Martin Clarke, the Earl of Porthampton, sat in the drawing room at Porthampton Abbey, listening to her father speak.

If he talks to me about the entail just one more time, she vowed to herself coolly, *I swear I shall blow my brains out.*

Kate knew all about the entail, since she had been hearing talk of it for most of her life, and she'd read her fair share of Austen. Chiefly, it meant that only male heirs could inherit her father's estate. Since there were none of those, it further meant that if she wanted to continue living the life she had grown accustomed to—and she did—and not see what was rightfully hers fall into outside hands, she would have to marry wealthy. And then, if luck were on her side, provide a male heir, posthaste.

In addition to being the eldest daughter, Kate was also the tallest and quite lean. The word "soigné" had been coined to describe creatures just such as her. She was fair-haired with keen eyes that reflected her high intelligence. In short, she was nothing like her father, who was on the stumpy side and balding, and who was fond of saying, "It troubles me not that none of my children resemble me, so long as each, a little bit, resembles her mother."

As the two sat side by side on one of the twin velvet sofas aligned perpendicular to the enormous fireplace, Kate regarded the books lining the room from marble floor to gilt-edged high ceiling. She had read many of the volumes herself and as she looked at them, she thought, not for the first time, that it was entirely possible her father had read none of them at all.

"Tonight at dinner," her father began, "there will be two men I should like for you to pay particular attention to. They are—"

But before Kate could learn who the two latest in the long line of what she privately thought of as "The Man Parade" were to be, her father was interrupted by the entrance of Mr. Ernest Wright, the butler, bearing the tea tray.

Mr. Wright had been with the household for as long as Kate could remember, and she knew he had been there even far longer than that. If she could be said to be fond of anyone outside of Father, it would be Mr. Wright, which wouldn't be saying much, since she really wasn't all *that* fond of anybody.

"Thank you, Mr. Wright," she said, her words and actions dismissing him as she reached for the teapot. "I shall pour."

"Very good, Lady Kate," he replied.

And yet the butler did not move from his position of attention, eyes straight ahead.

Father looked at the butler, then at his daughter, who widened her eyes to express her own lack of knowledge as she shrugged. Every time one thought one knew what to expect from the household staff—strict obedience, silence except when spoken to—they threw some spanner into the works.

"Was there something further, Wright?" Father prompted.

"Thank you, my lord." The servant all but sighed his relief at being asked. "There was a small matter that I did think I should bring to Your Lordship's attention."

"Yes?" Father was forced to prompt a second time when no more information was forthcoming.

Mr. Wright took in a deep breath before letting out with: "Someone has died, sir."

"Oh no!" Father cried. "Oh, I do hope it wasn't one of the members of the staff."

"I agree," Kate said. "Good help is so hard to find."

"It was not one of the staff," Mr. Wright assured them.

"Thank God for that," Kate breathed.

"It was one of the villagers," Mr. Wright said. "More specifically, a crofter—one of the tenant farmers on your land."

"I'm sure it is all very sad," Father said, "for *someone*. But surely people die every day, so I do not understand why you are telling *me* this."

"It is the way he died, my lord."

"The way…?"

"It would appear he was mauled and most of his heart ripped out so that very little of it remained by the time the body was discovered."

"His *heart*?"

"But the most peculiar part is that—"

"More peculiar than *that*?"

"—after the discovery of the body, after many had seen it and declared it dead in the yard, and after the widow said to leave it be until her nephew could be got home to help with the burial, and after the widow herself went back inside the house—"

"That is an extraordinary number of *after that*s, Wright."

"Indeed it is, my lord. And after all that, once everyone was inside and the widow was alone, she heard a sound from the doorway."

"I suspect it was someone coming to pay his or her respects," Father said.

"Hardly, my lord. It was the dead man."

"The one with no heart?"

Mr. Wright nodded.

"What did the widow do?" Father asked.

"She ran and got a shotgun, and then she shot him in the head until he was dead, my lord."

"But he was already dead," Kate pointed out.

Father considered for a moment. "Won't the widow hang for this?"

Both servant and daughter looked at him, perplexed.

"For what?" Kate asked.

"Why, for killing her husband," Father said. "I am fairly certain that in England, killing one's husband is still a hanging offense."

"Did you not hear what Mr. Wright said earlier, Father? The man was already dead!"

"Everyone does appear to agree on that part, Lady Kate," Mr. Wright said. "Everyone says the man was most definitely already dead."

"You see, Father?" Kate said, satisfied. "The widow will not hang. You cannot hang for shooting at someone already dead."

"Precisely," Mr. Wright agreed. "Everyone agrees that when the dead man was first found, while his heart was mostly missing, he most definitely did not have any bullet holes in him, although he does have them now."

Father looked thoroughly confused. "But if the man was dead, then how did he appear at the door?"

Mr. Wright and Lady Kate shared a look.

"Of course he didn't appear at the door, Father."

"But Wright said—"

"I know what he said, since I was sitting right here, but surely he meant that the widow only *thought* her dead husband had appeared in the doorway. The poor woman was no doubt so overcome with grief and terror that she only hallucinated her husband there."

"Most of the villagers agree with you, Lady Kate."

"I should think so. But wait. Only *most*?"

"I'm afraid there are others who believe that the widow was not hallucinating at all, Lady Kate. These others are now terrified at the notion of a dead man walking."

"But that is absurd!"

"I agree with you, Lady Kate, but you know how the villagers can be."

"I do indeed, Mr. Wright. They are, to a man, a superstitious bunch."

"Not only am I confused now," Father said with some annoyance, "but I also still do not know: *Who died?*"

"I'm sorry, my lord. I should have named the dead man earlier. It was Ezra Harvey."

Father considered briefly and then shook his head.

"Longtime tenant farmer?" Mr. Wright added helpfully. "Always quick with a joke?" He thought about this last, a rueful look overtaking his features. "Well, he was."

More consideration, more head shaking.

"Uncle to William Harvey?" Wright tried one last time. "William Harvey, who himself is known to the household as Will?"

"Will Harvey... Will Harvey..." Father tapped his lip. "Now, why does that name sound so familiar?"

"Because he is our stable boy?"

Kate gasped a smile as her elegant hand flew to her breastbone, sitting up even straighter if such a thing were possible. "The handsome one," she said, eyes flashing.

Kate couldn't have rightly said why she didn't admit immediately to recognizing Will Harvey's name as soon as Wright uttered it, because of course she did. Kate went to the stables nearly every day of her life, and every time she went there, Will Harvey was there, too. If, to Father, someone like Will Harvey was just a nameless person carrying out a necessary function on the estate, to Kate he was the person who took best care of that which she loved best outside of Father: the horses in general and, in particular, Wyndgate.

But it was more than that. When she'd been just three years old, she'd been taken to the stables for her first riding lesson. No sooner had the horse master got her seated than from the corner of a stall, a small voice was heard to cry with joy, "Horsey!" When questioned by the horse master, the little boy explained that he'd been playing on his aunt and uncle's farm but somehow, in his running and roaming, had wound up here.

"Horsey!" he'd cried again.

"Yes, well," the horse master had said, seeing Will Harvey's evident love and accompanying lack of fear as he walked among the great beasts, "you can stay for this one day, but then off you go back home. You can come back again when you're six—no, make that seven—and help out as a junior stable boy."

And so, for that one day in her life, Kate had had a friend—not her younger sister Grace, still a toddler at two, and so, useless to her; not her youngest sister, Lizzy, still a baby and so, more useless yet, but a real friend. Someone who loved horses as much as she had immediately loved them.

The event no doubt would have faded from memory, as most things experienced by three-year-olds do, were it not for the fact that for day upon day afterward, despite what the horse master had said, she'd looked for Will's return.

And when he didn't, he became a fixture in her mind, like an imaginary friend who might yet be made real. That day represented her earliest memory in life. There was nothing before it, not even memories of her parents, only after. Just one day, when she'd had a friend. But no matter how much she'd looked for him after that, he didn't come back for four years.

Then, seemingly out of the blue, he showed up and announced to the horse master, "I am seven today, and I am here for my job as junior stable boy."

Kate, already an accomplished rider for her age, slid off her horse to greet him, but with only one foot on the ground and one still in the stirrup, she had been approached by the horse master, who had whispered harshly in her ear, "That boy is not for you, Lady Kate. He is one of the help, and your father would be most displeased to see you treating him as anything more."

Oh! The bitter cruelty of being asked to give up the one friend she'd ever made!

But if there was one thing Kate loved more than the horses, it was Father. And so the line had been drawn. Will Harvey was a stable boy and Kate was a lady of the house, however young a lady she might be. Over the ten years since, they'd exchanged the occasional inadvertent smile because, both loving horses as they did, how could they not? But she would never cross that line again.

Still, while she might not immediately admit recognizing his name, as soon as Wright identified him to Father as the stable boy, the playful—and in some ways, more honest—side of her nature couldn't help but utter that line about him being "the handsome one," and so...

"Katherine!" Her father was outraged. "He's *a stable boy*!"

The stable boy, now grown almost to manhood, had

longish brown hair with a light wave to it and kissed by the sun, brown eyes that leaned toward green framed by sinfully long lashes, and a naturally muscular body made further so by labor. To see him ride was to envy the horse.

"Well," she said, unconcerned, "that doesn't stop his being handsome."

Father threw up his hands at this. "Is there anything else, Wright? And why did you bring me this news in the first place?"

Now it was the butler's turn to appear perplexed. "Why, because, as head of the household, head of Porthampton Abbey, and head of the entire village, you are not only the financial leader of everyone beneath you, but the spiritual one as well. In that capacity, I thought it only correct that you be informed about any major concerns—and I do stress *major*—the villagers have."

"Yes, yes, you have informed me and now I know." Father waved a dismissive hand. "The superstitious villagers fear a dead man walking." He rolled his eyes. "You may go now, Wright."

"Very good, my lord."

After the butler had bowed himself out, Father turned once more to the ongoing matter of his eldest daughter.

"Where were we again?" Not waiting for an answer, he continued. "Ah yes! Now, about that dinner tonight…"

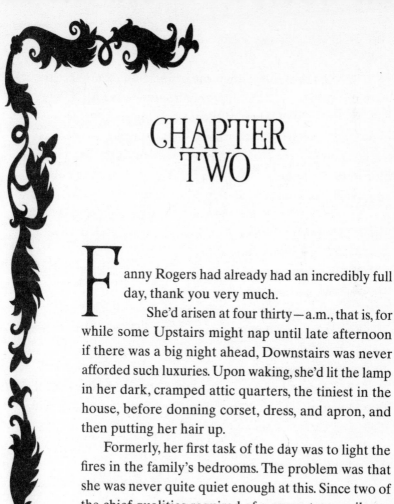

CHAPTER TWO

F anny Rogers had already had an incredibly full day, thank you very much.

She'd arisen at four thirty—a.m., that is, for while some Upstairs might nap until late afternoon if there was a big night ahead, Downstairs was never afforded such luxuries. Upon waking, she'd lit the lamp in her dark, cramped attic quarters, the tiniest in the house, before donning corset, dress, and apron, and then putting her hair up.

Formerly, her first task of the day was to light the fires in the family's bedrooms. The problem was that she was never quite quiet enough at this. Since two of the chief qualities required of a servant were silence and invisibility, and Fanny was not much good at either, this job was taken away from her and given to one of the housemaids, who didn't appreciate the extra work. Fanny, for her part, didn't mind in the slightest having one less thing to do, since she had so many tasks already.

After dressing, she made her way down to the cavernous kitchen to prepare the stove for the day ahead and put out breakfast for the servants in the hall just off the kitchen.

Then she woke the remaining housemaids and set to work laying fires in all the important rooms on the main floor. Despite her lack of talent at silence and invisibility, she was permitted to keep this task, since it did not intrude in any way on those still sleeping upstairs. First, she cleaned the fireplaces of residue from the day before, after which she put in paper and wood and kindling, finally setting flame to it.

From there, straight to the kitchen for an almost endless round of helping the cook, Mrs. Dorothy Owen—Dot to her friends—with anything and everything.

Clean the dishes from the servants' breakfast, help prepare the food for the family's breakfast, wash the dishes and scour the pots and pans afterward. And then repeat the process for lunch and dinner, with each meal more elaborate than the last.

By the time she finished her day, she would have worked at least seventeen hours straight with only precious few stolen moments to sit down. She did this six and a half days a week, for Fanny was the kitchen maid.

Fanny was seventeen, looked twelve, and had been with the household since exactly that age.

In fact, her only real break came at four in the afternoon, nearly a dozen hours after she'd first arisen, when the servants— or at least those who could afford to spare a few minutes from whatever current task was at hand—took their own tea.

On this particular day, those with the few moments to spare who were seated around the wooden plank table in the servants' hall included: Mrs. Ruth Murphy, the housekeeper, the big set of keys tied at her waist jangling even as she took her place at one head of the table; Myrtle Morgan, Her Ladyship Fidelia Clarke's personal maid; Agnes Hunt, the head housemaid whose chief task was tending to Lady Katherine; Becky Hill, another housemaid and the inheritor of Fanny's early morning task of lighting the fires in the family rooms; and Mrs. Owen, the cook.

Absent, because occupied elsewhere, were: Mr. Ernest Wright, butler; Mr. Albert Cox, Lord Clarke's valet; Jonathan Butler, the first footman; and Daniel Murray, the second footman.

Fanny sighed to herself over the absence of men—she did prefer the men to the ladies—and she sighed even harder over the absence of Jonathan Butler and Daniel Murray. Both were a bit past twenty, Fanny considered both to be passing handsome, and she would welcome either as a life mate, were she ever to be so lucky, as she very much wanted to be. Fanny dreamed of the day she would marry a passing handsome man who would take her away from all this, or at the very least, give her some company at night and cause to move out of her wretchedly tiny room.

Ah well. Even if no men were in sight, she could at least take this welcome break to burst out with what she had scarce been containing inside her little body for hours now.

"I think it must've been a vampire, don't you?" she gushed at the table, eyes open wide.

"What *are* you talking about, Fanny?" Mrs. Owen asked as she slathered a thick slice of bread with butter.

"Why, the thing that got Mr. Harvey," Fanny said, rearing back a bit as though Mrs. Owen might be daft. "Will Harvey's uncle." She sighed when she said the name, Will Harvey being one whom she found even more handsome than the footmen, even if Will Harvey smelled earthy and never wore a fancy clean suit of livery like the others did. "Did you not hear what the deliveryman said when he brought the things to the back door earlier? About the death of Ezra Harvey?"

"Of course I did, but—"

"What other explanation can there be?" Fanny said, eyes

wide once more. "You have a man with his heart ripped out, clearly dead, and then next thing, he's up and walking around again, forcing his wife to shoot him in the head."

Myrtle Morgan and Agnes looked decidedly queasy at this, pushing their plates away, while Becky shuddered.

"Fanny!" Mrs. Murphy admonished. "I hardly think this is—"

"I know what you're going to say, Mrs. Murphy," Fanny cut her off. "You're going to say that I shouldn't be saying such things while the others are trying to enjoy their tea. But I've read Mr. Bram Stoker's *Dracula*, you see, and the only explanation for how a dead person can then be not dead, however briefly, is if that person were attacked by a vampire to begin with and then became one himself." A puzzled look came over her face. "Of course, that doesn't explain how Mrs. Harvey could have killed him with a shot to the head—in Mr. Bram Stoker's *Dracula* it has to be either a sacred bullet, which I doubt Mrs. Harvey would have on hand, *or* a stake through the heart, or you can even decapitate it and stuff garlic in the mouth—but still, if there's a vampire loose in the village, don't you think we all ought to know about it so we can be properly prepared?"

"*Fanny!*"

The voice that admonished her this time did not come from Mrs. Murphy. This voice was male, which should have been welcome to her, except it came from neither Jonathan nor Daniel, the two passing handsome young footmen. Rather, it came from Mr. Wright, the butler himself.

"What is the meaning of this?" he demanded.

"I was only trying to explain to the others," she said, "how whatever attacked Mr. Harvey must have been a vampire, turning him into one, too, because that's the only possible explanation—"

"Enough!" Mr. Wright raised a firm hand. "Where *do* you get these ideas?"

Fanny began to explain again about Mr. Bram Stoker's *Dracula*.

"Enough!" If anything, the hand was firmer now; the voice certainly was. "I knew I never should have taught you to read. I forbid you to discuss this nonsense any further."

Of course, Mr. Wright was wrong. He hadn't taught her to read. She'd learned some in compulsory school, which she'd been in until age ten, and then taught herself the rest. *But, she thought, it might not be the best time to correct him on this matter.* Mr. Wright never liked being told he was wrong, particularly when he was already angry.

"All right, Mr. Wright," Fanny said, lowering her eyes to her plate.

But all the while she thought, *I could be right.*

CHAPTER THREE

Normally, Will Harvey enjoyed a good long walk, no matter how far and no matter what the weather. But when he'd received word earlier in the day that his aunt had sent for him, that something horrible had befallen his uncle, Will had borrowed one of the horses from the stables at Porthampton Abbey, riding hell-for-leather until he'd arrived at the little croft his uncle had tended for as long as Will could remember.

He'd dismounted to a scene of chaos. His aunt stood over the corpse of his uncle, still screaming—his aunt, not the corpse. There were villagers as well, too many to count, nor could he remember now who all had been there so he could name them in his mind. It had taken some doing, but eventually, he'd managed to piece together the story.

His uncle had gone out early, as was his habit, to do a bit of farming. But when late-morning teatime came and went, and he had not yet returned, Will's aunt had gone out looking for him.

She'd found him not far from the humble cottage, his body mauled by some animal, his heart ripped out. Her screams had been loud enough to draw the closest neighbors, and word had spread from there.

Everyone was adamant: his uncle had been dead. There was no possible earthly way he could have survived that gaping hole in his chest.

Will had been sent for, but it was a long walk to Porthampton Abbey on foot, and once there, it had taken the messenger some time to have Will located so he could deliver his sad message.

After the messenger had departed to find Will, some of the neighbors stayed behind with Will's aunt, at least until the hysterics had passed. But then they'd returned to their own homes, their own farms. Because, bad as they felt for Jessamine Harvey, there was ever the work, always more work to be done. From dawn until bedtime, it was the life of the farmer.

It was after everyone had gone that Will's aunt had heard a noise and, turning, saw a man—no, a monster, she'd said—standing in the open doorway. When he lurched her way in a menacing fashion, she didn't think twice before grabbing the shotgun and shooting him several times in the head. It was only when she was sure he was dead that her mind cleared and, recognizing the clothes she'd seen just that morning, knew it to be her husband.

If anything, she screamed louder this time.

The villagers came again, which was where things stood when Will arrived.

Everyone believed her. As crazy as her story sounded, everyone believed her.

They'd all seen Ezra Harvey dead, over there—they knew it to be true—and now he was dead in quite a different way, over here.

More than one villager clasped hands to breast and prayed.

How was such a thing possible?

A dead man walking.

But then one of the villagers thought to run to get Dr. Zebulon Webb—chiefly, the doctor to the Clarkes; secondarily, the doctor to the village—and when he arrived, he offered a different interpretation.

"Jessamine," he said, "grief, as I know too well, can take many forms."

The widow tried to interrupt, but even as he spoke gently, he would not let her.

"And *your* grief," Dr. Webb went on, "has taken the form of a hysterical hallucination."

"I know what I saw," she insisted.

"But what you have described is simply not medically possible."

"Explain this to me, then: If there is blood on the grass over yon, where he died, then how did the body get here?"

"Why, that is easy. In your hysterical grief, no doubt wishing your husband still alive, you dragged the body here yourself. As for the rest of what happened afterward? More hysterical grief. I am deeply sorry for your loss."

But not so sorry that he didn't excuse himself five minutes later to go home and change for a dinner engagement up at the abbey.

Not long afterward, the neighbors had dispersed. For a grieving neighbor, they no doubt would have stayed a bit longer. But for a neighbor whom the doctor described as hysterical? A word that sounded too alarmingly close to "insane" to their minds? Nobody wanted to remain too close to that. They'd been drawn along for a time by the madness, but now their minds had been cleared by the doctor's reassurances—the doctor was, after all, a man of science, wasn't he?—and it was time for them to go. As has been said, there was always the work.

Now, as for the past several hours, it was only Will and his aunt.

As night had fallen, he'd lit the lamps for her and as many candles as he could find—it didn't feel as though the sad home could possibly be made too bright now.

Then he'd sat in a chair next to hers before the fire he'd made in the small fireplace. And as he sat, he tried not to think about his uncle, or what remained of him, lying under a sheet upon the table in the kitchen, legs extending over the edge. It would be the next day before a hole could be dug in the churchyard to bury the body, and they'd not wanted to leave him outside where the animals might get at him. Or perhaps it would be more accurate to say: get at him *further*, Will thought, a laugh almost escaping. How could he think to laugh, even if it was only almost, at a time like this? With his uncle, whom he had loved, the only father he'd ever known, dead and in such a horrible fashion? It occurred to him then that he just might be near hysteria himself, and not the hysteria of mirth but of madness brought on by grief.

But he couldn't let any of that show. There was Aunt Jess to think about, to take care of.

Outside, when there had still been other people crowded around, Will had not had the opportunity to view his uncle closely. But when he'd carried him the few steps from the doorway to the kitchen table and laid him down there, he'd finally had the opportunity. He dearly wished now that he hadn't taken it.

He would not look again.

He wondered if his aunt was feeling the same near-hysteria he was at the thought of his uncle lying there, how he looked under the sheet.

Will stole a glance at his aunt. She was not yet forty, and while she had always appeared older than her years, tonight she looked twenty years older. He would have liked to comfort her, to offer some small sympathy in the form of an embrace, but her ramrod posture told him that, just now, such a gesture would not be welcome.

It had been so long since either had uttered a word that it came as something of a surprise when his aunt said, "You believe me, don't you?"

His instinct was to open his mouth and immediately reassure her—he could do at least that much for her, couldn't he?—but then it occurred to him that what she would want, far more than any reassurance, would be the truth.

Fifteen years ago, when he was but two years old, both of Will's parents had been taken by the influenza. With no other relatives able or willing to take on a child, he'd been taken in by his aunt and uncle, who'd never had any children of their own.

He didn't remember a thing about his own parents. But he knew everything about his uncle and aunt. His uncle had taught him the value of a hard day's work—to Will's mind, no man had ever worked harder than his uncle. His aunt had taught him the value of the truth—no woman had ever been more honest than she.

Perhaps he'd waited too long to answer, because his aunt spoke once more, this time on a topic wholly unrelated.

Perhaps, after all, she did not want to hear his answer if it would not be in her favor.

"Won't they be mad up at the house," she said with a gesture of her chin, as though the house might be just a few feet away instead of the distance it was, "that you never came back today?"

"They won't be," he said, "and if they are, it is of little matter."

"Little matter? And what would your uncle say if he could

hear you now? We're talking about your *job*, boy."

"And it is a job that I am extraordinarily good at. There are other grooms and stable boys at Porthampton Abbey, but even the master of the house has said: none are better, even if he never seems able to remember my name. So they will hold my job for me today. If you need me tomorrow, they will hold it then, too. However long I need, that long will they wait for me."

"You seem too sure of yourself, Will. Perhaps too proud, too."

And yet he could see, from the first glimmer of joy he'd seen in her eye on this most wretched of days, that she was proud of him, too.

He thought about everything this woman had been to him—she and his uncle both—and how steady she had always been, no matter what the world and life threw her way.

She had always been honest.

She had never been the slightest bit insane.

There were still so many questions, and yet...

"I find that I do not want to believe you," he began carefully, determined to make sure that each word rang true. "I do not want to believe you, because the tale you tell is so...*fantastical*, I don't wonder that others doubt its truth. And yet I further find that, based on everything I have ever known about you, no matter how impossible what you claim happened might seem, I cannot but believe that the impossible must be—*somehow*—possible."

She stared at him long and hard then, as though looking to see if he were only speaking so to humor her. Whatever she saw must have satisfied her, however, for at last her body lost its ramrod posture as she near collapsed with visible relief. No matter what else had happened that day, clearly the very worst was the sensation that no one believed her. And even if everyone else went on disbelieving her, perhaps even that would be all right so long as she still had Will and his belief.

"Thank you," she breathed.

And when he moved closer, she did permit him to embrace her.

Tears came then. Not like the hysterical ones earlier in the day; these were tears of pure sadness, and Will's eyes, at last, dampened, too.

"There's one more thing I need to ask of you," she said.

"Anything, Auntie."

"That…" She inclined her head toward the kitchen. "That… I cannot wait until tomorrow and the churchyard. I cannot think with it there. That… In the end, I swear, that was no longer him."

"Hush now," Will said. "It is all right." He took one of her work-worn hands in one of his, patting the back of it with his other. "Then we shall burn it."

CHAPTER FOUR

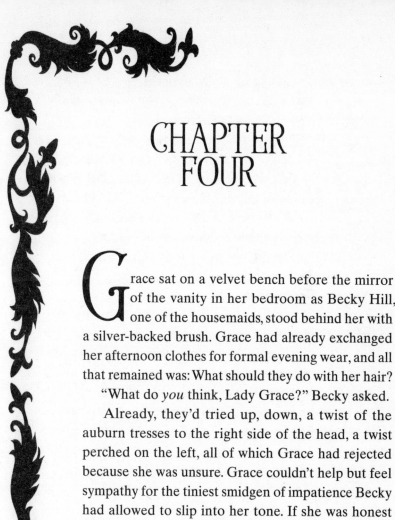

Grace sat on a velvet bench before the mirror of the vanity in her bedroom as Becky Hill, one of the housemaids, stood behind her with a silver-backed brush. Grace had already exchanged her afternoon clothes for formal evening wear, and all that remained was: What should they do with her hair?

"What do *you* think, Lady Grace?" Becky asked.

Already, they'd tried up, down, a twist of the auburn tresses to the right side of the head, a twist perched on the left, all of which Grace had rejected because she was unsure. Grace couldn't help but feel sympathy for the tiniest smidgen of impatience Becky had allowed to slip into her tone. If she was honest with herself—and she always tried to be—she'd have to admit that even *she* was impatient with her own inability to decide on such a simple matter.

"Oh," she finally said with mild disgust at herself, "just do whatever you think is best. I'm sure it will be fine."

Grace thought to herself how Becky, just a year older than Grace's own sixteen, always looked so tidy with every brown hair perfectly in place. Of course, Becky, most of the articles of her appearance dictated by uniform code, had little choice in the matter, but still.

"Well, *I* think you should just cut it all off!" came a giggling voice from the canopy bed behind her.

Grace swiveled the top half of her body to see her younger sister, Elizabeth—alternately Eliza, Liza, Lizzy, or Bess, depending on who was speaking to her, but mostly Lizzy—propped up on both elbows as she stretched out on her stomach across the bedspread, her legs bent at the knee so that her calves swung back and forth in the air.

"Lizzy!" Grace said, not unkindly. "You'll wrinkle your dress!"

"Oh, who cares about that?" Lizzy said blithely.

Grace well knew that her sister, younger by one year, cared little about her appearance. Not that she needed to. With her long black hair, worn down tonight as it was most nights, and her blue eyes, Lizzy could have worn sackcloth and ashes and she'd still manage somehow to look pretty.

Becky had dressed Lizzy and done her hair first, brushing it one hundred times before coming to Grace. The head housemaid, Agnes Hunt, would get Kate ready, putting the final touch in place just immediately prior to Kate's descending from the gallery to the waiting guests below so she might look as perfect as perfect could be.

"No one will be paying any attention to us," Lizzy said, stating the obvious as Grace returned to her reflection in the mirror. "Not that I mind. I would *hate* to be poor Kate."

"Hate" was not a word that Grace ever used lightly herself, although it was a word that tripped lightly off Lizzy's tongue. But then, most words did. Lizzy was given to chatter, not that Grace minded, for even when Lizzy uttered seemingly distasteful words like "hate," Grace could not be bothered by it, for Lizzy said it all so cheerfully. If only Grace could be so eternally cheerful or, at least, bolder in her speech.

She had to admit, though, in this instance, she agreed with Lizzy. She, too, would hate to be Kate. All the responsibility of being the eldest!

Grace knew that if her parents had had three sons instead of three daughters, those sons' paths in life would have been dictated by British tradition: the eldest would be the heir; the second would go into the British Navy; the third would enter the clergy. It was what people did. Grace could easily picture the same befalling her and her sisters had they been born male, but with a slight variation. Kate would be the heir, of course, but the other two would need to be flipped no matter what the birth order, with Lizzy—brave Lizzy—destined for the military, while Grace, who didn't have a brave bone in her body, would be consigned to the church.

They weren't boys, of course, but to Grace's mind, their destinies had still been prescribed early on and by their birth order: Kate, entitled and endowed with the mission to marry well and provide a male heir; Lizzy, as the youngest, allowed to traipse through life with no one much caring if she ever acquired any knowledge beyond basic manners, so long as she went on being adorable; and Grace, somehow lost in the middle.

Becky began to work on Grace's hair again, and it appeared as though the style she'd settled upon was the same one she'd had in the first place, before all the variations.

Which was fine with Grace.

"Did you know," Lizzy said, "that there are going to be *two* this evening?"

"Two what, Lizzy?"

"Why, two men, of course!"

"Two men? I'm sorry, I don't follow."

"For Kate! What were we just talking about?"

"I'm sorry, but I still don't follow."

"Well." Lizzy lowered her voice conspiratorially, even though only the three of them were in the room, and the solid door was firmly shut. "*I* heard Father tell Kate that there were *two* possible suitors coming to dinner this evening, one named Raymond Allen and the other Meriwether Young, and that Kate was supposed to be particularly polite to both of them." Lizzy considered what she'd said and then made a face. "I don't know about you, but I should *hate* to be married to a man named Meriwether. What would I call him? Meriwether? Merry?" She shook her head. "Not that I ever want to be married to anybody."

"How do you know all this?" Grace asked.

"Because I happened to be passing by the drawing room while they were speaking. Their hushed voices made it sound like whatever they were saying might be interesting, so I stopped to listen. Why? Should I not have done that?"

In the reflection of the mirror, Grace could see her sister behind her on the bed and the look of innocence upon her face. If it were anyone else, Grace might suspect it to be a faux innocence, but Grace knew in her sister it was genuine.

"When you heard them speaking privately," Grace suggested gently, "you might have kept walking. Did that never occur to you?"

"But why would I do that?" Lizzy countered. "And if they really wanted to talk privately, then why did they not do so in a less public place?"

Grace could not think of anything to defeat that logic.

"Do you know anything about either Raymond Allen or Meriwether Young?" Lizzy asked when her sister said nothing.

"I believe Raymond Allen is some sort of duke," Grace said. "But Meriwether Young?" She shook her head. "That one is a mystery to me as well."

"Poor Kate," Lizzy said again. "It was bad enough when suitors were paraded in here one at a time. But now they are coming in twos? What next—*threes*?" She shuddered. "Oh, I would *hate* to be poor Kate."

"Father is just concerned about the entail," Grace said. "Mother, too. They only want to ensure that Kate, as the eldest, will be provided for."

"The *entail*!" Lizzy spoke the word with a scorn that was rare for her. "That's all anyone ever talks about around here anymore. And if and when they *do* get Kate settled, what happens next?" She pointed a finger at Grace and then back at herself. "Will you, and then I, be subjected to the same bombardment of strange men, just to avoid the entail? Here is what I would like to know: If *this* was going to happen, then why did Father get an entail in the first place?"

"But Lizzy, that's not really how an entail—"

"And here is the other thing I would like to know," Lizzy said, cutting her off.

Grace waited for it. In her experience, whenever Lizzy got that particular look in her eye, whatever followed could only be what was termed a doozy.

"Why didn't Father and Mother have fourteen more children?" Lizzy said at last.

"Pardon? I'm not sure I follow."

"Well, Kate is seventeen, you are sixteen, I am fifteen." Lizzy ticked the sisters off on her fingers. "But why did they stop there? They obviously could have one child per year—that is the rate they had clearly established. So why did they not continue doing so for the past fourteen years if need be? Surely if they had done *that*, then they would have wound up with a boy child in there at least *somewhere*, and then none of us would have to worry anymore about the silly entail."

At this announcement, Grace's eyes met Becky's in the

mirror, and she could see that the housemaid was doing her best to fend off a laugh, as she herself was.

Grace wished she had the courage to explain to Lizzy exactly how procreation really worked, but all she could settle on was, still fighting the giggles, "I don't think it works quite like that."

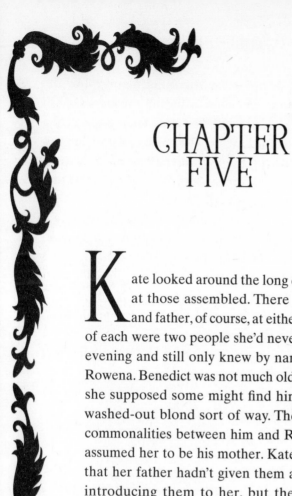

CHAPTER
FIVE

Kate looked around the long dining room table
at those assembled. There were her mother
and father, of course, at either end. To the right
of each were two people she'd never met before this
evening and still only knew by name, Benedict and
Rowena. Benedict was not much older than Kate, and
she supposed some might find him handsome in a
washed-out blond sort of way. There were enough
commonalities between him and Rowena that Kate
assumed her to be his mother. Kate found it strange
that her father hadn't given them a last name when
introducing them to her, but then, she'd arrived
downstairs so late, entirely missing the cocktail hour,
for Agnes would keep fussing around her until Agnes
was satisfied everything was perfect, that there'd only
been time for the briefest of introductions before
going in to supper.

In addition to her parents and the two mysterious
strangers, there were also on the opposite side to
Kate: Dowager Countess Hortense Clarke, Kate's
grandmother; Grace and Lizzy, of course; and Dr.
Zebulon Webb. There was also her mother's father, but
since, after introducing himself to everyone, whether

they'd met before or not—"George King; George, like the king, and King because of course"—he had a tendency to fall asleep wherever he was, even at the dinner table, it wasn't like he mattered all that much. When awake, he could sometimes be counted upon to keep Kate's grandmother on her father's side in line, but only if he remembered who she was and that his final mission in life was to dislike her.

Although there was ample elbow room on her side, Kate couldn't help but feel herself uncomfortably sandwiched between Raymond Allen to her right and Meriwether Young to her left. Regarding the latter, he was anything but what his name would imply, meaning that he was not young at all. Indeed, he looked even a smidgen older than Father, although it could just be that he was so portly. Kate fancied herself a person who knew how the world worked, and so she knew that sometimes, due to circumstance and for money and position— sometimes perhaps even for love—a young woman her age might find that life had landed her a husband far older than herself. Despite this knowledge, Kate was determined that *that* life should not become *her* life.

It was with relief, then, that when the soup course was completed and the Dover sole brought in on trays by footmen serving them with white-gloved hands, she turned her attention away from Mr. Young and all his nattering on about his various businesses in London. Now she could turn to Raymond Allen.

In his favor?

He was at least young and not merely by name.

Working against him?

He had an unfortunate pair of jug ears.

And carroty red hair.

One of those physical features might have been just barely tolerable, but both?

Oh well, she thought, *at least I won't be forced to practically shout my answers to him like I felt compelled to with half-deaf Mr. Young.*

Not that he really seemed hard of hearing, but he was so much older, it was simply easier for her to imagine him so.

Despite this asset of youth, Raymond Allen just didn't seem attractive to her in any way. For while it might be small-minded to dismiss a man for the regrettable size of his ears, it certainly was not a feature to recommend him.

Only good breeding and manners prevented her from sighing her dismay out loud. Honestly. If her parents were now going to parade suitors before her two at a time, one would think that would double the chances of her finding one to her taste. But these two?

Surreptitiously, she glanced around the room for at least some visual relief, and she did eventually find that. Sadly, the relief she found was in the form of the two footmen—whom she knew of only as the two footmen—standing at attention; unlike with the stable boy, she'd never felt any compulsion to learn their names. Not only were these two young, but each was handsome in a pleasing way, not like that stranger, Benedict. It was really too bad that neither could get her out of her financial pickle, but even though the way they held themselves in livery presented a good omen for how they might look in more proper formal dress, the idea of romance with someone from the serving class was laughable.

Before Kate could ponder this any further, Raymond Allen surprised her by actually saying something interesting.

"I took the train down from London today," he said.

"How marvelous for you!" she replied. "I do love London. I should make it a point to get up there soon."

"When I debarked, I heard the most interesting thing."

"Do tell. I enjoy hearing about interesting things as

opposed to those things that are not."

"People were talking about a mysterious event that occurred in your village earlier today. Something about a dead man briefly coming back to life?"

"Oh!" Kate exclaimed, truly delighted now. "You have heard about our dead man walking!"

"I hate to contradict you, Lady Kate," Dr. Webb interjected, "but that is *not* what really happened."

Then he proceeded with a tiresome account of how what people had *thought* had happened in the first place had not really happened at all; that it had all been the result of hysterical grief on the part of the dead man's widow and that no one dead had come back to life.

Even though Katherine had already guessed as much herself, and had said so earlier to her father and Mr. Wright, it would to her mind have made for more lively dinner conversation to have it the other way.

"What a shame," Kate said, still smiling. "I did so prefer the first version better."

"How can you make—what is the proper word—*light* of this?" her youngest sister spoke up, Lizzy's brow furrowed in rare outrage. "A man has died! A man whose nephew is employed by this household!"

"I do feel dreadful for poor Will Harvey," Grace added, although she did not meet Kate's eyes when she said this.

There were times when Kate wished one sister more courageous (not if Grace was going to defy her, of course) and the other more intelligent (had Lizzy really struggled to find a word as simple as "light"?).

Not to mention, so much fuss on behalf of the stable boy—she promised herself she would not think of him in any other way anymore, however handsome. A part of her did wonder, even worry, over the pain he must be feeling at the loss of his uncle. But then she tamped that part of herself down. Her job was to go on being bright and vivacious for the suitors, however ghastly those suitors might be.

"How typical of you, Grace," she said, "how typical and quaint to actually be bothered to know the name of the stable boy."

But then Kate noticed that it was not just her sisters who were showing disapproval at her words. Raymond Allen, an appalled look on his face, had turned to strike up a conversation with the person on his other side, and it wasn't even time to switch sides yet.

Was she really to be spurned by a carroty-haired man with jug ears?

It really was all too much, so it was with considerable relief when the whole sorry meal ended an hour later and it came time for the men to depart for their port—Grandfather had to be awakened first so that he could then go and drink—while the ladies retired to talk about the latest fashions and gossip among themselves.

Not that Kate was particularly looking forward to *that*.

Before the gender separation could occur, however, her father stopped her.

"Kate," he called. "Won't you come here?"

Standing with him were the two relative strangers.

"I'd like to properly introduce you to Benedict Clarke and Rowena Clarke," he said.

"Clarke?" she echoed, for the first time realizing not only were these two relative strangers strange, but they were also quite possibly relatives.

"Yes," her father said. "I received word late today of their existence. Benedict's father was a far-distant cousin and, apparently, Benedict himself is a male heir with a future claim to Porthampton Abbey."

As Kate shook hands with these new relations with as much grace as she could muster, already she could see her father's wheels spinning: *if Kate will only accept Benedict as her suitor, then all our problems will be solved!*

Meanwhile, all Kate herself could think was, *How dreary. Just like in Austen: Isn't there always a male heir?*

CHAPTER SIX

Raymond Allen stood with his hand on the knob of the door to his room in the bachelors' corridor—the portion of the guest area reserved for unmarried male guests to keep them separate from the ladies—and observed the two figures at the other end of the hall: Benedict Clarke and his mother, Rowena, exchanging some words before retiring for the night.

When Raymond first received the invitation for a weekend at Porthampton Abbey, he'd been excited. He knew that the earl must be looking for a husband for his eldest daughter, which was excellent timing, since he himself was in need of a wife. Then, when he'd arrived and seen that his only immediate competition was Meriwether Young, a much older and rotund man, he'd been positively giddy inside. This was a war he could win!

The aftermath of the actual war, which had ended just two years prior, should have presented him with lots of opportunities. There were nearly two million more women in England than men now, not to mention that nearly two million of the men who had survived the war had come home wounded: so, a surplus of single women. Not to mention further, he was a duke! Being a duke was the highest ranking, short of being king, and there were not too many of them, certainly not enough to go around to all the well-bred young women in need of a wealthy husband. Why, with another two hundred thousand Britons dying of the Spanish flu right after World War I, there should have been even more opportunities for him—it was as though people were dying for his benefit and convenience!

He felt mildly ashamed of himself for thinking of it in that way, but then, *he* hadn't started the war.

And yet for some reason, despite the presumably increased opportunities, it—*it* being romance with the prospect of marriage to follow—had never worked out for him that way.

But then the invitation to come here had arrived and with it, the idea of Lady Katherine Clarke. At age seventeen, she hadn't come out yet. Her presentation at court was still a year away—not that there'd been any such presentations since the war had ended, although hopefully they'd start up again soon—but she was such a striking young woman, and he'd figured if he got in early, maybe he'd stand a chance. Since death hadn't given him enough opportunities, he would need to make or take his own wherever he could find them.

And only Meriwether Young as competition? Laughable, how easy that should be!

But then…

But *then*…

Benedict Clarke had shown up unexpectedly.

Look at him, Raymond thought. *Not only will he fulfill the entail, thereby making him the one Martin Clarke will want to have marry Lady Katherine, but does he have to be so handsome? It's like looking at Apollo come down to earth. I can practically see the sun kissing his hair!*

Speaking of which, now Benedict was bending over to lay a kiss on his mother's cheek, and as he did so, Rowena touched a gloved hand to her son's face, tracing a gentle caress there.

Oh, this really was too much. Good looks *and* a mother who loved him?

Raymond Allen had neither of those things.

Raymond heard Benedict say cheerily, "Sleep well, Mother!" and then, although Raymond immediately twisted the knob and pushed the door open, before he could slide inside, Benedict turned and caught him standing there.

Now Raymond was in for it. The other man would probably demand to know what he was doing standing there, maybe even accuse him of snooping.

Which he hadn't been doing. Not really.

"Oh, hello!" Benedict called in a genial tone of voice. He began walking toward Raymond, lightly gliding his hand along the pink marble railing of the balcony, the gallery overlooking the entry hall far below. "I didn't see you standing there! Were you waiting for me? Perhaps you'd like a glass of sherry? I have some in my room."

As the other man drew to within inches, Raymond studied his face for any signs of the sarcasm he expected to find, either that or some other form of guile, but there simply wasn't any. If forced to describe Benedict's expression, Raymond would have to say it was open, honest, and overwhelmingly pleasant.

So on top of everything else, blasted good looks and a mother who genuinely loved him, Benedict Clarke was also *nice*? Oh, this really was too much.

"No, thank you for the offer," Raymond said hurriedly, entering his room now, "but we all have an early day in the morning—the hunt, you know—so I'll just retire now."

"Very well, then! I'll see you in—"

Raymond shut the door.

It wasn't so much that he didn't want to be friendly—in truth, it would be *nice* to have a friend—but it had already been such a long and trying day and night. And then there was the hunt in the morning. In these early postwar years, people as a whole were more reluctant to kill animals for sport. But it was still the done thing in big houses like this. Raymond didn't care much for hunting, didn't care much for guns in general really, but he'd heard Lady Katherine was a crack shot. Even if he felt his chances with her were greatly diminished since the advent of Benedict—probably hardly greater than zero, if he were truthful—he had to at least show up. He had to at least still try.

And they had said it was to be just birds and maybe small ground game; there weren't even supposed to be any horses involved, so that shouldn't be too bad. Not *too* bad.

But something that was bad?

"Parker?" Raymond called for his valet when he realized there was no one besides him in the room. He quickly strode to check the adjoining bath area, but there was no one there, either.

Like all good guests, Raymond had brought his own valet with him, so as not to place any undue strain on the household staff. While Raymond was at dinner, Parker would have spent that free time in the servants' hall or perhaps in the kitchen courtyard, enjoying a smoke, but he should have been up here by now. He should have been waiting *for* Raymond so he could wait *on* Raymond.

He began removing one of his cuff links but then thought, *This is preposterous—I'm a duke!*

Immediately, he crossed the bedroom and yanked on the bell pull cord to summon the butler.

While he waited, he regarded his reflection in the long,

standing mirror over in one corner. Well, he reflected, at least he was tall. Not for the first time, however, he found himself wishing that he'd been born into biblical times, when long hair on men had been the fashion. At least then he could have used it to cover his unfortunate ears. But as it were…

A discreet knock came at the door, followed by the entry of Mr. Wright.

"You rang, sir?" Mr. Wright said.

"Yes," Raymond replied. "I wondered if you might send up my valet, Parker?"

"He's not here with you?"

"Clearly," Raymond said, stating the obvious. "Otherwise, why would I have called you?"

"I don't know, sir, but I haven't seen Parker since this afternoon, not long after your arrival and his seeing you settled in. I assumed you'd sent him into town on an errand or something."

"Well, I didn't. And even if I had, surely he'd have returned for his dinner."

"It is odd, sir."

"Yes, very," Raymond agreed.

Except it wasn't. Raymond had a history of not being able to keep valets for very long, a tendency he'd inherited from his mother, a woman who could lose a member of staff as easily as another person might lose a lace handkerchief. So the only thing remotely odd about his valet's disappearing was that none of the previous ones had seen fit to quit without notice, departing without even asking for any money still due. And yet apparently, Parker had done exactly that, simply walking off into the sunset.

"I can send up one of the footmen to attend to you for the rest of the weekend," Mr. Wright offered.

"Oh, but that will take time. Couldn't you just…" Raymond

held out a shirtsleeve wrist and jiggled it a bit so that the cuff link shimmied in Mr. Wright's general direction.

"Oh no, sir. You'd be much better off with one of the footmen. And I know just the person for the job."

Before Raymond could object further, Mr. Wright was gone.

So now, on top of everything else, he would be subjected to having a footman act as his valet. Oh, this was too hard. Everyone knew that footmen were handsome creatures. The finer the house, the more handsome the footmen—and Porthampton Abbey was a very fine house indeed.

If Benedict Clarke hadn't made Raymond feel insecure enough about his looks, now a footman was going to come and finish the job.

In his frustration, Raymond sought again to remove one of his own cuff links. But he soon gave up, in even greater frustration.

He wasn't supposed to have to remove his own cuff links.

He was *a duke*!

CHAPTER SEVEN

The first footman, Jonathan Butler, and Daniel Murray, the second, were enjoying a late-night game of cards in the servants' hall when Mr. Wright entered.

"I'm afraid that the duke will need one of you to act as his valet for the remainder of the weekend," Mr. Wright announced. "It would appear that his own valet has gone missing."

"Who can blame him?" Daniel said, not bothering to look up from his hand.

"I'll go," Jonathan said, throwing down his cards and starting to rise. He'd been losing anyway.

"Thank you, Jonathan," Mr. Wright said, "but I think Daniel would be better suited to this particular job."

Isn't that just like old Wright? Daniel thought, tossing his own cards down. Someone else volunteers, so of course Wright would pick him instead.

"All right, Mr. Wright," Daniel said, knowing the butler hated it when he put it like that, slowly rising, slowly moving across the room.

"And don't dawdle!" Mr. Wright called after him. "The duke is waiting!"

Daniel just kept walking at his own pace, up the servants' stairs and through the green baize door at the top of it, moving through the house that he knew better than the home he'd grown up in. Now seventeen, he'd arrived at Porthampton Abbey when he was just twelve. He'd always been tall for his age, and so he'd lied about it, claiming he was sixteen in order to get the job of hall boy. His early duties were mostly scut work, all the odd jobs no one else wanted and Fanny was too small to do, and delivering Mr. Wright's breakfast. But he'd watched and learned, with an eye toward becoming a footman whenever a job opened up.

A few years after he started, it was easy enough to lie again about his age, for an entirely different reason, an entirely different sort of job.

For the past two years, Daniel had been second footman, and that suited him just fine.

His duties included greeting guests with the family, answering the front door, delivering messages to the village, serving in the dining room, and keeping the fires lit in whatever rooms the family were currently using. He also cleaned, ironed, laid out and packed clothes, did some mending, and removed change from pockets so Lord Clarke's clothes would hang better.

He liked that last duty.

What he didn't like so much was being assigned now to be the duke's stand-in valet.

Daniel considered his job, as a whole, to be not dissimilar to that of a great actor. A footman needed to act a certain way at all times whenever on duty and could relax, and even then just a bit, only when he was backstage with the other servants.

Oh well.

Daniel could act with the best of them.

He'd been doing it long enough.

Daniel knew that some of the other servants were always dreaming of life outside the big house; Fanny in particular. Daniel had once shared those dreams, but he'd seen enough of the world now, and he didn't anymore. If he could remain at Porthampton Abbey for the rest of his life, perhaps finding love and marriage with one of the female staff, that would suit him just fine. Maybe they could even live in one of the small cottages that peppered the farther reaches of the estate, those cottages reserved for tenant farmers and married staff.

Daniel liked the idea of marriage in general and liked the idea of females in particular; at least females didn't start wars and go around killing one another, which seemed a huge feature to recommend them. In addition to the female staff he knew from Downstairs, there were also the three daughters of the house, whom he glimpsed from time to time while carrying out his duties. But from what he'd glimpsed? Lady Kate was horrible and Lady Elizabeth was silly. Lady Grace appeared to be the best of the lot in that, if she was neither here nor there in the way her sisters were decidedly here and there, there seemed to be something downright decent about her. Some might find "decent" to be an equivalent to "boring," but Daniel had seen a lot that wasn't decent in the world, and for him it was anything but. Daniel would give a lot, he'd give everything he had, for a world populated with more decent people like Lady Grace. Still, when a person grew up with everything provided for her—money, a grand house, safety, *love*—it wasn't so much a wonder that Lady Grace was decent but that the rest of them weren't. Shouldn't they have been? Shouldn't they have been more *grateful*?

But now it was time for Daniel to leave off daydreams of a future and stray thoughts about the ladies of the house and get back on stage as he raised his fist to knock on the duke's door.

He needn't have knocked quite as sharply as he did, but Daniel liked to take his pleasures wherever he could find them.

"Enter!" a voice called.

Daniel did so, only to be greeted by the duke's surprised face.

"But you're so young!" the duke said. "I was hoping for someone more senior."

Immediately, Daniel bristled inside. No one else ever told him he looked young. As far as the rest of the household was concerned, he was something like twenty-one now. Besides, the duke didn't look much older than he was supposed to be himself.

"I'm old enough to have fought in the war," Daniel said, still bristling. "Were you there, sir? I feel like I may have seen you. Perhaps we shared a trench one time? It's always so difficult to remember who was with one and who was not, while one was being shelled. Don't you find that to be true?"

Daniel knew it was a low blow, just as he was sure he knew the answer, but he hadn't been able to stop the words from coming out of his mouth.

"No, I was not," the duke said. "I needed to stay at home to mind the family affairs."

"Of course, sir," Daniel said, just shy of snidely, but then he felt a touch of guilt upon seeing the blush of embarrassment color the duke's cheeks.

Of course the duke hadn't served in the war. A soft man like him would have died there. And a soft man like him would have been wise to not go.

Daniel hadn't been wise.

Three years ago, just fourteen years old, he'd gone, just in time for what would be the final year of the war. You had to be eighteen to sign up, nineteen to fight overseas. But if you didn't have a birth certificate, as many poor people didn't, a large sixteen-year-old could fake it. Or a large fourteen-year-old. The minimum height requirement was five foot three—Daniel cleared that easily, by ten inches. The minimum chest measurement was thirty-four inches—Daniel cleared that easily, too. Like the two hundred and fifty thousand other underage soldiers, Daniel had figured that he'd get some fresh air and good food and a bit of adventure.

He got more than he bargained for.

What had been embarked upon with great enthusiasm and dreams of glory had ended when he'd been forced to face grim reality.

He learned how to build trenches and use sandbags and toss a grenade, and he became all too familiar with the sight of death.

If he never saw another trench in his life, that would be fine with Daniel.

And if he wanted to make sure *that* never happened, that he never lost his cushy job at Porthampton Abbey, perhaps he'd better stop being so rude to this duke.

"What would you like for me to do first, sir?" Daniel offered solicitously. "Lay out your night clothes? Run you a nice warm bath? Perhaps I could help you with those cuff links?"

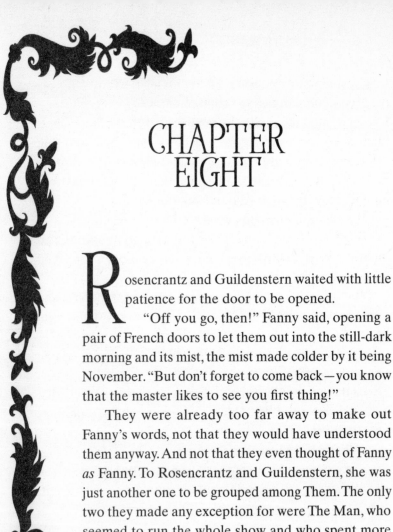

CHAPTER EIGHT

Rosencrantz and Guildenstern waited with little patience for the door to be opened.

"Off you go, then!" Fanny said, opening a pair of French doors to let them out into the still-dark morning and its mist, the mist made colder by it being November. "But don't forget to come back—you know that the master likes to see you first thing!"

They were already too far away to make out Fanny's words, not that they would have understood them anyway. And not that they even thought of Fanny *as* Fanny. To Rosencrantz and Guildenstern, she was just another one to be grouped among Them. The only two they made any exception for were The Man, who seemed to run the whole show and who spent more time with them than anyone else, and The Girl, who seemed to run The Man.

Rosencrantz and Guildenstern were cats, Persian cats to be exact, Persian cats having grown popular in Britain after being exhibited at the first cat show at the Crystal Palace in 1871. Not that they knew that, either, being cats and all.

What they did know was that sometimes Them tried to call Rosencrantz "Rosen*catz*," which they seemed to find very funny, but it had never stuck.

And they also knew they had the run of the place, the whole estate inside and out, unlike that poor unfortunate house cat who seemed to spend his entire existence in the kitchen, never getting to go anywhere. The house cat wasn't beautiful like they were, either. They were white from the mouth area down through the chest area and front, and gray in the upper face, back, and tail. They were also the very definition of the word "fluffy." The poor house cat had short hair by comparison and was just a tabby, a mackerel tabby— too common. Why, it wasn't even a real breed!

Rosencrantz and Guildenstern thought no more of the house cat, though, as they exercised their free rein, gamboling over the verdant lawns, the pleasure gardens, the rockeries, lakes, and croquet lawns. With the exception of the occasional pause for a little on-the-spot grooming, they only stopped long enough to take a piss by the tennis courts.

It was there, while they were doing that, that they saw the man.

Not *The* Man.

This man was one they had never seen before.

Or at least they didn't think they had.

So many of Them looked alike, particularly the men, like the ones with their similar suits who spent a lot of their time in the kitchen area of the house. Come to think of it, this man appeared to be dressed like they did.

But Rosencrantz and Guildenstern had never seen any of Them out here in the early morning, unless it was the one who always smelled like horses, and certainly not stumbling around so awkwardly like this.

Not unless they included the way The Man got on rare occasions very late at night.

The man lurched past them, almost as though he didn't see

them standing right there, and toward a stand of trees. Such peculiar behavior, even for a human. Immediately, their hairs stood on end, their backs arching, as though a grave danger were present. But then, humans got up to all sorts of behaviors that made no sense to Rosencrantz and Guildenstern, like using utensils to eat. And then there were the things you never saw humans doing, like chasing mice. It was a puzzle.

Oh well.

It was time for Rosencrantz and Guildenstern to head back to the house for their morning chin scratch. If they were lucky, The Man might give them some of his kippers.

CHAPTER NINE

K ate sailed into the drawing room, pleased with herself, past the two footmen lining the wall to wait attendance as if they were no more than wallpaper. The footmen might be extraordinarily pretty wallpaper, even she would acknowledge that, but still: wallpaper. She was pleased because immediately after breakfast, she'd hurried up to her bedroom so Agnes could help her change from breakfast clothes into her hunting costume, and further pleased with how she looked, a vision in black with just a touch of white: black veiled hat, a black jacket slit up the back, a white cravat at her neck, and even black jodhpurs under her skirt, although she wouldn't be riding today, wouldn't get to ride her most precious and favorite horse, Wyndgate, more's the pity—with this group, they'd be walking. She also had black leather boots and, clasped in one hand, a pair of black leather gloves.

Kate loved hunting, and with a little luck, she'd bag a fat pheasant for Mrs. Owen in the kitchen to dress and serve later. If she relished anything more than shooting things, it was enjoying the fruits of her efforts.

What did not please Kate at the moment was that with the exception of Father—who stood there ready for her in his scarlet coat and white breeches, black top hat and leather boots, white cashmere scarf and gold pin—none of the others had changed yet.

"I'm astonished!" she pronounced, hands on hips. "Why are none of you ready? We're losing the best part of the morning!"

The "none of you" included everyone who had been at dinner the night before: her mother, sisters, and grandmother; Grandfather, nodding in his chair; the newly discovered relatives, Benedict Clarke and his mother; the two suitors, Meriwether Young and Raymond Allen, the duke; and even Dr. Zebulon Webb. Not too many years past, the doctor would not have been welcome at a formal family dinner, never mind an entire weekend party. Back then, the doctor had been no more than just another villager performing a service, in his case someone to do something to keep them all healthy or help them out if one of them got sick. But the war had changed so many things, and this was one of them. Now, it seemed to Kate, almost anyone could show up at dinner.

"Grace? Lizzy?" Kate said hopefully. "You'll come, won't you?" The thing she was hoping for was that there would be more than just her to keep the two—now three, if you counted Benedict—suitors happy. "Come on, Grace. We'll just stroll around the place and shoot whatever we see. It'll be fun."

Grace shuddered. "That may be your idea of fun, but it isn't mine. Shooting small animals for sport." Grace shuddered again. "I think I'll stay behind with Mother and do needlepoint, thank you."

"Actually," Meriwether Young announced, as if anyone had asked him specifically, "I think I'll stay behind, too, look around the abbey a bit. I didn't get to see much of it last night, and I've never been before."

Well, that was a relief, and hardly a surprise, come to

think of it. The older rotund man didn't look like he could survive a brisk walk.

"I'd be happy to show you around," Grace offered.

Wouldn't she just, Kate thought.

"I suppose if others are staying behind," Raymond Allen began, "then perhaps I might also—"

"What about you, *Cousin* Benedict?" Kate said with false sweetness, cutting Raymond off as she regarded her handsome new relative. "Will you be staying behind, too?"

"I will come," he said with a smile, "but just for the stroll and to get some fresh air. I did serve in the last year of the war, and I find that hunting for sport no longer appeals as it once did."

He managed to speak his words without judgment of others, and yet Kate couldn't help but think: *how insipid.*

"Duke?" She turned to the other man. "I believe you were about to say you were going to stay with Mr. Young?" As insipid as the cousin was, it would be better if she only had him to keep entertained and not the duke as well.

"No, that wasn't it at all." The duke regarded Benedict as though taking up a challenge. "I was about to say that I'm going up to change now and shall be ready forthwith."

So it was to be Kate, her father, Benedict, the duke, and the doctor.

Kate cast about for at least one more female to entice into coming. "Grandmama," she said, "wouldn't you like to join us?" As soon as she issued the invitation, she couldn't help but laugh at her own desperation.

"You laugh," her grandmother said, "but I was quite a shot when I was a young girl. Still, I think my shooting days are over, at least for this lifetime. I shall leave the hunt to you young people." She paused briefly to cast an expression that managed to be both haughty and fond at her son in his red hunting jacket before adding a playful, "And Martin."

"I think I would like to go," Lizzy spoke up.

Kate had already forgotten all about Lizzy.

"I've never shot a shotgun before," Lizzy went on, "or any other gun, really, but I should like to try. I think it would be fun—you know, aiming at things and then possibly hitting them."

"*That's* the spirit, Lizzy!" Kate said, thinking: *two suitors, two daughters—at least now the math will work*, even though she hoped to end up with neither. "Why don't you run along and get Becky to find you a hunting costume? And everyone else who is coming: chop-chop! The morning is wasting!"

As Lizzy all but raced from the room, the other prospective hunters moving more leisurely, Mr. Wright entered.

"My lord," the butler said. "If I might have a word."

Kate drew closer to her father at this.

"Yes, Wright?" Martin Clarke said. "What is it?"

"It's…the stable boy," Mr. Wright said in a low voice.

"The stable boy?" Kate said. "The one whose uncle died yesterday?"

"The same," Mr. Wright conceded. He addressed his words to the earl. "He came to the kitchen. He demands to see you, says it's a matter of the greatest urgency."

"Oh," Kate said, "I do hope nothing is the matter with Wyndgate!"

"He didn't say what the matter was, Lady Kate, only that it was urgent, as I've already said."

"Well, then," Father said brusquely, "why haven't you shown him in?"

Mr. Wright looked scandalized as he lowered his voice yet further. "Because, sir, he *is* the stable boy."

The earl stared back at the butler.

"He's *dirty*, sir," Mr. Wright said. "We can't have someone like that just traipsing through the house!"

"But surely the maids can clean up after him if he touches anything."

For once, the butler stared back at his master as though *he* were the one in charge.

Kate laid a hand on the earl's arm. "I don't think there's anything else for it, Father," she said, finding herself feeling quite pleasantly eager at the prospect that suddenly lay ahead. "It looks like you and I will have to go to the kitchen."

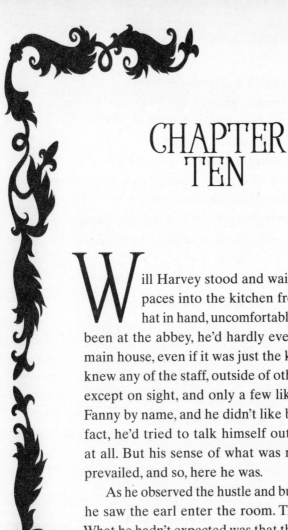

CHAPTER TEN

Will Harvey stood and waited, not too many paces into the kitchen from the back door, hat in hand, uncomfortable. In the years he'd been at the abbey, he'd hardly ever come inside the main house, even if it was just the kitchen. He hardly knew any of the staff, outside of other stable workers, except on sight, and only a few like Mrs. Owen and Fanny by name, and he didn't like being here now. In fact, he'd tried to talk himself out of coming today at all. But his sense of what was right and just had prevailed, and so, here he was.

As he observed the hustle and bustle of the kitchen, he saw the earl enter the room. This, he'd expected. What he hadn't expected was that the earl would have his eldest daughter with him.

Unlike with much of the staff, Will knew who all the family members were, by sight and by name, for they regularly came to ride the horses he tended.

And of course he knew who Lady Kate was, better than all the others. He still remembered that first time he'd met her, when they were both but three years old, that one day of friendship between them. When he'd returned to the estate four years later to claim his job as junior stable boy, he'd seen her again, and almost every day since then. But they'd never once spoken of that first day—he doubted she even remembered it as he did—their relationship settling into one of young lady of the house and worker on the estate, their only rare bond an exchanged glance and mutual smile in appreciation of something one of the horses had done. When he was seven, he'd initially felt stung by the change in her behavior toward him, so cool compared to his warm memory of her. Then he'd become resentful and, finally, resigned. After all, wasn't this the way their world was supposed to be? There was no point in wishing it different.

As the earl strode up to him without hesitation, Will hoped they couldn't see the evidence of the tears he'd cried the night before, anguished sobs he'd muffled with his pillow after he and his aunt had retired to their separate bedrooms. In the morning, Will had washed his face thoroughly, but you never knew. No matter how careful you were, you never knew what someone else might see in you.

"We were all so sorry to hear about your uncle's death," the earl said solemnly, a sincerely sympathetic expression on his face. "Such a horrible business, that. Ezra was with us for so many years. I cannot imagine this place without him."

Will could remember no particular closeness between his farmer uncle and His Lordship—indeed, it surprised him that the earl knew his uncle's given name. Still, he was willing to accept good wishes on the face of it.

"Thank you, my lord. I'm grateful for your kind words."

"Yes," Lady Katherine said. "We are all so very sorry."

He met her eyes briefly. Even with her face partially obscured by the black veil of her hunting costume, those extraordinary blue eyes were so piercing. Not to mention that while he was accustomed to village girls and farmers' daughters looking at him in a certain way, none had ever looked at him as boldly as this. Immediately, he looked away from that gaze.

"Thank you, Lady Katherine," he said. Then he added, "You're very kind," not sure he meant it.

"Mr. Wright said something was wrong," the earl prompted.

"Is it Wyndgate?" Lady Katherine put in. "Is he all right?"

"He's fine," Will said. "It's nothing to do with the horses. I came to talk to you about my uncle."

"I'm not sure I understand," the earl said. "We've already said we know what happened and that we are all very sorry." Realization dawned in the earl's eyes. "Are you here about getting time off? Because if you are—"

"It's not that, either!" Will said, beginning to feel impatience with these people.

"What, then?" Lady Katherine demanded, forcing him to look at her again.

"I came," Will said, "because I felt it my duty to warn you."

"Warn us?" she said. "That sounds ominous!" Strangely, she didn't appear disturbed in the slightest at the idea of something being ominous. He had to give her some grudging credit: unblinking bravery was a fine thing in a person. *Or perhaps*, he thought, *she is just being foolish*. "Do tell!" she urged with a smile and a flash of those blue eyes.

"The circumstances of my uncle's death were most unusual," Will began.

"Yes, we'd heard all about that, too," the earl said, practically brushing him off. "An unfortunate business... Your poor aunt... But what has any of that to do with a warning for *us*?"

Something in Will grew angry then. These people! As if strange tragedy could only come to the poor while *they* were above all that.

Still, he had to warn them.

"My uncle was dead," Will said, "and then he wasn't, and

then he was again."

"I really must stop you there," the earl said. "We have heard all about this, but surely even you must realize that to suggest such a thing is insane. It could never happen!"

"With all due respect, I don't think you understand, my lord. I'm not sure even I understand! But here is the thing: people go through their lives believing a thing could never happen. But never is only never until a thing does happen."

"But it *never* happened in the first place!" the earl said with some exasperation.

"My aunt saw it with her own eyes."

"Then she is delusional!"

"Are you calling her a liar?"

"Of course not! Did you not hear me use the word 'delusional'? The poor woman is grief-stricken. Of course she is imagining all this."

"I don't believe so, and I *do* believe her. Which is why I have come here and why I am concerned. Whatever this is, it's already happened once—to my uncle. What if it happens a second time? What if there is a danger of recurrence? So I thought it my duty to warn—"

"Yes, yes," the earl said brusquely now, all sympathy seemingly gone. "Now you have. And now I shall warn you. Were it not for the debt I feel I owe to your uncle and aunt for being such good tenant farmers all these years, and were it not for the even greater fact of you being better with horses than anyone we have on staff, I would dismiss you right now. No, let us have no more talk of this insanity." He nodded sharply. "Please extend our condolences to your aunt when next you see her. Good day."

"Good day to you, too, my lord," Will said, unable to keep a slight sneer from his voice as he addressed the earl's retreating back.

"You know," Lady Katherine said in a surprisingly soft voice, "we really are all so very sorry for your loss. If there is anything…"

She put one hand out, as though she might touch his arm, before letting it fall to her side. Perhaps, he thought later, it was the look on his face that made her drop that hand.

"And I thank you for it," he said stiffly, feeling a confusing combination of emotions: outrage, hurt, a rare vulnerability, "but there is nothing anyone else can do. My aunt and I—we take care of ourselves."

Will didn't particularly care to have anyone feeling sorry for him. And did she really feel genuinely bad for his circumstances or did she feel bad that, if the stable boy were insane, he might be sent away and then who would take best care of her favorite horse?

With no more words said on either side, Will watched Lady Katherine follow her father from the room.

Well, Will thought, *at least I tried.*

CHAPTER ELEVEN

Fanny watched Lady Katherine walk away, her blond hair contrasted stunningly against her black hunting costume, and she thought, not for the first time, that it simply wasn't fair. The daughters of the house had such beautiful hair colors: Lady Katherine's blond, Lady Grace's warm auburn, Lady Elizabeth's rich black. While she, like the housemaids, was stuck with mousy brown. Come to that, why were the footmen allowed to be so handsome while the female staff were all confined to being plain?

She'd been watching and listening to the exchange among Lord Clarke, his eldest daughter, and Will Harvey, but now that the first two had left and the third was about to depart the way he'd come, through the back door, she couldn't let that last thing happen.

Fanny hadn't had much occasion to talk to or even see Will Harvey in the past, but whatever she had seen, she'd always liked.

"Will!" she called after him as he placed his hand on the knob.

Will turned.

"I'm ever so sorry about your uncle," she said, twisting her hands together.

"Thanks, Fanny," he said. "You're very kind."

"Would you like to stay for a bit?" she offered. Then she gestured toward the long table. "Perhaps have a cup of tea with me?"

"*Fanny!*" Mrs. Owen admonished with a bark. "We're working here. *You're* supposed to be working here. This isn't some sort of...*teahouse!*"

"Mrs. Owen," Fanny said firmly, straightening her back. "I've already completed my morning's work. I've even packed up the hampers for Jonathan and Daniel to take for the barn luncheon Lord Clarke and his guests will be enjoying after the hunt, so I think I might be entitled to one measly cup of tea. And one for Will, too."

Mrs. Owen shot a quick glance at Will. "I'm sorry about Ezra, Will, sorry for your family's loss."

"Thank you, Mrs. Owen," Will said.

"All right," Mrs. Owen told Fanny, softening. "One cup of tea each." And then she hardened again. "But just one! And try to keep out of my way."

"Oh, thank you!" Fanny said, her shoulders inching up in pleasure at the prospect of doing something different for a change. "Why don't you go through to the servants' hall?" she suggested to Will. "I'll bring the tea."

A moment later, she did so, having found some leftover dessert from last night's dinner to bring on the tray, too.

But Will didn't appear to be interested in having anything sweet. Really, he didn't even seem all that interested in the tea as he sat there looking dejected.

Empathy caused Fanny's own expression to shift away from the pleasure she'd been feeling.

"Oh, you mustn't mind them too much," she said. "The earl and his daughter. Those people. *They* never think anything *we* have to say is important. Why, look at you. You try to help them, and they think you're insane!"

As soon as she uttered that last word, her hands flew to her mouth as though she might be able to push it back. She'd seen how Will's expression had darkened when the Clarkes had used that word. She certainly didn't want Will to think that she thought such a thing about him, too.

"It's fine, Fanny." He waved a dismissive hand. "If I stop and think, I can understand why someone who hadn't seen it with their own eyes wouldn't believe me."

"You didn't see it, either, though," Fanny said, again unable to stop herself. "Your aunt did."

"True," Will said. "But she did, and I believe her."

"I don't blame you. If it were my aunt, I'd believe her, too. Well, if I had an aunt." Fanny paused. "I believe you, Will."

He looked at her with gratitude. "Thank you, Fanny."

Fanny enjoyed that for a moment, someone actually thanking *her* for something. Then: "Do you think it was a vampire?"

Will had finally been about to take a sip of his tea, but now he stopped. "I'm sorry, what did you say?"

"A vampire! You know, like in Mr. Bram Stoker's *Dracula*? If a vampire bites you on the neck, you die for a bit, then you come back to life, only now you're a vampire, too, who wants to bite people and, you know, drink their blood."

Thankfully, Will didn't treat her suggestion with the same scorn Mr. Wright had when she'd raised the idea the night before, but he did shake his head.

"I don't think so," Will said. "No one said anything about there being any bite marks on his neck, and I didn't see any in that area myself when I...saw him."

"Oh." Fanny felt a bit disappointed. "Probably not vampires, then. Vampires are so obvious, it kind of makes you wonder why, once the evidence is there, anyone ever suspects anything else."

Fanny propped her elbows on the table and cradled her face in her hands, trying to think of some alternatives. While she sat there, a cat made its way into the room, a mackerel tabby, strolling the perimeter before eventually hopping into her lap.

"Who's this?" Will asked as Fanny petted the feline.

"This is Henry Clay," Fanny said proudly. "He's my mouser. You can't have a good clean kitchen without a great mouser."

Will reached out and gave the cat an experimental pat on the head. "Why Henry Clay?" he asked. "Seems like an odd name for a cat."

"It's the name," Fanny said, "of my favorite American."

"*You* have a favorite American?" Will said, laughing.

Even though it might be possible that he was laughing at her expense, Fanny was grateful to have been the cause of that laughter, given what Will had been through. Fanny knew what it was like to lose a beloved family member, knew it all too many times over. As far as family went, Fanny was alone in the world.

"What's so surprising about that?" she asked. "I have favorites when it comes to lots of things. Henry Clay—the man, not the cat—was a great orator and lawyer and politician. They called him 'The Great Compromiser.' So often, people have to find ways to compromise, don't you think? Anyway, he lived a long time ago and he had slaves, but he freed them in his will, so at least that's something. I like to think that people can change, don't you?"

"Well." Will appeared to be at a loss as to what to say to all that. "At least this Henry Clay seems friendlier than those two fluff balls I see roaming around the grounds sometimes."

"You mean Rosencrantz and Guildenstern?" Fanny guessed.

"Rosen...*what*?"

"Rosencrantz and Guildenstern." She jutted her chin toward the ceiling as though indicating the people of Porthampton Abbey who lived upstairs. "They come up with all kinds of crazy names, not like Henry Clay. Rosencrantz and Guildenstern are two characters from Mr. William Shakespeare's plays."

"You're not going to tell me you've read Shakespeare."

"No, I haven't." Fanny sighed, then brightened. "But I mean to. At least I've looked at the names on all the cast lists."

"How do you know all this?" Will said, clearly astounded.

"Because I read, don't I?" Fanny said. "Every day, whenever I'm supposed to be dusting the library, I take some time to look through the books. Might as well read as dust." She shrugged. "Besides, I don't think anyone else here reads the things, except maybe that oldest daughter. Sometimes I even smuggle books up to my room." She grew excited. "Say! Would you like me to smuggle some for you?"

Fanny regretted mentioning "that oldest daughter," because almost immediately, Will got a preoccupied look on his face and she even had to repeat herself, prodding him about her offer to smuggle books for him.

"I'll, um, I'll think about it," he said.

"Let me know." She sighed. "Those people," she said again, this time shaking her head at the foolishness of it all. "It's just like the *Titanic* all over again."

"I'm afraid I don't understand."

"The *Titanic*! It was this great big ocean vessel, biggest ever built, and even though everyone thought it could never—"

"Yes, I know about all that. But what I don't know is how *that* relates to any of *this*."

The *Titanic* had bothered Fanny for years—eight years, to be exact. Even though she'd only been nine herself when it sank, it still bothered her: the idea of all those people dying, in third class, in *steerage*, with no chance of survival simply because they hadn't been able to afford a better fare.

Fanny sought to explain all this, adding, "This is like that all over again. The poor, like your uncle, at risk for something, while the wealthy think they can get off scot-free *because* of their wealth. But even on the *Titanic*, even though almost all the poor died, not all the wealthy got away. Some of them died, too. Even some of the richest in the world, like that John Jacob Astor! So they were fools to think they could just go about their daily business and—"

"Where are they going on their hunt?" Will said, cutting her off with a chin jut toward the upstairs similar to the one she'd used earlier. If Will had seemed to grow preoccupied before, he appeared fully alert now, following her description of the wealthy thinking they were protected by that wealth but then dying anyway.

"How should I know?" Fanny shrugged. "But they're not taking horses and they are having a barn luncheon in the fancy barn, so it can't be too far from there."

Will tossed back the contents of his teacup, now likely grown cold, as he rose to his feet and headed toward the door.

"Where are you going?" Fanny asked.

"They may be fools," Will said, "but someone has to protect them."

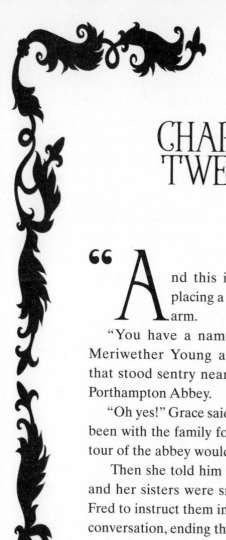

CHAPTER TWELVE

"And this is Fred," Grace announced, placing a fond hand on a metallic silver arm.

"You have a name for your suit of armor?" Meriwether Young asked, regarding the object that stood sentry near the interior front doors to Porthampton Abbey.

"Oh yes!" Grace said gaily with a laugh. "Fred has been with the family for hundreds of years. Why, no tour of the abbey would be complete without him!"

Then she told him a story about how when she and her sisters were small, Grandmama had used Fred to instruct them in the fine art of making polite conversation, ending the story with another laugh.

"You know, Lady Grace, you are quite pretty when you laugh. You are pretty when you don't, of course, but when you do..."

Grace touched the tortoiseshell comb in her hair with one hand while fiddling with the loose waistline of her calf-length peridot-colored Lanvin dress with the other.

When a good part of their party had retired to change for the hunt, Grace had retired briefly as well. Only in her case, it was to change out of her breakfast clothes into what she wore now. There were days when Grace lamented the need to change costumes so often—such a frivolous waste of one's time! Still, it was nice to receive a compliment, even if only from Mr. Young, whose paucity of hair looked as though it had been freshly slicked over to the left. Grace had stayed behind because she disliked hunting—anything to do with guns, really—and had been dismayed when he'd said he would stay behind, too. But then she had gamely offered to show him around. After all, wasn't that her duty? And now that they were in it, it wasn't turning out to be too bad of an experience.

"Thank you, Mr. Young," she said.

"Meriwether, please. Or better yet, Merry."

"All right, I'll try…Merry." She could feel the blush in her own cheeks as she spoke that last word. She wasn't used to men paying her compliments, not even from her parents so much—those were typically reserved for Kate.

"Yes, well," she said, hoping to brush off the awkwardness she was feeling, "let me show you some more of the place."

She led him from the doorway to the central grand foyer, so big it was like an interior courtyard with its tapestries on the walls, indoor palm plants, paintings, and sculptures. The grand staircase lay in front of them while the ceiling soared several stories overhead.

"If you look up," she said, "you can see the gallery lining the next level on all four sides."

"Oh yes, my bedroom is up there," he said, "so I saw a bit of it last night."

"But if you look up from down here," she said, craning her neck, "it's such an impressive sight, one of my favorites, what with the different levels. All the way at the top, in the attic, are the servants' bedrooms, although you can't see that level from here. Still, a truly impressive sight. Don't you agree?"

He glanced up, but only briefly, before casting his gaze downward with a shudder.

"I'm afraid I don't care for heights," he said. "Whether looking down from them or looking up at them, it is all the same to me. Whenever I do all I can think is what a terrible length that would be for a person to fall."

"Oh, dear!" Grace said, not unkindly. She could see that he was genuinely scared and, having no short supply of fears herself, she could empathize.

"Let's get out of here, then," she said, quickly ushering him to one of the many side rooms shooting off through the pillars of arched open doorways from the main courtyard.

But as she looked about the room she'd chosen at random, she wondered what she could really show him there that would be of note. Buttoned chairs, fringed lamps, plants, draperies, flowers in vases, centerpieces, carriage clocks, wood, marble, brass, a Lalique vase—would he really be interested in any of these items? She supposed the family coat of arms and the John Singer Sargent portrait of her mother that her father had commissioned from the American artist might be of some small interest, but only just barely. Maybe he'd like to see the music room? The smoking room, perhaps?

"I'm afraid," Grace said, laughing, "that when I volunteered to be your tour guide, I didn't take into account what a boring one I would be or how stodgy the place has become! Why, except for the gramophone, I don't believe a new piece of furniture has been brought here since 1890—perhaps even as far back as 1880!"

"That's quite all right," he assured her. "It's all fascinating enough to me. But perhaps you could tell me more about how the estate is run? I'm afraid I've spent most of my life tending to my businesses in London. As a result, I know precious little about the great country houses."

"Oh!" Grace said, mildly surprised at this request. "Let's see… Porthampton Abbey has well over a thousand acres."

"As much as all that?"

"Oh yes. And we are quite a self-sustaining entity. There's an estate manager who oversees the farms and tenant cottages and a gamekeeper who's in charge of the woodlands and the shooting. The farmers grow all our grains and such, and the home farm produces all our meats, vegetables, and herbs, and of course we have our own dairy. We have sheep, pheasants, partridges, geese, venison, rabbits, pike, and trout. As you can see, there's hardly any reason for us to leave the abbey at all, unless required to do so in order to preside over a village fair or some such. We even have our own small church on the grounds for those occasions, like this one, when we have weekend guests and so prefer not to go into the larger church in the village. After he's done with his service in the village, the vicar will come to us. You'll see that tomorrow—our smaller church, that is."

"It does sound impressive," he said, "particularly the wide assortment of livestock."

"I suppose it is," she conceded. Then she added with a laugh, "Would you care to inspect the pigs?"

"I don't think that will be necessary," he said, joining in her laughter before ending on a sigh.

"What's wrong?" she said, always sensitive to the feelings of others.

"Only that I came here with such high hopes."

"How do you mean?" she said.

"May I be frank, Lady Grace?"

"I wish you would, Mr. …Merry."

"I've been fortunate enough to be successful in life when it comes to my businesses. But sadly, I have been less successful in other things. Then, when your father's invitation arrived, and knowing your family's circumstances, I thought—maybe there's still hope yet for an old bachelor like me. Maybe there is still a chance for some love in this life of ours."

"Oh," Grace said. "Oh! You mean you and Kate."

"Yes, but then of course, no sooner do I arrive than I see another suitor has been invited—a duke, no less!—and then a long-lost cousin shows up, and a handsome male cousin at that. So I fear that any services I might have been able to provide to your family…" He let the idea trail off.

The entail. That was what he was talking about. In the absence of a son, the entire Porthampton Abbey estate would go to the nearest male relation. Mr. Young had clearly hoped to resolve that problem by marrying Kate and then, hopefully, providing a male heir through their union.

"You mustn't despair," Grace said.

"But now that Benedict Clarke has shown up…" Again, he let the idea trail off.

Yes, now that she thought about it, she had to agree with his assessment of the thing. Her father would want Kate to marry Benedict, thereby securing the estate for the foreseeable future, one way or another.

Of course, Martin Clarke would need to die first for any of this to become an issue, a prospect she shuddered at and hoped lay long in the future, but she did understand why it occupied her father's planning of what would happen to his estate.

"You know," Meriwether Young said when she failed to fill the silence, "I was not hunting a fortune. I have enough of one of my own, even if nothing like this." He gestured at the opulence around them. "But I had perhaps been hoping to find something resembling love."

"You mustn't despair," she said again, this time more

fervently. "Who knows how a thing will turn out before everything is said and done?"

"Perhaps you are right." Then light shone in his eyes. "Perhaps, not finding love with one daughter, I shall find it with another?"

Grace blushed at this, while thinking, *What an absurd idea!* "Why don't we go to the drawing room?" she suggested. "I'm sure Mother and Grandmama are there, and that there will be some tea laid out for us."

As they neared the drawing room, Grace could smell her grandmother before she saw her, what with her signature scent of Indian flowers.

Entering the room, she spotted her mother and grandmother in their typical midmorning occupation: one perusing the *Sketch* while the other consumed the *Tatler*. Soon, Grace knew, they would switch.

"Mr. Young!" her grandmother said, spotting them. "Why don't you come sit by me and tell me all the wretched things that are going on in London. As you can see"—here she waved her paper at him—"I do love a good nasty gossip."

"I'm not sure I know anything nasty," he said, taking the offered seat before adding gamely, "but if it suits you, I can certainly try."

As Grace observed Mr. Young kindly trying to accommodate her grandmother's request, she thought of what her elder female relatives' days typically consisted of: reading the gossip sheets, of course; a crossword; some oil painting; perhaps a walk around the gardens; endless changes of clothing. She could only conclude, as she always did: how boring.

Then she thought about what Mr. Young—Merry—had alluded to just a few moments ago. As the daughter of an earl, Grace knew she was expected to marry a man of equal or senior rank to her father. But there weren't many dukes around—although there was Raymond Allen, but then, he'd come for Kate as almost everyone did—and the king, well, he was already taken. Come to think of it, the earls she'd met were all taken as well.

But what of this Merry? She speculated. For a second daughter like her, no one would mind so much if she didn't marry a title when there were so few to be had anyway. He was kind. Why, look at the attentions he was paying her mother and grandmother. He was lonely, in need of a wife. Plus, young as she was, if she married him before Kate wed Benedict and if she—Grace—were to somehow bear the first male grandchild…

But of course, that would depend on her father dying first, and that was something, a fact she kept leaving out of the equation, no doubt because she hated to think of a world without him in it.

Something else she kept leaving out of the equation? The question of love.

She knew many married without it. Did her parents even love each other? She couldn't even say *that* with certainty, although she hoped so.

As Merry shot a hopeful smile in her direction, Grace let the notion of a different life—one in which she might live part time in London with an older successful husband, while possibly presiding over Porthampton Abbey the rest of the time—slip away.

Already she liked Merry well enough, and she did pity him his loneliness; she'd known loneliness herself. But let others, let Kate, marry for convenience or financial gain.

She, Grace, would hold out and marry for love.

CHAPTER THIRTEEN

Fanny carried Henry Clay into the library. The kitchen cat normally never got out of the kitchen, unless it was so early in the morning that the rest of the house except Fanny was still asleep, and Fanny imagined he relished the opportunity, no matter how undignified the manner of conveyance.

"Some are out hunting, while the others are having a late-morning tea," Fanny whispered to the cat as she set him down, "so I think you'll be safe with me. Only, if anyone comes in, you hide under the sofa and I'll pretend to be dusting."

Henry Clay blinked at her.

"I knew you'd understand," Fanny said.

Fanny figured Henry Clay liked her as much as he liked any human—more, even, since she was the only one who paid attention to him, who didn't just kick him out of the way whenever it was busy in the kitchen, which was pretty much always.

The kitchen maid regarded the kitchen cat as he sat on his haunches on the Persian rug, blinking at the sofas facing each other perpendicular to the fireplace. She hoped he didn't scratch them, since she figured if she were a cat, they'd be perfect for scratching the hell out of. But no. Henry Clay merely blinked around the cozy room with its writing desk by the window and its thousands of books.

"I agree," Fanny whispered. "Much nicer than the kitchen in here, isn't it? A person could get used to this." She paused. "Why do you think Will ran out so quickly like that?" She didn't wait for the cat to answer. "I'll tell you why. He likes Lady Kate. And I like him. Which one of us will get what we want? I'll tell you the answer to that one, too: neither. That's who. Because that's how the world works. But never mind all that now. This is not the time for love, Henry Clay."

Fanny turned away, fingering volume after volume on the shelves. "You can find answers to anything in books. What do you think, Henry Clay? They say Will's uncle didn't turn into a vampire, so that's not it. Perhaps a monster as in Mrs. Mary Shelley's *Frankenstein*?" She sighed. "No, Will's uncle wasn't pieced together with bits of other dead people, so that's not it, either." Then she got so excited about something, she stopped speaking softly. "Maybe I could glance through some medical books! I might get ideas there!" She pulled out a few volumes on medical diagnosis—really, there were so many books here and yet no one else ever read any—and waved them at the cat. "Shall we sneak these out with us?"

Henry Clay just blinked at her some more, causing Fanny to sigh, but then she smiled.

"Don't you worry about it, Henry Clay," she said, giving him an affectionate scratch under the chin before gathering medical books and cat up in her arms. "You're smarter than both those fluff balls put together. Why, they just sit and watch, waiting for their kippers. You, on the other hand? I'm sure when the time comes, you'll find something useful to do. You'll be a cat of action."

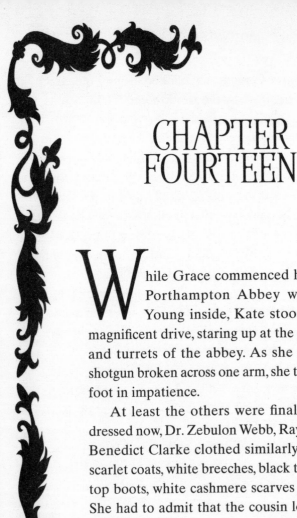

CHAPTER FOURTEEN

While Grace commenced her short tour of Porthampton Abbey with Meriwether Young inside, Kate stood outside in the magnificent drive, staring up at the pinnacles, towers, and turrets of the abbey. As she stood there, her shotgun broken across one arm, she tapped her booted foot in impatience.

At least the others were finally appropriately dressed now, Dr. Zebulon Webb, Raymond Allen, and Benedict Clarke clothed similarly to her father in scarlet coats, white breeches, black top hats and black top boots, white cashmere scarves with golden pins. She had to admit that the cousin looked handsome in his costume, while Raymond Allen appeared to be swimming in his. As for Lizzy, Becky had managed to piece together for her black boots, white breeches, and a black jacket with a scarlet waistcoat underneath. Kate had to further admit that her youngest sister did look smart, although she couldn't help adding to herself, *Too bad she's not actually smart.*

Kate was anxious for the hunt to start, but while her father and Dr. Webb already had their guns, and Benedict had said he didn't want one, Raymond

Allen was dithering over selecting his from the supply the gamekeeper had brought up and was showing to him now.

"You know," the duke said, "I do think I'd be more comfortable if Daniel chose for me."

"Daniel?" Kate said. "Who is *Daniel*?"

Just then, one of the footmen who'd been waiting attendance off to the side stepped forward, and Kate recalled something being said over breakfast about the duke's personal valet having pulled a bunker and one of the abbey's own footmen stepping in to help.

As Daniel selected a gun and sized it up, the duke informed the party at large, "Daniel was in the war, you know. He probably knows more about guns than all of us put together."

Had Daniel been in the war? Kate squinted at the footman. In her mind's eye, she summoned up a younger version, remembering him as a scruffy hall boy. Then he'd disappeared for a while. And now he was back, although she couldn't say for how long he had been. A year since the war had ended? Longer? She'd never paid much attention to the footmen before today. Handsome as they were, honestly, they all looked the same to her.

"Actually, I, too, was in the war," Benedict said, showing the first display of competition Kate had seen in him.

Good, she thought. *Competition is healthy.* Although why anyone should feel the need to compete with a footman, she had no idea.

"Yes," the duke said to Benedict, "but no doubt you were an officer, protected by your men. Daniel here, on the other hand, saw real fighting."

"Here you go, sir." Daniel handed the gun he'd selected to the duke, as though he hadn't noticed at all that they were talking about him. "I think this one should suit you."

"Thank you, Daniel," the duke said. "I'm sure it'll be perfect."

Daniel tilted his head and gave a slight bow as he backed away before turning on his heel. Once he started to walk, it looked as though he meant to keep going.

"Wait!" the duke called after him. "Aren't you coming with us? Aren't you going to attend to me?"

Daniel turned back. "I'm afraid not, sir. I need to help Jonathan bring the hampers down to the barn and help the others set up your luncheon there."

"Oh, I see." The duke sounded so disappointed.

"Daniel!" Lizzy called before the footman had a chance to start walking away again. "I've never shot a gun before. Do you think that, before you go, you could help me pick out a shotgun, too?"

Kate couldn't be sure, but she thought she saw a mild expression of scorn flit across the footman's face. Well, who could blame him? The idea of someone who'd never used a gun before going hunting was laughable, the height of foolishness, and she'd scorn Lizzy herself were it not for the fact that she wanted Lizzy along so she wouldn't have to deal with both the duke and the cousin herself.

Just as quickly as Kate spotted the scorn on the footman's face, it was gone, replaced by a bland expression of impassivity.

"Of course, Lady Elizabeth," the footman said. He then selected a shotgun and patiently showed Lizzy the rudiments of using it as the others waited—how to load it and all the et ceteras.

Daniel finished with, "I believe you're just meant to be shooting birds and the like today, so make sure to only aim at things above you and be sure no members of your party are in front of you when you shoot."

"Thank you, Daniel," Lizzy said with grateful good cheer, "I think I've got all that."

Honestly. Lizzy was now addressing a footman by his

given name and she was doing so with good cheer? Was this to be a *cheerful* hunt, then? It really was too much.

"Are we all finally ready?" Kate asked the assembly. When she was greeted with nods all around and some verbal assent, she added, "Good. Thank God it's Saturday."

"Why 'Thank God it's Saturday'?" the duke wanted to know.

"Because," Kate said, "at night and at Christmas and on Sundays we're not allowed to kill anything."

This is no kind of serious hunt, Kate thought. *Why, we don't even have a beater with us!*

Still, it was a beautiful day for a hunt.

Gorgeous, sunny, not a cloud in the sky—no sign of the rain that almost constantly plagued them. True, it was cold and extraordinarily windy, causing Kate's veil to annoyingly brush against her face, but one couldn't do a thing about the ever-present high winds at Porthampton Abbey. It was a fact of daily life one must simply grin and endure.

What was harder to endure was being forced to listen to her father and Dr. Webb behind her nattering on, chatting to the unarmed cousin they flanked, leaving her and Lizzy to be chatted to by the duke who walked between them.

Right now, he was going on about the inability to find good help. Not that she didn't agree with him, but did he have to whine about it? Like the wind, it was pointless to complain. She stopped listening, leaving it to Lizzy to offer sympathy, while she cocked an ear to the conversation going on behind her, all the while scanning the skies for something to shoot at.

"And you say you have a passion for croquet?" her father was saying to the cousin. "How fascinating!"

Kate didn't find it fascinating at all. Moreover, she could see where this was going. Father and Dr. Webb would ask the cousin questions and, no matter what Benedict replied, even if it were something completely idiotic, their responses would be, "How fascinating!" or "How interesting!" or "Aren't you clever?"

It was enough to make a person sick.

Never mind, she'd expected better from Father. Couldn't he see how transparent he was being? Clearly, having invited Meriwether Young and Raymond Allen to the abbey as potential suitors for her, now that he had the newly minted cousin on hand, he'd set his sights elsewhere: get the cousin to marry the daughter and everyone's entail problems would be solved.

She wondered how the cousin felt about her father's transparent plans.

And she decided she didn't care what the cousin thought—about this, or about anything else, really.

Then she thought, *What do I think about it? Why isn't anyone asking me?*

And then she decided that she really didn't want to think about any of this—marriage, entails—anymore, at least not right now. What she really wanted to do, was to shoot something.

Which she was being completely prevented from doing.

"Don't any of you know how to behave on a hunt?" she whispered in an annoyed voice at the group. "We've been out here for an hour, and you're all making so much noise, I haven't seen even a single bird yet!"

Before anyone could respond to her outburst, she peeled off and began heading to the left. "You keep going the way that you are," she informed the group, waving a dismissive hand at the path the others were cutting. "I'll head this way."

Raymond Allen began to follow her, but she stopped him with a gloved hand. "Really," she said firmly, "I prefer to hunt alone."

Reluctantly, the duke rejoined the men, who continued on with their talking walk.

Relieved to be rid of him, to be rid of all of them, Kate made her own way across the field. It was quieter now as distance grew between them, the voices receding, but as Kate scanned the skies for something to shoot, she heard footsteps at her side.

"Lizzy!" She whirled on her sister. "Did you not hear me tell the others that I prefer to hunt alone?"

"Of course I heard you," Lizzy replied mildly, before adding an eager, "but I want to hunt properly, too. And you're right, the others are making too much noise."

"Very well," Kate said, "but I'd be more comfortable if you kept your shotgun broken over your arm until you're ready to shoot something, which, in your case, I hope will be never. You are such a novice, you know."

"How do you mean," Lizzy said, as always refusing to show insult, "broken over my arm?"

Kate demonstrated, showing how the two main elements of the rifle could be partially separated, so that the hinge hung over her arm with the barrel pointed safely toward the ground.

"Oh," Lizzy said, "I don't think I want to do it like that. I'd rather just immediately be ready the instant I see anything."

"Fine," Kate said, exasperated. "Do it your way. But don't blame me if you shoot your own foot off."

"I won't."

"Now, do be quiet. As a matter of fact, it would be best if you walked behind me, making as little noise as possible so I can pretend you're not even there."

"All right," Lizzy agreed.

Kate proceeded to walk on ahead, past a stand of bushes. As she walked, looking upward, she positioned her shotgun, squinting one eye as she trained it on the sky overhead. Patience wasn't typically one of Kate's virtues, but she resolved that she would just do this until she saw the object of her desire.

It didn't take forever, at least. Soon, some flying creature came into view up in the distance. Kate froze, waited.

"Kate," she heard Lizzy speak from behind her; Lizzy, whom Kate had briefly forgotten was there.

"Shh," Kate hushed her.

Kate kept her eye on the sky. That bird needed to get closer for her to have her chance.

"Kate," Lizzy whispered again, this time with more urgency. Was there a rising panic to Lizzy's whisper? But what was there to *panic* about?

Kate ignored her, but then she felt the wind rushing at her from the right.

Only it wasn't the wind.

It was a body, a human body, crashing hers to the ground and then forcefully rolling her over and over until she and the other body came to rest behind the stand of bushes.

"Kate? Are you all right?" a male voice asked in a whisper.

She looked up to find the stable boy poised above her, his body on top of hers.

Kate had never even kissed a boy before, never mind had one lie on top of her, but she'd imagined—oh, how she'd imagined! And yet imagination was nothing compared to the reality of the masculine body and its hard length now pressing down on hers, which felt entirely natural somehow. Was it possible to swoon while lying down? That hair. Those lips just a breath away from her own. All she had to do was exhale and she was sure her lips would come into inevitable contact with his. But there were those eyes, filled with concern. Concern about... Wait.

Abruptly, Kate remembered who she was, who he was.

"Who gave you permission to call me Kate?" she demanded.

"I think when I saved your life, I earned that right," Will replied.

"What *are* you talking about? And why are we *whispering*?"

But before he could explain to her what he had meant by that, a shotgun shot rang out, followed by a scream.

Lizzy.

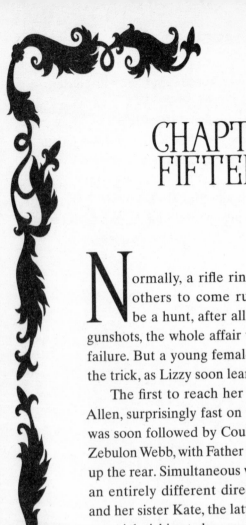

CHAPTER FIFTEEN

Normally, a rifle ringing out wouldn't cause others to come running. It was meant to be a hunt, after all. If there were never any gunshots, the whole affair would be deemed a sorry failure. But a young female screaming certainly did the trick, as Lizzy soon learned.

The first to reach her was the duke, Raymond Allen, surprisingly fast on those long legs of his. He was soon followed by Cousin Benedict and then Dr. Zebulon Webb, with Father panting a bit as he brought up the rear. Simultaneous with Father's arrival, from an entirely different direction, came Will Harvey and her sister Kate, the latter with straw and ground material sticking to her garments in various odd places.

"Lizzy, are you all right?" her father demanded, taking her in his arms. "What has happened?"

What *had* happened?

Oh, the morning had started out with such great promise! She'd never been on a hunt before. Honestly, she'd never been along for any of the fun and grown-up things her sisters, particularly Kate, were allowed to participate in. And then, when Daniel had shown her how to use a gun, *that* had been fun, although she'd never dreamed she would be called upon to use it so quickly nor in such a way. Still later, tramping around the grounds with the group, even though they hadn't been able to spot anything to shoot at due to the talking of the others, *that* had been fun, too. For a moment she'd thought that if that went on forever—the tramping and not shooting—that would be just fine. At least for once she was being taken seriously as a sort-of adult member of the group.

Not to mention, she'd known she looked just *smashing* in her hunting costume.

But then Kate had thought to peel off from the others in the hopes of actually shooting something, and Lizzy, wanting to be like and *with* her older sister, had gone along.

And then...

And then...

"*That* happened!" Lizzy cried, disengaging from Father's embrace as she sought to point over the shoulders of the party encircling her.

The others followed her pointing finger, and that's when they all saw what had happened: the motionless body, lying just a few feet away.

Dr. Webb broke off from the group.

"Is he dead, Doctor?" the earl asked as the doctor drew closer to the object of all their attention.

"I would say," Dr. Webb said, "that the man is quite dead. That is usually the case when a man has had his head shot just about clear off his shoulders."

"Lizzy, what happened?" Kate asked with what struck Lizzy as a surprising amount of concern, coming from Kate.

So Lizzy explained, as though just talking to Kate alone, about the excitement she'd been feeling and about how eager she was to follow where Kate led. Here Lizzy turned to include the wider group.

"Kate insisted I stay behind her, so as not to be a nuisance, which I didn't mind, not really. I didn't want to put myself forward, since I knew she had far greater experience with such things than I. But then she raised her shotgun, just keeping her head tilted toward the sky, looking for something to shoot at, for birds." Lizzy paused. "That's when I saw…him." As she pointed again, she shut her eyes as though reluctant to look upon what had happened, what she had done.

Lizzy felt herself engulfed by warring emotions: disgust at what she had done but a curious thrill of excitement as well. It was an astonishing thing to realize that as stupid and silly as others thought her, as she often thought herself, in the moment of danger, she hadn't cowered or run or waited for someone to save her; in the moment, she had reacted with action.

She shoved her feelings aside as she opened her eyes and continued. "He was stumbling across the field—toward Kate, really, since she was between us. I tried to warn her, I did, but she was too busy taking aim at the sky. Then when he drew closer, I tried to warn her again, but still she wouldn't listen. He was almost upon her, and I was about to scream, but before I could open my mouth, Will Harvey appeared from nowhere, pushing her out of sight and under those bushes over there."

"I was wondering where you'd come from," Father said, addressing the stable boy.

"After I warned you, back at the house," Will said, "and you wouldn't listen to me, I thought I'd just trail along anyway, stay out of sight."

"What warning?" the duke asked, but the earl ignored him.

"I thought I told you," Father said, still focused on Will, "that there was nothing to be concerned about."

"It's a good thing he ignored you," Lizzy said, "because

I'm sure he saved Kate's life."

"Yes," her father said gruffly to Will, "and I am sure we are all grateful to you for it."

Kate turned to Will, stunned. "Is that what you meant? By what you said before?"

Will looked away, seemingly unwilling to take credit. "Anyone might've done it," he said.

"But no one else was here!" Lizzy said. "Not to mention, once you rolled Kate out of the way, that…that…that *creature* turned his focus upon me. As he drew closer, I could finally see his eyes. They looked sick, really sick, *dangerously* sick… and…and…and…and I just shot him in the head!"

The full enormity of it all washed over her then, more forcefully than before, and her hands began to shake.

"My poor Lizzy!" Father cried out as he embraced her again.

"Poor Lizzy?" Kate said. "Try making it: bra-*vo*, Lizzy! The first time she shoots a gun, she saves my life *and* shoots a man's head off? I'd say there's hope for her yet!"

"Thank you, Kate," Lizzy said, grateful for her sister's kind words. "But here is one thing I'd like to know."

The others looked at her and she, in turn, pointed at the dead body, the soles of his shoes facing them.

"Who did I just kill?" Lizzy said. "Who *is* he?"

CHAPTER SIXTEEN

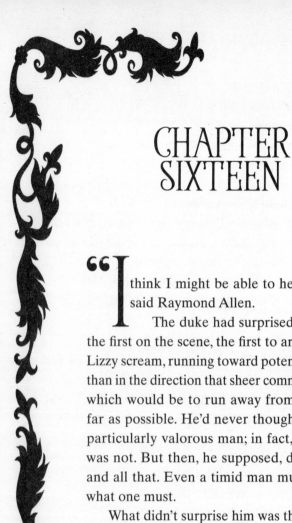

"I think I might be able to help you out there," said Raymond Allen.

The duke had surprised himself by being the first on the scene, the first to arrive after hearing Lizzy scream, running toward potential danger rather than in the direction that sheer common sense dictated, which would be to run away from it, preferably as far as possible. He'd never thought himself to be a particularly valorous man; in fact, he knew that he was not. But then, he supposed, damsel in distress and all that. Even a timid man must sometimes do what one must.

What didn't surprise him was that having spoken up, he was now being ignored.

He watched as the others approached the corpse, joining the doctor with varying degrees of trepidation.

"The color of his blood," Lady Elizabeth said, sounding confused. "Can that be quite right?"

"How do you mean?" Dr. Webb said. "What do you think is wrong with it?"

"Only," Lady Elizabeth said, still sounding confused, "when I cut my finger or some such, the blood that comes out is a much more lively vivid red, while his is dull as rust, the color of a brick, almost like what blood looks like after it's completely dried and it's no longer so...lively."

"Ah, I see what you mean," Dr. Webb said, looking briefly confused himself before hardening his expression into something more decisive. "Still, I'm sure it's all quite normal."

"But how can that be?" Lady Elizabeth pressed.

"Head wounds, you know," Dr. Webb said authoritatively. "They are different from any other kinds of wounds."

"So you've seen this before?"

"Well, no. I've never actually had any patients who were shot in the head before, but I suspect that if I had, they would look exactly like this."

And the duke suspected, or was beginning to, that the medical man might not quite know what he was talking about.

"But that smell," Lady Elizabeth went on, covering her nose.

"That is the smell of decomposition, my dear," Dr. Webb said.

"So quickly?" Lady Elizabeth asked skeptically. "Because I've seen a few recently dead things before, and—"

"As I said already—head wounds. They are quite different than—"

"Oh, look!" Lady Katherine said. "The man has livery on. Could he be one of ours?"

"I suppose it's possible," her father said. "But if so, which one could it be?"

"He's not one of yours," the duke said. And then, when no one appeared to hear him, "I *said*, he's not one of yours!" he practically shouted.

"He's not?" Lady Katherine said, looking surprised, and the duke wondered what surprised her more: that someone had contradicted her and her father, or that he was still there.

"Who is he, then?"

"I believe that must be Parker," the duke said, reluctant now to come too near.

"Parker?" Lady Katherine said. "And who is he when he's at home?"

"My valet," the duke said. "Or, at least, he was."

"Oh, that's right," she said, "you'd mentioned something at breakfast about his disappearing." She moved closer still to the headless corpse, seemingly not put off in the ways most of the others were. "But how can you be so sure?"

"Because the livery is all wrong," the duke said, gesturing vaguely with his fingers. "Or, if not *all* wrong, there are certainly differences." He enumerated what those distinctions were: a slightly different-colored this, a slightly different cut of that, and so forth.

"I suppose you're right," Lady Katherine said. "His livery is all dusty and dirty—not typically the Porthampton Abbey way. But are you quite sure he is not one of ours?"

A part of him couldn't believe they were having this discussion. She obviously didn't pay enough attention to her own footmen to notice the differences between hers and this one.

"Quite sure," he asserted vehemently.

"Seems such a shame," she said. "He decides to leave service and then he winds up like this?"

"None of this would have happened," Will Harvey spoke up, addressing his words to the earl, "if you'd listened to my warning." As though suddenly realizing to whom he was addressing his remarks, he added a hasty, "Sir."

"And what exactly was that warning again?" the duke asked.

"Yes," Benedict Clarke said, "I should like to know, too. If there is some sort of threat here, we should all be informed."

"I told His Lordship," Will Harvey said, "that I was concerned after what had happened with my uncle; you know, being dead, then not, and then dead again. My concern was that, having happened once, it could—"

"Yes!" Lizzy cried eagerly, snapping her fingers at the stable boy. "I'm *sure* that's why I reacted how I did!"

"How do you mean, Lizzy?" her father asked.

"Well, when the man, when this Parker started stumbling toward me after Kate was safely out of the way, I was practically frozen with fear. And then I saw those eyes—I could barely move, I was so terrified. I suppose a part of me must have remembered then; you know, what we'd heard last night at dinner: that Will's aunt finally killed his uncle with a shot through the head. I guess that must be why I shot there and not at some other part of his person. When he just kept coming at me, all I could think was 'Just shoot him in the head! That should do the trick! Just shoot him in the head!'"

"Once again," Lady Katherine said, "I feel compelled to say good show, Lizzy!"

"Thank you," Lady Elizabeth said. "But what about the threat?"

"What threat?" the earl asked.

"What Will described," Lady Elizabeth said. "Don't you think that this"—she gestured toward the dead man—"is just like what happened with Will's uncle?"

"But Ezra Harvey had his heart or some such ripped out first, before being shot by his wife later," the earl objected.

The duke wondered that they could speak so graphically and heartlessly about the fate of Will's relative with Will standing right there among them. When the duke shifted his gaze in that direction, it surprised him to notice that Lady Katherine was looking with concern at the stable boy as well. But for his part, the stable boy kept his gaze dead forward, his jaw hard.

"I don't see that at all, the idea of this being at all like that," the earl went on, turning to the doctor for confirmation. "Doctor?"

The doctor squinted some more at the corpse before concluding, "I quite agree with you, my lord. We all know that what your stable boy described happening with his own family—dead, not dead, dead again—*can't* happen medically. And as for this…"

"So there's no threat?" the earl demanded.

"None that I can detect," Dr. Webb said with a shrug.

"But I saw him!" Lady Elizabeth said. "I saw him with my own eyes! There was something really wrong with him!"

"I know what you think you saw," the doctor said, "and I believe that you believe that you saw it. But such things are simply not possible. This poor fellow, well, who will ever really know what happened to him? Perhaps he left the duke's service because he decided he'd had enough of working for the upper classes. And then, perhaps, he came back here, bitter, determined to take his vengeance *upon* the upper classes. No doubt, that murderous impulse was what you saw in his eyes. But beyond that speculation?" The doctor shrugged. "We cannot guess what was in his mind because he is no longer here for us to ask. All we can be certain of is that, whatever you're thinking this is, Lady Elizabeth, it's not that."

"W-will I hang for this?" Lady Elizabeth asked.

"Pardon?"

"I killed a man, didn't I?"

"Don't be absurd," her father said. "Clarkes don't hang! Besides, anyone can see it was a case of self-defense. You felt you and your sister were threatened, and you merely acted upon that threat."

"And as for those eyes," Dr. Webb said, "I suppose it's a

good thing you've pretty much obliterated them with that straight shot of yours, so now they can no longer devil you."

The duke felt himself experiencing astonishment and outrage on Lady Elizabeth's behalf. The medical man had been so dismissive of her, and even her own father had been to a certain extent—why, they'd practically patted her on the head!

He was about to voice some of his own thoughts on the matter, in Lady Elizabeth's defense. He might tell them that in the short time Parker had been in his service, nothing about the man had indicated he harbored any murderous impulses. On the contrary. Parker had been, in his experience, mostly just mild and bland and not a terribly good worker.

But he never got the chance, because Lady Katherine was saying, "Well, that's settled, then." And now, to his astonishment, she was raising the hem of the split-back jacket of her hunting costume a bit as she stepped right over the headless corpse before throwing over her shoulder, "Isn't anyone else ready for lunch?"

CHAPTER SEVENTEEN

Daniel couldn't believe what his ears were hearing.

The second footman normally kept his eyes straight forward on such occasions, but on this one, he couldn't help but shift his gaze just enough to look around at the others lining the walls—his fellow footman, Jonathan; the maids, Agnes and Becky, drafted into service to help the footmen at this supposedly informal barn "luncheon"—and he could see from the slightest shifts in their typical eyes-straight-ahead-seeing-nothing stances that none of them could believe it, either.

Apparently, someone—that valet of the duke's, Parker, whom Daniel had met only briefly—had tried to attack Lady Katherine and then Lady Elizabeth, and the latter had shot him dead.

Daniel couldn't believe that young Lady Elizabeth, whom he had taught how to use a shotgun only just a short time ago, had already employed it in such a deadly fashion, nor could he believe how gleeful they all seemed about it; he couldn't imagine, if Lady Grace were here, that *she* would react this way. Although at least, to Lady Elizabeth's credit, as they talked on and on, her expression had turned from one of eagerness to something resembling dismay at the role she'd played.

But then, after Parker was dead, apparently they'd all stepped over his body and come here for their luncheon!

"Well," Lady Katherine said now, "it's not like the body wasn't going to keep for a bit. What shall we do with it, anyway? Should we send it somewhere?" She turned to Raymond Allen. "Duke, do you know who his people were?"

Daniel had noticed that in addition to Lady Elizabeth's occasional expressions of dismay, the duke looked appropriately disturbed by what had happened. Daniel supposed it could be that it was his valet who'd been involved, but Daniel didn't think it was as simple as that. Perhaps there was more depth to the duke than Daniel had glimpsed upon first meeting him the night before? Or perhaps, even, there was greater depth to the duke than the duke saw in himself?

"To my knowledge," the duke answered with some sadness, "he hadn't any, so—"

"That's that, then," Lady Katherine said brightly. "And then," she said, eyes flashing as she returned to her recounting of what had gone on before, "Father banished the stable boy, told him not to show his face on the place again before tomorrow."

"The nerve of that boy!" the earl said heatedly. "He was trying to follow us here. He said he was sure we weren't safe. As if we needed him for protection!"

"Only you, Father," Lady Katherine said, "would tell a stable boy he couldn't come to a barn!"

"He did save Kate's life," Lady Elizabeth pointed out.

"Yes," Lady Katherine said, sobering, "I suppose he did." But that sobering lasted for only the briefest of instants before she was off again, laughing in her way about some other "madcap" aspect of the day.

Daniel really couldn't believe these people. But then, when he thought about it for a moment, he could. He, like the others he toiled with Downstairs, had seen and therefore knew all too much about the people he served overhead, while they knew precious little about those down below.

A man had died, and here they were all laughing over their luncheon. Well, most of them, at any rate. And were Lady Grace here, he was sure, she wouldn't be laughing, either. Still…

What a farce it all was! They'd gone on their little hunt, as they would do when guests came for the weekend, shooting at animals for sport—although he couldn't say that was completely wrong, since they did always eventually eat whatever they shot. Of course he supposed that wouldn't be the case today, since all that had been shot was a man. But then, after their shooting, they would come here to this "barn" for their luncheon, as though it somehow meant they were roughing it by not going back to the house for their midday meal.

Daniel himself had roughed it in the war, every day he'd fought in it, and this in no way resembled that. The Upstairs version of "roughing it" still included a long table covered with a fine cloth and set with linen, crystal, and silver. Not to mention the servants—Jonathan, Agnes and Becky, him—called into service to wait upon them.

Once more, Daniel briefly shifted his straight-ahead gaze to glance at his fellow servants: Jonathan, who was never too happy to lose to Daniel at cards, which he usually did, and yet who was always willing to play another hand; Agnes, whose job it was to tend to Lady Katherine and who did so more staunchly than any general protecting his country; and Becky, who waited attendance on both the younger daughters of the house and whom Daniel sometimes thought, when he thought about a future in which he would have marriage and family, might be the person he would have those things with. After all, who might he ever marry but another servant? He couldn't help but think that if war ever came to Porthampton Abbey, he'd rather have these three by his side to fight—come to that, throw in Fanny and Mrs. Owen—than all of Upstairs and their fancy guests put together. Well, maybe he'd want Lady Grace by his side, too, not that he imagined she'd be much use in a fight, but he couldn't see abandoning someone decent like her to the devices of the useless lot she'd grown up with.

Here they sat at their long table—Lady Katherine at one end, her father at the other, with Dr. Webb, Benedict Clarke, the duke, and Lady Elizabeth between them—consuming their "roughing it" meal, which consisted of what exactly? Cucumber sandwiches, cold turkey, asparagus tart, poached salmon, scones, blancmange, lemonade, ginger beer, lemon barley water, Turkish coffee. Oh, and a chocolate soufflé. A chocolate soufflé! Could anything be more ridiculous than that?

Even in a barn—a *barn!*—these people expected everything to be perfect.

Well—Daniel sighed internally—it wasn't for him to judge. All he needed to do was make sure his eyes were facing forward, that his expression showed none of what he was feeling, and to simply act his part.

Which was what he was doing when Mr. Wright entered the barn, the old man huffing slightly after his trek down from the house. Propped on his hand was a silver salver with some piece of paper on it. Daniel wondered it hadn't blown away in the day's strong wind. But then he thought ruefully, *Not even a folded sheet of paper would think to defy old Wright.*

Mr. Wright stopped just inside the entry, waiting to be noticed.

"Yes, Wright," the earl said. "What is it?"

"A call came for Dr. Webb," the butler announced, "and I have taken the message down for him."

"Well," His Lordship said, "bring it over, then."

The butler obeyed, and Dr. Webb removed the piece of paper from the silver plate, unfolded it.

He started to read, his brow furrowing as he did so. At last, he looked up.

"Apparently, I'm needed in the village," Dr. Webb said. "I'm sure it's nothing, really. There's been some small disturbance there caused by a sick woman. She refuses to come in to my surgery and they've called for me."

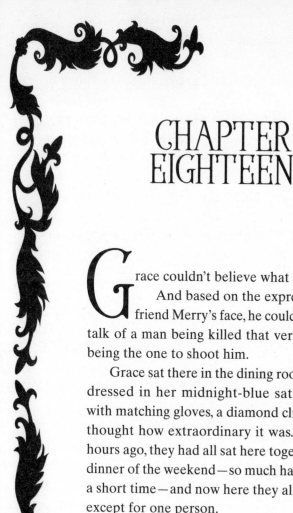

CHAPTER EIGHTEEN

G race couldn't believe what she was hearing.
And based on the expression on her new friend Merry's face, he couldn't, either. All this talk of a man being killed that very day and Lizzy's being the one to shoot him.

Grace sat there in the dining room with the others, dressed in her midnight-blue satin Vionnet dress with matching gloves, a diamond clip in her hair, and thought how extraordinary it was. Just twenty-four hours ago, they had all sat here together for their first dinner of the weekend—so much had changed in such a short time—and now here they all were again. Well, except for one person.

"Where is Dr. Webb?" she asked.

Her father explained about the doctor being called away to attend to one of the villagers.

"I told him," her father finished, "that he should take our car and driver and that the chauffeur might stay with him to ferry any messages back and forth if there was anything I needed to be notified about. There's a phone in the surgery, of course, but apparently the woman refused to come in, so he is attending to her at home. You know hardly any of the villagers have phones. Anyway, I'm sure there is nothing to be concerned about."

"Whatever the cause of his absence," Grandmama said, "I'm so glad the doctor is no longer with us. The people one finds oneself compelled to dine with these days!"

"Yes, Hortense," Grandfather, for once awake, said drily, drawing out the word, "I quite agree. In fact, I've been feeling that way at this table for many years now."

"I wish you'd consulted me before lending Dr. Webb our car and Ralph," Kate addressed her father, referring to the chauffeur. "What if I wanted to go somewhere?"

"Where would you need to go, my dear?" Father said. "We have all the entertainment we need right here. Besides, I don't see as how we'll have any need of the car before tomorrow, and even then not until late in the day when our guests will need a ride back to the train station."

"Before Lady Grace asked about Dr. Webb," Merry said to the earl, "you were about to tell us what you decided to do with the, er, body."

Grace shuddered. It was such a gruesome topic to broach, particularly coming from Merry. But then, when she noted the worried expression on Merry's face, she knew she couldn't blame him for asking it. She found that she, too, wanted to know how it had been disposed of. Anything was better than thinking about a dead man just lying out there somewhere, exposed to the elements and wild animals. Of course, nothing could hurt him, being dead already, but it was still awful to think about it.

"I told the gamekeeper to have a few of the gardeners bury him in one of the more remote gardens," Father said.

"How horrible!" her new cousin's mother, Rowena Clarke, said.

"I don't see why you would say that," Grandmama replied.

"It seems to me to be a fine use to make of a murderous valet. How better to continue serving than to become compost?"

"Are you always this insensitive and unkind?" Rowena asked.

"Yes, she is," Grandfather said.

"I'm sorry, my dear," Grandmama said, failing to look sorry at all as she ignored Grandfather and addressed her words to Rowena, "but what other way is there to be?"

"You'll have to excuse my mother-in-law," Mother said. "Her sense of humor can take some getting used to."

"Please do not apologize for me, Fidelia," Grandmama said. "And what, pray tell, is there to apologize for?"

"I don't know," Grandfather said, consulting the ceiling for inspiration. "Everything you've ever said or might say in the future, perhaps?"

"Be still, George," Grandmama said.

"Didn't the man deserve at least a Christian burial?" Rowena asked.

Grandmama considered this, but just briefly, before concluding, "I don't see how. I'm pretty sure that, once he tried to kill two of my three granddaughters, he forfeited all such rights. It's a good thing Grace wasn't there, too. Not that she'd ever allow herself to be placed in a position of potential danger or know what to do with herself if she were."

Grace waited for Grandfather to come to her defense, but she saw that he was already nodding off again. Who knew when he might be as lucid again as he'd just been? There was nothing else for it but to wince at Grandmama's words even as she had to acknowledge that this assessment of her was accurate. In her embarrassment, she cast her eyes about— anything other than the people she was dining with would do, really. And as she looked elsewhere, her eyes passing by the footmen lining the walls, something she saw made her stop and travel her gaze backward. Had that footman—the one called Daniel, she believed—been looking at her with something like sympathy? Was that concern she saw there? But no sooner did her eyes settle on him than his own shot straight forward as though seeing nothing.

"Shouldn't we be scared?" Grace asked.

"Of what?" Kate said.

"That two men have died!" Grace exclaimed. "And *how* they died..."

"I suppose such a reaction—fear—might be expected from others," Kate mused, as though seriously considering the suggestion. Then she snorted a laugh. "It's a shame we don't scare more easily."

"Yes, just dreadful," Grandmama added with a titter.

"I do think we've had enough talk of death for one evening," Mother said. That was so like Mother. Grace always imagined that Mother viewed her role in the family as that of the eternal peacemaker and that, no matter what happened in their world or in the outside world, her job was to keep everything smooth and pleasant and light for Father. "Let me tell you all about this story I read today in the *Tatler*..."

As Mother launched into her tale of London gossip, no doubt hoping to bring the talk back to something she thought more suitable for dinner conversation, Grace's mind wandered, so she barely noticed when Mr. Wright walked in with his silver salver.

But she couldn't help noticing when Father, having read whatever note Mr. Wright had brought to him, announced to the table at large, "It's from Dr. Webb. He says the case is a bit more tricky than he anticipated, but he is sure all will be well in the end, only he won't be joining us this evening."

"Well, we knew that already," Grandmama said with a laugh.

"Please send a note back with Ralph," Father told Mr. Wright, "saying that we wish him well with his medical situation and to send word again as circumstances develop or if anything changes."

"Dead bodies. Medical emergencies." Mother sighed. "This is not how I envisioned this meal going." She sighed again. "Perhaps you gentlemen would like to remain here for your port?" she suggested to Father, Benedict, Merry, and the duke. "We ladies will adjourn now to the drawing room."

Once there, Grace sought out Lizzy. She was concerned about how her younger sister was feeling after her hunting ordeal.

"I'm fine," Lizzy said. "Really, Grace, you mustn't worry about me so." Then Lizzy's expression shifted from one of blithe unconcern to something more serious and considering. "You know," she said, "come to think of it, I do think that today has taken its toll on me. Perhaps it's best that I retire early."

Lizzy excused herself from the group.

A moment later, Grace excused herself, too, thinking to go after Lizzy. Perhaps she needed some kind words of reassurance—truly, anyone in Lizzy's position would have done the same today or, at least, any *brave* person—or possibly a hug?

But when Grace caught up with Lizzy and saw her ascending the grand staircase, she noticed a smile playing on her younger sister's lips.

Was Lizzy up to something? And if so, what?

CHAPTER NINETEEN

The men had finally rejoined the ladies in the drawing room.

Little good that does me, thought Kate.

There the men all stood—her father, Mr. Young, the duke, and Benedict Clarke—clustered around together at one end of the room, brandy snifters in hand; Grandfather did love his brandy but was nowhere present, so perhaps Mr. Wright had escorted him up to bed already. No doubt, the remaining men were solving the problems of the universe. While here she sat, confined to the sofas before the fireplace with her mother, Grandmama, Rowena Clarke, and Grace. They were back to discussing the *Tatler*. Not that Kate minded a bit of gossip. She liked it just as much as any person, and she preferred hers fresh and juicy. But after such a day, she had hoped for something more stimulating.

It was too bad Lizzy had gone up so early. Lizzy might never be accused of being the sharpest knife in the drawer, but even she would have been something. At least with her there, they might have discussed what had gone on before. It was still hard to fathom that Lizzy—Lizzy!—had pretty much saved her life.

Well, after the stable boy had done it first.

She wondered, not for the first time, if he remembered that one day they'd spent together as friends all those years ago, and decided: probably not. It probably had never meant the same thing to him as it did to her.

Kate narrowed her eyes at the cluster of men, zeroing in on Cousin Benedict.

For the first time, it occurred to her: While Father might be designing that she marry Cousin Benedict to keep Porthampton Abbey in the family—*their* family, not Benedict's—might it be possible that Cousin Benedict had other designs? After all, couldn't he marry anyone he chose and still inherit after Father's death? And where would that leave her? Where would it leave all of them?

Perhaps, Kate thought for the first time, *I should give him a chance.* After all, he did represent the clearest and easiest path to what everyone in the household wanted, which was to secure the estate. And he looked so handsome in his dinner clothes. That was one thing you couldn't fault Cousin Benedict for: a lack of handsomeness.

Besides which, if she *didn't* take advantage of this opportunity, might one of her younger sisters—Grace seemed most likely—swoop in and take him off the market first?

Despite some few brief moments of closeness, Kate had never had much use for her younger sisters growing up. Grace and Lizzy had gotten on well enough with each other—why, at some points, they'd practically been a team! But Kate? She'd always been her own world, apart from the others. She'd had to be. Kate had always known she was destined for greater things. She was, after all, the eldest. She couldn't afford to be so eternally *nice* like Grace or as silly as Lizzy. She had the family's future to think of. But looking at Grace now...

Not that Grace was the swooping type. But despite

Grace's fears about, well, pretty much everything, she did have an unusually strong sense of wanting to do *right* by her family. So if Grace thought that Kate was not doing her duty, might she feel compelled to take over? Kate wouldn't give her the chance. Maybe she'd decide Cousin Benedict wasn't for her, no matter what was at stake, but that should be *her* decision, and hers alone.

"Excuse me, ladies," Kate said, rising from her place on the sofa and putting up a hand to make sure her hair was still perfectly secured in place before she made her way across the room. She knew she posed a striking figure in her emerald-green dress. It was always such a good color with her blond hair. Well, all colors were, really.

"Kate!" her father said as she approached.

"Lady Katherine," Mr. Young and the duke greeted her simultaneously, both formally and with some surprise, as though they hadn't all been together at the table not too long ago.

Kate noticed that Cousin Benedict didn't greet her with words, but merely with a slight tilt of his head and an appreciative half smile, which caused her to think there might be hope for him yet.

"You've decided to join us!" her father said.

"Yes, Father, I thought I'd take the opportunity of a pause in chatter about the *Tatler* to come over here and see what is going on in the real world. Cousin Benedict? Might I have a word?"

He showed only a mild surprise as he replied, "Of course, Lady Katherine."

With a hand on his arm—such a surprisingly strong arm; he said he'd been in the war, hadn't he?—she peeled him off from the group. And when she'd led him a sufficient distance away so as not to be overheard, she turned to face him.

"You know," she said, "you don't need to address me as Lady Katherine as the others do. We're related, after all. Although, thankfully, not too closely."

"What shall I call you, then?"

"Kate will do."

"Very well, Kate. And what was it you wanted to discuss?"

"I was wondering…" But suddenly it hit her. For once in her life, she hadn't thought far enough ahead. She'd thought only about getting away from the women and getting *to* him, to give him that chance. But now that she had him here, to herself, what *did* she have to talk to him about?

Then she remembered her training.

When she and her sisters were little, Grandmama had impressed upon them the importance of being able to hold down a decent conversation with anyone, no matter what their station in life, at any time. On sunny days, she'd had them practice on animals around the estate—plants, even! And on rainy ones, which were always far more frequent, they'd practiced on Fred, the suit of armor.

"The trick," Grandmama would say, "is to pretend you have an interest. Ask the other person questions about what you think is of interest to them, and ask those questions as though you might actually care. Like this: 'Fred, how is that suit of armor treating you today? Not too hot in there, I trust?' or 'Fred, how are you finding this wet weather? Best not go outside today, if I were you. I can't imagine rust is good for a man in your condition, don't you agree?'"

It was grand advice, this talking to others about what might interest them, not that Grandmama ever seemed to heed it much herself in social situations, but it did save Kate now.

"What do you do for entertainment, Cousin Benedict," she asked, "if you don't like to hunt?"

Peculiarly enough, having feigned interest in the asking of the question, she now found that she genuinely was.

"I like to read," he said.

"Oh!" she said, forcing herself to speak brightly. "How, er, interesting."

"I like to read whenever I have free time, whenever I am not required to do anything else."

"I see."

She liked to read as much as the next person, more than her other close relatives really, but to do it in one's spare time to the exclusion of all else? It did seem a bit much. It did seem a bit unbalanced.

"We have a lovely little library here at Porthampton Abbey," she said.

"Yes, I've seen it. A most impressive selection."

"And what do you like to read?" she asked, determined to keep trying.

"Oh, all sorts of things. Anything and everything, really. The classics, of course, all of Shakespeare…"

"*All* of Shakespeare?"

"There are only about thirty-seven plays. Well, and the sonnets."

"You know, I have read some Shakespeare."

"Really? Which ones?"

"The important ones, of course. Although I've never quite understood the appeal of *Romeo and Juliet*. That one is a puzzle to me."

"How so?"

"Only, how can two people fall in love so quickly, in love enough to die for each other in such a short time? It strikes me as silly."

"I take it you're not a romantic, then?"

"I don't know if I'd go so far as to say that. Now, why don't

you tell me more about all this reading you do? I find it so...
fascinating."

As he did so, speaking on what was obviously his favorite
topic, she studied his face, that handsome face, and that mouth
of his in particular as it moved to form words.

Kate may not have shared the depth of his enthusiasm for
books, but she did admire passion in other people. And as she
stole glances at that mouth, she found herself, inexplicably,
wondering what it would be like to be kissed by those lips.
They would no doubt be soft at first, but then, perhaps, it
would progress to a point where things were...firmer?

Kate had never kissed anyone before, never been kissed
in the way she was now imagining. Of course, she had some
notion of what married people got up to behind closed
doors. Her mother was modern in that way, and made sure
her daughters knew at a startlingly young age what might be
expected of them on their wedding nights so it wouldn't be the
surprise to them that it had been to her, although Kate was
never quite certain that Lizzy in particular had understood
what she'd been told.

And of course, she'd seen animals doing things around
the estate.

But the only kissing of the nature she was thinking on
now that she'd ever experienced was when she was younger
and she and her sisters would bend all their arms at the elbow
and then practice romantically kissing the crook formed at
the juncture of upper arm and lower, their eyes closed tightly,
mashing their lips around. It was one of the few times in her
life that Kate had felt at home with her sisters, free not to
be troubled by any concerns, free from the tyranny of being
eldest.

Kissing their own inner arms—how they'd laughed over
that!

Kate wasn't laughing now, though.

Because as she watched Benedict's lips moving, not registering the meaning of the sounds coming out of him, her mind went back to another pair of lips.

The stable boy's, as he lay over her beneath the bushes, his strong body pressing into hers.

What, she found herself thinking wildly, would it be like to kiss *those* lips?

CHAPTER TWENTY

Fanny had had barely a second to think all day, although when she had, she'd found herself thinking of Will Harvey.

They'd never talked as much as they had that morning. And she found that if she had liked him before, she liked him even more now.

Not to mention what she'd heard from Daniel and the others when they'd returned with the hampers following the barn luncheon. Apparently, after Will's talk with her, he'd followed the family and their guests on their hunt, hanging back so as not to be seen, but then jumping in just in time to push Lady Katherine out of the way of danger.

Kind, he was, and brave, too.

Fanny had to admit she wouldn't mind so very much if Will Harvey were to push *her* out of the path of danger.

Fanny couldn't imagine Lady Katherine would even bother to feel appropriately grateful or show gratitude to him for it.

Not that Fanny would want her to anyway, at least not too *much* a show of gratitude.

It was the time of day—late at night, really—when

it was Fanny's duty to help Mrs. Owen set the kitchen to rights. Agnes and Becky were upstairs, helping the daughters of the house get ready for bed. Daniel and Jonathan were in the servants' hall, playing one last game of cards before going up to the attic. Mr. Wright and Mrs. Murphy, the head housekeeper, were enjoying their nightly small glass of sherry in the butler's pantry.

"It isn't right," Fanny said, moving leftover food from larger serving dishes to smaller ones before storing them in the refrigerator. That refrigerator was such a wonderful invention. Mrs. Owen always said that back before Fanny had started working there, before the house had gotten one of the first ones of its kind for commercial use, they'd mostly had to throw out a lot of things. So wasteful. At least now things would last for a bit. Of course, Upstairs could never be allowed to have a leftover pass their lips, but she and the others down here might enjoy it for their lunches tomorrow.

"What's not right, Fanny?" Mrs. Owen said, adding in exasperation, "And watch what you're doing with those plates! I'd like some of that salmon for my lunch tomorrow, but I won't like it half so much if you drop it on the floor first."

"What Daniel and Jonathan said, when they were bringing in the dinner things after service." Fanny answered the question while ignoring Mrs. Owen's exasperation. She was well used to Mrs. Owen admonishing her. It didn't mean anything. "About them burying that valet in a back garden."

"It's none of our concern, Fanny. Our concern—"

"Mrs. Owen is right, Fanny!" a voice boomed.

Fanny looked up from her work to see Mr. Wright standing there, a small tray with two empty glasses with just dregs of sherry coloring their bottoms in his hand.

"How *dare* you question the judgment of His Lordship!"

Mr. Wright continued when she initially failed to respond.

"I only meant—"

"I know what you meant, Fanny, but it is simply not your place to say it."

"But they just killed him and—"

"And he was trying to attack Lady Katherine! I shudder to think what would have happened if Lady Elizabeth hadn't acted so quickly."

Fanny could well imagine him shuddering. They all knew how Mr. Wright felt about Lady Katherine, the first daughter of the house. Why, sometimes, you'd think he thought she was *his* daughter!

"They could have questioned him first before shooting," Fanny tried again.

"I doubt there was time."

"And to bury him in the garden…"

"Enough! I'm sure His Lordship was being facetious about that part. You know how humorous His Lordship can be."

She did not. Nor did she think he was being so in this case.

"But if it is true—" she started.

"Enough!" Mr. Wright said again, more forcefully this time as he held up his hand firmly to stop her going on, and even she could see there was no point in it. "And if you say one word about the *Titanic*—"

"I won't, sir."

"That's settled, then, and we shall speak no more about it." He put down the tray with its glasses on it, adding it to the pile of things yet to be cleaned. "The footmen have gone up to bed and Mrs. Murphy has gone to her room and now I shall retire, too. Fanny. Mrs. Owen." With a curt nod, he took his leave.

"What are we doing about breakfast in the morning?" Fanny asked Mrs. Owen, hoping to make peace with at least one person and seeing as how she knew food was Mrs. Owen's favorite topic.

"I don't know," Mrs. Owen said with a hearty laugh. "I suspect we'll be eating it, I suppose! Isn't that what you do with breakfast?"

"I meant for them," Fanny said, gesturing with her chin toward the ceiling and the people who lived their lives above it.

"Oh, Fanny." Mrs. Owen sighed. "I can't even think about that right now, I'm that tired. Let tomorrow take care of tomorrow; we'll come up with something. No doubt Her Ladyship will go over it first thing with Mrs. Murphy and then we'll be notified last minute on what they've decided."

Fanny could see that Mrs. Owen was tired, dead on her feet really. Well, Mrs. Owen wasn't getting any younger.

"Why don't you go on up?" Fanny suggested. "I can finish down here by myself."

"Are you sure?" Mrs. Owen looked about with warring expressions on her face: eagerness to rest but reluctance to leave Fanny with so much mess.

"I'm sure. Sometimes I think I'm better when I'm on my own. It helps me to think."

"I know I yell at you a lot, and you mostly deserve it," Mrs. Owen said, laying a hand briefly on Fanny's arm before passing her by, "but you're a good girl, Fanny, and no one truthful could ever say any different."

And then Fanny was alone.

She scrubbed and scoured stubborn stains off all the pots and pans.

As she performed these duties, she thought some more about the things Daniel had said while bringing in the serving plates from dinner.

Daniel had said that when they talked about having the

valet buried in the garden, they'd mostly all just laughed about it. So maybe Mr. Wright had been judging it accurately, and that part was merely a joke?

Not that it seemed much of a joke to Fanny. None of it did.

But Daniel had also said that not all of them had laughed. Lady Grace hadn't. Nor had Mr. Young or the duke or even that new cousin of theirs, Benedict Clarke. Fanny had only seen the cousin briefly the day before on his arrival and had caught a few glimpses of him since. He was handsome. And if he hadn't laughed then maybe he was even nice, too. Or, at least, nice for one of *them*.

The scrubbing and scouring done, Fanny cleaned off all the countertops until you could eat off them. Then she got out the broom and swept, followed by wet-mopping the whole place until it was so spotless, you could eat off the flagstone floor, too.

Fanny was just about to finally go up herself—perhaps she could stay awake long enough to look at those medical books she'd secreted in her attic room earlier in the day?— when she felt warm, furry bodies, doing a dance between and around her ankles.

She looked down to find Henry Clay there, Rosencrantz, and Guildenstern, too. The latter two didn't typically go to the kitchen if they could help it—they preferred the posher parts of Porthampton Abbey even though there was all that food downstairs—but even they knew where to go if it was late at night and the rest of the house was asleep.

"You need to go out one more time?" she asked aloud as though they might answer her. "All right." She opened the back door for the trio, who initially, suddenly, seemed reluctant to step outside. "Well, go on, then!" she urged. "But be quick about doing your business. Some of us still have to get up and work here in the morning."

They scampered.

As they did so, Fanny herself stepped outside for a breath of fresh air and a look up at the stars. There were so many, and they were so pretty, but it was also so cold and, shivering against it, Fanny rubbed her palms up and down the length of her upper arms for warmth.

There came a sound some distance away, and Fanny looked toward it, catching a glimpse of a figure moving. Was that a long cloak flapping in the wind? Who was that? Who would be out there this time of night?

Fanny's spine stiffened, and she was filled with a sense of alarm. Was this some sort of threat? Something to do with what had happened to Will's uncle? Was this like the duke's valet, Parker, who'd tried to attack Lady Katherine and Lady Elizabeth? She remembered what Will had said after the death of his uncle: that there might be more. And he'd been right. There'd been the valet, just that day. And where there was one, and then two, wouldn't it be logical to conclude that there would, most definitely, be more? Was it that *more*, coming for her right now? Were the cats in danger? She squinted into the darkness, searching for those furry little bodies, hoping to hurry them inside to safety. If need be, she'd risk herself to save them.

But then Fanny realized that whoever the figure was, it was moving away from the abbey, not toward it. She let out a long breath she hadn't even realized she'd been holding in. That was all right, then. Whatever was out there, so long as it went in the other direction—let it just go away.

Now the cats were all circling her ankles again, only this time wanting in. She stepped aside to give them access to the house and, as she did so, she saw an envelope lying on the ground a few feet away from the doorway. Perhaps the cats had scattered it when they first scampered out?

She picked it up, turned it over.

It had His Lordship's name on the front of it.

When had it come? And who had brought it? Fanny shrugged, bringing it inside. Perhaps Ralph, the chauffeur, had come with it during dinner service. Sometimes it got so loud in the kitchen, what with all of them scurrying around to make sure that everything was perfect for Upstairs, you couldn't even hear your own thoughts, never mind a knock on the back door. Perhaps Ralph had come and, not wanting to wait, had left it there.

Fanny took the letter to Mr. Wright's pantry and set it down on his table with another shrug. Let Mr. Wright take care of it in the morning, she thought. He'd know what to do.

CHAPTER TWENTY-ONE

Lizzy should never have come upstairs so early. She hadn't thought about how many hours she'd need to wait.

What she *had* thought was how badly she wanted to talk to the one person who might understand what she was going through and also about how badly she simply wanted to get away from the rest of them.

How they'd laughed at the barn luncheon and then at dinner! And how she had laughed, mostly, along with them!

But inside, she hadn't been laughing at all.

Oh, Lizzy knew what they all thought of her. She knew none of them believed her to be terribly bright. And she had to admit, most days she didn't think herself very bright, either. But even she wasn't dim enough to not realize that something terrible had happened here, something not normal, and yet the rest of them were for the most part behaving as though everything was fine.

She'd killed a man today.

No matter the circumstances, how could she not be changed by that fact?

Oh, how she wanted to talk with the one person

who might understand.

But then she'd escaped to her room, with Becky following soon after, to help her get ready for bed and to draw her bath for her.

Lizzy hadn't minded the bath part. How many had she had today? That one made three. There had been the one before breakfast and another after the barn luncheon. She'd really needed that one. It had only been after she'd shot the valet that she'd noticed the stench. Perhaps, when he'd been coming toward her, she'd been too scared to mark it? Well, whatever the case, she certainly had marked it afterward. The stench of something rotting.

Is that what human death smelled like? She supposed it might be different than with the animals she'd seen. And Dr. Webb had assured them it was all quite normal. But would a body start to rot so quickly? The others hadn't said anything about it when she'd mentioned it to Dr. Webb, except to place the backs of their hands to their noses, as if they could keep it out.

But she couldn't keep it out.

Maybe it was because she'd been the one to kill him, but it felt as though that rotting stench had permeated her clothes and skin, invaded her very being. Even the second bath after the barn luncheon hadn't fully eradicated the sense memory in her mind, although the third finally helped.

Then, after the bath, Becky had assisted her in getting into her nightclothes—her silk gown and velvet robe—and she'd climbed into bed.

But not before asking Becky to hunt her down another pair of riding breeches—definitely not the ones she'd worn that day, no matter how well they might be laundered; she never wanted to see any of those clothes again—and bring them up to her.

If Becky found the request odd, she didn't say, and she had done what was asked of her as she always did.

Finally, Lizzy had been left alone in bed to wait, for hours if need be, with only the thoughts in her own mind to occupy her.

Some would have said it wasn't much of a mind, but it was the only one she had.

Lizzy worried she might drift off to sleep and miss her opportunity, but she needn't have worried. There was simply too much for her to think about.

The hours ticked by, all too slowly for her.

At last, there came the sounds of footsteps, first just a few and then more, making their way through the house as her family and their guests retired to their rooms.

Still, Lizzy waited, hoping to give the servants ample time to put the house to rest.

When she thought she had given it enough time, when she couldn't wait any longer, she got up from her bed and removed her nightclothes, replacing them with the breeches and a shirt Becky had laid out to go with the breeches. She pulled on boots and, taking up a cloak, threw it around her shoulders, tying it at the neck before putting the hood up.

It felt odd, dressing herself, but Lizzy supposed a person could get used to it if she had to.

Then Lizzy stole out of her room, pulling the door closed softly behind her, padded down the grand staircase on cat's feet, crossed the marble floor, and went out the great front door, closing that softly behind her as well. Then she tore off running until she got around behind the abbey, running faster than she'd ever run in her life, not even stopping when she heard a door open in the distance behind her and the sound of Fanny talking to the cats. She didn't turn. She didn't want to be seen.

Lizzy kept running until she'd gained the farther reaches of the estate, where the cottages of the tenant farmers would be. Which one, though?

She'd toured this part of the estate before—all the sisters had, with Father. It was something you did from time to time, making sure all the tenant farmers were happy enough, that everything was operating as it should be.

She thought now that she remembered which one it was. The cottage, right here, with all its lights out.

That was no surprise. No doubt the whole world was sleeping by now.

Well, except for her.

Out of breath and panting, pulse pounding and heart racing in her chest from her run, Lizzy raised her hand to knock. Oh, she did hope she had the right place. If she didn't, this could get very embarrassing for her very quickly.

The door to the cottage opened.

"Lady Elizabeth," Will Harvey said, wearing what he usually wore about the estate, as though he'd never been to bed at all. "What are you doing here?"

CHAPTER
TWENTY-TWO

Will Harvey couldn't believe his eyes.

Lady Elizabeth Clarke, standing on his doorstep in the middle of the night as though she'd come for—

Oh, who knew what she had come for? Nor did he give her time to tell him before he grabbed hold of her arm, all but yanking her inside and then shutting the door and latching it firmly behind her.

"You silly girl!" he couldn't stop himself from saying. "Don't you realize yet that it's not safe out there?"

"Of course I realize that," she said, shaking him off. "Why do you imagine I ran all the way? Now do you think you might turn on a light or something? It is rather dark in here."

Will grudgingly obliged, although there was no light to be turned on, only candles to be lit; there was no electricity in the cottages.

Now that there was some illumination, Will wondered what Lady Elizabeth saw as she looked around the small cottage. His aunt had tried to make it a home for them, in and around the rest of her other work on their plot of land, but he knew it was no doubt meaner than any home the youngest daughter of the house had ever been in. Why, Will had been in the kitchen of the abbey earlier, so very many hours earlier, and he had to admit that his family home couldn't compare in terms of fineness even to that.

Oh, well. He certainly wouldn't apologize for it. Who cared if she didn't like it? He hadn't invited her here in the first place!

"First you call me Lady Elizabeth, then it's 'you silly girl,'" she said. "How about we split the difference and make it Lizzy?"

"I don't think I can do that."

"Oh, do try!" Lizzy urged. "It will be impossible to have this conversation with you if you don't!"

Will's aunt had been known to sleep through just about anything. Jessamine Harvey had slept through the knock at the door and their initial exchange of words. But once Lizzy raised her voice, even Auntie couldn't sleep through that.

"What's going on?" his aunt said, rubbing at her eyes as she came out of her room in her threadbare white dressing gown.

The cottage only had two bedrooms, his and the one his aunt had shared with his uncle until his death, to go with the one larger room that included kitchen area and sitting area.

"Oh, Your Ladyship!" his aunt said. "Would you care for some tea?"

Leave it to Auntie. You'd think she'd be ruffled and rattled by any visitor in the middle of the night, particularly this visitor, and yet here she was behaving as though being called on thusly was a daily occurrence for her.

"No, thank you, ma'am," Lady Elizabeth said, "but please, call me Lizzy. I don't want to put you to any trouble."

"Oh, it's no trouble for me, Lizzy. Will can get the fire going again in an instant."

"Well, if you're sure…"

"And would you care for a biscuit with that?"

"Yes, now that I think about it, I think that tea and a biscuit would be just lovely."

As his aunt busied herself with heating this and getting a small plate for that, and he lit the fire, he looked at Lady Elizabeth—fine, *Lizzy*—more closely, and he could see that she didn't want tea or a biscuit at all. She'd already refused the first before his aunt pressed her. So what had changed her mind? Perhaps, he conceded grudgingly, she'd seen that refusing Auntie's hospitality—even if the acceptance of it meant a diminishment in the Harvey family's own meager supplies—would offend his aunt too much, and it was an offense she didn't want to give.

It was possible he was mistaken, but was she being *kind*?

"Oh, this is lovely," Lizzy said, taking a hurried sip when she'd been handed a cup, "perfectly hot, too."

He knew it wasn't—the lovely part. His aunt, for all her strengths as a human being, made perfectly wretched tea. Although how a person could foul up tea, he'd never been able to figure out.

"Do you mind if I sit down somewhere?" Lizzy asked. "Only, I had such a long run."

"Of course, of course," Auntie said. "Take the chair closest to the fire."

He saw Lizzy hesitate. Perhaps she didn't want to take their very best? But then, no doubt again concluding that refusal was the greater crime, she accepted.

His aunt sat in the overstuffed chair across from her and he settled on the arm of that.

"Now you must tell us," Auntie said. "Why are you here and what can we do for you?"

"Yes," Will said urgently, no longer able to contain the question that had been burning inside him since first finding her on his doorstep, "is Kate all right?"

"Kate?" Lizzy drew back in puzzlement. "Why would you think it's something to do with *Kate*? She's fine. Or at least she was last time I saw her." Lizzy leaned forward, turning her attention to Will's aunt as he breathed an internal sigh of relief.

"It's just so awful!" Lizzy cried out. "Did Will tell you what happened today?"

"Of course he did, pet. That must have been horrible for you." Here Auntie leaned forward and grasped one of Lizzy's delicate hands in both of her work-roughened ones.

He marveled at his aunt: calling Lizzy, a daughter of the estate, "pet"; touching her as though she were Annie Mason, the farmer's widow who was their closest neighbor, come by for a cry after some loss. But then, that was his aunt all over. If Queen Mary came to the door in need of something, Auntie would treat her just the same.

Still, he half expected Lizzy to recoil at her touch, as he'd sensed Kate doing as he lay on top of her earlier in the day, protecting her. Not that it had been like that at first. At first Kate hadn't seemed to mind the contact at all, nor had he, if reluctant truth be told. In fact, it had almost seemed as though she were pressing into him, which hardly seemed necessary, since he was already on top of her, pressing her into the ground. Despite the danger at hand, he'd enjoyed the sensation of close contact very much indeed. But then she'd cooled and…

Well, it didn't bear thinking about.

What did Lizzy see when she looked at his aunt with her prematurely grizzled gray hair?

But rather than what he'd half expected, Lizzy leaned forward, too, placing her other hand on top of his aunt's.

"*Thank* you for saying that!" Lizzy said. "That's why I came here. I *knew* Will would understand. And I suppose if I'd taken the time to stop and think about it, I'd have realized that you'd understand, too, given what you've been through."

"Of course we do," Auntie said.

"That man," Lizzy said, "the one I killed today, he was already dead."

"I believe you. I saw it myself with my Ezra."

"But how is such a thing possible?" Lizzy said.

"I don't know." Auntie shook her head.

"And the toughest part," Lizzy said, "well, maybe not the toughest, but still very bad, is that no one up at the house is taking this seriously, or almost no one. Even Dr. Webb—"

"I saw that doctor," Will said, "heard him, too. You expect more from a medical man. You expect him to be more, I don't know, open-minded, maybe even to have an idea or two about what might be going on."

"Well," Lizzy said with a laugh that was only the tiniest bit bitter, "if we're expecting that, then clearly we're expecting too much from Dr. Webb! Perhaps some other medical man—"

"But the way he dismissed you!" Will said, now feeling outrage on her behalf. "When *you* were the one who saw—"

"Just like I did with Ezra," Auntie put in.

"First," Will said, "there was just the one."

"And now," Lizzy said, "there've been two. And where there's two…"

She let her voice trail off, perhaps reluctant to finish the thought herself. So Will did it for her.

"There could be more," he said. "Which is why I was so upset that you'd come here, at night, like this. We're safe enough inside, or at least so far we've been, with the doors closed. But out there…?"

It was his turn to let a thought lie.

"But don't you see?" Lizzy said. "I felt I had to come! To at least talk to someone who would understand, someone who would believe me, because there's no point in trying to talk to them."

"We understand, pet," Auntie said, "and we do believe you. But it will be morning soon. Hadn't you better get back before they notice you've gone?"

"I didn't think about the time," Lizzy said, looking mortified. "How awful of me, to keep you up late, interrupting your sleep when you have your own life to attend to in the morning."

"I don't mind," Auntie said. "I'm no longer sleeping as well as I once did. Hadn't you better walk her home, Will? She came all this way by herself. She mustn't go home that way, too."

Will excused himself to his bedroom, grabbed a thing or two, and returned.

"What's that?" Lizzy said, pointing to the pistol in his hand.

"A pistol," he answered.

"Yes, I know that. But what is it for?"

"Insurance."

If they were living in normal times, Will might have relished the opportunity to walk a pretty girl home. He'd have taken the long way, strolling at the most leisurely pace possible so that he might prolong the pleasure of having her at his side.

But these were not normal times, so instead he found himself rushing, protectively holding her hand as he hurried her along, racing against the house waking up and discovering that the youngest daughter had spent a part of the night down in the small cottage of the stable boy, racing against whatever might be there outside with them.

Not to mention, as a daughter of the house, Lizzy was not for him. And besides, she was Lizzy.

"But what do you think it is?" Lizzy whispered. "Dead, not dead, dead again—what is happening?"

"I don't know," Will said. "I'm not a doctor."

"And the one we have is all but useless."

"Maybe it's some new disease," Will said, "something the world has never seen before."

"Maybe," Lizzy said doubtfully, as though she were unsure just what to think. "Anyway, we're close enough."

Porthampton Abbey lay not far ahead.

"You should leave me here," Lizzy said. "If someone does see me coming, better that they see me alone."

"All right." He jutted his chin toward the abbey. "I'll stand watch until you're safely inside."

"But Will?"

"Yes?"

"Don't listen to what my father said. I know he sent you away yesterday and told you not to come back before today. And for all I know, he'll send you away again! But don't listen to him. Find a way to be here. We need you here. *I* need someone here, someone who understands."

"All right," Will said simply again.

Lizzy started to leave him, but he stopped her. He couldn't believe he'd nearly forgotten the most important part.

"Here," he said, laying something in her hands, the other thing he'd grabbed from his room back at the cottage.

"What's this?" she asked.

"It's a pistol."

"Yes, I do know that, but—"

"Keep it on your person, Lizzy. Keep it on your person at all times, *especially* whenever you go out of doors."

He watched her look at the gun for a long moment, realization sinking in, before she shifted her gaze up to his.

"It's your insurance," he told her.

CHAPTER TWENTY-THREE

Breakfast was a simple affair that day.

Or at least, it was as simple as it ever got with *this* lot, Daniel thought, setting out buffet offerings for the Sunday morning meal. They'd have their food, and they'd go to their church, waiting to have their big meal later once they'd returned, that larger repast no doubt involving the proverbial fatted calf.

Or possibly a real one.

Hands covered with spotless white gloves, Daniel and Jonathan placed chafing dishes on the marble-topped mahogany sideboard, lighting the oil burners underneath to keep the food warm. The chafing dishes contained kedgeree, made with smoked haddock, rice, eggs, oil, butter, and parsley; eggy bread; fluffy eggs; bacon; and a small plate of kippers, which only His Lordship tended to appreciate.

Honestly, it was enough food to feed an army.

These people were always eating food and there was always so much of it, which made little sense. It wasn't as though they really did anything all day long, certainly nothing a person might term "work."

As for Daniel's breakfast, Jonathan's and the rest

of the servants', too, that would need to wait until after the family was finished. And the dining room cleared. And the kitchen cleaned. And a few other chores done. Then, it being Sunday, they might enjoy some kedgeree and bacon for a treat, too.

His Lordship was the first to arrive at table, and Daniel thought that if His Lordship weren't careful, he'd be popping the buttons on his waistcoat soon. Lady Katherine followed shortly after.

Daniel knew that even with guests in the house, Her Ladyship would take her own breakfast on a tray in her bedroom and eat it in bed, just like she always did. As for the others, he expected they'd be along soon enough. He'd already been upstairs, earlier, helping Raymond Allen get dressed for the day, although the duke had been disinclined to come down right away.

On Sundays, the family always helped themselves. Well, what would be the point of a buffet if they didn't? But Daniel and Jonathan still needed to stay at attention, just in case anything else was needed or some sort of food emergency occurred.

Once His Lordship and Lady Katherine had filled their plates with whatever they wanted, they sat at the table. Since no one else was there yet, they actually sat close together. Lady Katherine picked up a slice of bacon with her fingers, pointing it at His Lordship's own overgenerous helping of it, which he was about to attack with knife and fork, and said, "You know, Father, if you eat much more of that, you'll be popping the buttons on your waistcoat," before taking a crisp bite.

Sometimes it wasn't easy being wallpaper, no matter how good an actor Daniel fancied himself because, hearing her say that, he wanted to burst out laughing. And he did like that, for all her properness, Lady Katherine ate her bacon with her fingers. Was there any other way?

To His Lordship's credit, rather than taking offense, he laughed along with his daughter.

"I suppose you are right, my dear," he said. "But I've always found it difficult to turn down more of anything I like. I *always* want more."

Nice for some, Daniel thought, *to have that choice*.

Just then, Mr. Wright entered, bearing a note on a silver salver and looking uncommonly flustered.

"What's the matter, Wright?" His Lordship said.

"I don't know how this happened, my lord. Apparently, another note came from Dr. Webb, but it's only just been brought to my attention now. Fanny found it on the ground outside the kitchen late last night and she put it in my pantry. I'm so sorry—"

"No need to be. Besides, there's nothing to be done about it now. Let's have a look."

His Lordship took the envelope from the salver and, picking up Lady Katherine's unused knife, slit it open. As he perused the contents, his brow furrowed.

"What's the matter, Father?" Lady Katherine asked. "Has something happened?"

"I honestly can't say. Dr. Webb has simply written, 'Things have taken a bad turn for the worse—situation in the village much more dire than I first thought.'"

"That sounds ominous," Lady Katherine said, "and not in the usual good way."

It sounded ominous to Daniel, too. And unlike Lady Katherine, Daniel had never found anything ominous to turn out good. He wondered that His Lordship didn't leap out of his chair, immediately set about trying to determine just what exactly the doctor meant and how it might affect them.

"Whatever it is," His Lordship said, "I'm sure Dr. Webb is capable of dealing with it. Still, perhaps after church—and lunch, of course—I should take a ride down to the village and have a look around."

"Are you sure that's safe?" Lady Katherine said.

"*Safe?* Why wouldn't it be?"

"Why, because of all the things that have been happening lately."

His Lordship merely gazed back at her blankly.

"What happened to the stable boy's uncle," Lady Katherine prompted. "What happened with the valet yesterday. What Dr. Webb writes of now, things in the village being dire…"

"Oh, that."

"Yes, that."

"Well," His Lordship said cheerfully, "we can't let a few stumbling blocks make us forget who we are."

"A *few*—"

"You know, my dear, as lord of the abbey, it is my duty to make sure *all* under my care are safe. We are British! We must never give in to fear! And anyway, I'm sure I will be safe enough. But that's for later. For now? Church! If the rest of those laggards don't come down soon, we'll all be late and miss it. I still need to change, myself, and you do, too."

Daniel knew that His Lordship was exaggerating. No matter how late they might be, *they* wouldn't miss anything. On Sundays when there were guests in the house, the family didn't bother going to the church in the village. Rather, they went to the stone structure on the far reaches of the property. After performing an early-morning service in the village, the vicar would go there to perform a second private service for the family and their guests. And so church would come to them.

"Wright," His Lordship said, wiping his mouth with his linen napkin before laying it down beside his plate, "have

Ralph bring the Rolls up."

The church may have been on the property, but it was a vast property, and it wouldn't do to have the ladies walk so far in their Sunday clothes, particularly Her Ladyship and the dowager countess. Oh, and that guest, Rowena Clarke. There was something about Rowena Clarke that caused Daniel to keep forgetting about her.

"I'm afraid that won't be possible," Mr. Wright said, looking flustered once more.

"Not *possible*?" It was rare that His Lordship was told that something he'd requested wasn't *possible*.

"I'm afraid the Rolls isn't here, and neither is the driver."

"But I don't understand."

"I would guess, my lord, that the car and its driver are still with Dr. Webb."

"I suppose you are right. I did say I would lend them to him. But I did not say that he could have them *forever*!" His Lordship was clearly outraged, but despite the flaws Daniel saw in his employer, he had to admit that at least his bad moods never lasted for more than a few moments. Soon, the clouds would part and his expression would turn optimistically sunny again, as it did now.

It probably helped that the cats had just sauntered in.

"Rosencrantz and Guildenstern!" His Lordship said. "How good of you to join us! Would you care for the rest of my kippers?"

Well, of course they would.

His Lordship set the china plate down on the carpet for the felines, giving them each a pat on the head, before returning his attention to Mr. Wright.

"Never mind," His Lordship said. "I'm sure Ralph knows what day it is—Sunday!—and that he is expected here to drive us. He'll be back in time. I'm sure Ralph won't let us down."

CHAPTER TWENTY-FOUR

G race was late coming downstairs.

She'd been *almost* ready when, halfway out the door of her bedroom, she remembered she'd wanted to put on a particular set of earbobs to go with her church costume. That costume consisted of a cream-colored Chanel with a blush-pink sash at the waist, silk stockings, side-button shoes, and a hat to match the color scheme of the dress. She was adjusting the hat on her head as she hurried down the grand staircase to join the others below.

"You're a vision, Lady Grace," Merry told her. Then he added with a smile, "But why did no one tell me there was a particular dress requirement for church here at Porthampton Abbey?"

Grace looked around at the assembly. The guests all clad in typical church attire, Merry and Benedict Clarke and the duke in dark suits with Rowena Clarke in a lavender dress, while her family all wore cream with the occasional touch of pink, as she did, even Father, who had also donned a cream-colored duster coat over his suit. Why, the hats alone could be their own separate subject! Hers with its pink ribbon. Kate's surprisingly romantic one, wide-brimmed and decorated with pink flowers, Mother's felt cloche, and Grandmama's perched on her head at a jaunty angle. The only one slightly out of fashion step was Lizzy who, for some reason, had put on a long dark cloak over her own cream-colored dress.

"I'm sorry." Grace laughed. "I suppose I should have warned you. Only, we've always done it this way. It makes us feel closer to God when we go to church, purer somehow."

"I doubt," Kate put in with an arched brow, "that God is ever fooled by us."

"Whatever the reason," Merry said, "you all look beautiful. It makes me feel as though this might be summer, even though I know that it is not, and we're going to a garden party together."

"Yes, well, now that we are all here." Father clapped his hands. "Shall we?"

Behind them, the butler cleared his throat.

"What is it, Wright?" Father said.

"I'm afraid, my lord, that Ralph still isn't back yet and, therefore, neither is the car."

"Oh, that's blasted inconvenient!" Father said.

"Language, Martin," Mother said. "Mr. Wright? Please send down to the stables for a few traps. I suppose today we'll have to go to church the old-fashioned way."

"Wright," Father said, "please *don't* send down to the stables for a few traps."

"But how on earth will we get there?" Mother said.

"We shall go the *truly* old-fashioned way," Father said. "We shall *walk* there. Besides, it's a lovely day out."

"That's me out, then," Grandfather said, shuffling away before anyone could stop him.

"We can send for a trap for just you, George!" Father called after him.

"Never mind," Grandfather said, waving a hand to the side while never turning; once Grandfather was set on a particular course, it was always difficult to turn him. "I'll have an early drink and an early nap and I'll put my dancing shoes on before you return."

"It's not a lovely day at all!" Mother said to Father. "It's misty out and positively dreary."

"Oh, a little mist never hurt anybody," Father said. "Wright, could you fetch my walking stick?"

The butler left and then returned with the requested item, silver-handled of course.

"I'm not sure about this, Martin," Grandmama said skeptically. "To suggest we all take some sort of…outdoor exercise. Are you sure you are quite right in the head?"

"I am. My eldest daughter informed me over breakfast this morning that I was in danger of busting the buttons on my waistcoat. Well, we shall see about *that*."

"I fear I am too old for such energetic adventures."

"Does that mean you'll be staying behind? With George?"

"Don't be ridiculous! The day I'm as slow as that old man is the day that I am dead. I'm afraid, Martin, you'll all just need to walk at my pace. Grace, lend me your arm. I don't imagine that you'll ever go too fast for my liking. And I further don't imagine God can do without me."

CHAPTER
TWENTY-FIVE

Raymond Allen checked his long-legged stride once again to accommodate the far shorter one of his chosen walking companion, the rotund Meriwether Young. Why, even the dowager countess, up ahead on Lady Grace's arm, was making faster progress toward the church than they were.

When the weekend had commenced just two days ago, the duke had fancied himself and Mr. Young as rivals, operating against each other to achieve the same prize: the beautiful hand of Lady Katherine in marriage. But now, he figured, they were in the same boat, and that boat was sinking fast.

"Well, I suppose that's us out of it, then," the duke said with a chin nod to indicate Benedict Clarke walking ahead beside Lady Katherine, his head leaning close to hers in conversation. Or as close as it could get to hers, given that wide-brimmed hat she had on her head.

"Oh, I needed to at least try, but I knew that I was never in the game, not really," Mr. Young said with an endearing self-deprecating laugh. "After all, what chance could there ever be for an old, short, fat businessman from London?"

"You're not that old," the duke said, in an effort to be reassuring.

"Thank you for that," the other man said, laughing again. "Now, if only we could do something about the parts of me that are too short, too fat, and too untitled, perhaps I will make another run at Lady Katherine yet."

The duke had to admire Mr. Young his ability to look at his life's situation with a sense of humor. Thinking of his own situation—that despite his wealth and title, he'd no doubt die without ever knowing real love or being loved—he found little to laugh at.

"Daniel?" the duke called over his shoulder. "Do you think you might hold that umbrella a bit steadier? I think my top hat is getting mist on it."

"Yes, Duke," came a voice from behind, followed by the requested adjustment.

Back at the house, before they'd set out on this impromptu walking journey, the duke had asked Daniel to accompany them to church as his valet.

"But I'm not your valet at the moment, Your Lordship," Daniel had said. "I've helped you get dressed for the day and now I'm back to being the footman, and my presence is required here to help the others get everything set out for your luncheon following your special, private church service."

"Did you and the other staff already go to church in the village early?"

"When would we've had the time? We were busy getting your breakfast."

The brief exchange that followed brought home to the duke something he hadn't thought of before: that while the Clarkes and their guests would enjoy their special just-for-them church service today, the circumstances of the weekend meant that the staff would have to do without completely.

There would be no God for the staff this weekend.

"Oh, I see," the duke had said, feeling unaccountably chastened. But then he shook off the feeling. It wasn't *his* fault that things were the way they were. "Yes, well, I'd still like you to accompany me."

What the duke was thinking was that when they'd gone outside of the abbey for their hunt the day before, Daniel hadn't accompanied him then even though the duke had asked him to, and look how *that* had turned out. Now that they were to be going outside of the abbey once more, he certainly didn't want a repeat of that performance!

"I doubt Jonathan and the others will appreciate the extra bit of work, what with my hands gone, but if that is what you wish, Your Lordship."

"It is. And do you think you might find something else to call me besides 'Your Lordship'?"

The footman had simply stared back blankly at this.

Honestly! Was it that hard to understand? "Only," the duke had explained, "when there's more than one titled person in the vicinity, it does get confusing for me. I always find myself thinking, 'Are they talking to me or one of the other ones?'"

"What do you propose I should call you instead?"

The duke had brightened considerably at this. "Duke would do nicely!"

Someone else who had brightened considerably? Daniel, upon spotting Lady Grace in her church finery when they'd all assembled in the entry hall. Well, perhaps "considerably" was taking it a bit too far. Did Daniel ever do anything considerably? Such a cautious young man, even for a footman, footmen not exactly being known for their risk-taking. Why, if they were possessed of derring-do, would they even *be* footmen? The duke didn't think so. But Daniel had certainly brightened a bit, before stoically turning his gaze away—the duke was certain he'd seen that.

And now here they were, in front of the family church. It was made of stone, and despite its modest size, it still did manage to contain its allotment of spires and stained glass on the exterior with pews and stone floor as they entered the interior.

"This is cozy," he said to his walking companion. Then he indicated the pew all the way at the back, near the doors they'd just entered through. "Shall we?"

"Yes," Mr. Young said with a laugh, "I suppose the back of the room is the place for the likes of us."

The duke watched as the earl and countess, the dowager countess, the three daughters, and Benedict Clarke and his mother took seats at the front, although the youngest daughter, Lady Elizabeth, seemed to be sitting off to the side a bit in that cloak of hers. But no sooner had Lady Grace gotten her grandmother settled than she rose again, making her way to the back of the church, where she squatted slightly before whispering to Mr. Young, "Merry, wouldn't you like to sit up front? With us?"

Now, why didn't I think of that? the duke thought. *Maybe if I asked people to call me something less formal, I'd endear myself to them, too? But what would that be? Raymond? Ray?*

"You are so thoughtful," Mr. Young said, patting her hand where it rested on the edge of the pew. "But having walked so far and finally sat down, I fear I must at least remain seated and rest until the service is over. These old bones, you know."

Looking disappointed, Lady Grace returned to the front.

The duke thought about what Mr. Young had said, *Until the service is over...*

Once it was over, there would be the luncheon, followed by the trip to the train station, and this part of his life—this brief interlude—would be at an end, part of his past.

But for the service to be over, it would have to start first. And for it to start, there would need to be a vicar.

Where was the vicar?

Simultaneous to this thought arising in him, he noticed the family members up front beginning to grow restless, and it occurred to him: when they'd arrived at the church, there'd been no vicar to meet them at the doorway, to greet them with a godly word or two. Why, there hadn't been a horse or a trap outside or even a motorcar—if the vicar were really well compensated—to indicate that anyone else was here at all and that the vicar had arrived to perform the duty that had been requested of him. He wouldn't have just appeared out of nowhere. There had to have been some sign of a conveyance, and yet there wasn't.

Well, if there was no vicar, there would be no service, surely. So now, not only would there be no God today for the staff—like Daniel, standing behind them to the side of the closed church doors—but there would be no God for any of them, either.

"I'm sure the vicar has an excellent reason for not being here," Martin Clarke said in a booming voice as he rose to his feet. Then he made his way the short distance from his front-row seat to the altar. "In his absence, I shall perform the service. I may not be a vicar, but I think I've seen enough of these in my lifetime to know how the thing is done, and as the Earl of Porthampton..."

If only he himself, the duke thought, were capable of adopting such a take-charge attitude. Perhaps then his life might have turned out differently. Never mind Daniel, he supposed he could do with a little derring-do, too.

Of course, as the Earl of Porthampton, Martin Clarke was not only a landowner with a title, he was also, in a very real sense, the spiritual center of Porthampton Abbey, the entire village really.

Why, look at him now, the duke thought, leading a religious service at the drop of a hat and even giving a little sermon—and he did it all so well!

"What a lovely service that was!" Fidelia Clarke said to her husband as he stood near the doors at the back of the church greeting the congregants as though he really were the vicar.

"If we ever lose Porthampton Abbey, Martin," the dowager countess said, "I do believe you could support us all as a snake-oil salesman."

"Bite your tongue, Mother, we shall never lose Porthampton Abbey," the earl said, but he said it with a good-natured laugh.

It was easy to see that the earl was pleased with himself. Well, who could blame him? To have that confidence, that ability to just get up and speak before a group unplanned, to offer consolation and hope and...

"Truly lovely," Mr. Young was saying now, seizing his turn to congratulate the earl, following which, he nodded at Daniel, indicating the church doors. "Can you get those for me?"

Daniel obliged, and Mr. Young stepped out.

The duke patiently waited his turn to offer the earl his compliments. After all, he didn't want to be the only one caught out not saying some kind, congratulatory words.

But before he got his chance, he heard Mr. Young's voice, shouting a greeting from the other side of the church doors, which had been left ajar.

"Dr. Webb!" Mr. Young called out with real joy in his voice, as though he'd just discovered gold. "You've made it back! So everything in the village turned out all right, I trust?"

Dr. Webb?

The duke forsook the opportunity to congratulate the earl, electing to go outside instead and see what was going on. The others must have had the same inclination, for soon they were all crowded around the exterior in their Sunday clothes.

What the duke saw then was disturbing—there was no other word for it.

Dr. Webb was lurching toward the church out of the mist, something terribly off about his halting gait. More specifically, he was lurching toward Mr. Young.

"Are you all right, Dr. Webb?" Mr. Young called, the former joy in his voice replaced now with concern for the other man.

"Merry!" Lady Grace called out a warning. "Don't go any farther!"

"But can't you all see?" Mr. Young said, still walking forward. "Poor Dr. Webb is sick."

Yes, Dr. Webb was sick. His clothing and general appearance were all disheveled. And he smelled bad, too, the duke realized, as a rotting stench made its way to his nostrils, which flared in response. Why, the smell was similar to that which had enveloped the dead valet, *his* dead valet, yesterday. Perhaps Dr. Webb had acquired the wretched smell while tending to some poor person in the village?

Dr. Webb still lurched, his arms spreading out now as Mr. Young approached.

"Merry, *please*!" Lady Grace cried. Then she moved to step forward herself, no doubt to try to stop Mr. Young, but Benedict Clarke held her back, catching her with one arm around the waist.

And now Mr. Young was opening his arms wide, too, as though to warmly greet the returning doctor, but when their bodies met and the doctor embraced him, he immediately began to chew on the closest part of Mr. Young's body that was available to him, which, in this case, happened to be his upper arm.

The duke watched, frozen in horror as no doubt the others were, too, as the doctor chewed through Mr. Young's jacket and shirt, straight down to the flesh beneath. It might have been almost comical, were it not so downright horrifying. Among the things you never expect to see in life: one human being attempting to feed on another like an animal.

Mr. Young screamed and struggled, but he was no match.

The group outside the church took a single step forward, en masse, in a hesitant fashion, as though unsure what to do but wanting to do *something*.

It was easy to know what to do about the typical hazards of daily life, even for a duke: someone falls, you help them up, or you ask a servant to do it, and all the other et ceteras. Far more difficult, though, to react quickly, to know what to do about a shocking sight one never could have imagined seeing in this world—one person of your acquaintance chewing on another person of your acquaintance. Indeed, it would be just as shocking if it involved two human beings one didn't already know at all.

Later, the duke would think, *If only someone had reacted quicker. If only I had reacted quicker.*

But there is no proper and logical reaction to the unimaginable.

"Stand back!" a voice shouted, a *female* voice, and the duke followed the direction of the sound only to find Lady Elizabeth in the process of pulling a pistol from somewhere in her cloak. Then she strode forward and struck a stance, legs spread as she gripped the pistol in both hands.

"Lizzy!" her mother cried.

"Dr. Webb, let go of poor Mr. Young this instant!" the dowager countess cried.

"Don't shoot Merry by mistake!" Lady Grace cried.

At this last, Lady Elizabeth's steady grip began to waver, and she shifted the gun a bit.

A shot rang out and the duke saw, he *saw* Dr. Webb take a bullet to the arm.

But the strangest thing happened then.

Or *didn't* happen.

The doctor didn't react at all. Even though there was now a bullet hole straight through his arm, he did not cease chewing on Mr. Young except to shift his teeth to a fresh spot.

Mr. Young screamed yet louder, a horrible sound to hear.

He's been shot and he's not hurt at all! the duke thought in giddy horror. *And now he's trying to bite Mr. Young in the head!*

Lady Elizabeth shot the pistol a second time, this time striking Dr. Webb in the shoulder, but again her efforts failed to elicit a response. It was as though the doctor hadn't felt the impact at all, or the pain that should have surely followed, even though there were now two holes in him. Indeed, while something resembling blood was now coming out of him, like you'd think would after being struck twice with bullets, it wasn't the gush of vivid red you'd expect, but rather a slow ooze of sludgy rust.

Mr. Young had ceased screaming and struggling, merely lying limp in Dr. Webb's arms, which was somehow worse than his wretched screams had been.

But the duke had no opportunity to register what that might mean.

For now Lady Elizabeth was striding boldly forward, her pretty church hat whipped off her head by the wind in the process, and there came shouts for her to stop, to proceed with caution, but she didn't stop until she was right behind Dr. Webb—rotten-stench Dr. Webb, who was taking another bite out of Mr. Young—at which point, she placed the pistol directly to his skull and pulled the trigger.

CHAPTER TWENTY-SIX

Well, that did the trick, Daniel thought.

He watched the doctor—having been shot in the back of the head after having already been shot twice in two places but to no effect—fall to the ground. And then Mr. Young, poor Mr. Young, no longer held in place by the doctor's death grip, fell to the ground, too.

If he hadn't seen what had unfolded with his own eyes, he would never have believed it.

He *had* seen it, and he still didn't believe it.

Daniel had heard about what had happened to Will Harvey's uncle. And he'd heard about what had happened to the duke's valet, Parker, yesterday at the hunt. And then he'd been there, standing attendance, when the earl had read out loud each of the doctor's increasingly alarmed missives. A part of him had known then that there was some further threat out there, somewhere, but he had never imagined anything like this.

Now Lady Grace was escaping Benedict Clarke's hold on her and hurrying forward, falling to her knees, heedless of the damage to her pretty clothing, as she knelt on the ground beside the fallen Mr. Young.

"He's still alive!" she yelled. "Somebody help him, *please*!"

Daniel waited and waited, waited for someone with more authority to step in and take over.

This wasn't his job.

Even if it was Lady Grace out there now, and how he would have liked to help her, it wasn't his place to do so. And anyway, wasn't there someone else more equipped? Someone with the proper training?

But how could anyone be properly equipped, trained, for such an event? And unfortunately, the only one with any formal medical schooling, the doctor, was dead.

It's not my job, it's not my job, it's not—

Oh, blast these people!

Daniel hurried toward Lady Grace and Mr. Young, tearing off his jacket and waistcoat as he ran.

Blast these bloody people!

Reaching them, he tore off his white shirt and then ripped a long shred off it, using his teeth.

Then he settled on his knees beside Lady Grace—it would be hell trying to get the grass stains out of his trousers later—and proceeded to fashion a tourniquet in an attempt to stanch the flow of blood coming from Mr. Young's arm.

So much blood.

Daniel had hoped, after the war, to leave the sight of such things behind him forever.

And yet now, here he was again.

"I'm all right, Daniel," Mr. Young said, feebly attempting a brave smile.

To so many people, to most of the people he worked for, Daniel was just wallpaper. And yet here was Mr. Young, on such short acquaintance, already bothering to know his name.

"It's just a flesh wound," Mr. Young said.

"Please don't talk, Mr. Young," Daniel said. "You need to

preserve your strength."

"How does he know how to…" He heard a voice behind him.

"He was in the war," another voice said. "Perhaps he learned a few things there?"

Oh, he'd learned some things all right. Any soldier, if lucky enough to survive, had learned a few things, however rudimentary, about staving off disaster. And so he'd known how to fashion a tourniquet. But that head wound, from where Dr. Webb had been…*chewing*. Head wounds were always tricky things, difficult. And he didn't have any supplies out here. Not to mention…

Out here.

Daniel cast his eyes about.

They were all so vulnerable *out here.*

He didn't see anyone else but them, anyone else out there in the mist, but how could one ever be certain?

"Quick," he said, "everyone back into the church."

"But what about Merry?" Lady Grace asked.

Daniel had initially acted, in part, because of her. But since joining them, he'd been so absorbed with helping Mr. Young, he'd half forgotten she was even there. Now, at her words, he was reminded of her presence. And when he looked at her, he was surprised to find her looking back at him—not through him, like he was wallpaper, but *at* him, like he was worthy of respect and admiration, wonder even. He thought a person could get lost in those eyes of hers.

But this was no time for such thoughts, and he tore his gaze away.

Daniel knew he couldn't carry him all by himself. It would be rough and awkward hefting a man of Mr. Young's size. Not to mention that with his wounds, it would be best to move him gently, and for that he'd need help. He was about to direct Benedict Clarke to help him—he seemed most fit for the job—when Raymond Allen stepped forward unasked.

"Do you think you should take the upper part while I take the lower, or the reverse, or what exactly?" the duke asked.

Between the two of them, they managed the job.

Once inside the church, they laid Mr. Young on the cold stone floor as gently as possible. Now that everyone was safely inside, Daniel moved to the doors.

"When I go out," he said, "shut this and bar it behind me, and don't open it for anybody until you hear my voice and are sure it's me back again."

"But where are you going?" Lady Grace asked, the concern in her voice evident. She'd dropped to the floor beside Mr. Young and was cradling his head in her lap, heedless of the cold stone beneath her, heedless that she was now adding bloodstains to the grass stains on her cream-colored frock with its blush-pink sash at the waist.

He imagined other young women of her station would be more concerned with keeping their appearance pristine. And yet those stains and her heedlessness of them only served to make her that much more attractive to him.

"We can't get him back to the house like this," Daniel said, indicating Mr. Young with a jut of his chin. "He's not well enough to walk and it might not be good for him to be carried such a distance. Besides which, it may not be safe for any of us to walk—you know, *out there*. I'm going to go get a trap and horses."

Before anyone could say anything else, he stepped out, pulling the church doors shut behind him.

Then Daniel took off running, the cold wind whipping at his naked chest, running faster than he'd ever run in his life.

CHAPTER TWENTY–SEVEN

race settled beside Merry, who had been gently laid down the length of one of the bench seats of the trap.

When Daniel had returned with Will Harvey at the reins driving the trap, Daniel had said that before anyone else, they should get Mr. Young safely back, but there had been room for a few more.

"I want to go with him," Grace had said. "He's my friend."

Kate had made a stupid joke then, something about, "Only Grace would take the occasion of a man getting bitten in the arm as an opportunity to see if there might be some possible romance in it." No one had laughed, but for once Grace hadn't minded being the object of her older sister's bizarre sense of jocularity. She sensed that even Kate might be frightened now and that, feeling such an unfamiliar emotion, she might be responding to it by resorting to her typical tricks.

As for Lizzy, she did not seem as shaken by having killed Dr. Webb as one might think. Come to think of it, Lizzy had killed two men now—two men in two days!

But she couldn't think about Lizzy anymore as she

settled into the seat beside Merry. She couldn't even think about Daniel and how brave and wonderful he had been. She only wanted to get Merry home, back to the abbey, where she could more properly tend to him.

"Who else is coming on this round?" Will Harvey had asked, with a questioning look at Lizzy, the pistol still in her hand, as though he were somehow and for some reason specifically concerned about her.

Before anyone else could answer or step forward, however, Raymond Allen did.

"I'd like to go, if I may," he said.

"Are you scared we won't come back for you?" Will Harvey said with what could only be described as a slight sneer. "Because I assure you, I will get everyone back safely."

As Grace focused her attention on Merry, she could only imagine the looks on her parents' and Grandmama's faces, that they should live to see the day when a stable boy might address a member of the British peerage in such a fashion.

She waited for one of them, or for the duke himself, to rebuke Will, but the rebuke never came.

Grace looked up briefly enough to catch the blush coloring the duke's face as he replied without rancor, "I've developed a feeling of kinship with Mr. Young in our short time together, and I would merely like to see that he is well."

Grace could certainly understand this, for those were her sentiments exactly. It seemed to her that while family abounded, friends were hard to come by in their world. And if one was lucky enough to find a friend, even a relatively new one like Mr. Young, it was one's job—privilege, even—to take care of that person.

And so Raymond Allen had joined them, sitting on the seat behind her and Merry.

Grace didn't notice much about the journey. Her attention

was too focused on Merry, and she did worry that every bump and jounce of the trap might hurt him further. Considering the severity of the attack he'd endured, he didn't appear to be suffering much, only wincing slightly at some of the more violent jounces.

But, preoccupied as she was, even she couldn't miss the look of shock on Mr. Wright's face as they'd reentered the abbey, and the stable boy and still-shirtless footman carried one of their guests up the grand staircase.

It had taken two more trips in the trap for Will Harvey to transport everyone safely back to the abbey.

Now here Grace sat, beside Merry, who lay in the bed in his room, as she bathed his head wound with hot water Daniel had directed Fanny to bring up from the kitchen in a basin.

"We should put some alcohol on that," Daniel said. "On his arm wound, too, so it doesn't get infected."

"Get whatever we need," Grace said. "We have to do whatever we can to help Merry get better."

Daniel went.

Raymond Allen remained, standing to one side, not really doing much of anything. Well, you couldn't say he was terribly useful, but at least he cared.

"I was only trying to help Dr. Webb," Merry said, "and he bit me! But I suppose he wasn't feeling well. I know that when I am not feeling well, I can get so cross."

"Hush," Grace said. "Preserve your strength."

"You're right, my dear," he said. "We're safe now."

"Yes," Grace said, watching as his eyes gently fluttered shut. "We're all safe now."

CHAPTER
TWENTY-EIGHT

Even Kate had to admit: she *had* been rattled.

Well, as rattled as she ever got about anything.

Seeing Dr. Webb in that...*condition* of his. And then seeing poor Mr. Young step forward in his misguided attempt to help the medical man, who was clearly beyond any help. Finally, seeing Lizzy, *Lizzy*—again Lizzy!—be the one to finally put a stop to it all by shooting Dr. Webb in the head.

Well, first she'd shot him in the arm and then the shoulder, but that hadn't done much good.

And where had Lizzy gotten that pistol from anyway?

And why had the stable boy looked at Lizzy and her pistol like he was specifically concerned about her?

Oh, it didn't matter anymore. Because now they were back inside Porthampton Abbey. They'd all changed out of their church clothes; Kate, for one, hoped she never again saw the garments she'd worn that wretched morning for as long as she lived. Not even the hat.

They were about to eat their luncheon with Father doing his typically wonderful job presiding over all, just as he'd presided over the service at the church, and all was back to being right with her world.

Kate looked around the table and saw that three of the party that had gone out together that morning were absent. Mr. Young, of course. The duke, who had insisted on staying upstairs to see if Mr. Young or Grace needed anything. Well, he was no great loss. And Grace herself, who had insisted that she be the one to nurse Mr. Young back to health. It was as though Grace thought that no one but her could be equal to the job when really any of the household staff could have sat watch and done it. Why, even the stable boy could have.

The stable boy.

Why did everything keep coming back to him?

When Will Harvey had returned to collect another round of them from the church, she'd taken the seat up front with him before anyone else could, behind the horses, holding her hat in place against the wind. Being in that position had caused her to remember that she hadn't ridden since before their guests' arrival, all the way back on Friday.

She'd said as much, ending with, "Later on today, after our guests have departed, I do think I might take Wyndgate out for a ride. Please see that he is ready for me."

"I don't think so, Lady Kate."

She'd been about to ask what he meant by that, but then she'd been struck by how he'd addressed her. At least now he was back to calling her Lady, but she was not sure how she felt about the Kate part. The rest of the staff called her Lady Katherine, as well they should.

"It might be wiser," he'd gone on, "for you to just stay put until things are more…*settled*."

How patronizing!

She would most assuredly have pointed this out to him, but by then they were pulling up in front of the abbey.

She'd leaped down from the trap. She certainly would not wait for him to come around to help her—perhaps hand her down, or even grab her by the waist and swing her down—not that he appeared inclined to do so as he remained seated, holding the reins. *Well!*

She'd turned, fully intending to give him a piece of her mind, tell him exactly what she thought about his patronizing words and his rude arrogance and lack of basic manners. But when her eyes met his, she was shocked to find naked concern there. Concern for her.

Kate hadn't known what to do with that. She was accustomed to a world in which she was expected to lead the way somehow, a world in which people looked to her, not one in which anyone worried *about* her. She wasn't sure if she should bristle at this or merely thank him. Having finally decided on the latter, however, she'd opened her mouth to do so only to find she was too late, for by then he was snapping the reins and making clicking noises at the horses and driving away.

And now she was here at luncheon and Father was saying, "You know, Lizzy, when I first saw the footman place that shotgun in your hands yesterday, I thought 'Oh, good. Now Lizzy will learn to use a gun, too. Perhaps one day, she shall even bag a bird!' But I never dreamed... By the way, where did you get that pistol?"

Lizzy opened her mouth, only to be cut off by Mother.

"Martin, *please* stop talking about it! I would like to have one meal pass without it being spoiled."

"Of course, my dear. *Although*..." He paused to cut into his rare roast beef. "You do realize that with Dr. Webb, er, *gone*, we will need to find another doctor to come work in the village?"

"I suppose you can call London tomorrow for a referral," she said.

"Well," Grandmama said, "while I do not approve of the way he went, I for one am not sorry to see Dr. Webb go. I never did condone having him as a guest to dine here with us, and when we do secure a new village doctor, I hope you don't plan on making the same mistake with him."

Rowena Clarke looked properly horrified at Grandmama's words. Kate tried to figure out which part she would find most troubling before concluding: probably all of it.

If only Grandfather had been there, he might have challenged Grandmama, if he remembered to do so. But despite his earlier promise to have his dancing shoes on by the time they returned from church, he hadn't come down for lunch.

"Speaking of guests," Father said, "I suppose that, after luncheon is over, someone will have to round up Ralph to drive our guests back to the train station. Although I suspect Mr. Young will stay on for a day or two, until he gets his health back."

Kate wondered: Had Father gotten a good *look* at Mr. Young as he'd lain there on the ground, and later on the stone floor of the church? She doubted he'd be well enough to travel in a day or two. Maybe not even a week or two! Maybe even—*sigh*—not ever.

"I suspect," Father was adding, "the others will feel ready to get away, much as they've no doubt enjoyed their stay with us."

"Father," Kate said, "what makes you think that Ralph is back?"

Father raised his eyebrows at this. "But why wouldn't he be? I'd lent him and the car to Dr. Webb, and obviously he's not with Dr. Webb anymore. So he must have returned."

It seemed that no one knew what to say to this undeniably optimistic assessment, and into the silence that ensued, no pins were heard to drop but there did come the sound of a throat clearing.

Kate looked to the wall and saw a footman standing there. Not the one who'd ripped his shirt off and proved himself to be otherwise useful earlier. This was the other footman— Jonathan, she thought his name was?

"Do you know something?" she demanded. "Speak up if you do."

"Only," the footman said, eyes still straight ahead, looking at no one, "Ralph never did return, the car either."

"Are you sure of this?" she pressed, eyes narrowed.

"As sure as I can be of anything," was the answer.

"But," Father said, clearly perplexed by this turn of affairs, "where can Ralph be?"

"Maybe," Lizzy said, speaking up at last, "whatever happened to Dr. Webb has happened to Ralph, too."

Kate recalled the letter from Dr. Webb that Mr. Wright had brought in that morning when only she and Father were at the breakfast table, the letter that said that things had taken a bad turn for the worse and that the situation in the village was much more dire than Dr. Webb had first thought.

It occurred to Kate then, something none of the others had mentioned.

When the vicar had failed to show up for their private service, they'd just assumed it was a matter of little importance, since Father had been able to step in and temporarily fill the vicar's shoes. It wasn't as if their souls depended upon it. And certainly, none of them imagined there was anything sinister behind the vicar's absence.

But what, Kate wondered, *if there was?*

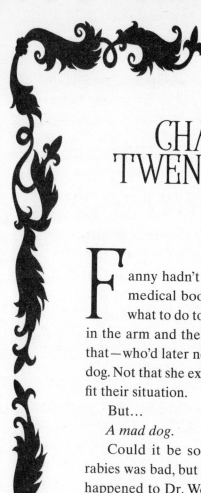

CHAPTER
TWENTY-NINE

Fanny hadn't had time to read enough of the medical books the night before to discover what to do to help someone who'd been bitten in the arm and the head by someone—a doctor, at that—who'd later needed to be put down like a mad dog. Not that she expected to find anything to exactly fit their situation.

But…

A mad dog.

Could it be some form of rabies? She knew rabies was bad, but could it do to a person what had happened to Dr. Webb? Fanny didn't think so. And then there was the part, like with Will's uncle: dead, *not dead*, dead again. For sure that wasn't rabies.

She did think that the hot water she'd been asked to take upstairs for Lady Grace to use in cleaning the wounds was probably a good idea. If they could get it hot enough, that would help. And the alcohol Daniel had thought to ask for to use as a disinfectant would probably help further, she believed.

What she couldn't believe was that despite the events of the day, the Upstairs folk were in the dining room having their precious luncheon; Daniel was back to helping Jonathan serve; and she was back in the kitchen, expected to do everything as though this were just any normal Sunday.

As if nothing had changed!

One abnormal thing that was good: Will Harvey was in the kitchen with her.

He'd come to the back door not long after returning the rest of the party home. He'd told her that one of *them*, one of the daughters had said that he should come here to the kitchen for a decent lunch as a reward after the extra effort he'd expended helping them out of their "little jam." The idea of feeding him or rewarding him seemed more the sort of thing that Lady Grace or Lady Elizabeth might generously think up, Fanny thought, but that condescending "little jam" part, *that* was all Lady Katherine. Not to mention, it diminished Will's role in it, as though he hadn't played a part in saving her life again, not to mention everyone else's.

"And then she wanted to go out riding this afternoon," Will was saying as he tucked into the rare roast beef before him.

Fanny was about to ask him who "she" was but then realized she didn't need to. He was no doubt talking about Lady Katherine—or Lady Kate, as he apparently called her now. It occurred to her then that Will Harvey thought that he disliked Lady Katherine when, in reality, he kind of did. Like her, that is. Which was too bad, since Fanny kind of liked Will.

Oh, well. She'd known all that already, hadn't she? The only one who appeared to be oblivious to it was Will.

"Fanny!" Mr. Wright's voice came at her. "What *are* you doing?"

"I'm sorry," she said, hastily rising to her feet. "But what am I doing wrong now, Mr. Wright?"

"You're feeding the stable boy rare roast beef! Why, that is what His Lordship himself is eating right this second!"

Oh. That's all it was.

"I'm sorry, Mr. Wright," she said again, not really feeling sorry at all. "I know I should've waited for lunch to be completely over, so I could be sure that any food left over really was left over, only I didn't think you'd mind in this instance."

"Not mind? How could you imagine that?"

"Because Will Harvey saved Lady Katherine's life again today, didn't he? When he made sure she got back safely, along with all the others."

Mr. Wright opened his mouth and shut it, twice, like an old frog trying to catch a fly but failing the speed to do so.

"I suppose that, just this once, you're right, Fanny."

It was a small victory, but it was all hers.

"But don't let it happen again!" Mr. Wright admonished, raising a forefinger high to underscore his point. "Just because things have been…a little off lately, it doesn't mean this household will fall to pieces. It doesn't mean that now we will start dishing up fresh meals to all and sundry willy-nilly."

"Of course not, Mr. Wright," Fanny agreed, casting her eyes downward, not so much because she felt the sting of his admonishment but because she didn't want him to catch her smile.

"I should think not," he huffed and was gone.

"You know how to take care of yourself, don't you, Fanny?" Will observed with respect.

"If I don't, who will?" she said. On another day, she might have felt the bitterness of her situation. But not now. It seemed to her that being able to take care of oneself, whether there was anyone to help or not, was the best way for a person to survive.

Speaking of survival…

"They had me take hot water up for Mr. Young," she

said, "for them to clean his wounds. But now I'm thinking I should fetch some cool water, too? After all, if his wounds get infected, he'll run a fever, and—"

Fanny stopped talking at the sight of Lady Elizabeth entering the servants' hall and the *astonishing* sight of her taking a seat at the table with them.

Lady Elizabeth had on a white cotton dress with blue stripes, cinched at the waist, a far more casual garment than she'd typically wear for a Sunday luncheon. Why, it practically looked practical.

"I hope you don't mind," Lady Elizabeth said, by way of asking permission for the seat she'd already taken. "Will, I was hoping I'd find you still here. Did you enjoy the lunch?"

Lady Elizabeth invited him? Fanny had been sure it was Lady Katherine. Perhaps Lady Elizabeth had meant "little jam" in some other way, then? One that was not in any way insulting?

"It was fine, and I thank you kindly for it," Will said, wiping his mouth with a napkin, which he then discarded beside his empty plate. "Are you feeling all right? After this morning?"

"Of course. I'm perfectly well. Or as well as one might expect."

"What is it, then? Do you need more bullets?"

Fanny thought she would fall off her seat at that one.

What? Will Harvey had given Lady Elizabeth the gun she'd used to kill Dr. Webb after he'd taken bites out of poor Mr. Young?

"Of course I need more bullets," Lady Elizabeth said, sounding mildly dismissive as she added, "and I'd be grateful if you got more for me. But this isn't about that."

"What, then?"

"The others," Lady Elizabeth said. "I still don't think they grasp the enormity of what's going on. Cousin Benedict just now suggested it might be mustard gas. He said that he'd seen mustard gas do awful things to people during the war."

"If he was so close to the mustard gas"—Fanny couldn't stop herself from butting in—"then why wasn't he affected by it, too?"

"You know," Lady Elizabeth said thoughtfully, tapping her lip with one beautifully elegant finger, so unlike Fanny's; Lady Elizabeth may have fired a gun and killed a man—make that two men—but she'd never had to scrub pots and pans, "*that* is a very good question." Lady Elizabeth shrugged. "I may have gotten things confused. People tell me I do that a lot. I suppose it's possible Cousin Benedict merely said he'd heard a lot about mustard gas somehow or read about it in the papers."

She shrugged again. "Anyhow, after Cousin Benedict said whatever he said about mustard gas, I naturally pointed out: 'But where would the mustard gas have come from? And why would it have affected only Will Harvey's uncle, the duke's valet, and Dr. Webb?' Then Kate laughed, told me to stop playing doctor, and the others laughed at what she'd said to me, Mother asked if we might talk about Paris instead, and that's as far as it got for that round."

"I know they're not taking it seriously enough," Will said, "but what's to be done about it?"

"I think you should move in here," Lady Elizabeth said.

Fanny felt her jaw drop open.

"I know Father will never approve," Lady Elizabeth said, "so I needn't bother even trying to ask. There's no point. But maybe you can move into the servants' quarters, in the attic, with no one else really knowing about it. It seems like it would be safer for you, and I know it would be safer for us." She blew out a soft breath before hastening to add, "Just until this all blows over, which I'm sure will be very soon."

Lady Elizabeth had used the word "this." Fanny was sure Lady Elizabeth had no idea just what exactly "this" meant here, and she was equally certain that she had no clue, either.

Only that it was bad.

So far, she didn't know what this was, only what it wasn't:

Not vampires.

Not rabies.

Not mustard gas.

It was a start. Fanny supposed if she had time enough, one by one she could rule out every other possibility until the only one remaining had to be the answer. She suspected, though, that they didn't have that kind of time. Worse, she was beginning to suspect that what they were seeing was something unlike anything the world had ever seen before. So while medical books might provide inspiration for treatments, the whole answer would never lie there.

Or at least, not until someone did discover all the answers and then write an entry for those medical books like nothing that had ever before existed, one that no human could have imagined in his or her wildest dreams.

If Fanny had only thought earlier that she might fall off her seat, she really did fall off her seat now when Lady Elizabeth turned and, focusing her eyes on Fanny, said, "Fanny. Maybe you can help."

CHAPTER THIRTY

Lizzy couldn't believe what she'd heard at lunch. After she'd said what she'd said, about how maybe what had happened to Dr. Webb had happened to Ralph, too, she'd thought that surely then they'd all take the threat seriously.

What had happened with Will's uncle—only his aunt had seen that.

And what had happened with the valet, Parker—only she had witnessed that.

So maybe in their minds, it was logical to disbelieve what they themselves had not seen?

But at the church—they'd all seen that.

They'd all been there to witness the changes in Dr. Webb; witness what Dr. Webb had done to poor Mr. Young; witness what she, Lizzy, had been forced to do in order to stop it.

Sure, they'd acknowledged the individual parts of what had happened that morning. They'd even praised Lizzy for her part, what they referred to as her bravery. But they had not and would not acknowledge the whole.

When she'd tried to suggest, at lunch, that they should consider things more seriously, they'd all but laughed at her.

"But I shot him *twice* first!" she'd cried. "And he never stopped what he was doing—he never reacted at all! It was only after I finally shot him *in the head*—"

They'd found a way to laugh at that, too, found a way to make excuses, excuses that made no real sense at all, provided answers for none of this, and yet they deemed them acceptable.

Then there had followed Cousin Benedict's blind-alley suggestion about mustard gas. She did think that he had at least been sincere in his suggestion, trying to find a solution to her problem for her—as she'd begun to notice males always tried to do for females—but she was certain he was wrong. How could mustard gas have found its way to Porthampton Abbey? And even if it had, how could that mustard gas be so terribly selective?

Was it even made of mustard?

And now that it was teatime, and they were all gathered before the fire in the parlor, even Grandfather, she couldn't believe that it was still going on.

"I'm sure there's some explanation," Father said now, "for what happened to Dr. Webb."

"Well, of course there's an explanation," Lizzy said, feeling exasperated, "but what do you propose that might be?"

"How should I know?" Father said. "Perhaps he was taken with a madness?"

"So," Lizzy said, "Will Harvey's aunt was crazy with grief and thought she saw something that wasn't real, the valet was taken with a wanderlust that caused him to walk away from his employment without notice followed by a madness that caused him to try to attack Kate and then me, and now Dr. Webb was taken by a madness—perhaps brought on by too many hours trying to heal villagers. You're saying all of that is what's happened and you further think none of it is in any way related?"

"Lizzy," Kate said, "I did not bother to count the words, but I do believe that is the longest speech you've made in your life, and most of it was even coherent."

It was so like Kate, to make fun of her intellectual weaknesses like that.

For the first time in her life, it occurred to Lizzy to wonder: Was she really stupid? Or did she only think herself so because other people kept telling her she was and she believed them? Was it possible that they all only thought of themselves, however each of them did, in the ways in which they assumed the world viewed them? And was it further possible for any of them—her, specifically—to retrain their minds to think differently of themselves?

"Lizzy," Mother said, "I don't think you should talk to your father like that."

"Oh, I don't know, Fidelia," Grandmama said. "I rather like this new Lizzy. She shoots guns, she kills inconvenient people for us, she speaks her mind. Well, just so long as she doesn't speak any of it to me."

Yes, Lizzy thought, *that is exactly right. I* am *a new Lizzy.*

"You know," Rowena Clarke spoke up. "As fun as this weekend has been…"

"Yes, you're right," Father said. "We should see about getting you and Benedict and the duke back to your various homes."

"And how do you propose to do that?" Lizzy asked.

Father rose, went to the wall, pulled a cord, and waited for Mr. Wright to appear.

"Yes, my lord?"

"Wright," Father said, "please send one of the servants into the village."

"Into the village, my lord?"

"Yes, Wright, that's what I said: the village! And ask

whoever you send to look around, perhaps starting in the vicinity of Dr. Webb's surgery, to see if they can find the Rolls-Royce and then bring it back here."

When Mr. Wright did not immediately respond, Father added, "It shouldn't be that difficult to find. It's the only Rolls-Royce Silver Ghost around here—it's the only Rolls-Royce around here of any kind, I'm sure!"

Lizzy did not think she'd ever seen Mr. Wright squirm before. Indeed, he'd only ever been prompt in his determination to fulfill any of Father's requests, no matter what or how outlandish they might be. But he definitely appeared to be squirming now as he replied, "I'll *try*, my lord. But I don't think—"

"What do you mean, *try*?"

"There's been some talk among the staff..."

"What kind of talk?"

"After what happened today... Once the stable boy got everyone home safely... I just think that people are scared to go outside right now."

"Scared to... What nonsense!" Father sighed, as though the weight of the world and everyone's foolishness in it sat on his shoulders. "Servants will be superstitious and have their fears. If there's nothing to be done about it right now, then there's nothing to be done. No doubt, we can sort out our transportation problems in the morning. If need be, we can call up to London and have a car sent down from there." He turned to his guests, once again the genial host.

"I hope you won't mind too terribly much staying on with us for just one more night," he said.

What, Lizzy wondered, *can they possibly say in reply? What choice do they have?*

"How generous of you to have us," new cousin Benedict replied.

"I know!" Father said, his eyes filling with delight at some notion he'd no doubt just come up with. He turned to his father-in-law. "Remember what you said earlier, George?"

"I'm not even sure I remember earlier," Grandfather said, "much less what I might have said then. What did I say?"

"Oh, come on, you must remember! You said that by the time we got back from church, you'd have your dancing shoes on." Father paused. "We could have a dance!"

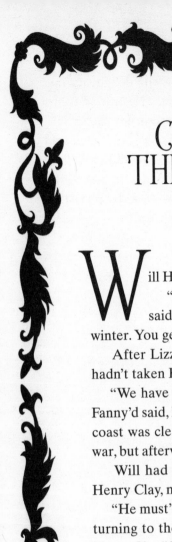

CHAPTER THIRTY-ONE

W ill Harvey took in his new accommodations.

"It's pretty drab up here, I know," Fanny said. "And hot, too, even though it's nearly winter. You get used to that."

After Lizzy had made her suggestion earlier, it hadn't taken Fanny long to fulfill it.

"We have plenty of rooms available in the attic," Fanny'd said, leading him up the back stairs once the coast was clear. "We had more servants before the war, but afterward... Hey, where did you come from?"

Will had looked down to find the kitchen cat, Henry Clay, moving back and forth between them.

"He must've followed us up," she told Will before turning to the cat. "Don't let Mr. Wright catch you, Henry Clay," Fanny said, "wandering around the main part of the house during the daytime. He'll have your head first, and then he'll have mine, too."

When Will stood up straight now in the room, his head just about touched the ceiling.

"Now *that*," Fanny said, making the bed up for him with fresh sheets, "I never get used to. Compared to Downstairs? Sometimes, when I'm working in the early hours of the morning, before anyone else is awake, I sometimes just walk around with my head tilted back"—here Fanny tilted her head all the way back to illustrate—"gazing up at the high ceilings, and I just marvel—oh, to have all that space above your head, as your God-given right, every day of your life!"

Will had to admit that even at home in his meager cottage, there was at least a little more space over his head than there was here in the attic.

"And all the colors they get to have," Fanny said. "It's so drab where they keep us—it's like we're not allowed to have any real color at all!"

He knew what she meant. When he'd dropped off the family and their guests earlier in the day, through the opened front doors he'd glimpsed colors beyond. And then of course he'd been the one to help Daniel carry Mr. Young gently up the grand staircase and to his room on the gallery. Will hadn't loitered, but in his brief time inside the family part of the abbey, he'd seen how vividly colorful so much of it was when taken in comparison with the drabness of the kitchen area and what he was seeing now here in the attic servants' quarters.

"At least you've got fresh sheets now," Fanny said, slipping a cotton case over the pillow.

Will had spent more time with Fanny in the last few days probably than in all the time he'd known her, but as her hands moved to smooth out the wrinkles in the cotton-covered pillow she'd just laid down, for the first time he noticed something about her.

"Fanny," he said. "Your hands. Did you burn yourself today?"

"Today, yesterday, and every day for as long as I can remember before that," she said with a laugh. "I burn them on the stove, I burn them on the range, I burn them taking things out of the oven. And if the water's too boiling hot when

I go to wash something, I burn them some more. And if I'm not burning them, they're getting chapped and cracked when I clean the copper pots—I use salt, vinegar, sand, and flour. And, of course, it's my job to create the daily supply of salt by rubbing a large solid block of it through a sieve. I don't think that helps much, either."

She looked down at the twin objects of their discussion, holding the backs of her hands at a distance so she could study them. "Not exactly like Lady Elizabeth's beautiful, delicate hands, are they?" she said with a rueful grin. "Or Lady Katherine's, come to that?"

Why had she mentioned Lady Kate?

Hearing her name on Fanny's lips caused his heart to race, but almost immediately, he pushed that feeling away.

"No, they're not." Will couldn't help but agree; anything else would be a lie and Fanny would never believe him. "But," he added, "they're fine enough hands, just as they are."

Fanny, perhaps unused to compliments no matter how meager, blushed and put her hands behind her back. "So," she said, "are you going to live here forever now?"

"Hardly," he said. "I'll just stay until things get better."

He said it, even though he was no longer sure when that might be.

A part of him felt guilty. If there was something bad going on out there—and he had no doubt that there was—then shouldn't he go home to Aunt Jess? Protect his own?

But the truth was, Aunt Jess was the most capable woman he'd ever known. Why, she'd been the one to first teach him how to shoot a gun, not his uncle. And when push had come to shove, Aunt Jess had even killed her own husband, however impossibly hard that must have been for her, because it needed to be done. If anyone could protect herself, Aunt Jess could.

And besides, Lizzy had asked.

And most of these people were so hopeless.

He didn't think that Lady Kate was hopeless, though. She might be stubborn, proud, and vain, but she was also intelligent and strong, with a spine made of steel. He'd known she was different, special, from that one day he'd met her when they were both three—it was why she'd remained stuck in his mind from that day until the one some four years later when he'd returned to the stables to begin his apprenticeship at the age of seven. It occurred to him to wonder, now that he was in the house: Which, among its many rooms, was hers? Where did she go to sleep at night? Where did she lay that beautiful head?

"You'll just sneak around?" Fanny pressed. "You'll, I don't know, go out to the stables when you need to and then sneak back here?"

Will shrugged. "Pretty much."

"I'd best be off before they start to miss me." Fanny looked around. "Where did Henry Clay go?" Then she shrugged, too. "That cat." Fanny outlined her mouth with those cracked hands as she called softly, "Henry Clay! Don't get caught by Mr. Wright!"

Then she laughed, and Will found himself laughing along with her, an extraordinary thing on such a day.

But he sobered up quickly enough when Fanny said, "Mr. Wright's the one you have to worry most about. Don't you get caught, either."

CHAPTER THIRTY-TWO

Grace sat before the mirror in her bedroom, watching her reflection as Becky arranged her hair from behind.

Just two nights ago, she'd been in the same spot, only Lizzy had been with her then and the atmosphere had been playful; happy, even.

How much had changed in such a short time.

Then, if there had been the prospect of a dance ahead, rather than just another chance for a couple of new rivals to take up positions against each other in the hopes of winning Kate's hand, no doubt she and Lizzy would've been even happier.

But now?

How could anyone think it a good time to have a dance?

How could *she*?

And yet here she was.

Grace had first learned of the dance from Kate, who'd taken the time to come to the sickroom to tell her, although Kate had seemed reluctant to step over the threshold, as though whatever was wrong with Merry might be catching, which of course it wasn't. He was merely wounded. A person couldn't get sick from simply being around someone else's wounds.

"How's our patient doing?" Kate had asked brightly from the doorway. "Much better, I hope?"

"It's hard to tell," Grace said. "I *think* he is. Mostly he sleeps, drifting in and out. When he's awake, he tells me stories."

"Really? How fascinating!" Grace was sure that despite Kate's bright smile, she found it anything but fascinating. Kate had never had much patience or sympathy for other people's illnesses, nor even her own come to that.

Oh well, Grace had thought. *At least Kate's trying.*

"What kind of stories?" Kate asked.

"Oh, nothing earth-shattering, I suppose. Just tales of growing up in London, ambitions he once had, dreams he'd hoped to see fulfilled."

"And he still will!" Kate had said with surprising vehemence. "Now, let me tell you about the dance Father is planning for this evening..."

That's when Kate had explained that it was to be no ordinary dance. Apparently, Father was upset there were so few in the party. He did want there to be something festive, to take people's minds off the unpleasantness of the day, but he also wanted to make up the numbers so it wouldn't look too depressing in terms of the sparseness of attendants.

"He said," Kate had told her, "that he wants it to be like the Servants' Ball."

"How do you mean?"

"You know what the Servants' Ball is! During the week between Christmas and New Year's, we let them have their own party so that there's a festive occasion for them, too, and the family pops in but only stays for half an hour, just to put a jolly face on things."

"Yes, I do know all that. But how is *this* supposed to be like *that*?"

"Well, not exactly. More like the reverse."

"I'm afraid you'll have to speak clearer, Kate, because you've really lost me now."

"I swear, you're getting dimmer than Lizzy, Grace!"

"Actually, it's seemed to me that Lizzy's been getting a bit brighter lately. Who knows? Maybe Lizzy has been bright all along, only none of us ever gave her a chance."

From Kate's expression, Grace thought she didn't like this.

"Somehow I doubt that," Kate said, confirming Grace's suspicion. "And it's not really that much of a leap, is it? To go from not bright at all to only very dim?"

Sometimes, when Kate spoke like that, Grace could swear she sounded just like Grandmama.

"Anyway," Kate continued, "there is to be a dance—in the music room, naturally, because there at least we have the gramophone, but if we did it in the ballroom, we couldn't ignore how few in number we are for a party or the fact that we have no live entertainment—and the servants will join us. You know, the footmen. And all the rest, I suppose. With the footmen, there'll be more choices in terms of dance partners. This will all be after dinner, of course."

The footmen. Daniel would be there, then. Still.

"I don't think I'll come down for dinner tonight. I think I'd rather stay here."

"Fine. But afterward? You'll come down for the dance, won't you?"

A part of her would've liked to say yes. A part of her would've liked to join the others in having a regular jolly time and pretending that none of this was happening. And an even bigger part of her would have liked the opportunity to thank Daniel, properly, for all he had done earlier in the day. But…

"I don't think so. What if Merry wakes and needs something?"

"One of the servants—"

"Yes, but I—"

As though underscoring Grace's point, Merry stirred then, but just as quickly, he settled back down into sleep.

"You see?" Grace said.

"What I see is that once again, you've elevated your own importance. Oh, you can be *such* a martyr, Grace!" Kate had cried in frustration and then she'd flounced off.

"Am I?" Grace asked. "Being a martyr?"

Grace posed the question to the only other conscious person in the room, whom Kate had not even bothered to acknowledge as being present.

But perhaps she hadn't seen him there?

Or maybe she had, and she'd chosen to ignore him anyway, which would be just like Kate.

"I don't think so," the duke said, stepping forward from the shadows. "But I do think you should go to the dance. It sounds like it could be good fun for you."

"But who will stay here with Merry if I do that?"

"I can stay," the duke had offered. "It may surprise you to learn this about me, but when it comes time for filling out dance cards, no one is ever quite eager to have theirs filled up with *my* name. Somehow, I doubt I'll even be missed. And I've seen those handsome footmen of yours here at the abbey. If given the choice, even *I* would rather dance with one of them than be stuck with myself."

Grace would have expected to find bitterness in his expression, but then, as she studied him more closely, she saw none there. It was just an acceptance of facts. Grace could understand that. She'd had her own facts she'd needed to find ways to accept in life.

Indeed, his smile had been generous as he'd added, "Really. You must go. Mr. Young and I will be fine here."

At the time, Grace had felt unable to turn down what, for the duke, represented a generous offer.

Now, however, as Becky stood behind her, trying her hair this way and that, Grace thought: *Do I even want to go at all?*

CHAPTER THIRTY-THREE

"I think it's delightful using the gramophone instead of having live performers come in," Kate said to her father as he led her around the dance floor. She was attired in a deep amethyst sleeveless silk dress. In her hair, there was a matching forehead band with peacock feathers attached at the back, while Father, she thought, looked spiffy in his white tie and black jacket, as did Cousin Benedict. "It gives Wright something to do."

"Yes," Father said. "You know, it's surprising, really. Wright is usually so resistant to any small changes, and yet since he's got the hang of the thing, he no longer wants to let anyone else touch it—not even me!"

"Too bad, though," she said. "With Wright refusing to make metaphorical entries on any dance cards, it leaves Mrs. Murphy without her natural partner."

"Yes, well." It was clear Father knew something should be done about the situation, but perhaps not quite just yet. "Shouldn't you be dancing with Benedict?"

"Father!" She laughed. "You are so transparent!"

"Well." He gave a rueful grin. "Someone has to think of the British Empire."

"If you're determined to do it, I see no reason why the rest of us need to worry our heads. Besides, why dance with anyone else when I can dance with my favorite partner?"

It was true.

Kate knew that one day some man would come along to take over the primary place in her life, but that day hadn't come yet. And until then? Who better to dance with than the man who had taught her?

She smiled at the memory of being little, her father gently teaching her the various dance steps she would want to know when she grew older. How patient he'd been with her—even when she insisted on leading!

But her brow furrowed and her smile disappeared as she said, "Do you think we're doing the right thing?"

"Kate." He pulled back a bit as he examined her face more closely. "It's not like you to ever doubt yourself. And anyway, what 'right thing' are you talking about?"

She struggled with her thoughts, with forming the accurate words, but the impulse to be vague about that which was so scary was too strong.

"This...*thing* that happened today with Dr. Webb. Do you think we're right to pretend that—"

"No one is pretending anything!" he said, speaking words more sharply than he was accustomed to with her, more sharply than she was accustomed to hearing from anybody. "No matter what is going on, we must never forget who we are!"

His tone softened a bit as he added, "There is nothing going on here. And if it were, it would be nothing I couldn't protect you against. Haven't I always protected you?"

She had to admit he had. Of course he had.

"Of course!" she said brightly, determined to shake off her unease. "How silly of me. Now, what shall we do about the others?"

"Others?"

"Everyone is supposed to be dancing. And yet so far, family is just dancing with family, while the servants are hanging back against the walls. We must mingle, Father! How will anyone else know what to do if we don't lead the way?"

"I suppose you're right."

"Aren't I always?"

"And I suppose you want me to dance with Mrs. Murphy, give her a little spin around the place?"

"I consider it your duty as head of the household."

"I know," he said, looking down like a reluctant little boy. "But whenever I dance with her every year at the Servants' Ball, she always steps on my feet."

"Then you must move your own more quickly," Kate said, twinkling her eyes at him fondly as he released her.

"And I suppose you'll ask Benedict to dance?" he said.

Kate had a wild thought then. Since family could dance with staff on this occasion, if the stable boy were here, she could ask *him* to dance. What would *that* be like? *But he'd never be here*, she reminded herself. *He'd never be anywhere in this house unless it was the kitchen.*

"Of course not," she said. "Cousin Benedict is busy with Mother. Besides, I'm going to ask Wright to dance—give someone else a chance spinning the gramophone!"

Daniel stood with his back against the wall, posture ramrod straight, eyes forward, as he might when called upon to serve at a meal.

He knew what was expected of him: to join in the fun. But as good an actor as he fancied himself, even at the annual

Servants' Ball he found these situations so awkward. Why bother? Was he supposed to pretend they were all equals, for what amounted to little more than five minutes, only to go back to being wallpaper?

He'd seen Lady Katherine approach old Wright a few minutes ago and place her gloved hand on his forearm, asking him to dance. Wright rarely could muster resistance to the charms of his favorite Clarke daughter and yet in this instance, he'd shaken his head vehemently, determined not to relinquish his control of the gramophone. So then Daniel had observed Lady Katherine make straight for Jonathan and, bold as you please without even asking permission first, take his hand to lead him out. Daniel watched, feeling a chuckle form inside, as Jonathan awkwardly sought for where exactly on Her Ladyship's person he was meant to place his hands without giving offense.

"Excuse me?" a tentative voice said. "Daniel, isn't it?"

Daniel shifted his eyes downward to see Lady Grace standing before him in her aquamarine dress, so striking against her auburn hair. It was enough to take a person's breath away.

He nodded.

"Do you mind?" She held out her hands, still tentative. "The others, or at least those who want to, have all paired up, and I find myself without a dancing partner."

Daniel tore his gaze away, looked around the music room, and saw that she was right. The countess and her father and the dowager countess and Benedict Clarke's mother were all seated on the sidelines in white crushed-velvet Queen Anne chairs with gold trim, but as for the others? The earl had just shifted from Mrs. Murphy to Myrtle Morgan, Lady Clarke's maid; Benedict Clarke was dancing with Mrs. Owen; Agnes and Becky were dancing with each other, giggling over who should lead while tripping over each other's feet; even Fanny was taking a turn with the earl's valet, old Albert Cox.

And Lady Grace, while not possessing the bold determination of her elder sister, did look like she wouldn't take no for an answer. Plus, she *was* Lady Grace.

There was no way out of it.

Not that he necessarily wanted one, but it was vaguely terrifying to be so physically close to her, dressed as she was, to smell her scent on the air.

"If you like," he said at last, recognizing how ungracious he sounded even as he said the words. Still, he came back to the idea that this, like the Servants' Ball, was meant to be fun for the servants, too. And yet where was the fun if one had no choice in the matter? If he had his way, it would've been him asking her to dance, not the reverse. But he'd never be so bold.

He'd been laughing inside at Jonathan's discomfort a moment earlier. But now that it was his turn to feel discomfort, he was no longer laughing.

Where was he meant to place his hands?

If Lady Grace were someone else, if she were one of the village girls encountered on a night he'd gotten off to go to a dance in the village, or Becky even, he'd know exactly what to do. He'd place both hands around Becky or some village girl's waist, firmly, and spin her off into a reel. But with Lady Grace, where—

"I think," she said, taking one of his hands and positioning it on the small of her back, and he felt a thrill go through him at the startling physical contact between them even if there was the thin fabric of her dress separating his hand from her skin, "you put this here." Then she took his other hand and placed it on her shoulder. "And put that one there." Then she positioned her own hands on him, creating a mirror image.

"There! I think that should do it!"

The first steps in the dance that commenced could only be termed awkward.

Daniel had no idea where to let his eyes settle. He certainly couldn't look at her. That would be too forward. Not to mention, he'd managed to glance at her once tonight, but if he allowed himself a second time, how could he ever stop? Now, if it were a village girl, or Becky—

"Do please look at me," she said, only instead of the command that the words might indicate, her voice was entreating.

With great reluctance, he did so.

"Daniel," she said, gazing up at him. "I know this is awkward for you. It's awkward for me, too. I've never asked a man to dance with me in my life—not even Father!"

Every time someone referred to him as a man, Daniel found himself wanting to object, "I'm not a man yet—I'm only seventeen!" But then he had to remind himself that to everyone else in the world, in *this* world, he was supposed to be older.

"Look," she tried again, "I only asked you to dance because I thought someone should thank you."

Daniel was completely taken aback by this, so much so that it stopped him in his dancing tracks and he ceased moving his feet for a moment. "Thank me?"

"Of course! Everything you did earlier today, from the moment you came forward to help Merry—"

He began moving again. "Anyone might've done the same."

"No." She tilted her head to one side, considering, then shook it slightly. "I don't think so. Maybe others wanted to help, but no one else came forward, not like you did."

"That's not entirely true. You did. You went to help Mr.

Young before anyone else even moved."

"Of course," she said, as if there'd been no choice in the matter, when there must have been. "He's my friend. But you? What is Mr. Young to you? No one knew you were capable of that. You could have just hung back. No one would have ever known."

Inside, he bristled at this. She'd come forward because she thought it the right thing to do. So why should she think that it wouldn't have been the same for him? And yet he knew he hadn't wanted to come forward, not at first. How he'd wished at the time that there was someone, anyone else to do it.

"And then," she said, when he didn't reply, "afterward, you ran for help. At risk to yourself, when no one else had even thought of it, you ran for help. You're not going to tell me *that* wasn't brave! I know what bravery is when I see it. I've never had any myself, and I've always felt the lack."

He didn't think that was true. She could have cared about Mr. Young and still been too cowardly to go help him. Most people would've been. But he couldn't figure out a way to tell her this.

"Anyone else might have—"

"—done it. Yes, you've said that already," she said thoughtfully. "But somehow, I don't think that's quite true."

"I suppose in the war, I…"

He let the thought trail off. Now, why had he said *that*? He never spoke of the war to anybody.

"Yes," she said. "I heard you were in the war. So I suppose someone needs to thank you for that, too. Thank you, Daniel, for fighting in the war, and thank you for today." Lady Grace had always struck him as the timid sort, when taken in comparison with her overly confident older sister and her high-spirited younger one, so it surprised him when she looked him straight in the eye as she said, "I simply thought someone should thank you for what you've done. I suspected no one else would, and now I have."

Before he could say anything further, perhaps another sentence beginning with "Anyone might've," she'd slipped away from him and was gone.

Lizzy's dancing companion leaned down and whispered just above her ear so she could feel the exhale of his breath against her skin.

"Do you have your gun on you?" he said playfully.

A few moments ago, Cousin Benedict had approached her.

"One sister is otherwise occupied," he said, indicating Kate, who had finally persuaded Mr. Wright to dance with her, leaving Father to awkwardly man the gramophone, "so I thought I'd give another one a try." He held out his hands. "Care to give it a go?"

She supposed she should have been offended. Who ever wanted to be second choice? But his expression when he'd asked her had been so genial, and it wasn't her nature to take offense. If another sister was what he wanted, though, why hadn't he tried Grace? Then she looked around and saw Grace dancing with the footman, Daniel.

"You mean to say," she'd said, "*two* sisters are otherwise occupied, so you're resorting to the only one left?"

But she'd laughed when she said it, adding, "Oh, all right," as she took his hands.

And she surprised herself by laughing again now.

"No, I don't have my *gun* on me!" she said. It was somewhat thrilling to find mirth in anything on such a day. But then Lizzy had never been the sort to be kept down for long. "Where would I put it?"

"I don't know. In your dancing shoe, maybe?"

She pulled a face. "It would never fit there, and besides," she added, feeling the sober mood of earlier in the day overtake her again, "we're indoors. I don't need it when we're in here. It's only when we go outside, when we go out...*there*."

"Do you really think there's a threat?" he asked earnestly. "Or that it's so great?"

"Oh, I don't know," she said. "Dead people who aren't and then are, people who get shot and don't react to it at all, people who need to be shot in the *head* to finally be stopped—what do you think?"

A veil of sarcasm wasn't the way Lizzy typically chose to view the world; sarcasm was more Kate's thing, really, but there, she'd said it, and she wouldn't be sorry.

Except she was.

"I'm sorry," she said. "I don't know why I just took it all out on you like that. It's just frustrating, no one listening, after the things I've seen the past two days."

"If it's any consolation," Benedict said, "I saw what you saw today, too."

"And yet you don't seem bothered by it. And the others, they won't admit to seeing anything, at least not anything out of the ordinary."

If Will Harvey were here, she found herself thinking, at least they could talk about the practicalities, like the fact that they'd at least learned something today from that business with Dr. Webb: when people got like...*that*, you had to—most definitely, positively, and certainly—shoot them in the head.

But having mentioned it once already to Benedict, she found herself disinclined to discuss with him any further the idea of shooting people in the head. He seemed so nice, and she was spoiling his good time.

"I've already seen my share of extraordinary things," he said, adding, "in the war. Horrible things that I'd just as soon not think about anymore if I can help it."

"But not like this," she couldn't help but persist.

"No," he had to admit, "not like this."

His expression had grown grave, and even though she'd wanted people to take her ideas seriously, Lizzy found that her impulse was to wipe that gravity away.

"So," she said with a smiling chin nod in the direction of her oldest sister, "do you like her?"

Here, thankfully, he laughed again. "Well, I know I'm meant to…"

"But do you?"

"How should I know?" He shrugged. "I've only just met her, really." He shrugged again. "I've only just met all of you."

She was about to point out that you could feel as though you'd gotten to know someone rapidly given the right—or wrong, as it were—set of circumstances. She found herself feeling that way, in a sense, about Will. Although she wouldn't tell Benedict that part. But before she could say anything at all, she saw a small hand, chapped and cracked, reach over the top of his shoulder and give him a tap.

They stopped dancing as Benedict turned and Lizzy saw the owner of the hand, Fanny, standing there.

"Oh!" Benedict said, surprised. "Did you want to dance? With me?"

"Well," Lizzy said, grateful to be laughing once more, "I don't think she's here for me."

• • •

"Fanny," she said, introducing herself in answer to his first question. "I'm the kitchen maid," she said, in response to his second before she'd given him a chance to ask it.

Oh, why did I do this? she asked herself now. *Why did I ask him to dance?*

But she knew why.

Because he was tall.

Because he was incredibly handsome.

Because she knew that she could.

Sure, Jonathan and Daniel were incredibly handsome, too, but she could dance with them anytime she wanted to, or at least once a year at the Servants' Ball, and she had; she'd even danced with them at village dances upon rare occasion. But when would she ever get another chance to dance with someone like Benedict Clarke?

Never. That's when.

Yet now that she had him here, her hand not even all the way up on top of his shoulder, instead resting against his chest: What could she talk to him about? What did she know of interest in the world? All she knew was the kitchen at Porthampton Abbey. Would he really want to hear about how she cleaned the copper pots and pans?

She didn't think so.

"So, Fanny," he said, "what do you like to do when you're not working?"

For once, Fanny was grateful for Upstairs. Their breeding was so good, they could make conversation with a potted palm tree if need be, which was about what she felt like at this point: a potted palm.

"I like to read, sir," she said eagerly, remembering that she did have a subject of interest to her outside the workings of the kitchen.

"Do you?" he said, his expression mildly surprised but

also pleased.

"Yes, I learned how at compulsory school. Of course, I had to leave when I was ten, but the reading part of things stuck with me."

"And what do you like to read?"

"Shakespeare."

"Shakespeare!"

"Well, not the actual plays."

"No, of course not."

Was he laughing at her?

"I have read all the cast lists, you know," she said heatedly.

"The cast lists?"

"I think they're called dramatis personae. Anyway, I know all the characters, which is how I know that Rosencrantz and Guildenstern are named for two of them."

"Rosencrantz and—"

"The cats. Of the house. Have you not seen them running around the place? They will take His Lordship's kippers whenever they get the chance. Not like my Henry Clay. He knows to stay in the kitchen."

"And Henry Clay is…"

"My cat. The kitchen cat. Am I not being clear enough in my speech?"

"No, you're quite clear. I'm sure it's just me. When you started talking about Shakespeare, I was—"

"Are you laughing at me, sir? Because I know I haven't *actually* read the plays yet, only the cast lists, but I will get around to it, I promise you."

"I have no doubt that you will, Fanny. And when you do, I look forward to the conversations we might have. I assure you, I was not laughing."

And yet he was smiling when he said it, kindly though.

"I don't blame you, sir," she said. "I'd laugh at me, too, I suppose. Talking about reading things that I haven't actually read yet, it's too funny."

"Well, what have you actually read, then, if not Shakespeare?"

"Today I began some medical texts."

"Medical…"

Fanny clapped a hand over her mouth.

After showing Will Harvey to his room earlier in the day, she'd slipped into her own room to get in a bit of reading, and she'd started one of the books. She had. But then her thoughts had drifted a bit to Will down the hall from her now. Having seen his room, he'd no doubt sneaked back down the stairs and gone to the stables, because where else was a stable boy supposed to be during the daytime? But she suspected he'd sneaked back into the house by now and was way upstairs in his room.

She knew that Lady Elizabeth had wanted this, because she fancied him to be somehow useful. But it occurred to Fanny now that he wouldn't know where anything was inside, and how useful could he be if he didn't? Maybe she should wake him up early in the morning, when everyone else was still asleep but her, and take him on a little tour of the place?

"Fanny?" Benedict Clarke said. "You were saying something about reading medical texts?"

"Was I?" she said. "I don't think so, sir."

This won't do at all, she thought in a panic. If he knew about the medical books, he'd know she'd taken them from the library. If anyone knew she'd taken something from the library without asking permission first—and who would ever give her such permission?—it'd be her job.

She may've thought she was better than her job, and she was, but that still didn't mean she was prepared to lose it.

"I think if you thought you heard me say something like

'medical,'" she hastened to add, speaking as fast as she could, "it must've been 'medicine,' and I would've been talking about Mr. Young, who perhaps I should check on now to see how he is. Sir."

Then Fanny fled.

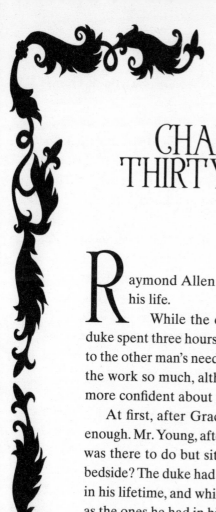

CHAPTER THIRTY-FOUR

Raymond Allen had never worked so hard in his life.

While the others danced downstairs, the duke spent three hours with Mr. Young, alone, tending to the other man's needs. He found that he didn't mind the work so much, although he did wish he could be more confident about the way he was doing it.

At first, after Grace left them, it had been easy enough. Mr. Young, after all, had been asleep. So what was there to do but sit in a comfortable chair by his bedside? The duke had sat in many comfortable chairs in his lifetime, and while this one wasn't quite as nice as the ones he had in his palatial bedroom back at his own home, it could've been worse.

But then Mr. Young had wakened. Despite the wounds to his arm and head, both of which had been bandaged, and despite the horror of having been… *chewed upon*, Mr. Young was calm and in a surprisingly chipper mood.

"You say the others are having a dance?" he asked in response to the duke's own reply upon having been asked where Lady Grace had gone to. "How lovely." Mr. Young closed his eyes, and a smile played around the corners of his lips as he said, "If I were down there, I think I should like to dance a Viennese waltz."

"Who would you ask to dance it with you? Lady Katherine?"

Mr. Young opened one eye and regarded him with it. "A few days ago, I would have said yes. But now I think I would choose Lady Grace. Or possibly even Lady Elizabeth. That one looks like she might be fun and know a thing or two about dancing."

"When you're all better, perhaps there will be another chance, and then you can make your choice."

"Yes, when I'm all better." Mr. Young laughed, but it was without rancor. "As if even then there would be a choice for me, anyone who would say yes, among beautiful ladies." Mr. Young moved his lips against each other, and the duke could see that they were very dry.

"Oh! I didn't even think! Would you like some water?"

Mr. Young allowed as how that would be lovely.

The duke reached over to the bedside table and lifted a glass and a pitcher of water from it, filling the one from the other. He placed both back down and then he rose and, as gently as he could, raised the other man to a sitting position against the headboard. Then he held the glass to Mr. Young's lips so that he might drink from it.

Look! he thought, as though he were someone else observing his own actions from outside his body. *I'm helping someone! Oh, if only Mother could see me now—she'd see that I'm not just decorative, but that I can be useful, too.*

When Mr. Young had had enough refreshment, he waved the glass away, and the duke found a napkin with which to wipe his chin. The napkin had been from a tray that had been brought up earlier, while Mr. Young was still sleeping, and it also had a bowl of soup on it and a silver spoon.

"Oh!" the duke said. "I forgot all about that, too! There's

some soup here." He frowned. "I'm not really sure what kind, and I'm sure it's grown cold, but if you like—"

"Perhaps in a bit," Mr. Young said, waving a feeble hand to stop him fussing.

"All right."

The duke reclaimed his seat, wondering: *what to do, what to do…*

He didn't have to wonder for long, however, because, perhaps refreshed by the water, Mr. Young was now in a talkative mood. He told the duke story after story about his childhood, so different from the duke's own and all of which the duke found fascinating.

Perhaps it was that, the duke's surprising—to himself— interest in someone else's life story that prevented him from noticing at first. But when he did, it was inescapably obvious: Mr. Young was nattering and nattering at an increasingly fast clip without ever stopping for any response from the other person, as one would normally do over the course of a conversation. And as he did so, perspiration sprang to his forehead, soon turning into rivulets of sweat coming down his face.

Mr. Young obviously had a fever and was perhaps even delirious.

What to do, what to do…

The duke leaped from his seat and commenced pacing the room in a dither.

What to do…

He could yank on one of the bell pull cords, summon a servant from the kitchen. But wasn't everyone else at the dance, the servants, too?

He could run downstairs—the music room, he thought they said it was—but wouldn't it take a long time to get there and back again with someone to help? And he didn't want to leave Mr. Young alone, not for that long.

Besides, what could anyone else do? It wasn't as though, even if he could run down there and back again, lickety-split, there was a doctor in the house for the duke to bring back with him. Nor was there a doctor anymore in the village to convey Mr. Young to. Or even a car to get him to the village if there were.

He shouldn't have to deal with this! Someone, anyone else should! Other people took care of such things—it was what other people were there for! But then, what was the point in spoiling everyone else's good time?

What to do…

In the end, the duke realized that there was nothing for it but for him to handle it himself. He'd volunteered for the job, after all.

First, he dampened the napkin with cool water, laying it across the feverish man's brow. Almost immediately, Mr. Young slowed his nattering, which the duke took as a good sign. But then, having drawn closer, he noticed that the sweat must have come out of the pores of Mr. Young's entire body, drenching the nightshirt he'd been put in earlier and even dampening the sheets below. Now the sweat seemed to have subsided, but Mr. Young couldn't just be left there in all those damp clothes and sheets like that.

What was a duke to do?

The duke did the only things he could do. He hurried to his own bedroom, not too far down the same corridor, and ripped the sheets from the bed there. Then he raced back with them. Upon reentering Mr. Young's room, he located another nightshirt in the wardrobe. Then he removed his own jacket, waistcoat, tie, and cuff links, loosened his collar, rolled up his sleeves to the elbow, gently shifted Mr. Young's body around until he was successfully able to remove the wet sheets, shifted him around some more to replace the wet sheets with fresh ones, and gently removed Mr. Young's soaked nightshirt, replacing that with a fresh one, too.

Phew!

Being so close to Mr. Young's body like that, the duke did notice a slightly unpleasant smell coming off him, and only politeness prevented him from pinching his nose against the sudden assault of it. He supposed it must be all that sweat or the wounds even—wounds could smell, couldn't they?

Once he'd settled Mr. Young back down, everything nice and fresh again, the duke stepped back from the bed, relieved to be away from the closeness of that smell and guilty at feeling that relief.

"There!" he said with forced bright cheer. "As good as new!"

"Thank you, my friend," Mr. Young said, clearly feeling better now, although he did look very tired. "You're very kind."

The duke was moved by his words. He couldn't remember a time in his life when anyone had referred to him as their "friend." And "kind"? If no one else had ever called him friend, he surely never would have thought to refer to himself as *kind*.

"I'm feeling a bit better now," Mr. Young said. "Perhaps some of that soup…"

The duke fussed with getting the bowl and spoon and a napkin for any stray drips. Then he filled the spoon partway and held it to the other man's lips.

"I'm sorry it's cold now," he said, "but my nanny always said that a good soup could cure just about anything, so I think you'll find…"

The duke let the sentence trail off when he realized that now he was the one who was nattering on and he had no idea how to finish the sentence. What would Mr. Young find in eating soup? That it was, in fact, soup?

"Tell me a story," Mr. Young said.

"A story?"

"Yes, you said you had a nanny, which is no surprise. I never had one myself, and I just wondered what that must be like. Surely you must have some happy stories about that time in your life."

Did he? The duke racked his brain for one, finally settling on a story involving his nanny and him and a pony that didn't end too, *too* badly for him. Well, he supposed, he could always leave out the ending part.

So the duke told the story to Mr. Young, between feeding him mouthfuls of soup. Before the bowl was empty or the story finished, Mr. Young had fallen asleep.

The duke, careful to do so quietly, set the bowl, spoon, and napkin down on the bedside table and then settled back into his seat, keeping his friend company while he slept.

They were still like that when Fanny came in.

"I came to see how Mr. Young is doing," she whispered.

"He was a bit restless before, feverish, too, but he seems to be a bit better now," the duke whispered back. "He took some soup."

"That's nice," Fanny said. "Mrs. Owen always says that a good bowl of soup can cure just about anything. Since I'm here, though, if I may, I might as well just…"

She gestured toward the bed with both hands, and he nodded his permission, although he wasn't quite sure what she had in mind.

Fanny stepped right up to the bed, her nose only wrinkling slightly at the smell he'd already grown accustomed to; it surprised him to think how quickly a person could get used to changing circumstances, whether it be a foul smell or even being called upon to take care of someone else when a person—a duke, no less!—had never done such a thing before.

But as Fanny's confident hands flew around, tucking and straightening a sheet here, plumping a pillow there, all without disturbing the sleeping patient, the duke saw that those hands were far more capable than his had been.

And he saw something else.

"Your hands!" he said. "Have you hurt yourself?"

The little maid launched into something of a speech then, a whole litany beginning with "Today, yesterday, and every day before that" and ending with something about rubbing a large block of salt through a sieve to create the household's daily supply. In between, there were a lot of other things, about boiling water and about copper pots and even vinegar. He wasn't sure. He hadn't followed it all because, well, it was a lot to take in. And clearly, it was a speech she'd given before.

When he didn't immediately reply upon her completion of it, she held her hands away from her, studying their backs before offering them to him, presumably for inspection.

"Not exactly a fine lady's hands, are they?" she said with a rueful grin.

"No," he said honestly. "No, they are not." Then he thought about what he'd just seen those hands do—flying all around Mr. Young, helping and never hurting—and he thought about something he'd never given any consideration to before at all: how much the life of someone like Fanny was spent taking care of other people, and how many hours spent in simple good, honest labor. "But they're beautiful hands all the same," he found himself adding.

Before she could respond, the footman entered. Or was he the valet, his personal valet now? No, he was back to being the footman. It was so hard to keep it all straight. Best to just think of him as Daniel.

Daniel, too, just wanted to see how Mr. Young was doing. So the duke and Fanny filled him in, and just as they were finishing, Lady Grace entered, too.

If she was surprised to find him there in his shirtsleeves, she didn't show it, but then she caught sight of Fanny and Daniel.

"Oh!" she said with a surprised smile. "I didn't know there was a second party going on up here!"

There was nothing censorious in her expression or the tone with which she invested her words, but Fanny must have imagined one there, for she dipped a quick curtsy, bowing her head as she said, "I'm ever so sorry, Your Ladyship. I know I should've asked permission before coming up here. Only I wanted to see how Mr. Young was doing, and I didn't want to bother anyone by asking. I hope you don't mind."

"Of course not, Fanny," Lady Grace said. "Your concern does you credit." She turned to Daniel. "I suppose you came for the same reason?"

Daniel simply nodded—rather stiffly, the duke thought, even for him. Was there something about Lady Grace that made Daniel feel particularly awkward?

No doubt deciding they were no longer needed now that Her Ladyship was there, Fanny and Daniel moved to depart the room.

"Oh, Fanny!" the duke called her back.

Fanny turned.

The duke indicated the pile of discarded laundry, including the sheets he'd removed from the bed earlier and Mr. Young's sweat-soaked nightshirt.

"I took the sheets from my own bed to replace his," he finished, after explaining why he'd removed them in the first place. "I hope that was all right?"

"It's fine," Fanny said, gathering up the heap that practically dwarfed her behind it. "I'll be sure to get some fresh ones for your room right away."

Then she was gone.

"*You* changed the sheets?" Lady Grace said, sounding amused.

"Yes, and his nightshirt, too. Oh, and I also gave him some soup."

"How enterprising of you! And kind, too."

He felt himself sitting straighter in his chair at her words as a rare feeling of pride came over him.

"Yes, well," he said. Then he gave her a full report on his night of nursing, ending with, "He looks to be more peaceful now. He might even sleep through the night. I think the worst is over."

"That's a relief. Now, why don't you give up your seat and let me take over."

Peculiarly, he found himself reluctant to leave. It was rather nice feeling useful.

"I could stay…"

"Nonsense. You've done your part. The others are still dancing. Why don't you join them?"

"I suppose I could. But why don't you come with me? I really do think he'll just sleep now."

"I promise I will. I'll even dance with you when I do. I just want to sit with Merry for a bit."

"All right then, although I suppose I should put on a fresh shirt first." He gathered up his rumpled jacket, tie, and waistcoat, and his cuff links, and headed for the door.

Once there, he turned back.

"When Mr. Young and I were talking earlier, just the two of us," he said, "he told me the most amazing story."

"And what was that?"

"Did you know he made his own fortune? I always thought people just inherited them. What an extraordinary man!"

CHAPTER THIRTY-FIVE

How awkwardly Daniel reacted, Grace thought, *when I came upon him earlier in Merry's room.* Was it possible that he had felt the same exhilarating surge she had downstairs, in the music room, when she'd placed his hand on the small of her back? No, she told herself, it was not possible. He no doubt merely felt awkward at being caught upstairs when no one had sent him there.

The duke was right—Merry was an extraordinary man, Grace thought, sitting beside him now as he slept, and he had been extraordinarily kind to her.

Oh, how cruel the world was sometimes! That some people should have so much while others like him, who were kind and deserving, should go through their lives without ever finding love.

Well, now that he was feeling better, once he recovered he might still find it yet. It wouldn't be with her—he was far too old for her, more like an uncle, really. He was too old for Kate, too. What had Father been thinking?

The entail.

That's what he'd been thinking, an idea that she was sure must be as far from everyone else's minds as it was from hers now, now that so much else had happened.

The entail! What a laughably small problem!

And yet Father had been worried about it, and so he had brought in Merry, the duke, too, in the hopes of solving it. The arrival of Cousin Benedict had potentially resolved that issue, leaving Merry without a chance.

No, he was too old for her, but he might yet find someone who would be suitable. And for now, she would be his friend.

She cast about in her mind, considering older women in her acquaintance but not too old. Perhaps she could come up with someone and then play matchmaker? She'd never done anything like it before, but she figured, just because she might be hopeless at finding love for herself, it didn't mean she'd be hopeless at finding it for someone else.

Rowena Clarke! Benedict's mother—*she* was alone in the world! Perhaps…

"Grace?"

"You're awake!" she cried, pleased.

But then she saw that his hands were shaking horribly as they clutched at the sheets and his teeth were literally chattering in his head as he stuttered out the words, "Wh-wh-wh-what is ha-ha-ha-happening to me?"

She placed her hand on his forehead, and it was ice cold. She grabbed on to one of his shaking hands, and that was ice cold, too. But the room wasn't. The temperature there was fine.

Grace rubbed one of his hands and then the other between her own.

"I'm so cold," he said.

"Yes, I can see that, Merry. I'll just—"

She started to rise from her chair. She was going to go and find some extra blankets from another room; she would grab every blanket she could find, but he stopped her, hanging on to her hand in a desperate grip.

"Please," he said. "Don't leave me."

"No, of course not. I was just going to—"

"*Please*, Grace!"

What else could she do?

What was there to be done if he was freezing but couldn't bear to be left alone?

Gently, she pulled back the sheets and climbed into bed beside him, without even taking off her dancing shoes first. He rolled over halfway, so he was on his side facing away from her, and she rolled over in the same direction. She pulled the sheets up over both of them, then she wrapped her arms around his thick waist, pressing the front of her body into his from behind in the hopes of transferring some of her warmth to him.

Since she'd first learned about what married people did, she'd always imagined that one day she'd lie down in bed with a man, but she never imagined that the first time she did so it would be like this.

"That's better, Grace," he said, feebly patting at her hands that encircled him. "I feel so much better now."

But his teeth were still chattering, so loud she could hear them, and he felt so frightfully cold.

This close, he smelled, too, bad, but she didn't mind that.

"I'm glad," she said, forcing cheer into her voice.

"Tell me a story," he said. "Tell me something about growing up here at Porthampton Abbey."

So she did.

She told him a story of Kate and Lizzy and her when they were just little things, the same one she'd told him when she'd taken him on a tour of the abbey, about Grandmama training them to be able to talk to anybody, no matter what the other person's station in life, by making them have conversations with the suit of armor, Fred.

The irony of it! She'd been trained to make conversation, and here she couldn't think of a fresh story to tell, one she hadn't told him before.

But it didn't matter. Merry didn't appear to mind, for as she talked, the chattering in his teeth gradually silenced, the trembling throughout his body slowly subsided and stilled, until finally, there was no movement at all.

Good, she thought. *He's sleeping. Sleep will heal him.*

But when she removed her support from behind him, his body fell backward awkwardly against the bed, and she saw that his mouth had frozen open in an unusual position and his eyes were wide, vacant and unblinking.

She almost screamed then.

She'd never seen a dead person before, not someone she cared about, and it did scare her, making her heart race faster.

But she did care about him, so she forced the fear to flee, and then all she could think was, *Merry*.

He'd actually been quite a nice man. He'd only ever dreamed of finding love.

Merry.

Even though he'd never been married nor had any children, he must have had some family back in London, some friends who would miss him, not to mention that his affairs would need to be settled. No matter what was going on here, they would need to do the right thing by him and calls would need to be made.

Merry.

She placed her palm over his face, gently closing his eyes, and then she laid a soft kiss on his cheek.

She should tell the others, she thought. Everyone must know.

But then she thought: *Why?*

They were all still dancing, having their good time.

Just because she was sad now, why spoil it for everybody else? She would rejoin the others downstairs, but when she did, she would say nothing of what had just transpired up here.

Morning would come again soon enough. There would be time to tell everybody then.

CHAPTER THIRTY-SIX

Not long after one of Them exited the bedroom, Rosencrantz and Guildenstern slithered their way in. They'd seen some food brought in there earlier in the evening, but they'd never seen it come out again, and they thought there might be some left for them. Any extra meal you could take without anyone seeing you was a gift. Although sometimes, it was even more fun being spotted but then managing to escape with the food before you were physically caught.

They smelled it, in the dark broken only by the strip of hall light behind them and by some small bit of moonlight peeking in through the heavy draperies, before they saw it.

The thing on the bed.

Rosencrantz and Guildenstern had enjoyed lots of experiences with dead things. Mostly, they'd been the agency for those deaths. But this, now, *this* was something different.

This dead thing was changing.

CHAPTER THIRTY-SEVEN

"Father," Kate said with a laugh, "when you decide to do a thing, you certainly don't go at it by half measures, do you?"

"I like to think that about myself," he said, still huffing and puffing slightly after his exertions. "But to what exactly are you referring in this instance?"

"When I suggested that you should dance with Mrs. Murphy, I didn't mean you should feel the need to dance with *all* the female help. After she came back from wherever she disappeared to, you even danced with Fanny!"

"Yes, well, in for a penny, in for a pound. And you know, the pound is worth so much more." He gave a last big exhale. "Although I must confess, that Agnes of yours can dance—that girl wore me out!"

"I think everyone's a bit worn out now," Kate said, assessing the music room, in which everyone had finally ceased dancing, preferring to talk in small groupings, and even Mr. Wright had grown a little lackluster in his manning of the gramophone. There had been at least a few minutes' gap between when the last record ended and this one began.

"I think," Father said, "that some refreshments are

in order and then to bed for all of us."

"I quite agree. I'll just tell Mrs. Owen to—"

"No, don't do that," Father said. "I mean, of course Mrs. Owen will need to organize the food end of things, and Fanny will need to help her, but I have another idea."

"Which is what, exactly?"

"It's what you said before." He tapped his forefinger against his lips. "About not doing things by half measures."

"I'm afraid I don't follow."

"When I said that we should have a dance this evening and that we should include the servants, as a diversion for every one of us from all this unpleasantness this weekend, well… It's not much of a diversion for the servants, is it, if they immediately have to go back to waiting on us?"

"It is what servants are for, Father. If they did not serve us, how else would we know that they are servants?"

"Yes, of course. But wouldn't it be more—oh, I don't know—*festive*, if we were to pitch in, too?"

"Festive?" Kate narrowed her eyes. "What are you proposing? That I chop up some beef and Mother can roast it in a pan? That Lizzy whip up a blancmange and Grace— well, I can't think right now what Grace might be good for, but give me some time and I'm sure I can manage to come up with *something*."

"Of course that is not what I am proposing—don't be absurd! I already indicated that Mrs. Owen and Fanny would still need to do the more…*kitcheny* things, and of course the footmen would have to carry any heavy trays." He put his hands in front of him and then slowly separated them outward, as though laying out whatever scene he was envisioning in his head. "Then everything could be set up in the front parlor—no, make that the back parlor. Since the servants will be joining us, it might as well be in a less formal room. Plus, you know, less nice things for them to muck up. And then—"

"You want us to take our refreshments with the servants? And we're supposed to *help out* somehow?"

"Am I not making myself sufficiently clear, Kate? I want this to feel festive! For just a few minutes, it'll be a real holiday for everybody, like a Christmas before Christmas. So we will assist the servants in bearing the refreshments to the back parlor. I promise you, it won't be anything too difficult on our end, just the smaller things and I can, oh, I don't know, carry a lemon or something."

Kate lifted her eyebrows so high, she could practically feel them hit her hairline. "A lemon?"

"For tea! Some people take lemon in their tea, you know."

"Yes, I do. And I also know that, sometimes, you are too good for this world."

"Hardly. Now, then…" Father looked around the room, his eyes eventually settling on the person he sought. "Wright!" he called across. "A word over here, please, if you would!"

When Wright did as had been requested, Father explained his little plan, at which point the butler stiffened and said, "With all due respect, Your Lordship, but have you gone *insane*?"

"Has Martin gone *insane*?" Grandmama said a half hour later as she used her cane with her left hand while carefully conveying a small pitcher of milk in her shaking right hand.

Kate had never pictured her grandmother and Wright having much in common in terms of ideas—or in anything else, really—but in this, it would appear, their attitudes were as one.

The whole group had processed up from the kitchen and were now making their way through the house and toward the back parlor. It was a snail's progress with their three remaining healthy guests and the rest of the family except for Grandfather carrying small items ahead, while the servants with their far more burdensome trays took up the rear. No matter that it might make sense for the servants to go on ahead to set things up and ease their burden, it wouldn't do for them to pass their betters.

"He thought it would be fun," Kate said brightly.

"*Fun.*" Grandmama invested the word with scorn. "'Fun' is a nice juicy bit of gossip that you didn't expect to hear that day and coming from a quarter from which you never expected to hear such a thing, preferably that Rowena Clarke person, who strikes me as someone who fancies herself above it all. 'Fun' is an enemy finding herself in a preposterously embarrassing situation. 'Did you know you had your hat on backward or is that the fashion in Paris these days?' But this?"

"The others seem to be enjoying themselves," Kate said with a chin nod ahead.

It was true. The rest of the family and guests bearing their small items, even Father with his lemon—they all appeared to be having a jolly time; well, except for Grace, who was doing her part by carrying something, but only in a half-hearted fashion and with a somewhat grim and distracted look upon her face. But outside of her? They all seemed happy enough. Indeed, Cousin Benedict and Rowena Clarke appeared to consider it quite the good game, occasionally trading their items between themselves, something along the lines of "You take the sugar bowl for a bit and I'll carry the little silver dish with jam in it with its tiny spoon shaped like a silver pineapple."

"Then they are simpletons!" Grandmama said. "And why did Martin get to carry the lemon? Come to that, why are there not more lemons? How will we ever get by with just the one?"

"It's symbolic," Kate said. "I'm sure the servants are bringing more."

"I could have carried a lemon," Grandmama huffed, "instead of this ridiculous milk pitcher." As she said it, the pitcher wavered some more. "And why aren't you carrying anything?"

"Because I'm walking with you and making sure you are all right."

"If that is the case, then you should be looking after that other grandparent of yours. He cannot be trusted to carry anything."

"Which is why he isn't and why I am blessed with the distinct pleasure of accompanying you."

"Do you think I am feeble? Do you think me incapable of carrying a small pitcher of milk without dropping it?"

Kate sought for the politic answers to both these questions, but before she could come up with something, Grandmama was on the attack again.

"And why is Fidelia the only one besides you and that wretched father of hers to be carrying nothing? Martin doesn't need minding. Shouldn't she be contributing to all this *fun* we are having, too?"

Now this Kate did have an answer for.

"You know that all Father ever expects of Mother is that she look beautiful and be happy."

As far as Kate was concerned, her parents had a perfect marriage.

"He spoils her," Grandmama said. "He always has, much to my chagrin."

Those walking ahead had already stepped onto the black-and-white large-checked marble floor beneath the gallery, which they would need to cross to get to the back parlor beyond. But suddenly all progress stopped and there appeared to be some kind of commotion going on, and she could hear a thumping coming from upstairs.

Kate left her grandmother's side and pressed through, in order to see what was going on, arriving just in time to discover the duke pointing at something overhead.

Kate looked up to where he was pointing, at a portly figure clad in a nightshirt who appeared to be moving in an unsteady fashion toward the pink marble railing of the gallery.

"Look!" the duke said. "It's Mr. Young! He's made a complete recovery!" Then concern filled his voice. "But are you sure you should be out of bed, Mr. Young?"

"It can't be," Grace said, dumbstruck. "This isn't happening. It's simply not possible."

"What *are* you talking about?" Kate demanded.

"That can't be Mr. Young up there." Grace paused, gulping. "Merry is *dead*."

CHAPTER THIRTY-EIGHT

"**D**ead? What *are* you talking about?" Lizzy heard Kate demand of Grace a second time.

"The man can't be dead," Grandmama said, having used her cane to pry her way through the others so that she now had a view from the very front row, spilling only a little milk along the way. "Even I, with my aging sight, can see. Why, he's standing right up there."

"M-Merry," Grace began in a halting fashion. "When I went up to check on him earlier. I was with him. And then he died. It was horrible. So how can he…"

"If you thought he had died," Father said, sounding mildly peevish, "why didn't you tell anybody?"

"I didn't want to spoil your good time," Grace said, apology and regret written all over her.

"Only you," Kate said with derision, "would leave out such a vital bit of information for such a trivial reason. And now, as you can see, you were wrong anyway."

"Yes, but," Grace started, her eyes clouded with confusion. "Unless…perhaps I was mistaken? I'm not a doctor, after all, so maybe…" Lizzy felt that her sister seemed to be filling with hope, but then two things happened, almost simultaneously.

The duke started to move forward, walking toward the foot of the grand staircase, while the figure above moved closer to the railing, peering down at them.

"No!" Grace cried, and Lizzy could see that whatever the reason, whatever Grace was seeing that they weren't, somehow all hope had left her now.

"No!" Grace shouted more urgently as the figure drew yet nearer to the railing above. "Don't you understand?"

Lizzy had seen the valet, Parker, with her own eyes; Dr. Webb, too. Parker and Dr. Webb had obviously been a menace; anyone who was paying attention could see that. But she couldn't bring herself to think that this situation was anything like those situations. Mr. Young didn't seem menacing at all, merely questing somehow. And besides, as she'd told Benedict earlier: the threat was all out there. It wasn't, could never be, in here.

And yet…

"What is it, Grace?" Lizzy said, forcing herself to ask the question gently while inside she could feel only a sense of rising urgency. "What don't we understand?"

"Yes, Grace," Kate said haughtily. "Do tell us what only you are perceptive enough to see."

"Merry is…" Grace started. "Merry *was* terrified of heights. He told me so himself when I took him on a tour of the abbey. He couldn't even bring himself to look up there from down here the other day. Merry—if this really were the Merry I knew—would never be able to bring himself to look down here from up there."

The man above was now pressed against the railing, arms stretched outward over the marble, grasping at air, as though he would walk right through the railing and reach for them if he could.

From this great distance, Lizzy couldn't see his eyes, but suddenly she was certain about what she would see if she could: the same thing she'd seen in Parker's eyes and then Dr. Webb's. Oh, how could she have been so stupid? When Dr. Webb bit Mr. Young, he must have somehow transmitted whatever was wrong with him to the other man, like a disease, an infection passed from one person to the next. And then they'd brought Mr. Young back here, to the house. She'd thought they were safe here, inside...

But they weren't, not anymore.

"Perhaps Mr. Young is just delirious," Cousin Benedict said. "I'm sure there must be some reasonable explanation."

"No," Grace said. "I—"

"What is that cat doing up there?" Mr. Wright called out, indignant.

"Henry Clay!" Fanny shouted from behind.

Lizzy could just glimpse, between the gaps in the marble railing, a furry object moving at high speed toward the man.

The man must have been stumbled up somehow by the cat, for now he was tumbling up and over the railing, and then his body was falling, flailing in the air, falling from that terrible height, until it crashed to the black-and-white marble floor, just barely missing the duke.

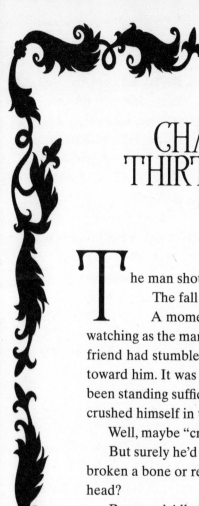

CHAPTER THIRTY-NINE

The man should have died.

The fall should have killed him.

A moment ago, the duke had stood there, watching as the man he'd come to think of as a sort of friend had stumbled over the railing, crashing down toward him. It was just sheer luck that the duke had been standing sufficiently out of the way as not to be crushed himself in the process.

Well, maybe "crushed" wasn't the right word.

But surely he'd have been badly injured. Perhaps broken a bone or received a really nasty conk on the head?

Raymond Allen took a step toward the crumpled body of Meriwether Young, facedown and still on the floor. Oh, to find a friend, only to lose him so quickly!

"Don't!" the duke heard Daniel cry out and other voices, Lady Grace's distinct among them, repeating the entreaty.

The duke ignored them. Why *were* people always trying to tell him what to do? He merely wanted to lay a hand of benediction on his friend, his poor dead friend. Where would be the harm in—

Mr. Young's hand shot out toward the duke as

others began to scream. There was the sound of porcelain breaking. How well the duke knew that sound! In his own home, porcelain was always breaking. It did seem to be his lot in life to hire only the most clumsy-fingered of servants, but oh how he missed home now—home! The duke looked toward the direction of the sound briefly enough to see the shattered porcelain and spreading milk near the dowager countess's feet and cane.

Oh, why was his mind filling up with such nattering nonsense like the problem with clumsy-fingered servants when—

The duke felt his feet take a few scuttling steps in retreat, moving out of the way as Mr. Young lifted his head from the floor, although his eyes were still directed downward. Now that he was so much closer, the duke could smell the wretched rotting stench coming off him in waves. Worse, although unpleasant smells were never, well, pleasant, the duke saw now that Mr. Young's legs were twisted at improbable angles to each other and yet he dragged his body upward onto his elbows and lower arms, inching himself toward the duke, occasionally shooting out an arm as though to grab on to whatever part of him he might catch.

The duke couldn't believe his eyes, and yet what choice did he have?

He was going backward, Mr. Young kept coming forward, the two of them caught in a circular pattern, with Mr. Young a grotesque crab seemingly in pursuit of the duke's feet.

The duke could see that Mr. Young's body was broken. Now that he'd had a moment to get over the shock and study him more closely, he could see that even his neck was at a bizarre angle that would normally be indicative of death.

"I should have brought my gun!" he heard Lady Elizabeth shout in frustration. "Why didn't I bring my gun! I'll just go and—"

In his peripheral vision, the duke saw her break from the group that had been frozen in place at the sight of this bizarre tableau. Lady Elizabeth was edging around Mr. Young and him on the left, inching toward the grand staircase, presumably to get the promised gun. Mr. Young had now managed to raise his face so that he was no longer looking downward, and the duke could see his eyes: milky with death and yet also, somehow, *hungry*. And then Mr. Young darted that head forward, even with its broken neck, teeth bared, snapping at him in hunger and frustration, and the duke knew that if Mr. Young could catch him... Well, he didn't want to think about that just now. But suddenly, that gun couldn't come quickly enough for him.

Whatever Mr. Young had been in life, he was that no longer.

But something in Lady Elizabeth's progress, as she neared her goal of the foot of the stairs, must have attracted Mr. Young's attention. For now his focus on the duke's circularly retreating feet had been broken and had instead been shifted upon Lady Elizabeth.

Lady Elizabeth, in their short acquaintance, had never struck him as the type to experience fear, yet she certainly looked fearful now as she backed away from that grasping hand.

"Father, do something!" Lady Kate cried.

He noted that Lady Kate hadn't cried out when *he* had been in immediate danger, but who could blame her? He'd pick Lady Elizabeth over himself any day. And Lady Elizabeth was Lady Kate's sister, after all.

"What can I..." His Lordship started to say, waving the lemon in his hand impotently as if holding the fruit in one hand precluded him from taking action with the other.

Or maybe, like all of them, he simply had no idea what to do.

The duke thought that people liked to think they'd be brave in any emergency, but you honestly never did know what you were capable of until you were actually faced with one, did you?

This was like what had transpired at the churchyard so many hours ago. Was it possible that both events were part of the same day? Then, people had been frozen, too, except for Mr. Young, who'd stepped forward to help Dr. Webb, only to get bitten and turned into...*this* as a thank-you; and Lady Grace, who'd moved to help her friend Mr. Young where he fell because he *was* her friend; and Daniel, who'd helped with knowing how to make a tourniquet and then had been further helpful by running for the trap and horses so they could all be safely transported back here.

Well, come to think of it, the duke wasn't so certain anymore that Daniel should be thanked for bringing Mr. Young back safely. It might have been better, for all of them, had they finished off Mr. Young when they had the chance. If only they had known what was to come. For surely, it wouldn't have just been better for all of them. Surely, it would have been better for Mr. Young, too, for the duke couldn't imagine his friend—*his friend*—wanting to survive *that*, only to turn into *this*.

But even Daniel, whether his bravery be ever true or occasionally just a tad misguided, might not know what to do in a situation like the one they were now confronted with.

One of the maids shouted, her voice reaching a high pitch and causing Mr. Young's head to point like an Irish setter, the sudden noise drawing his attention away in that direction. Now there was more shouting and cries of, "Somebody, do something!" The duke was quite sure that one of the people crying that out was him.

As the entire group drew backward, with only the duke and Lady Elizabeth as offshoots, vastly separated like cast-off stars from some cluster constellation in the night sky, the duke heard Lady Elizabeth coo in a twinkly voice, "Mr. Young. Over here, Mr. Young."

Whatever fear she'd been experiencing before was visibly gone now as she, with clear deliberation, drew the monster's focus back to her.

A thumping, the sound of running, came from above. Who could it be? Weren't they all here? Then a voice shouted from the landing at the top of the stairs, "Lizzy! Are you all right?"

"I'm fine, Will," Lizzy called back calmly, not turning around. "But unless you've got your pistol on you, I don't think you can help at the moment, and you might make things worse by getting any nearer."

"The *stable boy*?" Martin Clarke said. "What is the stable boy doing here? And why is he calling my daughter 'Lizzy'?"

Lady Elizabeth ignored the question and, reverting to the same seductively twinkly voice she'd used on Mr. Young a moment ago, urged the others through gritted teeth, "Now, will someone else please find a weapon? I don't think I can keep doing this all night."

"Martin?" the dowager countess called.

And yet, still, all His Lordship had was his lemon.

It occurred to the duke then that it wasn't fair. Lady Elizabeth was doing all the hard work, and what were the rest of them doing? They were letting her.

"Yoo-hoo!" the duke called, trying on his own imitation of Lady Elizabeth's seductive voice. "Oh, Mr. Young! Over here! Yoo-hoo! I say, yoo-hoo!"

Well, the duke thought, *that worked perhaps a little too well.*

For now, not only was the monster facing him instead of Lady Elizabeth, but the monster had even managed to find a bit of speed in those broken bones as it made for the duke, and Lady Elizabeth screamed, "Will someone please find a weapon!" and then Her Ladyship, Fidelia Clarke—Her Ladyship!—was prying the spear-like weapon with its hatchet-like end out of the hand of the suit of armor and His Lordship was crying out, "Fidelia, what are you doing to Fred?" and she was crying back, "I'm trying to save our guest!" and when she was on top of Mr. Young she swung the curved hatchet-like end downward, severing an arm, but that didn't stop the dead human crab, not even for a second, and Lady Elizabeth shouted at her mother as that lady raised the weapon once more, "The head, Mother, it won't work otherwise; be sure to cut off his head!" And now Fidelia was hacking at it, lifting the weapon and bringing the hatchet-like end of it down repeatedly, like an executioner on the first day on the job, attempting to succeed until getting the thing right, and then at last, at last, the head was finally severed and it came away from the body, rolling to a stop, but even though it had stopped rolling, its teeth were still snapping as though to bite anything that would just come close enough to those snapping teeth, and Lady Elizabeth screamed to her mother, "I shot the others *in* the head, so maybe it's not enough to simply cut *off* the head?" and then Fidelia raised her weapon once more and cleaved the head in two, and the snapping teeth finally ceased their horrible snapping, and Lady Elizabeth stood over the head, pointing to both parts of it, her voice a mixture of exhaustion and triumph as she exclaimed, "Now, surely, no one can argue with *that*!"

CHAPTER FORTY

Daniel wanted, *wished* he could go to Grace.

She stood there alone, tears falling down her cheeks, gently sobbing at the sight of what had become of her friend.

"Fidelia!" the dowager countess said in a peremptory fashion. "What do you think you are doing?"

Daniel couldn't blame the dowager countess for her reaction. In all his years in service at Porthampton Abbey, he'd never known the earl's wife to be anything other *than* a wife: a benevolent presence who wanted nothing more dearly than for each meal to pass successfully with nothing unpleasant said. Who in their right mind would have ever suspected her capable of something like this? But then, Daniel figured, you never really did know what people were capable of until pushed, did you?

"Well, someone had to save them," Lady Clarke said, then she let fall her weapon, putting out her arms to embrace her youngest daughter.

"Lizzy!" a voice called, and Daniel looked up to see Will Harvey racing down the grand staircase.

"I'm fine, Will," Lady Elizabeth said from her mother's arms. "There's no need to worry."

"What is the stable boy doing here, will someone tell me, please?" His Lordship said again in a booming voice. "And why is he calling my daughter 'Lizzy'?"

Daniel saw Will freeze, on one of the steps near the bottom, at this.

"He's my friend," Lady Elizabeth said, gently pushing her mother away.

"Your *friend*?" Lady Katherine said with some emotion Daniel couldn't quite identify. Was it scorn? Or was it jealousy?

And was it just him, or did Will suddenly look like he felt guilty?

Lady Elizabeth ignored her eldest sister, adding to her father, "He's here because I invited him. I invited him to come stay with us."

"You did *what*?"

"What choice did I have? No one else was taking the threat seriously. He was the only other person who appeared to, the only one who seemed to know what was going on. He even gave me a pistol—"

"So that's where that came from," Lady Katherine said coolly.

Again, Daniel noted the guilt in Will's expression. But why should he feel guilty? By giving Lady Elizabeth that pistol, he'd no doubt saved all their lives back at the churchyard or, at the very least, some of them.

"I don't care what he gave you or what choices you thought you had or didn't have," His Lordship said heatedly, "one of them was not to invite someone—a stable boy, no less!—to come stay in my house."

"It's just the attic," Lady Elizabeth said in a small but defiant voice.

"I don't care if it's the rooftop! Is this or is this not still my house?"

"Yes, Fa—" she started to say, but he wouldn't let her finish.

"You!" His Lordship waved his hand dismissively in the direction of Will Harvey. "Be gone. Get out of here now."

"Where do you propose he go?" Lady Elizabeth asked.

"Why, outside, of course," His Lordship said. "He certainly can't stay here."

"And you can't send him out there, either," Lady Elizabeth said with steely resolve, hands going to hips. "No one knows exactly what's out there anymore—none of us do, and it wouldn't be right."

"I'm not sure," Lady Katherine said, "that in the entire history of the universe, anyone has ever uttered the sentence 'Lizzy is right.' I'm afraid, though, I'm going to have to be the first, because she is. Father, you can't send him out there. You couldn't send a dog out there now."

His Lordship pursed his lips together for a long moment, before announcing with no small degree of exasperation, *"Fine."* Then he waved his hand at Will Harvey again. "But you, go back upstairs or to wherever you've been hiding, and don't let me see *you* again until morning. Once it's daylight, we can decide what to do about you."

"Thank you, Father," Lady Elizabeth said, and with only one backward glance—did his eyes linger longer over Lady Elizabeth or Lady Katherine?—Will Harvey went.

Daniel looked over and saw that Grace was no longer sobbing but that tears were still falling from her eyes.

He wanted to go to her—someone should—but he couldn't, of course.

And earlier, just a short time ago, when the threat had come among them, he hadn't been able to do anything about that, either.

He couldn't believe he hadn't done anything. Even just moving from his position at the back, holding his tray, would have at least been *something*.

And yet he hadn't. He'd been frozen. Even in war, that had never happened to him. So why now? Of course, in war, action had been obvious. Someone else, on the other side, is trying to kill you, and so you must kill that person first if you possibly can, and the reason that you are fighting in the first place is because people who are far more powerful than you have decided that it is a good idea for you to do so for some reason. All right, so maybe that wasn't necessarily understandable, either, but this? Nothing he'd ever seen before, not even in war, had prepared him, *could* have prepared anyone for *this*.

The sight of someone who'd been alive, then dead, still capable of movement without pause even after an arm had been severed, only stopping once the head had been removed. And then even that was not enough. It wasn't until the blade had penetrated the skull that the teeth had finally stopped their awful snapping.

And yet Raymond Allen—the duke, of all people!—had managed to act, bravely trying to draw Mr. Young's grasping hand and snapping teeth away from Lady Elizabeth.

Before tonight, Daniel wouldn't have imagined the duke to have it in him. And yet he had, when no one else did.

Daniel promised himself, if he had another chance…

But now, Daniel saw, the duke was bent over, hands on his knees, breathing in and out rapidly as though his heart might explode within his chest at any moment. Daniel didn't know what to call that, medically, or if there was even a name for it, but he'd seen it happen in the war. A man might act bravely in the moment, but then, as soon as the dangerous moment had passed, this would happen, as though the man were now experiencing all at once the crashing fear of everything that might have gone wrong.

He was about to go to the duke and offer assistance when

old Wright instructed, "Fanny! Can't you see that His Lordship the duke is struggling? Fetch him something to drink!"

"We have some tea right here, Mr. Wright," Fanny said.

"No," Mr. Wright said firmly, "that's probably gone cold by now. And anyway, water would be better. If you don't have any plain water here, then fetch some from the kitchen."

Before she could move, before any of them could, there came a knocking at the front door to Porthampton Abbey.

Everyone jumped a little at that, even Daniel.

Who could it be?

The earl looked all about, as though perhaps they had somehow lost one of their party and that person was now outside, but no one was missing.

"I don't think we're expecting anyone else this evening, are we, dear?" the earl finally said, turning to his wife, who shrugged.

Now the pounding came louder, more insistent.

"Well, Wright?" the earl said. "Open the door."

"But Your Lordship…"

The pounding increased yet further, as though a barrage of fists were attacking the door now.

"Do you not hear me, Wright?" the earl said in a voice that would brook no arguments. "Answer the door. That is what we do in this household, and it *is* still my household: when someone knocks at the door, we answer."

"Very good, my lord."

With a stiff bow, Wright obeyed.

Once the door had been opened, the barrage of pounding fists was replaced with a barrage of voices, as people Daniel recognized without necessarily having spoken to them before—farmers, their wives and children, even a few villagers—shouted things like, "Let us in!" and "You don't know what it's like!" and "You *must* let us in!"

Daniel couldn't help it. At the sound of the panic in their

voices, he felt panic rise in him. It was like something contagious.

And yet old Wright never wavered. Standing there in the doorway, a bulwark against disaster, barring their entry. They could have gone around him, of course they could have, and yet they didn't.

Daniel couldn't blame them. For all his referring to him, at least in his own head, as "old Wright," the butler was a formidable man.

And now that formidable man was telling the crowd outside in a calm but firm voice, "No, I'm afraid you can't come in. Now, go back to your homes. You'll be safe inside there. Run along now. In the morning we'll sort this all out. Run along."

A part of Daniel was surprised to see them turn away from the door. Wouldn't people fight more, struggle? Wouldn't *he* fight more? And yet the other part of him wasn't surprised. He'd seen things like this in the war, too. If a commanding officer were commanding enough, no matter how ridiculous or dangerous the order given, most people tended to obey the voice of authority. Even if it meant going to their own deaths.

And as old Wright not only closed the door now but drew the bar down across it, the other door, too, Daniel couldn't help but think that old Wright had been correct in his decision.

Because now, you just never knew any longer with people, did you?

"Anything for me to worry about, Wright?" the earl asked.

"I don't think so, Your Lordship," Wright said, back on an even keel as he brushed one white-gloved hand against the other as though the act of barring the door might have gotten some dust on it.

"Very good," the earl said. "Now, shall we have our refreshments?"

"Refreshments, my lord?"

"Yes! Refreshments! Surely everyone still needs sustenance?"

"But what should we do about…?" Old Wright indicated the headless body and the bodiless pieces of head with a sidewise gesture of his own noggin.

"Oh, we can worry about that in the morning. After all, it's not like the poor man can hurt us anymore now, can he?" As he said this last, the earl waved his hand once more, before realizing it was the hand that still held the lemon. He made a face of disgust at it before holding it out with two fingers in the direction of Wright. "Please do something about this," he said, dropping the useless fruit into the butler's waiting hands. Then, to family and guests at large, and with a two-handed invitation gesture toward the back parlor now that both hands were finally free, "Come? Shall we?"

Old Wright, lemon now in his hand, turned to Fanny.

"Fanny! What are you still doing here? Didn't you hear me tell you? Go fetch His Lordship the duke a glass of water!"

"Right away, Mr. Wright."

Fanny departed quickly. But then, a moment later: "You know," the duke said, "maybe it'll be quicker if I just go with her—you know, get the water in me faster."

Daniel watched everyone disperse—family, guests, staff—then he straightened his back, assumed his role, and bore his tray into the back parlor.

Once there, seeing Grace, he wished again that he could just set his tray down, go to her, and comfort her.

But he couldn't do the latter two.

Well, at last and at least, he was finally able to put the tray down.

CHAPTER FORTY-ONE

Grace stood apart from the others in the back parlor, half listening, half grieving.

"You know, Fidelia," Grandmama was saying, "I could have done that, too, if I'd only gotten to the ax first."

"But you didn't," Grandfather said, sounding smugly satisfied, "because you didn't think of it first, and even if you had, you wouldn't have been quick enough. You probably couldn't even lift it."

"Harrumph. I'll have you know…"

Grace couldn't believe they were bickering over this.

"Oh, who cares who got there first?" Mother said. "So long as one of us did what had to be done. Now who wants tea? Something a little stronger? I know I would like both."

Tea? Something *stronger?* Grace had only had sips of "something stronger" a few times in her short life and while she could see where some might find it fortifying, she didn't think anything could fortify her now.

Did no one care that Merry was dead? No one but her?

Kate was flirting with Benedict, which was in no

way surprising. With Merry dead and the duke gone to the kitchen with Fanny to get a glass of water, who was there left for Kate to flirt with?

Even Lizzy, who had come so close to being attacked herself, was behaving as though nothing of great import had happened. Or, at least, nothing that couldn't be dealt with as a matter of practicality.

"No, Father," Lizzy said, "I won't explain again what the stable boy is doing here, in this house, in *your* house. As you said, let's handle that in the morning. Now, the way I see it…"

And here Lizzy launched into a long speech about people getting somehow infected when bitten, so it was vitally important to avoid getting bitten, and, of course, if someone was bitten, he would then get sick and die, as Merry had done, at which point, you had to be sure to cut off his head but be sure to penetrate the skull, too, or shoot him there, so maybe, if you knew someone had been infected, you should just go ahead and cut off his head and deliver a final cut to the skull or shoot him right away, because you were only going to have to do it later anyway, it was just a matter of time and who knew how much time you really had, so why not do it first and remove all threat?

"Listen to Lizzy," Kate said. "If I didn't know any better, I'd swear she fancies herself some sort of doctor now!"

"I do not!" Lizzy said. "It's just—"

Grace stopped listening, so now she was no longer half listening, half grieving. She was all grieving.

At the church, she'd cradled Merry's head after he'd been injured. And later, she'd held his body as he died. But what was there for her to hold on to now?

Father had said they could worry in the morning about what to do about what was left of Merry, but she knew that wouldn't be the case. He couldn't be allowed to remain out there like that. You could hardly get from one place to the other downstairs without passing over the marble floor beneath the gallery; you couldn't even come down or go up the grand staircase without seeing what was left of him there. While they were in here, enjoying their *refreshments*, Mr. Wright would no doubt slip away at some point and see to the disposal. He'd probably enlist one of the footmen, possibly Jonathan, to help him.

And that would be that.

The servants.

When they'd first adjourned to the back parlor and all had been set up, Father had urged the servants to partake. He said it was what he had intended all along.

The servants had looked reluctant at first, but eventually, under Mother's gentle entreaties, most had been persuaded. Mrs. Owen looked perfectly thrilled to be eating rather than cooking for once. The maids had said yes to Mother's offer of something stronger, Agnes and Becky giggling all the while. Even Mr. Wright had accepted a cup of tea, although she noticed he just stood there, uncomfortably holding the saucer and cup. Mr. Wright would no doubt rather die of thirst than run the risk, however small, of dribbling a drop of tea on his pristine uniform while in the presence of the family.

Grace looked around some more and saw that one servant still had not partaken of anything, preferring to stay where he was accustomed, his back to the wall, eyes staring at some invisible point in the middle distance: Daniel.

But when she took in his face, she saw that rather than adopting his typical eyes-straight-ahead posture, his face was slightly turned in her direction. And when she looked specifically at his eyes, his gaze met hers completely and he smiled a sad smile.

Well, Grace thought, *at least one person cares.*

CHAPTER
FORTY-TWO

Fanny knew she had to hurry.

While those who lived their lives upstairs, their guests—well, the ones who were still alive—and even the rest of the staff had retired to the back parlor, Fanny knew she had little time to get done what she needed to get done before some of the latter group began to straggle down and back again, returning to the kitchen.

For all she knew, Mrs. Owen or Mrs. Murphy was making her way there now. Or—heaven forbid—Mr. Wright.

The nerve of Mr. Wright!

To stand at the doorway, sending people away, as though it were his house.

Not that Fanny minded that part so much. It had always struck Fanny as wrong that the earl and his family had so much space when others had so little. It was only fair for Mr. Wright to think of it as his, too. After all, didn't he do as much as anybody, more than the family, to keep the place running?

But Mr. Wright had stood there and spoken not just as though he was speaking for the earl. He'd done it as though he were speaking for everybody.

Well, he certainly wasn't speaking for her.

So she would do whatever she could.

But that didn't mean she wanted to be caught doing it.

Which is why it came as a great shock when: "I'm sorry to interrupt," the duke said from behind as she entered the kitchen, determined to make straight for the back door, "but weren't you supposed to be getting me a glass of water?"

Fanny half jumped, placing a hand to her chest as though she could still the racing of her heart.

"I'd forgotten you were back there," she said.

"Apparently."

Fanny felt time slipping away. She was losing time!

"I just need to…" she started to say, torn between doing what her job prescribed that she do—his bidding—and what she wanted to do: get to that back door.

"If I could have it now, please," the duke said, amiably enough, "I would be most grateful, since as you can see, I am rather—"

"Fine," Fanny said with ill grace, locating a glass and pitcher of water, filling the former from the latter, finally all but slamming the glass into his hand. "There you go. Drink up."

Only he wouldn't drink fast enough. He seemed content to take a sip, delicately wipe away any moisture from his lips with the back of his hand, take another sip…

Bloody hell! Why would he not just drink the thing down?

"You'll feel better faster if you drink that faster," she suggested.

"But then I might choke. It's better and safer to sip."

"You'd be more comfortable if you sipped it safely with the others in the parlor."

"Walking while sipping isn't particularly safe, either."

"Nobody likes standing around a kitchen."

"I suppose it could use a spot of color, but other than

that…" The duke shrugged. "Doesn't seem too terribly awful to me."

Well, of course it didn't to him, but that was only because he had a choice in the matter.

And now, having made the choice to come here, he simply wouldn't leave.

Fanny couldn't wait any longer. Already, she'd probably waited too long.

Could she trust him, though?

She didn't have a choice.

She left him standing there with his half-empty glass of water as she hurried across the kitchen, at last achieving her goal of reaching the back door.

"What are you doing?" the duke called to her from behind.

Fanny turned to him just long enough to say, "I'm saving as many people as I can. This won't turn into the *Titanic*—not on my watch!"

Then she flung open the back door.

CHAPTER
FORTY-THREE

The *Titanic?* the duke wondered. What could Fanny possibly mean by that? And "save people"?

But there was no time for him to figure out the answer to this puzzle, for now Fanny was actually *leaving* the building, running out into the night.

Without thinking, he raced to the doorway himself, although when he got there, he couldn't bring himself to cross the threshold. Who knew what was out there?

"Fanny!" he yelled after her. What could that girl possibly be thinking? "It isn't safe!"

But the sole answer he got was her voice, in what could be described only as a whispering shout, calling into the night, "Yoo-hoo! Is anyone still out here?"

He felt so vulnerable standing there in the open doorway. What if there was a threat out there? What if there were more like Dr. Webb and Mr. Young, just lurking? He thought to close and bar the door then, in order to save himself. But even though he knew it was the cautious thing to do, maybe even the right thing for him and everyone else in the house, he couldn't do that to Fanny. He couldn't leave her out there alone.

"Fanny!" he cried. "Get back here this instant!"

He felt despair overtake him as he realized he could no longer see her little form in the fog-shrouded darkness.

Would he need to go after her?

Then the duke heard murmuring in the distance, and he squinted against the fog to try to see something, anything. A few moments later, his efforts were rewarded when he saw Fanny emerge from the fog, leading a small contingent of people. As they drew closer, he saw they were rather grubby-looking people, perhaps amounting to no more than twenty in number.

"Fanny," he demanded, "what are you doing?"

For answer, she stepped over the threshold, but before those behind her could do likewise, she turned to face them, hands held up.

"Now," she said in a quietly commanding voice, "we need to do this in an orderly fashion, so please line up here."

He thought they might charge her then. It was clear they were all desperate to get in. And yet something in her voice and the way she held herself caused them to meekly obey. Who knew that someone so small, a kitchen maid no less, could possess such commanding authority?

The first in line was a man who took his hat off before Fanny, holding it nervously in his hands.

The duke was sure he'd seen women and some children among the group, too. Shouldn't this man, shouldn't all the men have let those women and children go first? For whatever this was?

But Fanny seemed to take no notice of the man's gender, merely requesting that he bend over a bit. The man complied, although he did want to know, "What's this for, then?"

Fanny stood on tiptoe, running her hands through his hair and inspecting his scalp.

"Just checking for lice," she whispered softly. "Can't afford to have an infestation, now, can we?"

An infestation? Of *lice*?

But the duke could see that it wasn't just that. While Fanny's hands went through the man's hair, her eyes were also examining all around his neck and any other exposed parts, sliding her hands down until she was holding his hands in hers, looking at them closely on all sides, even pushing his sleeves up a bit before looking steadily into his eyes, searching.

Seemingly satisfied with what she'd found, or hadn't, she leaned into the man and whispered, "Now, you haven't been bitten anywhere that I can't see, have you?"

"No, of course not," the man said, shaking his head vehemently.

The duke wondered how she thought she could take him at his word. Couldn't he be lying?

But Fanny merely looked deep into the man's eyes once more and, again seeming satisfied, told him, "You're all right then. You can come through."

She stepped aside, and once the man was in the building, she gave him directions to a staircase and told him to use it.

"But step as quietly as you can," she cautioned him. "I'll be up soon as I can to get rooms and sleeping arrangements sorted out."

Rooms? What was Fanny thinking? *Sleeping* arrangements?

The man tipped his head to her before placing his hat back on it and proceeding to do as she'd directed.

"Fanny, what *are* you doing?" the duke demanded again. He *would* be heard this time. He *would* receive an answer. He *was* the duke!

"Why, I'm saving as many people as I can," Fanny said, as though it were the most reasonable thing in the world, before turning her attentions to the next person in line, a girl, possibly no more than twelve years of age. "Next?"

"But you can't do that!"

"Watch me."

"But Mr. Wright said—"

"I know what Mr. Wright said," Fanny replied as she inspected the girl's scalp and other exposed parts. "But he's wrong. Don't these people have as much right to survival as anyone else?"

"Perhaps, but—"

"There's no perhaps about it."

"Fine, but—"

"There're no buts, either."

Satisfied that this girl was acceptable to enter, too, Fanny let her pass, directing her to the stairs just as she had the man.

"Look," Fanny said before turning to the next person. "You have a choice: you can report me or you can ignore me, pretend you haven't seen any of this." She paused. "Or you can help me." Then she shrugged, as if it no longer mattered what he decided to do, and continued with her work.

Help her?

He wasn't about to…

Oh, blast it all to hell.

The duke reached for the person next in line behind the one Fanny was examining. But then he thought of something.

As he had earlier in the evening, when he'd removed Mr. Young's perspiration-soaked bedding, the duke took off his own jacket, waistcoat, and tie, removed his cuff links, and rolled up his sleeves, opened his stiff collar.

There. That was better.

Then, with tentative fingers, he began going through the scalp of the woman who bent her head before him, gingerly going over the parts of her he could see. Whatever else he might find, he certainly hoped there wouldn't be any *lice*.

The duke and Fanny were in this position, examining

farmers and villagers side by side, when a voice behind them boomed, "Fanny! Stop what you are doing this instant!"

"I don't think so, Mr. Wright," Fanny said, not even bothering to look up as she continued.

"I turned these people away!" Mr. Wright said.

"And I'm letting them in," Fanny said. "Look," she added, and the duke recognized the calm, reasonable voice she'd employed with him earlier. "We can't just let people die. Don't you see, we're responsible for them, too?"

"What I see here is insubordination! What I see is insurrection! What I see—"

"What are you going to do about it, Mr. Wright?" Fanny said. "Fire me? Order me out into the night, too?"

The duke wondered: Would Mr. Wright do that? Could he be that cold…to Fanny?

But then he saw the butler color at this. "No, of course not. But I know what the earl would want, and the earl would not want—"

"Ah, but you see, Mr. Wright," the duke said, drawing himself up to his full height and authority, although he did feel a bit silly doing so in rolled-up shirtsleeves and an open collar, "it doesn't matter in this instance what the earl would want, because a duke outranks an earl, and I am the duke." He paused. "And I want this."

He heard Fanny gasp, and then came a sound that was shocking on such a night: Fanny giggled.

Seeing Mr. Wright's expression, the duke was tempted to join her, but where would be the authority in that?

So he forced himself to look as serious as possible as he added, "The way I see it, Mr. Wright, you have a choice: you can report us to the earl, you can ignore what you've seen here, or you can help us."

"I shall need to think about this further," Mr. Wright said, sounding like his usual self-important self, but there was no real heat left behind the words.

"You do that, Mr. Wright," the duke said. "And while you're doing it, please get out of our way. Some of us are trying to work here."

The butler half bowed and stepped back, turning on his shiny heel. As he turned, the duke heard him mutter to himself, "Perhaps I didn't see anything. Maybe my eyes were just playing tricks on me. Perhaps I just need sleep..."

When he was gone, Fanny burst into giggles again, and this time the duke joined her.

But a moment later, the laughter stopped. He looked up and saw her expression had turned serious.

"What is it?" he asked.

"Oh, nothing," she said, but there was a forced blitheness in her tone.

His eyes shot to what she was looking at, and then he saw it, too: a mark on one of the hands of the woman Fanny was now examining. The woman had wild gray hair that made her look quite old, although on closer inspection, the duke guessed she was not much over forty and maybe not even that.

"If you would, please," Fanny said, taking the woman by the elbow and positioning her to one side of the remainder of the line.

"Is there something the matter?" the woman asked, concern in her eyes, which, the duke noted now, looked a bit feverish.

"No, not at all," Fanny said, still blithe. "But it's my job to get everyone properly sorted, and what a job it is!" Fanny scanned the remaining people, which included only a few more men and a young boy. "I wouldn't want to make any mistakes!"

Those last few went quickly and without incident, and

then the gray-haired woman was in front of Fanny once more.

"Now, may I—"

"I'm so sorry," Fanny said sincerely, and she even took the woman's hand—*that* hand—in both of hers as she said it, giving it a reassuring pat. "But I can't let you in, not this evening. You see, we only have so many beds available, and the ones reserved for females are all full already."

"But I could sleep on—"

"Go back to your home, Mrs. Harvey."

Mrs. Harvey? But wasn't the stable boy...

"You'll be safe there, I promise," Fanny said. Then she added soothingly, "Someone will be along in the morning to fetch you, just as soon as I get this silly bed business sorted out. I'm sure I'll be able to find one for you then."

The duke thought the woman would fight Fanny, put up some resistance, but she simply removed her hand from Fanny's and began walking away, into the night. Perhaps the fever in her made her too weak to fight.

"Oh!" Fanny called after her. Then she grabbed a heavy copper frying pan from the wall and hurried it over to the retreating woman. "Here you go, Mrs. Harvey!" She placed it in her hands. "Something to protect yourself with as you walk!"

A moment later, Fanny was back inside. And once inside, she shut the door firmly behind her and then bolted it.

"That frying pan won't protect her, will it?" the duke asked, already knowing the answer. Fanny had no doubt given it to the woman so she'd have a false sense of safety, so perhaps she wouldn't think to further resist being turned away.

"Of course not," Fanny said.

"And we couldn't save her?"

"Didn't you see her hand? She'd been bitten."

"Dr. Webb, after he turned into whatever he turned into, bit Mr. Young," the duke said, figuring things out as he spoke the words aloud. "Lady Elizabeth stood reasonably close to both Parker and Dr. Webb, but she never caught it, whatever it is. But Mr. Young got bit and…"

He let the thought hang there.

"That's what I figured," Fanny said.

How smart she was! And not only that, she'd figured it out ahead of him.

"I couldn't let her in here," Fanny said, looking sad but resolved. "She'll be dead by…whenever. And then, once she is, she'll be one of them. I wish I could've saved her somehow, but—"

"You did the right thing, Fanny."

He could see that she knew he was right. And he could also see that it didn't help any.

Suddenly, Fanny smiled, surprising him.

How could she smile at a time like this?

But then he thought, if there was one thing he was learning about Fanny, it was that you couldn't keep her down. Not for too long.

"Look at you," she said, grinning.

"What?"

"In your rolled-up shirtsleeves and everything."

Now that he thought about it, in his rolled-up shirtsleeves and open collar, he felt like a pirate! A swashbuckler!

No, more important than that, for the first time in his life, he felt like a man.

"First you changed the sheets for an invalid earlier," Fanny said. "Now this."

"Yes, well, I…" He could feel the blush suffuse his face all the way to the tips of his jug ears.

He saw her gaze shift to one of those big appendages, no doubt drawn by their coloring.

"I like your ears," she said, surprising him.

"What?" He felt self-conscious, both hands instinctively moving to cover those twin objects of so much of the scorn in his life.

"I like them. Your ears."

"But I've always hated them."

"Why? They're so substantial, the way ears should be. Mine are so small, like little seashells." She made a face.

He let his hands fall away from his own ears as he studied hers. She was right. They did look like little seashells, but she was wrong to make a face over them, for they were pretty ones at that.

"I've always thought," she said, when he didn't respond immediately, "that ears—everyone's—are funny things, ridiculous really, the way they stick out the sides of people's heads like an afterthought, slapped on at the last minute when someone realized they might be useful."

"How extraordinary! You know, I've never thought about it like that, but I do believe you're right."

"Of course I am."

Earlier, he'd complimented her hands, and now she'd complimented his ears. What a world this was turning out to be!

"Now," Fanny said, "if you're still inclined to help, let's go upstairs and get everybody sorted. Who knows how long Mr. Wright will agree to ignore what he's seen? And the more established they all are in the house, the harder it'll be for anyone to get them out."

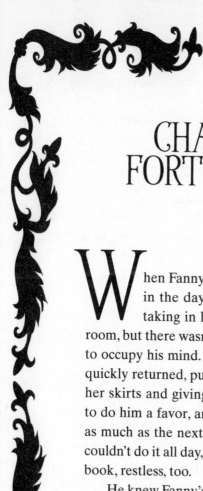

CHAPTER FORTY-FOUR

When Fanny had left Will in the room earlier in the day, he'd sat down on his new bed, taking in his surroundings. It wasn't a bad room, but there wasn't much to it, nothing with which to occupy his mind. After leaving before, Fanny had quickly returned, pulling a book from somewhere in her skirts and giving it to him. She no doubt meant to do him a favor, and he supposed he liked reading as much as the next tenant farmer's nephew, but he couldn't do it all day, and soon he grew bored with the book, restless, too.

He knew Fanny'd said for him to be careful not to get caught, particularly by Mr. Wright. But what was he supposed to do, just sit up here all day and night, until Fanny or possibly Lizzy—although he couldn't quite see how that could happen—came for him and told him he was needed?

He'd decided to go out. He wanted to check on the horses. Someone had to; he doubted anyone else would think of them at a time like this—unless it was Lady Kate, but then she'd only think about riding one, not the work of actually taking care of it—and if he didn't, who would? The horses couldn't feed themselves.

The trick would be not being seen, which would require stealth and luck.

Both had been working in his favor in terms of his exit.

After leaving his room, he'd tiptoed to the top of the servants' staircase, waiting until any footsteps echoed into the distance before scooting down. Instead of going all the way to the bottom, which he knew would leave him in the kitchen where there would likely be activity going on, he'd stepped through a side door on one of the landings. There, he'd found himself in more luxurious surroundings with rooms that led to grander staircases. He wasn't sure quite where he was — there'd been no time yet to ask Fanny for a tour, although that would have been a good idea; perhaps tomorrow? — but by stopping and listening repeatedly before proceeding forward, he managed to make his way through the warren of rooms, going ever downward when he saw a staircase, while always avoiding *the* grand staircase.

At last, he found himself in an empty parlor somewhere at the back of the house. Back here, some of the rooms had long doors leading outward, and it was easy enough to slip out of one. It wasn't locked on either side, and it occurred to Will that while they no doubt barred the front door at times, anyone could get in and out back here if they thought about it.

Once outside, Will made for the stables.

He knew he should be worried about possible threats, but the misty fog from the morning had cleared by then, and he could see all around him as he crossed the great lawn. Besides, he'd witnessed Dr. Webb attack Mr. Young, so now he knew what such an attack looked like. Dr. Webb had moved relatively slowly, lurching in his gait. The trick was to not let them get too close to you, not to let them surprise you. But Will would be vigilant, and he was confident that if he spotted anyone who looked or smelled like Dr. Webb had, he could outrun that person. Or thing. Whatever you would call it.

Not to mention, Will had thought to bring his pistol with him before exiting his new room.

At the stables, Will had been relieved to find the horses were all well, particularly that Wyndgate was, as Wyndgate was his favorite. He knew the horse was Lady Kate's favorite, too, which served to make him feel warm inside: the idea that, no matter what they might not share, could never share despite the way she somehow haunted him, at least they had their love of this animal in common.

Will wasn't sure what he'd expected to find: that the horses had been slaughtered by some malevolent force? The horses with gaping wounds or human bite marks all over them?

Whatever he'd imagined he might find, thankfully, that was not the case.

So, maybe whatever these new creatures were, dead humans come back to life with a desire to devour others, perhaps their violent impulses didn't extend to animals? Or at least not in terms of attacking them with their teeth?

Will certainly hoped so. It was awful enough being a human trying to sort out this awful mess. He didn't see how a beast could understand it, however smart might be that beast, like Wyndgate.

The horses taken care of, Will had set off to return to the main house and his room in it. And he almost made it, he almost did. But where stealth and luck had held for him earlier, this time only stealth did, for upon finally wending his way back through trial and error to the posh side of the door that led to the servants' staircase, no sooner did he push through it to the other side than the luck part failed him.

On the other side, he encountered two of the servants — Jonathan and Becky, he thought they were — coming downward.

They'd been laughing together when he first spotted them,

but spying him, they immediately stopped.

Now the jig was surely up.

It was a phrase he'd encountered for the first time that day. It had been in the book Fanny had given him, a detective story, and when he'd read it he hadn't understood what it meant, no doubt because his mind was not fully engaged by the words on the page before him; there was too much else to think about.

Well, he certainly knew what the words meant now, he thought, as his eyes met those of Jonathan and Becky in turn to find them staring back at him.

Instantly, he felt embarrassment at the disparity between his stable garb and their pristine house clothes. Anyone could see he didn't belong up here.

Now the jig was truly up.

Jonathan and Becky would fetch Mr. Wright, who would throw him out, whereupon he'd be rendered useless to Lizzy. And the others. And Kate.

Well, he supposed he could always sneak back in again.

But that wasn't the point.

Because once caught, Mr. Wright would be more vigilant, meaning the mere ability to be stealthy might not be enough.

And yet neither Jonathan nor Becky screamed out his presence, alerting others.

Instead, Jonathan tore his gaze away from Will and, turning to Becky, said, "So. Bex." Bex? Was that some sort of friendly nickname? "I was about to tell you. Last night, when Daniel and I were playing cards…"

Whatever else got said was lost as Will watched, dumbfounded, as Jonathan and Becky turned away, continuing down the stairs, soon laughing again, as though they'd never seen him there at all.

Huh.

Will decided then and there that he rather liked Jonathan and Becky. Or Bex. They seemed like jolly sorts.

Will puckered his lips, a smile twinkling in his eyes as he continued on up the stairs. If he weren't worried about being overheard, he'd have whistled out loud.

After Will's narrow escape on the staircase and his subsequent return to his room, he'd laid his pistol down on the small dresser and laid himself down on the bed.

He hadn't planned on sleeping—there was so much still to think about—but so much had already happened that day, and so much of it had been exhausting...

He awoke to the sound of shouting.

Many voices shouting, somewhere in the house far below.

Will raced from his room, in a hurry to get to whoever was shouting, whoever needed help.

Only just roused from sleep and being in that great hurry: no doubt, those were the two reasons he'd left the pistol behind on the dresser, where it was of use to no one.

Which was why when he arrived on the scene, that horrific scene—Mr. Young, turned into something even worse than Dr. Webb had been; Lizzy in danger—he'd been as impotently useless as that lemon in the earl's hand.

And then everything else had followed.

He'd wanted to go to Lizzy then, afterward, to at least make sure she was all right. He felt so responsible for her. After all, he'd been the one to give her the pistol. He'd been the one to put the idea in her head that she might be somehow equipped to fight whatever lay ahead. But her mother had her.

And then he'd seen the look on Lady Kate's face. Did she not understand that he felt responsible for Lizzy, who had been in direct and immediate danger of attack from Mr. Young, while he'd seen Kate to be relatively safe at the time, and anyway, he trusted and respected that Kate was strong enough to take care of herself? But then the earl sent him back upstairs to the attic and he'd gone, like a little boy who, having behaved badly, needed to be dealt with later.

Again, he waited.

And waited.

Now, though, there came the sounds of footsteps and then more footsteps coming up the servants' staircase.

He thought that he should remain hidden and not risk being seen, but then he realized: What was the point any longer? His jig was already up. The earl had seen him, everyone had, and he'd no doubt be evicted in the morning.

So when it sounded like there were more footsteps of people out there than there could possibly be servants in the house, he opened his door and had a peek.

What he saw were farmers he knew there, some villagers, too.

"Will!" someone shouted at him. "Will Harvey!"

And from another person: "You thought to come here ahead of us? You were always a clever boy."

He was about to explain that he hadn't been clever, but before he got a chance to, they were telling him things: about attacks on the farmers; attacks on the villagers; how a menace had come among them that no one understood and the only thing they'd thought to do, those who could get away, was to head for the greater safety of the abbey.

The people he spoke with said there were more like Dr. Webb and Mr. Young out there, but none could say how many. Just more. And more today than there'd been yesterday.

Every so many seconds, another farmer or villager would come up the stairs to be added to their group in the hallway, and more greetings of reunion would follow, leaving Will little time to ask the things he wanted to know: Just how bad was it out there, really, beyond this idea of "more"? Who had let them in the house? Surely it wasn't Mr. Wright. And most important of all, where was Aunt Jess?

But then what must have been the last of the lot joined them, and a few minutes later there was Fanny and—Will had to blink at this!—the duke, jacketless and with shirtsleeves rolled up, there to help organize everyone, Fanny showing people which rooms they could use and directing the duke on where to find and then set out linens and the like.

Before people could be dispersed to their rooms, Will raised his voice above the din: "Has anyone seen my aunt Jess? Jessamine Harvey?"

His uncle and aunt, the only parents he'd ever known. They'd taken him in when his own parents had died. And while one might think that to be expected behavior in all families, as Will had grown he'd learned that wasn't always the case. He'd heard of other orphans turned away by family members who said they already had too many mouths to feed. And no one had judged them poorly for this. Rather, people had accepted that you do whatever you need to do to protect the survival of those closest to you first, no matter the cost to others. But who knew what ever became of those other unlucky orphans.

Will, on the other hand? He'd been taken in by his uncle and aunt, even though they didn't have to do it, because they believed it to be right, no matter the cost to themselves. More than that, though, beyond a roof and food, they'd given him love. For Will's part, he'd been grateful to them for providing him a place to live and warm food. But more than that, he'd loved them back.

"That's funny," said a large man with white muttonchops,

who Will recognized as Silas Powell, the village publican. "I could've sworn Jessamine was in our group."

"Well, she's not here now," said Lottie Richards, one of the tenant farmers' wives. "And who can really say if she was with us before? I know I was so busy running for my life, I doubt I'd have noticed if the king of England had been with us and then left."

"I suppose you're right," Will said. "There must've been lots of confusion." Then: "Fanny? Did you see her tonight? With the others?"

"No," Fanny said, not lifting her eyes from the task currently at hand, which was fitting a case to yet another pillow. He smiled at the sight. It was as though Fanny'd gone and opened up her own boardinghouse here, or a hotel even. He'd heard of those: grand places where people could go and, for a price, spend the night and get treated like, well, those who lived in the abbey got treated every day. "I'd have said if I had," Fanny added, still not looking up.

"Your Lordship?" Will turned to the duke. "Have you seen her?"

"I wouldn't know if I had, would I?" the duke said, his eyes likewise fixed to his task, which in his case was handing sheets to one of the village women. You wouldn't think such a simple task would require such intense focus and concentration, but then, Will told himself, the duke had no doubt never performed such a menial task in his life and perhaps he merely wanted to get it right. "I've never met the woman."

"I'm sure," Fanny said, "that wherever she is, she's fine, Will."

"I'm sure you're right," Will said. "Wherever she is, I'm sure Aunt Jess can take care of herself."

CHAPTER
FORTY–FIVE

Kate sat before the vanity mirror in her bedroom as Agnes stood behind her holding the silver-backed hairbrush. Agnes had already helped her out of her evening clothes, then slipped the silk nightgown over her head. Now, having taken the peacock-feather forehead band and pins out, she was brushing her hair. One hundred strokes. And they were only at around twenty-four.

Had there ever been such a long day?

Thankfully, days like this didn't come along every day and hopefully never would again.

Surely tomorrow would be better.

"Agnes?" Kate asked. "What are the servants saying?"

Kate was aware, on some level, that the servants had thoughts and feelings about things, too, just like anyone else, she supposed, although their jobs demanded that they maintain a stoic front at all times. Of course, those thoughts and feelings were no doubt informed by silly superstitions and wrongheaded beliefs. Still, Kate found, she was curious.

Agnes kept her eyes on her work. Thirty-nine. "How do you mean, miss?"

"Come now. It's me. You can tell me. Surely, they must all be saying *something* after all that has happened."

"Well, naturally people are scared..."

"Scared? Why?"

"Why, because of what you just said! 'All that has happened'! The thing with Dr. Webb...that awful thing poor Mr. Young turned into... Why, there's not even a doctor in the village anymore if one of us got very sick! That is, of course, if we ever can get into the village again. Aren't you scared, miss?"

"Of course we'll get into the village again! And no, I'm not scared, not in the slightest."

"But how is that possible?" Agnes said, pausing in her stroking at fifty-two.

"I don't know! I'm just not. And you shouldn't be, either. It's ridiculous to be so fearful of things that are outside of one's control."

"Perhaps, miss, but it's because it all seems so out of our control—*that's* what I find scary."

"Don't be—"

Kate had been about to admonish Agnes, use the word "ridiculous" again, possibly toss in a "silly" or two, but then it occurred to her: if Agnes had stopped mid-stroking, at just fifty-two, the poor girl really was concerned.

"Do people think we're not doing enough?" Kate asked, looking at Agnes in the mirror until the other girl became compelled to meet her eyes.

"No, of course not, miss," Agnes said. "Besides, what can anybody do if no one even knows what's really going on?"

Kate turned in her seat.

"It will be all right, Agnes," she said. "I promise, you'll be taken care of. I won't let you down."

Then she reached for the brush.

"But we still have—" Agnes started to object.

"Forty-eight more to go, I know," Kate said, relieving her of the silver-backed item. In doing so, her hand accidentally touched up against Agnes's and for the briefest of moments Kate thought to cover the other girl's hand with her own, to offer that comfort. But no. That would be taking a good thing too far. So instead she added brightly, "We'll just add it to the morning's lot. One hundred and forty-eight strokes seems to me a fine number to start the day with, and tomorrow will be a fine day, I promise you."

"Then I'll just…" Agnes moved to begin arranging the bedsheets and things on the great canopy bed, but Kate stopped her there, too.

"Leave it," Kate said. "I think I can turn down my own sheets for just this once. It's been an impossibly long day for everybody. And you must be tired, too."

"I am," Agnes said. "If you're sure…"

"I am."

Once Agnes was gone, Kate did turn down her own sheets and climb into bed. But sleep did not immediately come. Without the maid's silly fears to contend with and comfort her over, Kate was left with her own concerns.

Kate had told Agnes that she wasn't scared, but was she?

Kate thought about it for a long moment and then decided that, no, she was not.

What was really bothering her was this: Was she really destined to wind up with Cousin Benedict?

Mr. Young was obviously out of the picture. Not that he'd ever been in it. But after tonight? She thought about that crab-like creature he'd turned into and shuddered. She didn't want to think about that. What if Mother had never thought to grab that weapon from Fred? She couldn't believe the rest of them had frozen. She couldn't believe *she* had frozen.

No, even if what had happened to Mr. Young hadn't

happened, he would still never have been in the picture.

But Kate had seen a few other things tonight, too, perhaps none so dramatic as the transformation of Mr. Young, but still.

The stable boy, Will Harvey, had come charging down the stairs, no doubt imagining himself some sort of romantic hero destined to save the day!

And he'd been calling Lizzy's name as he ran.

Lizzy!

Why had the stable boy been so concerned about Lizzy? Again, Lizzy! It seemed suddenly as though wherever Kate turned, Lizzy was shooting someone or saying something shockingly not stupid or, now, capturing the attentions of the stable boy. He'd been worried about Lizzy, but hadn't he been worried about her at all?

And then later, in the back parlor, Kate had seen the glance that had been exchanged between Grace and the footman, Daniel. Leave it to Grace to make eyes at a footman. Not that she, Kate, would ever want one for herself. But still. At least the footman was handsome.

Not like the duke. True, he had behaved somewhat bravely in trying to draw Mr. Young's attention away from Lizzy and on to himself. But then he'd gone and had that awful attack of nerves afterward, needing to go with Fanny to the kitchen for a glass of water in order to steady himself. So: not handsome. Not brave.

So where did that leave Kate?

It occurred to Kate for the first time that maybe the stable boy was only so worried about Lizzy because Lizzy was the type of person who required worrying over while she, Kate, he regarded as fearless, invulnerable, and in need of no one's concern?

Of course she'd told Agnes that there wasn't anything to be scared of. And there wasn't.

But if she were being honest with herself, she had to admit that while she might hope tomorrow would be a better day, it was quite possible that they wouldn't be getting out of here then, maybe not even anytime soon, nor would there be any new visitors coming to them.

Or, not anyone they'd necessarily want to see.

Which meant no immediate opportunities for fresh suitors, which in turn meant...

Stupid bloody entail.

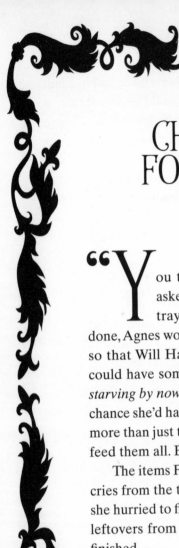

CHAPTER FORTY–SIX

"You told Lady Katherine what?" Fanny asked Agnes, loading items onto the large tray Agnes was holding. Once she was done, Agnes would need to bring it up the back stairs so that Will Harvey and the farmers and villagers could have something to eat. *Those people must be starving by now*, Fanny thought, but this was the first chance she'd had to do anything about it. They'd need more than just the one tray, however large and full, to feed them all. But at least it was a start.

The items Fanny was loading it with, ignoring the cries from the three cats standing before the door as she hurried to finish before Mrs. Owen returned, were leftovers from Upstairs's breakfast, now thankfully finished.

No matter what else was going on in the world, Upstairs would still have their nice breakfast.

And no matter what else was going on in the world, Fanny would still be expected to do her regular work. There was always the work.

Already this morning Fanny had risen before anyone else, lit some fires, did some dusting, read a little, helped Mrs. Owen prepare breakfast, did everything else that was normally required of her on a Monday, all the while ignoring the entreaties of the three cats whenever she came across them.

She knew what they wanted: to go out. But Fanny couldn't, wouldn't let them.

Before Agnes could answer Fanny's question, and before Fanny could finish what she'd been doing, Mrs. Owen's voice came at her from behind.

"Fanny, what *are* you doing with all that food?"

Fanny groaned inside. This was what she'd been hoping to avoid.

Usually, once breakfast service was finished, Mrs. Owen took a little break to do, well, what a person needed to do from time to time, the same thing the cats wanted to do right now, had wanted to do for hours. And whenever Mrs. Owen did it, she always took her time.

Fanny knew she couldn't keep the presence of twenty extra people upstairs, all with mouths to feed, a secret forever. But she'd hoped to get a little further than just one meal. Twenty extra mouths to feed was normally no problem at all for a house such as this. Why, on any given weekend, Upstairs might have that many guests! There was always plenty of food. There had never been any lack here. But Fanny knew Mrs. Owen wouldn't take kindly to it being these particular mouths.

Mrs. Owen didn't know yet about them being up there. With the exception of Mr. Wright, none of the senior staff did. All the senior staff—Mr. Wright; Mrs. Murphy; Albert Cox, the earl's valet; Myrtle Morgan, Lady Clarke's maid; and Mrs. Owen—all had their bedrooms on this basement floor of the house, not on the attic floor with the rest of them. Fanny'd always supposed things were arranged thusly because they were all so old and it would mean fewer stairs for them. So none of them had reason yet to know about the extra twenty.

But now Fanny saw, if she was ever going to pull this off at all, she'd need to enlist Mrs. Owen's help.

So Fanny told her.

"Are you insane, Fanny?" Mrs. Owen said.

"I suppose it's possible that I am," Fanny replied. "But not because of this."

"You're taking food out of the family's mouths!"

"But I'm not. These are things they were done with."

"Then you're taking things out of *our* mouths!"

"Only a little bit. And we have so much in the house."

"Well, we won't have for long, if you keep up at this rate."

"What do you mean by that?"

"We have a lot, for the time being, but it won't last forever. What if we're trapped here? What if none of us ever get out of here again for more supplies?"

Fanny hadn't thought about that.

Was it possible? Would they never get out of here again?

It was scary to think of, but after a moment, Fanny pushed the thought away as she tightened her resolve.

"That doesn't matter," Fanny said.

"Doesn't matter?" Mrs. Owen's pudgy hands went to her ample hips. "How can you say it doesn't matter?"

"Because it doesn't. Those farmers up there, they've worked this land all their lives. Don't they have a right to the fruits of it? Don't they have as much right as anyone else in this house does, to eat, to survive?"

"What about Mr. Powell, then? You said he's here, too. Well, he's not a farmer. What's Mr. Powell ever done for anybody?"

"I don't know. He's the publican." Fanny thought about this. "He serves beer to people when they go into the village, which some of the farmers and villagers find essential: that he serves them beer." She thought about it some more. "And he's a human being."

"A hu—" Mrs. Owen stopped herself. "Does anyone else know about this insane scheme of yours?"

"Actually—"

"Fanny, what are you doing!" Was there no end to people asking her that question? This time, it came from Mr. Wright.

"Why haven't you let those cats out?" Mr. Wright said, not giving her a chance to answer. "They're making an infernal racket!"

"But they need to be kept safe," Fanny said, worried now, panicked even. "It's not safe out there, you know it isn't."

Henry Clay had been so brave last night, coming up behind Mr. Young like that, causing him to topple over the marble railing. How could Henry Clay've known that a fall from such a height wouldn't kill him? Or destroy him? Or whatever you called putting an ending to something that had already died once? After doing that, Henry Clay didn't deserve to be put at risk. And Rosencrantz and Guildenstern. While they might not hold quite the same place in her heart that Henry Clay did, she was fond enough of those two privileged fluff balls. She certainly didn't want to see them dead.

She tried to explain as much to Mr. Wright.

"And what do you propose?" Mr. Wright said when she'd finished. "That they do their business inside? That they be allowed to *piss* all over the abbey? No matter what else is happening, standards must be maintained. Anything less is chaos."

Before she could say anything further, Mr. Wright strode to the back door and turned the knob with his white-gloved hand.

"Well, go on," he told the cats, who scooted out, but for once, they didn't go far.

"There," Mr. Wright said, observing the cats as he stood

in the doorway, arms folded. "You see? That's how you do it. You just let them out and then you stand guard and wait. It's a lovely day, clear, you can see anything that might come at you."

The cats finished with their business and, disinclined to scamper about as they would normally, trotted back in.

Mr. Wright shut the door and bolted it. "You see?" he said again. "Now, where is tea? His Lordship and the others are gathered in the drawing room, and they are ready for it now."

Tea? But they'd just finished breakfast!

"Ah!" Mr. Wright said, spying the tray in Agnes's outstretched arms. "There it is!" Then: "But those are just leftovers from breakfast. That will never do. Mrs. Owen, please see to getting the tea organized and do be quick about it—His Lordship is waiting. I'll be back in a trice for it."

"But Mr.—" Mrs. Owen started to say.

"Whatever you want right now must wait," Mr. Wright said. "Honestly, I don't know what's going on in this house anymore. Did you not hear me? His Lordship is waiting!"

Then the butler was gone.

"He doesn't know what's going on in this house anymore?" Mrs. Owen muttered. "Well, that makes two of us. And I don't want to know any more than what I know already. I'll just put my head down and do the work, that's me settled."

At last, Fanny turned back to Agnes, loading the last few items she'd set aside onto Agnes's tray. Oh, those poor people up in the attic. So hungry they'd be by now.

"I told her we were scared," Agnes said.

"What?" Fanny said vaguely, looking it over just one more time to make sure that everything she wanted was there.

"You asked, before, 'You told Lady Katherine what?' And now I'm telling you again. I told her we were scared."

"Why would you do such a thing? She doesn't need to know that. Especially since it's not true. I'm not scared."

"Even if you're not, Fanny, I am, and the others are, too."

Fanny did know that. Of course she did. Even though the others were going about their normal business, performing all their daily duties, Fanny knew that fear had taken over most of them. She could see it in Becky's eyes. She could hear it in Jonathan's voice, laughing too hard at something that wasn't all that funny to begin with. And now Agnes, coming right out and saying it.

"But it's going to be all right," Agnes said.

"How do you know that?"

"Lady Katherine said. She promised. She said she'd take care of us."

"And you believed that?"

Agnes nodded.

"Oh no," Fanny said softly. "We need to take care of ourselves."

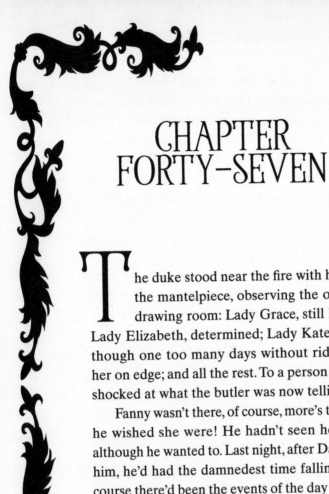

CHAPTER FORTY-SEVEN

The duke stood near the fire with his elbow on the mantelpiece, observing the others in the drawing room: Lady Grace, still looking sad; Lady Elizabeth, determined; Lady Kate, restless, as though one too many days without riding had put her on edge; and all the rest. To a person they looked shocked at what the butler was now telling them.

Fanny wasn't there, of course, more's the pity. How he wished she were! He hadn't seen her yet today, although he wanted to. Last night, after Daniel had left him, he'd had the damnedest time falling asleep. Of course there'd been the events of the day to relive: the awfulness with Dr. Webb. The even greater awfulness with poor Mr. Young. But more than that, there were the words Fanny had spoken to him. No one had ever paid him such a fine compliment before.

"Fanny did *what*?" the earl said.

The duke noted that Mr. Wright had mentioned Fanny and no one else when he'd given his report. Why had he said nothing of the duke's involvement? Was he made of glass? Of course not. The duke knew he'd seen him there, spoken with him, too. What then? Did his actions not matter? Then it occurred to him.

Mr. Wright might be quick to tell on Fanny, figuring it to be his duty, but he'd be less quick to say anything about him. He was, after all, the duke. *Huh*, he thought. *Well, that's a good privilege.*

Privilege or not, it wasn't fair. It wasn't fair that Fanny should hang alone when they had acted together.

Even if it had been all her idea.

He was about to say as much—not the part about it all being her idea, which would not be very gallant of him, but rather that they'd enacted the idea together—but then he thought: *Am I really brave enough to speak out?*

He thought he was. Maybe. But maybe not. May—

But it didn't matter any longer what he thought, for now the butler was speaking again.

"I know, my lord. And I would have told you about it earlier, but you see, you were having your breakfast. I know how you hate to have any meal spoiled with unpleasantness, most particularly the first meal of the day. I simply thought it could wait a bit. Shall I throw them all out now?"

Throw them—

"Of course we can't do that," someone said, a female voice, and the duke was surprised to see it belonged to Lady Kate.

"We can't?" the earl said.

"No, Father. It's our duty. It's *your* duty as head of not only the abbey but all of Porthampton itself. We must do whatever we can."

This struck the duke as surprising, coming from Lady Kate. She hadn't exactly impressed him as one who cared overmuch about other people. But maybe something in all this had caused her to change a bit, to think more generously about others? Or maybe, he thought, it was exactly the word she used: "duty." As a member of the British Empire, one could never escape it. *Duty*. To what's right. To what's the done thing. To being, simply, British. Well, the duke supposed, he had that sense, too.

The earl looked as though he were still stuck on the outrage he'd felt earlier, unwilling to give it up, and the duke thought for sure he would overrule her, however much she was his obvious favorite.

But then: "Kate's right, Wright."

The butler could ill disclose his shock. "She *is*?"

"Of course," the earl said. "It is our duty, now that they're under our roof. Although I do wish someone had thought to ask me about this first. It is, after all, still my house."

"And if they had asked you," Lady Kate said teasingly, "you'd probably have said no."

"You're probably right, my dear," the earl confessed with a rueful grin. "But now that they are here, Wright, do see that they're comfortable and have everything they need, but not too comfortable. We don't want them to think they'll be staying on forever once the danger has passed and everything has been returned to normal."

Did the earl genuinely believe, the duke wondered, that the danger might pass with any sort of speed or that anything would ever be normal again?

"Very good, my lord." The butler all but clicked his shiny heels. "As you wish."

"Now, then." The earl clapped his hands together. "I think what we need here is a plan of action."

"A plan of action?" Her Ladyship said.

"My, that does sound overly ambitious," the dowager countess added. "And all before I've had my tea."

"Be that as it may," the earl said. "We've been putting this off, no doubt because none of us wanted to face the truth of what is happening. But after the events of last night, we can put it off no longer. We must organize! We must prepare a line of defense! Toward that end..." Here, the earl turned to Benedict Clarke. "Benedict, might we enlist your help?"

"My help?" Benedict said.

"Of course! You're the only one here who's been to war. I thought perhaps that, with your training and skills..."

"Yes, well, I-I don't..." came the stammered reply.

"No, no, no, no, no! You're doing this all wrong!"

It was only when all heads turned in his direction that the duke realized he hadn't merely thought those words, but rather, they'd actually flown out of his mouth.

"You had something to add to the discussion, did you?" the earl asked him.

Did he? Have something to add?

Once upon a time, the duke thought he had been born into greatness. He was a duke, after all! How much greater could one get? Well, king. There was that. But then, as he'd started to grow up, he'd realized that greatness hadn't come along to accompany the title. And those times the possibility of having it thrust upon him had occurred? He'd pretty much run the other way. But now, in this moment, could he reach for it? Could he do and say the things that needed to be done?

He thought of Fanny's ears, and he found that he could.

To the earl, he said, "I don't mean to offend you, but you're making a hash of things." Then he turned to Benedict. "Look," he said, "I don't mean to be rude, and you're a fine enough chap, or at least you seem to be, but you're simply not the right man for the job."

"And who is?" the earl said.

"You can't possibly be suggesting yourself," the dowager countess chortled, peering at him, "can you?"

"No, of course not. The person I'm suggesting is Daniel."

"Daniel?" the dowager countess said. "Who, pray tell, is this *Daniel*?"

"Your footman," the duke said, feeling some impatience.

"Yes, but which one?"

"The one who tore off his shirt to bandage Mr. Young yesterday," Lady Kate provided, smiling when she mentioned the part about him tearing off his shirt. "It was quite thrilling, actually."

"Oh," the dowager countess said thoughtfully.

What was she thinking, the duke wondered, that like her granddaughter, she too found it pleasing and thrilling when the footman ripped off his shirt?

"Look," the duke tried again. "I'm sure that Benedict is well-meaning and I hate to be rude, I wouldn't want to give offense—"

Benedict Clarke waved a hand. "None taken, I assure you."

Well, that was a relief, at least.

"But I do think Daniel knows more about what may be required here. He saw more, did more in the war. He has real military training, and I think his instincts are exemplary. I just," the duke finished, "think he's the best person for the job."

"Well," the earl said, "I thank you for sharing your opinion on this matter with us, and I will take it under advisement. Now then. Where was I? Benedict—"

"I don't think you're hearing me right," the duke said.

"Of course I am," the earl said peevishly, "but this is still, as I have already been forced to point out once today, my house."

"And I am still the duke."

"Pardon?"

"It pains me to say this, but I outrank you. You are an earl. I am the duke. So unless you want to bring the king in here to overrule me, I suggest we do this my way."

"This one." The dowager countess pointed a wavering

finger at him. He'd always thought it was considered rude to point at people—he'd been taught as much by his nanny—but he didn't correct her. "This one, I think, is a dark horse."

"You think I've been rude?" the duke said, the realization of what he'd just done hitting him for the first time.

"Of course not," the dowager countess said. "One can never be too rich or too rude. But to look at you, with those ears, one would never suspect there was any intelligence between them. Although now that I think about it, the sheer size of them does lend itself to better listening and, one would hope, better learning."

"What are you saying, Mother?" the earl asked, still peevish. "What has any of this to do with his ears?"

"Nothing, Martin. But I do believe he's right."

"You can't be serious!"

"If we need a line of defense, what does it matter who organizes it? The footman or even the stable boy, it is of no concern to me. All that matters is our survival. We do want to survive, don't we?"

"Yes, of course, but—"

"I say we get this footman person in here right now," the dowager countess said, "this Daniel person, although I do hope he can manage to keep his clothes on this time. Martin?"

"I suppose you're right, Mother," the earl said grudgingly. "Wright? Go fetch Daniel and tell him we'd like to see him for a word."

While most of this conversation was taking place, the butler's usually stoic expression had gone through a series of transformations, most containing at least some element of shock. Now he merely looked resigned.

"Yes, my lord."

The butler turned to go.

Speaking of the stable boy…

"Mr. Wright!" the duke stopped him.

"Yes, Your Lordship?"

"After you've sent Daniel in, please fetch Will Harvey as well and tell him we'd like to see him. Now that I think about it, I believe he could prove quite useful, too."

Lady Kate's lovely eyebrows arched at this but it was impossible to read what she was thinking.

"As you wish, Your Lordship," said Mr. Wright.

That's right, the duke thought, pleased, watching Mr. Wright go, *I* am *Your Lordship*.

Daniel arrived first.

The duke invited him to sit in an actual chair, which he seemed flustered by, finding the suggestion confusing. Once he'd finally been persuaded that he could sit in their presence without fear of reprimand, the duke explained what they wanted from him as Daniel listened intently.

"Yes," Daniel finally said when the duke was finished. "I do have some ideas."

CHAPTER FORTY-EIGHT

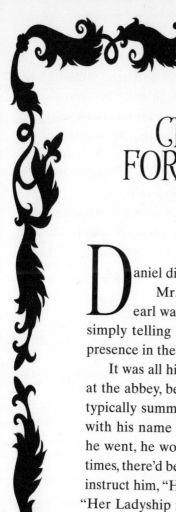

Daniel did indeed have some ideas.

Mr. Wright hadn't explained what the earl wanted with him, even when he'd asked, simply telling him that His Lordship required his presence in the drawing room.

It was all highly irregular. In the years he'd been at the abbey, before the war and since, he was more typically summoned by a pull cord that rang a bell with his name below it in the servants' hall. Once he went, he would be told what was needed. Other times, there'd be no bell and old Wright would simply instruct him, "His Lordship requests you do this," or "Her Ladyship requests you do that." Or, since the duke had come for his visit and then lost his valet, "His *Other* Lordship needs…"

But to be told to go without being given a reason?

What could it be?

Perhaps they intended to fire him for failing to do anything last night when Mr. Young attacked, for just standing there like a stupid block of salt holding his even stupider tray?

And what would he do if that proved to be the case?

When the weekend had first started, he'd been thinking how, after his experiences in the war, he never wanted to leave the abbey if he could help it, unless it was to go into the village on a day off or for a dance; that he would be content to live out the rest of his days here. Now he would still be content to do so, to stay here forever, particularly since he no longer had any desire to go into the village, not after what Fanny had told them about what she'd learned from the farmers and villagers who had come to stay in the attic: that there were more of them out there like Dr. Webb and Mr. Young.

Well, of course there were more.

Who but a fool could have imagined otherwise?

And if he were to be fired now, how would he make his way out there, alone in a world that was likely now unrecognizable as the only one he had known?

It would be worse than the war.

And yet if he had to, he knew he would do whatever he needed to in order to survive, just as he had before, for as long as he could.

But as it turned out, the earl hadn't wanted to fire him.

On the contrary, Daniel thought, as he'd sat there—sat there! he was sitting! among them!—right in their presence. On the contrary, and here his mind turned practically giddy at the duke's surprising request, it would appear they wanted to *promote* him!

So, yes, Daniel had some ideas, based on what he'd seen in the war, his military experience being a fact that these people clearly hoped would be the thing that might save them all. The duke even said that he, Daniel, would be granted free rein of any resources he deemed necessary. He knew they must be feeling desperate when Will Harvey joined them, sent there by Mr. Wright as he had been; as soon as Will entered, Daniel noted his eyes went immediately to Lady Katherine, and hers to him, but then each looked quickly away. The duke said that, like with the resources, Will would be at his disposal, too. They all would be. But to be calling in the stable boy, whom Daniel could tell the earl didn't care for, not one bit, they must be feeling truly desperate.

But as he laid out those ideas, one by one, although most of the group were receptive, encouraging, rapt, or intrigued, respectful even—in particular the duke—each one was met by the earl with something along the lines of: "Are you quite sure about that?" or "That can't be right!" or "But won't that just be a lot of bother?"

And it occurred to Daniel for the first time: *I have my work cut out for me.*

"But this isn't what I told you to do."

"I know that," Will told Daniel. "You want me to stay here and help train the others."

"Yes, that's exactly what I want."

After the meeting, the others had dispersed, but Daniel had asked Will to stay behind so they could talk.

Will couldn't believe he was meant to take orders from a footman. In the past, the only people he'd ever taken orders from were His Lordship or sometimes Mr. Wright, acting on His Lordship's behalf.

"What I don't want," Daniel said, "is for you to go out looking for more weapons. We have plenty right here."

"Yes," Will said, "but how long will that last? We don't have an endless supply. We don't know how many of *them* there are out there, how much we might need. The farmers and villagers, some of them came armed, but they left their homes so quickly, and even the ones who did bring a weapon, it's just the one. I know there will be more weapons left in their houses, ammunition, too. So I'll just go out there and see what I can find, gather whatever I can carry, and bring them back here."

"But it's not safe."

"I'm young and I'm strong and I can outrun any situation I might encounter. And I have my pistol with me." He paused. "I should do this now. It may not be safe, but do you really think it's going to get any safer later?"

"It might."

"You know it won't. We've been lucky so far."

"Lucky?"

"Yes. Since my uncle's death, there've been only Dr. Webb and Mr. Young and Parker, stragglers. But there will be more coming, you know it. Just like the farmers and villagers found their way to us, eventually *they'll* manage to find their way to us, too. You know I'm right."

"I suppose…"

"And anyway, the family have gone to have their lunch." Oh yes, they had, because… Well, the less said about that, the better. "So what better time for me to go? I'm not needed here right now, and I could do some real good. I promise I'll be back in time to do whatever you need me to."

"All right." At last, Daniel relented. "But be careful. You're the best person I've got. We can't afford to lose you, and…"

Daniel let the sentence hang there, but Will knew how it would have ended: "…I don't want to see you turn into one of *them*."

Well, Will thought, *I don't want that, either*.

"Of course I'll be careful," Will said, feeling the smile break across his face. "Do I look like the sort of person who would take unnecessary risks?"

And Will *was* careful, although he knew that even being out here was a risk, but it was one he found necessary for more reasons than those he'd given Daniel: Will wanted to find Aunt Jess. She might be the most capable woman he knew, in terms of handling any ordinary disaster that life might throw her way, but this?

Besides, how bad could it be?

As it turned out, it could be very bad.

Once he'd crossed the great lawn and achieved the outer reaches of the estate where the tenant farms were, he saw that the situation had grown very bad indeed.

Everywhere he looked, there was evidence of people fleeing for their lives: doors left open, tools left out mid-work.

And then there were the bodies.

People half eaten, people with their heads gone.

Will didn't bother about the latter. But the former? He made sure to put a bullet in each one's head before they had the chance to wake again.

And the worst part?

Outside of the sound of his own weapon firing, it was dead quiet. Deserted. It was now as though no one had ever lived there at all.

Some of the dead he recognized based on a body part or an article of clothing: people he'd grown up with, people he'd known his whole life.

Will wondered where *they* were.

Having decimated the small population of farmers, had they moved on elsewhere? Had they further invaded the village, with its far greater population?

Will didn't want to think about that.

Will moved from cottage to cottage, entering each with

trepidation. What if one of *them* was still there? Lurking inside?

But each turned out to be empty, unless there was a body inside, headless or seeming dead and needing to be shot. From each, Will gathered up whatever weapons there were to be had and placed them in the sack he'd brought along for this purpose before moving on to the next.

Will saved his own cottage for last.

If pressed, he wouldn't have been able to answer quite why that was. Maybe he was putting off the inevitable? He hadn't seen any evidence of Aunt Jess among those he'd encountered, thankfully, and he didn't find her in their cottage, either, although on the table there did sit a peculiar item: a great copper frying pan, shiny and unlike anything they had ever owned. It was somehow almost sinister, how pristine it was in the humble cottage, how out of place. But he couldn't spare a second thought for its presence. There was still work to do.

Will gathered up the other weapons he knew they had there, before leaving, careful to shut the door behind him. No matter what was going on, no matter what others were doing, when you left a place you still shut the door.

A part of him was relieved as he set off back toward the abbey, feeling only slightly burdened; the sack now full, he carried a heaping armload of weapons as well, with several rifles slung over his left shoulder. He'd been hoping to find Aunt Jess, but at least she wasn't among the fallen or those who looked dead but were yet to change. He wasn't sure which he'd have found worse.

But she hadn't been anywhere to be seen, which meant that she must still be out there somewhere.

Will was sure as he'd ever been that Aunt Jess could take care of herself.

Hadn't she always?

She'd certainly taken good care of him.

Over the course of the rest of Will's walk back to the abbey, he encountered only one moving thing, unless you included the remaining leaves shifting in the trees from the strong wind.

From the side, stumbling toward him, was a figure similar to Will in shape and size. As the figure lurched closer, Will recognized him as someone from the tenant farms, a boy his own age, Samuel Chapman.

Outside of that one perfect day with Lady Kate when they were both three, Samuel Chapman had been his first friend after he'd come to live with his aunt and uncle. In their early years, they'd played together, laughed together, making up their own games as they raced each other, gamboling over the fields. Samuel Chapman had been his best friend.

Samuel Chapman, the boy, with his long, curly blond hair flowing out all around him as they raced against the wind together, his smile so wide and bright it had been like a second sun.

But this Samuel Chapman no longer resembled that one, except in the merest of details. This one looked like decay; smelled like it, too, his once-sparkling blue eyes now gone cloudy and yet somehow, hungry, too.

Will stood, waited.

He could have run, gotten away easily enough, but he didn't.

Will had never imagined killing another man, had never imagined killing anyone. He knew people, other young men, who had dreamed of fighting for their country, fighting for anything, really. But not him. Will had been too young to go fight in the last war, and he'd always hoped that he'd be too old to go by the time the next one came around.

But Samuel Chapman was no longer a man, and now the fight had come to Will.

It had been different with the other ones, just now, back at the farms. They'd needed shooting, but it wasn't as though they were moving at the time. It wasn't as though there was anything about them to trick you into believing that they were part of a living universe.

It wasn't like this.

When Samuel Chapman was nearly upon him, the sheer reek of him slamming Will in the face, Will dropped the sack and the rest of his weapons, keeping only the one that he held in his right hand, raising it and shooting Samuel Chapman in the head point-blank.

Will watched Samuel Chapman fall.

Then Will gathered up his supply of weapons and moved on.

K ate heard the clinking sound before she caught a glimpse of the cause of it.

The suit of armor, Fred, was on the move.

After lunch, many of the others had gone off to have their first lessons, all of which involved some sort of shooting. Kate loved shooting as much as the next person—more, really, than any of them—but like Grandmama before her, Kate was the best shot in any bunch, and she didn't need any practice.

So instead, she'd come to the library, going there with Daniel to discuss strategy. Kate had asked Daniel if the stable boy would by chance be joining them for their strategy session, but Daniel had said that the stable boy had already gone out on an errand. She'd masked her disappointment as she wondered at the wisdom of this—was it safe for him to be out there alone?—but Daniel had assured her that he was armed and then they'd settled in for their discussion.

And what a discussion it had been—and the plans he'd drawn up!

It was hard to fathom that a footman should have such ideas in his head, and that he'd be able to express them so clearly, even writing things down on paper—and so neatly!

But Daniel had gone, and now there was that clinking noise, and...

Kate rose from her seat at the table, leaving the plans behind as she crossed the room and lifted up the face mask on the suit of armor to see who was inside Fred.

"Father!" she cried.

"You were expecting somebody else, maybe?"

"No, of course not. But what are you doing in there?"

"Well, that Daniel did say we were to prepare ourselves."

"Yes, but when Chekhov said that thing about not hanging a gun on the wall in the first act unless you intended it to go off later, I don't think he meant for it to apply to suits of armor as well."

"I'm just trying to do my part. And I did think Fred might come in useful." He clanked his arms about a bit to demonstrate, laughing all the while.

"Father." She narrowed her eyes shrewdly at him. "Are you trying to sabotage us?"

"No, of course not! How can you even think such a thing? But we can't just be nothing but doom and gloom all the time. And when has a little bit of levity hurt anybody?"

"Never mind that now. Come here and see what Daniel has drawn up."

Kate was pleased when Father obeyed her, following her

to the table, although his gait was awkward and he did clink so much.

"Look!" Kate said, pointing at the pages.

"What is it?" Father asked, but then the face mask fell down again and she was forced to lift it for him and then hold it in place while she attempted to show him what she wanted him to see.

"You see here?" she said. "He's marked off some places, all along the perimeter of the estate and at various random points within the main property. He says we might want to dig trenches there."

"Trenches? But won't that spoil the look of the place?"

"What does that matter right at this moment in time? Don't you see? Those trenches would perform two functions for us. First, some of *them* might fall into the trenches and then get caught there, trapped, until we can get to them—you know, they don't seem terribly bright when they get into that state, and once fallen, they might have difficulty finding their way out again. *Or*, we could also use them to hide in ourselves, should it come to that. We could lie in wait with our weapons and, if need be, pop up and shoot them. Do you see how brilliant this all is?"

"Oh, surely, Kate, it won't come to that. We won't ever need all this"—he waved a clinking silver arm dismissively—"this *bother*. Did you not hear me say as much earlier?"

"I did, but we have to be prepared, Father. At the very least, we must find a way to secure the perimeter. Perhaps arrange for a series of sentries to patrol it with weapons in order to keep a lookout for incoming threats? The farmers and villagers we've taken in should be good for that. Daniel says—"

"Oh, who cares what *Daniel* says?"

Kate was about to say, "I do, Father." But then it occurred

to her: What was the point?

Earlier, the duke had accused Father of making a hash of things. At the time, she'd bristled at those words. Who was this young man, no matter that he might outrank an earl, to come into their house and say such things to *her* father?

But now she saw that perhaps the duke was right. Father might make a hash of things, if they let him.

There was little point in arguing, however. Much better to mollify him, send him on his merry way, and then...

And then do whatever needed to be done.

"You're right, Father," she said brightly, patting him on one silver arm. "It's a silly plan. We don't need it." Then she gently, lovingly, lowered his face mask until it was back in the position it had been in when he first entered. "Now, why don't you get out of that thing? You must be sweltering there, inside Fred."

"I suppose you're right. Once I slip out of this thing, perhaps your mother and I can go for our walk."

"Father, you can't be serious!"

"But we go for a walk every weekday. Why should this one be any different?"

"You must promise me, Father, that you won't today. It's too dangerous out there."

"Fine." Then he gave out a sigh so loud, it echoed its resignation metallically within the confines of Fred. *"Fine."*

"Tell me again: Why do I need to do this?" Grace said.

Grace stood in a long-neglected room on the far south side of the abbey. It was the north where the family did most of their living. Grace knew there had been a time when the whole abbey had been used, when her ancestors had employed enough servants to fill all the attic bedrooms, including the ones now used by the farmers and villagers who had come to stay. Back then, the abbey had been like its own small kingdom. But time had gradually changed that, the last war further reducing things, so now these rooms on the south side saw very little use.

When Daniel had told Father that he needed some space in which members of the household could practice their use of weaponry, that it was too dangerous for them to do it outside but it had to be done, Father had mentioned these rooms.

"There's one in particular," he'd said. "It has a massive tapestry on the wall that I've never been particularly fond of. You can shoot the whole thing up, for all I care."

And so here they were: Grace holding a rifle against her shoulder, while Daniel urged her to shoot the whole thing up.

"Everyone needs to learn," Daniel said now.

"Yes, but why?" Grace said. "I've never wanted to know how to shoot anything, and I still don't want to know."

"Well, we're all being called on to do things we've never wanted to do."

She supposed that was true.

"And you never know," Daniel went on. "You're safe enough, for now, so long as you're inside. But who knows what might happen later? And do you really want to be a prisoner in here for the rest of your life?"

The rest of her life?

"No one knows how long this will go on," Daniel said. "It may end quickly, and I certainly hope it does, or it could go on for a long time. In any event, you must be ready. We must all be ready. At least if you learn how to defend yourself, it will be possible for you to go outside if you want to. Now, let's try again. You see that huge stag on the far right corner of the tapestry?" He pointed. "Let's see if you can hit that."

She tried, she really did. Daniel had shown her how to clean the weapon and load it and demonstrated for her how to use it. When she'd been awkward with the weapon, he'd even put his arms around her from behind, his hands covering hers as he guided her in the proper way to hold it. She knew that what they were doing was meant to be serious business, but the feel of his hands on her hands, his breath against her neck, and the sensation of his body coming lightly into contact with hers from behind—she couldn't help but wonder if it gave him the same feelings, the same stirrings it gave her, just like had happened when they'd danced together.

Still, it was a serious business. And a part of her wanted to please him, she really did. But after taking aim, as she went to pull the trigger, all she could picture was that instead of a tapestry stag, it was a real stag standing there and, unwilling to watch the beautiful creature die, she squeezed both eyes shut as she fired rather than simply squinting the one.

"Did I hit it?" she asked anxiously, opening her eyes.

"Let's just say we're going to need to work on your aim a bit more," Daniel said with a rueful grin. He pointed to a hole in the tapestry that was about as far from her intended target as one could get.

"Oh, I'm hopeless at this!" she cried.

"You're not. And if you are, it's only because you don't appear to want to be good at it. But all you need is some practice. Well, that, and maybe learn to keep at least one eye open."

"You've just had *so* many more years to get used to doing such things," she said. "I'll never catch up."

"'*So* many'?" He smiled. "You make me sound ancient. Just how old do you think I am?"

"Why, you're twenty-one."

"And who told you that?"

"It's just something I heard," she said. And she had. She'd heard it when she'd made a point of seeking out Mr. Wright after lunch and asking him. At the time, she'd thought: *He's five years older than I am. He's almost a third again as old as me.*

"Well, you heard wrong," Daniel said.

What? Was he even older than that?

"I did?" Grace said.

Daniel studied her for a long moment, as though weighing something. Finally: "I'm seventeen," he said.

Just a year older than her?

"But how is that possible?" she said. And how could Mr. Wright be so far off?

Then he told her a story: about lying in the first place to get work in the house; and then lying again later on so he could go to war.

"I wish I hadn't done that last part," he said. "And you mustn't tell anybody about this. Or, at least, I hope you'll choose not to."

"I won't if you don't want me to. But why would they care?"

"Because I lied to get the job in the first place. Because I've been lying ever since. If that got out, they'd fire me."

"I hardly think so," she said, finding herself laughing for the first time since Merry died. And then died again.

"You don't?"

"Of course not!" She laughed again. "You've grown too valuable. No one would fire you now!"

"I suppose you're right."

"But if you were worried about getting fired," she said, "why did you tell me?"

"I'm not rightly sure. I've never told anyone about that before, not even Jonathan, and I work more closely with him than anybody. I guess I just felt like I could trust you. And I didn't want to lie to you."

He'd lied to everyone, he'd lied to everyone else for years, but he didn't want to lie to her?

"I'm glad you told me," she said. Then she thought of something. "Daniel," she asked, "what's your last name?"

It seemed odd to be having such a conversation with someone, a conversation about fears and trust, and yet not know the last name of the person to whom one was speaking.

He just looked at her.

"Is that a complicated question?" she asked, suddenly feeling self-conscious.

"It's not," he said. "It's just…"

"Just what?"

"In the years since I've come to live here, I've practically forgotten I even have one. Sure, in the two years I was away at war, all the other soldiers and officers called me only by my last name. But here at the abbey? As a footman? Like the rest of the help, except for senior staff, I've never been granted the dignity of a last name. Here, I've only ever been Daniel."

It was, quite possibly, the most he'd ever said to her at one shot.

"Well, I'd like to know what it is, Daniel-who-isn't-twenty-one-but-rather-seventeen."

"It's Murray," he told her.

"Daniel Murray," she repeated softly.

Then she raised the rifle so that the butt of it rested against the shoulder of her silk dress.

"Show me again how to use this thing, Daniel Murray," she said, smiling. "I can't promise I'll be any better at it now than I was before, but at least I can try."

. . .

"Nothing like a little archery to get the appetite going!" Lizzy laughed.

She was in a different long-neglected room on the south side of the abbey than the one Grace and Daniel had used. Father had directed her there, saying, "I've never cared for the tapestry in that room, either!" He'd said it jocularly enough, and she'd laughed with him. But then she'd been troubled when his mood had seemed to sharply shift as he added, "It doesn't matter anymore anyway, though. Why not just shoot the whole place up?"

She'd been troubled then, but she was laughing now for she was, indeed, shooting the whole place up!

"I'm *good* at this!" she said, quite pleased with her use of bow and arrow. She'd aimed at the stag. She'd hit the stag!

"You are," Cousin Benedict said, smiling. "But then, when Will Harvey suggested this, I thought you would be."

When Will suggested a bow and arrow for her, explaining that it was obvious she had talent with guns but that she should practice with other weapons in case one day their ammunition ran out, she'd expected him to be the one to accompany her, to teach her.

And then she'd been disappointed when he had not, telling her that Cousin Benedict should accompany her instead.

"But is that what Daniel wants?" she'd objected. "Didn't he say that you—"

But whatever Daniel might have said, it didn't appear to have made much of an impression on Will Harvey, who'd already hurried away.

Now that she was here with Cousin Benedict, though, she found she was having a fine time.

After the meeting in the drawing room earlier in the day, Kate had said something to her about Cousin Benedict turning out to be "a disappointment." She'd further gone on to say, "You'd think the man would have more fight in him. Did you see the way he just let the duke take his role away from him and give it to Daniel instead?"

On the one hand, Lizzy knew it was impolitic to pose the question to him. On the other hand, she just really did want to know.

"Doesn't it bother you?" she asked.

"Doesn't what bother me?"

"Father was all prepared to have you lead us, but then the duke stepped in and gave all the power to Daniel."

"I don't know about *all* the power," Benedict said, genially enough. "But no, it doesn't bother me in the slightest."

"I just would have thought…" But Lizzy let the thought trail off, unwilling now to cause offense.

Was Kate right, then, in what she'd implied? Was Cousin Benedict, after all, a bit of a coward? If that were the case, Lizzy didn't want to make him feel worse by pressing him about it. Bad enough for him to know himself to be a coward; he didn't need her to be going on and on about it, as she knew she had a tendency to do about things. No, she'd just raise the bow, nock another arrow, and—

"Why would it bother me?" Benedict said, stopping her. "We all want the same thing: for us to be safe. And who better to be in charge of that than the person who seems to know more about it than anyone else here? Which in this case happens to be Daniel. Don't you think it would be silly of me to insist on power over everything merely because I had the good fortune to get born to a higher station in life than he did?"

"Good *God*!" Lizzy said, stunned.

"What?"

"You're…you're just so…*sensible*!"

"And is that a crime?" Cousin Benedict laughed.

"Not at all. But it's not exactly something you see around here every day."

"Well, I suppose we're no longer living in times that are like 'every day.' If this were every day, or any day, I'd want to sit by the fire, feet up on a stool, a good book in my lap, perhaps gazing out at the lawn every so often." Benedict sighed. "How I long for such a day."

"Sounds lovely," Lizzy said. Then she wrinkled her nose. "Well, except for maybe the book part, unless it happened to be a particularly exciting one."

"Book or no book, *that's* not going to happen now. We must all do our part, and I am content to do mine." He paused. "Do you mind if I take a turn with that?"

"You mean this?" Lizzy indicated the bow and arrow.

"Yes," Benedict replied. "Daniel said we must all be prepared. And Daniel is right."

Lizzy handed the items over, and as he accepted them from her, she noticed that he grasped them rather awkwardly. Had he never shot a bow and arrow before? And here he'd been sent along to tutor her! As he tried, and failed, to nock the arrow perfectly the first time, Cousin Benedict appeared to notice something.

"What are those on your feet?" he asked.

"You mean these?" Lizzy said, shifting one foot to the toe and then tilting the ankle of that foot against the ankle of the other, as though modeling the worn dirt-encrusted lace-up black boots she now wore on her feet. "It's all the rage in Paris. I call them my sensible boots. Do you like them?"

. . .

"I still have to get the wine properly decanted!" Mr. Wright cried. "With everything that's been going on here today, I clean forgot. Oh, I do hope His Lordship won't be too displeased if the wine isn't fully decanted."

Mr. Wright hurried off to his office, bottles in hand, there to perform his ministrations.

In the past, Fanny had found Mr. Wright to be a bossy man, a stern man, an overly officious man. None of that had bothered her much, not even when he was yelling at her, which he so often was. It was his job. But now she found herself thinking for the first time, *What a silly man.*

Did he think it mattered anymore now what state the wine was in?

Fanny had had her small tastes of wine in the past, knocking back the dregs of Mr. Wright's and Mrs. Murphy's glasses when those glasses had been brought to the kitchen for her to clean after their nightly tipple. Those dregs had ranged from sherry to whatever grand wine the family and their guests had been enjoying at dinner if there was any left over; it wouldn't do for the family to be served leftover day-old wine the next night, and so Mr. Wright and Mrs. Murphy would finish the rest, sometimes sharing it with Mrs. Owen if there was enough. And Fanny got the dregs.

As far as Fanny could tell, it was all bitter, and whether it was served straight from the bottle or allowed to rest in a crystal decanter for a long time first, it wouldn't change that fact. The one good thing about wine was that it left you feeling a bit soft around the edges afterward, the world gone pleasantly a little blurry.

Fanny didn't want her edges softened now, and she

couldn't see any advantages in letting the world go a little blurry. On the contrary, she felt as though she needed to see it all as clearly as possible in order to survive everything that was going on.

But no matter what else was going on, Fanny was expected to behave as though none of it was. She still had to cut up the vegetables just so ("No, Fanny!" Mrs. Owen cried. "I said to dice those carrots! What do you think Her Ladyship is, a stevedore?"); she had to help make sure nothing being served included any food items Upstairs might have partaken of in the last twenty-four-hour cycle of meals ("Didn't they have some salmon yesterday, Fanny?" Mrs. Owen said. "Oh, it's so hard to keep everything in my mind today, and I can't remember where I put yesterday's meal cards. Best to just toss that salmon. We can do something instead with the trout.").

And now here was Mr. Wright, that silly man, worrying about his wine.

What did any of it matter now?

Fanny said as much to Mrs. Owen as they worked, side by side.

"People still have to eat, Fanny," Mrs. Owen said. "And I'm sure His Lordship would feel that there's no reason why they shouldn't still do it nicely. And I, for one, happen to agree with him. Just because the world's going to hell in a handbasket, there's no reason for us to stop cooking proper meals, nicely served up."

Now Mrs. Owen was sounding like Mr. Wright.

"So stop your moaning about, Fanny, and all your... *philosophizing*, and get back to work. I could use some help with these trout here. They won't clean themselves."

Fanny went back to work. She worked and she worked until all the food preparations had been made and the other servants had brought the series of courses upstairs. She worked straight through until dessert was brought up and then, rather than retiring with the others for a quick bite, she went to do something she'd been wanting to do all night.

She hurried back into the kitchen a short time later, rushing to put her apron on over her dress so that they could commence with the cleaning up.

"What *are* you wearing, Fanny?" Mrs. Owen demanded.

"Yes, Fanny, what *are* you wearing?" echoed Mr. Wright, walking into the kitchen, a thoroughly empty decanter in his hand, a thoroughly disappointed look on his face.

"Do you like it?" Fanny said, putting one hand to the shoulder of the scarlet-red garment. She'd have put it on earlier, had been eager to, but she hadn't wanted to get food stains all over it. Now, though, she figured it would be safe to wear it during the cleaning-up part. A little soap and water wouldn't hurt it any, not like greasy fish might.

"No, I don't *like it*," Mr. Wright said. "It's not your uniform!"

"That may be," Fanny retorted, "but if the world's coming to an end, I'm damn well not going to greet it in a maid's uniform."

Mr. Wright narrowed his eyes at her. "Where did you get that dress?"

"Lady Lizzy—"

"You *stole* from Lady Lizzy?" This from Mrs. Owen.

"You take that dress off this instant!" Mr. Wright commanded.

"This instant?" Fanny countered. "And what? Do you want to see me in my knickers?"

"No, of course not!"

"But you said—"

"What I meant was that you should leave this kitchen, go

to your own room, and *then* take off the dress."

"But it wasn't like that—I didn't *steal* anything. You know, there are always things they have put aside, things they've outgrown or are tired of; things they set aside that they might give to Agnes or Becky as a present come Christmas."

"You're not Agnes or Becky," Mr. Wright said, "and this is not Christmas."

"I do know that. But it wasn't anything she was going to be using anymore. As a matter of fact, when Lady Lizzy caught me—"

"Lady Lizzy *caught* you?" Mr. Wright said.

"Yes," Fanny replied, defiant. "And if you'd just let me finish, you'd know that when she did, she said it was fine for me to take it, that she was glad for me to have it, but did I by any chance have a spare pair of the black lace-up boots I always wear in the kitchen. She said Agnes and Becky's side-button shoes were pretty enough, but that mine were ever so much more practical and would I be willing to give her a spare pair of mine if I had one. Lady Lizzy said she thought they'd be more practical than anything she has for what might lie ahead."

"Lady Lizzy asked…" Mr. Wright shook his head, like a dog coming in from a downpour, like he'd had too much wine to drink and could no longer trust his own ears although, sadly, he'd had no wine.

"We *traded*, Mr. Wright," Fanny said. "Lady Lizzy and I *traded*. So everything is even-steven and there's no reason for you to—"

"Hullo!" a cheerful voice called out from the foot of the staircase that led to the Upstairs part of the house.

It was the duke.

"What a lovely dress you have on tonight, Fanny," he said.

"Thank you," she said, stunned.

"But I do think you'll want to lose the apron," the duke said thoughtfully.

"Lose the apron?" Mr. Wright said.

"Yes," the duke said. "I was thinking… While it's important for everyone upstairs to be armed, and to know how to properly use those arms, the servants need to be trained, too. We must ensure everyone's safety."

"You mean even me?" Mrs. Owen said, pointing at herself. "I've only ever strangled a chicken and then hacked its head off with a knife, but I've never fired a gun before."

"Which is why you must learn!" the duke said brightly, encouragingly.

"What is our world coming to?" Mr. Wright muttered uselessly, empty decanter in hand.

"Yes, well," the duke said, still brightly, "be that as it may." Then he turned to Fanny in her red dress. "I thought we'd start with you, Fanny."

The duke knew he shouldn't be thinking this, not with everything that had gone on and might yet go on. All right. Fine. *Would* go on. For there was little to no doubt that there would be some very dark days ahead. Days so dark, none of them might survive it all.

And yet…

And yet…

"This is so much *fun*!" he cried. "I can't remember a time I've ever had so much fun in an evening, not in my entire life!"

It was true.

His entire life, relatively short as it might have been when taken in comparison with someone like the earl or Mr. Wright,

had been positively Hobbesian if one were to only take out
the poor part, meaning it had been solitary, nasty, brutish,
and short.

Father dead very early. Mother as cold as a stone castle
in winter. A nanny who was only a touch warmer than that.
A series of governesses and tutors, coming to their home to
teach him all the things there was no father there to teach
him, none of them staying for very long—Mother was a hard
woman to work for. Then, starting in adolescence, being
trotted out to meet girls, potential mates, or having them
trotted in to meet him. None of those girls had ever shown
the slightest bit of interest, no matter how grand his home,
no matter how grand his title. Finally, coming here three days
ago—just three days ago! the mind reeled—with the last-ditch
hope of Lady Katherine.

Well, that hadn't exactly worked out.

So, to now, after all his solitary and brutish misery, not to
mention all the nasty sport other boys had made of him when
he was younger—what with his jug ears—and sometimes
when he was older, too; after all that, to find himself in this
room on the south side of the abbey, engaging in target
practice with Fanny; Fanny, whom, despite the seriousness
of their circumstances, seemed to be delighting in this as
much as he was—

"It's no laughing matter," a voice said; a voice that was,
clearly, not laughing.

Ah yes. Will Harvey was there as well. Too bad, that.

"Yes, I know it's not," the duke said. "I only meant—"

"This is serious business," Will said.

"Yes, I do know that, too," the duke said.

And the duke did know that.

No matter what Mother, others, and now Will thought of
him, the duke wasn't some silly simpleton.

He'd seen what had happened to Dr. Webb. Even if he hadn't really known Dr. Webb, it had still been awful. And he'd seen what had happened to poor Mr. Young, more awful still because he had gotten to know him a bit. Really, the whole thing was dreadful, almost too dreadful to contemplate. But you had to. You couldn't just put your head in the sand. There was too much at stake, and the duke knew exactly what was at stake: their entire way of life, the world as they had ever known it to be.

He knew what they could all lose if mistakes were made, like Dr. Webb had when he'd failed to take the initial death of Ezra Harvey seriously; like poor Mr. Young had when he'd stepped forward, misguidedly, to help Dr. Webb without any thought to his own risk. So of course you had to take it all very seriously. And yet he was finding that you couldn't let it overwhelm every second, consume your thoughts through every breath you took so that all became darkness and fear. Why, if one couldn't still take delight in the things that made life worth living, then what was the point in waging the battle at all?

No, he was not a simpleton. He'd been smart enough to choose Daniel to lead them, hadn't he?

Oh, how he wished Daniel could have come along to tutor him and Fanny instead. He knew Daniel would have taken it seriously, of course he would have, but he wouldn't have been quite so grim about it. Will Harvey, on the other hand...

But there'd been little choice in the matter. After all, they did need to permit Daniel to take a short break for some sustenance *sometimes*.

Still...

"You know," Will said to him, "you already have plenty of experience with guns, what with the hunting you lot do and all. Perhaps you should let Fanny give it a go?"

"Oh! Of course!"

The duke stepped away, stood off to one side as Fanny lifted the weapon, took aim.

"You know," the duke said, thoughtfully tapping his lower lip, "if left to my own devices, I'd have picked out something for you in a pastel: perhaps a soft pink or a pale yellow. But now that I've seen you in it, I find that bold red suits you right down to the ground."

Fanny didn't take her eye off the target, although the duke did note a blush coloring her cheeks. It was a pretty blush, but he wasn't so taken with it that he didn't feel the uncomfortable presence of other eyes.

"What?" he said, looking over to find Will staring back at him with disapproving eyes. "Nothing's so serious that a man can't pay a maiden a compliment, is it?"

"It is and you shouldn't."

"I'm sorry, I don't follow."

"It is that serious and you can't, not when you're a duke and the maiden in question is an actual maid."

What? The impertinence!

But was Will Harvey right? Should he not have said that? But it was true…

Now, though, it was Fanny's turn to cast disapproving eyes on someone. Much to the duke's surprise, the person she chose to cast them on was Will Harvey.

"Who died and put you in charge?" Fanny demanded.

"Daniel said—"

"That you were to train us. He didn't say anything about you having the right to tell other people what they can or can't say."

"Yes, but—"

"And if you didn't want him paying me a compliment, then

you should have thought to pay me one first yourself. I *do* look nice in this dress!"

Good show, Fanny!

Then Fanny hefted the rifle to her shoulder once more and blasted a hole in the tapestry, right where Will had told her to.

"Good show, Fanny!" the duke said, laughing as he clapped wildly. "Good show!"

W hat an extraordinary day it had been.

Daniel lay in his bed, reliving it.

It had really begun when he'd been summoned to the drawing room and been informed that he was to be some sort of leader. It had been a lot to take in—simply being invited to sit among them had been a lot to take in—and the wonders had only increased from there.

Sitting with Lady Katherine in the library, being invited by her—no, she'd *insisted* that he take the main place at the writing desk, while she pulled up a smaller chair beside his, watching as he drew up those plans, his ideas for the perimeter defense.

He hoped to set up that perimeter defense in the morning. It would take a while to dig all the trenches he wanted dug, but at least they could institute some sort of patrol system along the edges of the estate, using armed farmers and villagers. He'd have liked to get it done today, but there had been so many people to train in weaponry first.

There'd been Grace in the afternoon, of course. More a pleasure than a job, that, particularly when he'd put his arms around her from behind, felt her soft hands beneath his. Had she felt what he did? Then later, after Will had worked with Lady Lizzy and the duke, and after his own dinner, he and

Will had worked with some of the other servants.

Agnes and Becky had mostly giggled their way through it. This had clearly irked Will, who'd reminded them of how seriously they needed to take things. Daniel, on the one hand, agreed. Well, of course they should take the threat seriously. But what did Will want? That they take it so seriously that they move through the rest of their lives in a state of constant fear? Who would that help? Besides, it was nice to hear people just giggling, to hear Agnes and Becky just being girls.

Then it had been Jonathan's turn.

In the years they'd worked together, Jonathan had had no quarrel with Daniel, not even all those times Daniel had beaten him at cards. And yet he'd sounded a bit bitter when he said, "You were missed at dinner service this evening."

Well, of course Daniel hadn't been there. He wondered who had been there in his place. Had one of the maids, although maids never attended in the dining room, been pressed into service?

"Looks like you've misplaced your jacket," Jonathan said.

Daniel hadn't misplaced it, but he had removed it when he'd been drawing up plans for Lady Katherine—the buttons on his jacket kept banging against the side of the desk as he tried to write and it had been annoying. And later on, it felt only natural to remove his bow tie and collar, to roll up his sleeves when he began working with the weapons.

"Next thing you know," Jonathan said, "they'll have you eating dinner with them."

But they hadn't called him in to do that, nor had he eaten meals with the other servants as had always been his custom.

He ate alone.

Now Jonathan was making him feel bad about things that were not his fault, things beyond his control, and Jonathan was even bristling a bit as Daniel showed him how he wanted him to do things.

"I have shot one of these before," Jonathan said.

Will laughed from the side—at Daniel, Daniel felt.

"Of course you have," Daniel said, in a tone he hoped was polite, respectful. It was obvious Jonathan was feeling some jealousy; Daniel couldn't really blame him for it, and Daniel further didn't want to do anything to exacerbate the situation.

"Well, it's been a number of years," Jonathan added sheepishly, having discharged his weapon but hit far wide of his mark.

Now Will was laughing again, only this time it was at Jonathan's expense.

"You've worked so hard today," Daniel said to Will, still keeping the same polite tone he'd used with Jonathan. *God, I'm a great actor*, he told himself. *Used to be, I had to feign polite subservience for Upstairs. Now I have to feign polite solicitousness so as not to ruffle the feathers of Downstairs.* "Why don't you go on up? I can finish down here."

"And why don't you stop telling me what to do?" Will said.

Daniel felt as though he'd been slapped. "You don't like me very much, do you, Will?"

"I don't really know you *to* like you or not."

"Still."

"I suppose I just always thought, particularly after Lizzy invited me to come here, that when it finally came to it, *I* would have a more central role in things; a leading role, even."

"They did ask you to help, too, you know."

"Yes, to help *you*."

"You know, I didn't ask for this."

"Still." Will paused, his expression shifting from its usual state of proud stubbornness to one that was almost wistful. "I suppose, too, that I also thought, in a perfect world…"

"Yes?"

"I don't know. I suppose I thought things might be different in that perfect world." He gave a rueful laugh, falling just short of bitter. "Well, you know what they say."

"And that is?"

"If wishes were horses…"

"…beggars would ride."

Another rueful laugh, then: "Exactly."

"Well, perhaps in this new vastly imperfect world, we may yet get that chance."

Daniel smiled and was half shocked to see Will smile back at him.

"Why don't you go on up?" Daniel suggested again, more gently this time.

This time, Will went.

Despite that exchanged smile, that last good moment at the end, once Will was gone, the air almost immediately felt clearer. Daniel had never had much to do with Will in the past, before all this happened, but he'd always seemed to be a serious sort. Now, though, it appeared as though something more was going on, something deeper and beyond the petty jealousy both Will and Jonathan seemed to be experiencing, the kind that naturally follows when one of your own is suddenly raised a bit over you.

Daniel wondered how he'd feel if Jonathan—or, God forbid, Will—were suddenly granted leave to give him orders. He had to admit, he wouldn't like it.

Still, as the air cleared with Will's departure and, left alone, Jonathan and Daniel fell into their old ways together, Daniel decided that was something he'd need to make note of and watch out for.

Who could be depended on? And who might be…trouble?

Surprisingly, Lady Katherine had fallen into the former group. If at first she'd had a problem accepting that he might have more knowledge of a subject than someone high-born like Benedict Clarke did, once he'd demonstrated for her that he did have that knowledge, she'd been all ears. Indeed, it had been she who had warned him about one who surprisingly fell into the latter group.

Late in the afternoon, she'd pulled him aside and said, "I could be wrong, although I should point out that that never happens, but I do believe Father might not be entirely on board with the rearrangement of power in the house. You'll be careful, won't you? I know he doesn't mean any harm, but he can be disruptive."

He'd thanked her for telling him and left it at that. What else could he do? He couldn't argue with her. If he did, she'd no doubt get mad at him. And he couldn't outright agree with her, either, because then, even though she'd brought it up, she'd probably get offended on her father's behalf.

But he could see then that she was onto something.

And later, he could see that Will was someone he needed to look out for, too, because he was bothered by something on his mind and he was moody and he was Will. Jonathan also needed to be looked out for, because he was understandably jealous. And old Wright had to be looked out for, because some things never change.

If only they could all be as easy as the females had been: Lady Katherine, who'd been surprising in her agreeableness; Lady Lizzy, who it was impossible not to like; and Grace, whom he found it hard to stop thinking about, and so he had to force himself to do it.

Like when, as Jonathan was leaving the room, the dowager countess entered.

Even she was easier to deal with than some of the men.

"Hello?" she said. "Is this the place I am to report to for my military training?"

"I don't think it's necessary… That is to say, I don't think anyone means for you to…"

"Do not be ridiculous. Daniel, is it? Now, hand me a weapon. I will show you how it's done."

And she had.

Turned out, she was the best shot he'd had all day.

"*Oh!*" she said, placing one silk-gloved hand against her chest as she closed her eyes in what could only be described as a state of bliss. "That is the most fun I have had in years." She opened her eyes, looked into his. "Do you know how I do it?"

He shook his head.

"I simply picture the faces of my enemies, those people who annoy me most. Bull's-eye every time. The list is long, you know, and the opportunities to do something about it like this are far too few. I shall sleep with this pistol under my pillow tonight."

"I'm not sure that would be the safest place for it."

"My nightstand, then. Once armed, we should keep those arms close by at all times. Now then."

She turned to go, but he could see her falter a bit, perhaps done in by her exertions.

Without thinking, he offered his arm to her. With the exception of Grace, he'd never touched one of them before.

The dowager countess looked at the crooked elbow as though he were offering her a rotten piece of fruit.

"You know," she said, "I usually decline all offers of assistance. It does not do to give your enemies the idea that you've gone weak. I find that to be particularly true with Fidelia's father. That man rankles me so. Well, when he can manage to stay awake and remembers *to* rankle." Then she smiled. "But as the person attached to the arm is so handsome, how can I refuse?"

Then she slipped her right hand, pistol and all, into the crook, using her cane with her left.

"Where are we going?" he asked. He could see now, although she'd never admit it, she was tired, a little wobbly, too.

"Back to the drawing room. Let them see me arrive in style for once."

After conveying her there, he'd moved to leave them immediately, all of them dressed in their typical smart evening wear: white tie and black tail for the men, fancy dresses and fashionable accessories for the women, with the exception of the black lace-up boots on Lady Lizzy's feet.

"Won't you stay a bit, Daniel?" the earl called him back. "Please, do give us a report."

Daniel started to give one, and the earl even interjected with a few questions, but Daniel could tell he wasn't really listening to the answers, and then the earl cut him off with, "Yes, I'm sure you're doing a splendid job. Well! Tomorrow will be another big day for you. No doubt, you'll be wanting your bed now"—effectively dismissing him much as he'd tried to dismiss Will earlier.

"To the attic?" Lady Lizzy said.

"What, my dear?" the earl said.

"Will Daniel be sleeping in the attic?"

"Where else would he sleep?"

"Only, it doesn't seem quite fair, does it? Given all he's doing for us."

Daniel liked her for that.

"Come to think of it, why should anyone sleep in the attic?" Grace said. "It must get so hot up there in the summer."

And Daniel liked Grace even more then for that. She not only thought about him, whom she now knew, a bit, more than anyone in the house had ever known him really, but she also thought of the other servants, whom she did not know.

"Yes, well, then it is a good thing it is not summer," the earl said. "Good night, Daniel."

Daniel smiled in the darkness of his bedroom now. He'd been relieved the earl had settled the matter. While a nicer bed and a larger room would be, well, nicer and larger, it had been bad enough, earlier in the evening, when he'd eaten his dinner alone. It had been as though he were caught between worlds: not a part of Upstairs, although he was mixing with them now; no longer a part of Downstairs.

And yet somehow, responsible for all of them.

It was a lot, but he wouldn't shrink from that responsibility.

And tomorrow would be a new day.

CHAPTER
FORTY-NINE

If this menace had never come to Porthampton Abbey, Lizzy thought, looking down and admiring her feet, *perhaps I would have had to invent it. Otherwise, how would I ever have wound up with such a lovely pair of boots?*

The boots she had traded Fanny the red dress for were worn almost through in spots, but still, they were way more practical than the footwear Lizzy was typically expected to wear. Heeled satin shoes were fine enough for dancing, she supposed, but it wasn't like a person could get much else done while wearing them.

Now, if only she could persuade Father to let her wear some sort of trousers every day and not just when she went out riding, which didn't seem likely to happen anytime soon. Yes, now that she had these boots, trousers would be the next ticket for her. But where to find a pair in her size? It wasn't as though they'd be out shopping anytime soon, either. On the contrary, it seemed as though they might now be expected to spend the rest of their lives alternating between just their bedrooms to sleep, the dining room to eat, and the drawing room to talk, with no deviations.

In fact, the drawing room was where Lizzy found herself now, ruminating on her pleasing footwear and future clothing options. Another breakfast had passed, and now they were all engaged in another chat about what had been done and what still needed to be done.

She supposed she should be more focused on what was being said, but as interesting as this had all been in the beginning, it was tough to maintain an attitude of high alert at all times. Perhaps if she could practice more weaponry?

"Lizzy," Kate hissed from one side on the sofa, "I know your boots are a source of endless fascination for you, but do try to pay attention. This could be important."

Ouch.

"...so I was thinking that if we begin by setting up some farmers and villagers with guns on the west side of the estate," Daniel was saying, "and then space them out every—"

"Yes, yes, this is all very fascinating," Father said, clapping his hands against the arms of his chair, "and I'm sure you'll do an excellent job with it all. Now then. I do believe it's time for my daily walk."

Father could be so impetuous.

Lizzy knew people thought Kate took after Father, that they were of a similar nature, and she thought so, too. But she also thought that in this, his tendency to impetuosity, there was something of him in her, too. Whereas Grace—who knew who Grace took after? Still, even Lizzy could see that this wasn't a good idea.

And Kate, who so often disagreed with Lizzy—well, Kate disagreed often with everyone, really—clearly concurred.

"Father," Kate said, "not this again. You can't be serious!"

"Of course I can," he said, rising. "No matter what else is going on, we should not give up on the things that define us. We must not surrender our freedom. You don't expect me to remain cooped up, a prisoner in my own home forever, do you?"

It was as though Lizzy could see the gears of Father's brain cranking along: *We are British. We will not give in. We will have our daily walk. Otherwise, civilization is at an end.*

"Fine," Kate said, "you're serious. Then the problem is that you're not taking the threat seriously enough."

"Of course I'm taking things seriously! But would it help matters any for me to set fire to my hair and then run around like a scared little maniac screaming as flames fly off my head? We must go on. We can't give in."

"No one is suggesting that you give in, Father," Kate said, "only that you be sensible."

"Yes, you are suggesting I give in!" Father boomed. "You are suggesting I abandon our way of life, the only way of life I have ever known, and give in to fear. Did Henry the Fifth let fear stop him at Agincourt?"

"Of course not," Kate said, "but he did have an entire army with him."

"Well, then. What of King George and Queen Mary? Did they let a little thing like the Great War keep them from going out among their people? Did they give in to fear and stay cooped up inside their palace?"

"Actually," the duke put in, "that's pretty much exactly what they did."

"Fie on them, then! I should hope that when the next war comes, and there is always a next war, that whoever sits on the throne then will be brave enough, *British* enough, to leave the palace and go out among the people to offer them comfort, whatever the personal risks."

Actually, Lizzy thought, *I think* this *might be the next war.*

"But you're not talking about leaving the abbey to give comfort to anyone," Kate objected, clearly growing exasperated. "You're talking about taking a stupid walk."

"And are you suggesting," the duke said, "that you are somehow more British than King George and Queen Mary?"

"Huh," Father said reflectively. "I never thought of it like that, but I suppose I am."

Before anyone could say anything further, Mother rose, too.

"Good," Kate muttered under her breath to Lizzy. "Now she'll overrule him."

"Your father is right," Mother said, slipping one hand through the crook in his arm. She looked a little frightened as she said this, which in itself was shocking—when had Mother ever shown fear about anything?—but then her quavering, over-bright smile settled into a firm and steady one as she added with resolve, "If Martin says we should go for our daily walk, then we shall go for our daily walk."

For the first time, Father looked uncertain.

"You know, that's not necessary," he said, stumbling the words out. "I said that I would go, but I never meant to imply that you... That is to say..."

"Of course it is necessary." She patted his hand. "Where you go, I go."

"But it's sheer madness!" Kate objected.

"Martin," Grandmama said, "you know how I *hate* to point out the error in anyone else's ways..."

Lizzy couldn't prevent a snort at this startling announcement, and judging by the several similar noises she heard, others in the group couldn't, either.

"But I do feel the need to ask," Grandmama went on, "are you sure you're behaving quite sanely? Have you perhaps misplaced some of your marbles? If that is the case, I'm sure we'd all be most happy to help you hunt for them."

"Please," Mother said steely, "do not speak to your son in

that fashion." Then she turned to Kate. "Nor you your father."

Father looked as surprised as any of them. But then he patted the hand holding on to his arm as he said, "Thank you, Fee."

Lizzy hadn't heard Father call Mother that in a long time, it seemed, not since before all this started. "Fee" was something he'd always called her when particularly pleased with something she'd said or done, and it rang now as an old familiar.

Still, could no one stop Father?

As though all heads were attached to the same puppet master's strings, they swiveled as one now to face the duke.

The duke had stepped in once before, pulling rank to say that Daniel was a better choice to lead their military campaign than Cousin Benedict would be. Surely the duke would intervene now.

"What?" the duke said. "Don't look at me. Even if I thought it was madness, and I do, what can I say about it? It's still the man's home, it's still his castle. I only got involved before because there was a better choice to be made that involved all of us. But if he wants to walk, far be it from me to stop him."

"Thank you so much for your permission," Father said icily, with a sarcastic tilt of his head.

"At least wait until we've fully erected the perimeter defense," Daniel said.

"I will not wait," Father said petulantly. "I've already waited long enough."

"Then at least take a bodyguard with you," Kate said.

"An armed guard would be best," Lizzy added, thinking, *Perhaps I could do it?*

"Yes," Grace said. "Why not take Daniel?"

"I will not take *Daniel*!" Father shouted. He must have

realized how he sounded, for almost immediately he added with some impatience and a dismissive wave of the hand, "Daniel is busy. He has more important things to do now than stand attendance, escorting an old couple about as they stroll around their property."

"Well, you must take someone with you," Kate insisted.

Maybe me? Lizzy thought.

"I know!" Kate snapped her fingers. "The stable boy?"

Father opened his mouth, no doubt to object, as he'd objected to every sensible suggestion they'd made. But then he must have seen all their faces aligned against him and realized he had to make some sort of concession.

"Fine," he muttered at last with little grace. "We'll take the stable boy."

CHAPTER FIFTY

I f the earl didn't look like he wanted Will Harvey to accompany them out here as he and Her Ladyship took their little stroll, well, it wasn't as though Will exactly wanted to be there, either.

Normally Will loved to be outdoors, practically lived his life there, particularly on such a glorious day: a crisp, cold one, and with a sky overhead like a blue-and-white marble.

But he'd prefer not to be out there like this.

In one of their few unguarded moments together yesterday, Daniel had mentioned to Will that as a footman, he'd always felt like little more than wallpaper. Will had been surprised at this declaration. As the stable boy, he'd never felt that way. True, he was still a form of servant, but one people actually talked to and even showed respect for; whenever Lady Kate came to the stables, which was almost daily before this all started, even she deferred to his opinion if it was something to do with Wyndgate.

These fancy people needed him to care for their most highly prized animals, and they had a high regard for what he was able to accomplish. His job had been an important one, far bigger than that of someone whose role it was to convey a tray of tea safely from one area of the house to another. You could always get another footman, but you couldn't so easily replace someone who was a master with horses, someone like Will. In his job, Will had never felt like wallpaper before in his life.

But he felt like wallpaper now.

Trailing with his pistol, vigilant, behind these two married stiffs.

Marriage.

Over the years, Will had had occasion to see the earl and Her Ladyship together from time to time. Theirs had never impressed him as a real marriage, not like the one he'd observed all his life between Aunt Jess and Uncle Ezra—poor Uncle Ezra whom he'd not even had time to properly mourn yet.

Aunt Jess's and Uncle Ezra's lives had been bound together by hard work, mutual affection—no, not just mere affection; it had been love, a lifetime of it—and their joint desire to see Will healthy and happy in the world. But these two? What had they ever known or shown but stiff formality? Why, he doubted they even slept in the same bed.

"I do hate to see you worrying yourself about things you cannot change," Her Ladyship was saying now as she patted the earl's hand. "You can only do the best that you can do."

What was that?

Will had heard those words before, if less formally said. .

When there was some concern over something at the farm—would the crop come in on time? Was there some sort of blight?—Aunt Jess would always say, "Now, Ezra, I'll not have you worrying yourself sick. You've done your best and no one can ever say different."

Aunt Jess would offer Uncle Ezra comfort and he would take it. They were always a team against whatever the world might throw at them.

And then Uncle Ezra would thank her and kiss her, laying his lips on hers despite the little boy in the room.

And now the earl was thanking Her Ladyship, pressing his lips to hers, heedless of the young man standing guard behind them, heedless of Will.

Was it possible that these two were something more than just incredibly lucky and wealthy? Was it possible that these two loved each other, after all, were a team together against the world in the way that Aunt Jess and Uncle Ezra had been?

Later, Will would think, *If I hadn't been so shocked at the sight of them kissing...*

Later, Will would think, *If it had been a man — it had only ever been men who changed before...*

Later, Will would think, *If it had been anyone in the world other than Aunt Jess...*

Will heard the sounds before he saw the cause of it, rustling in the bushes, far off in the distance from Her Ladyship's side, and then the sound of feet.

He looked over to see three figures coming their way, two men and one woman, their clothes ragged, their hair wild, the woman's gray; not stumbling, but rather, running with only the slightest of hitches in their strides, the woman faster than the other two, as though despite that hitching stride she would race to him, to be reunited with him as fast as was humanly possible.

"Aunt Jess!" Will cried, realizing who the woman was, joyful — joyful! — and washed over with relief at finally seeing her again.

It had been so long; he had waited to see her again for *so* long.

In his excitement, he held his arms open wide for her embrace, dropping his pistol in the process.

But she ignored his open arms, and by the time he registered what he was really seeing—*not Aunt Jess, not like this*—the creature that had once been his closest living relative was practically flying like a wolf through the air toward Her Ladyship. The moment her feet had left the ground and before Will could properly react, the earl shoved his wife out of the way and to the grass, sheltering her body with his—much as Will had done with Kate, so long ago now it seemed—and on top of the earl's body thudded the form of Aunt Jess.

Will scrambled on the ground for his pistol, all the while keeping his eyes trained on the others as the earl writhed in an effort to escape the questing, snapping teeth of his attacker, even as he steadfastly protected his wife's body with his own—how the reeking stench poured off her—and the two men, the other two *creatures* drew closer. And now he had the pistol in hand once more, rising to his feet, and Will finally had his arm up and was shooting, once, twice, at the heads of both men who were only mere steps away before they too would reach the earl and Her Ladyship, and they were falling.

Then Will was pointing his arm downward, laying his gun against the creature's skull and cocking his pistol. At the sound, so close to its ear, the creature stopped and looked up at him, teeth bared, its expression a horrible gaping rictus, angry at being disturbed. Will saw the skin then, up close for the first time, an ashen gray color like nothing living. Still, he searched those eyes, hoping to find some remnant of the person he knew. But his search was in vain, for all that was there in that milky inhuman gaze was death and savage hunger.

With an anguished cry but a hand that never wavered, Will pulled the trigger, putting a bullet through the brain of the creature that had once been the only real mother he had ever known.

The sound of the shot rang deafening in his ears, the silence that followed still more so.

Then: "I think it is all right now, my dear," came the earl's muffled voice. "The danger has passed, thanks to Will."

The earl pushed the creature off him, off them, rolled off his wife and onto his back, looked up at the perfect sky. Her Ladyship pulled herself over to him, lay her head on his chest. Then the earl looked at her, regret filling his eyes.

"I am so sorry, Fee," the earl said. "I almost killed you with my foolishness."

"But then you saved me," Her Ladyship said, raising her head and smiling at him, "so now you are even with yourself." Then she lifted his hand toward her mouth, as though she would kiss forgiveness into him, but then stopped.

"Look," the earl said, seeing what Her Ladyship was, seeing what Will saw now, too: his ring finger, on the tip of which could now be seen a small set of bite marks. "That woman must've *bitten* me."

CHAPTER FIFTY-ONE

No matter how deep the emotions Will was feeling, a loss so vast and oceanic there would never be sufficient words to articulate it, he couldn't allow himself the luxury of the indulgence of those feelings. There could only be the sense of urgency to act, for he was responsible for these people.

Will couldn't believe what had happened, couldn't believe he'd been so careless.

He shot his eyes all around, looking for others, but none were in sight.

Still, how long could they expect to stay safe?

"Your Lordship," he said, trying to think of words that might seem kind to the older man, words that would not alarm him, "it's been a lovely walk, but now perhaps it's best that we get you and Her Ladyship inside."

"Yes, of course," the earl said, instantly agreeable. "Why didn't I think of that myself?"

He hurriedly rose to his feet, extending a hand gallantly down for his wife, but no sooner had she grasped on to it than he stumbled, his other hand going to his forehead.

"I feel…" he started to say.

"Oh, dear!" she said. "You look woozy!" Then to Will, "I think His Lordship has gone woozy."

She's so calm, Will thought, *so extraordinarily calm.*

But then, he remembered, he'd seen this woman cut off Mr. Young's head with a hatchet on Sunday night.

Her Ladyship shrugged her shoulder up under the earl's armpit to keep him from falling and put an arm around his waist. Then she started trying to walk with her burden. She stopped, looked at Will.

"Do you think you might help?" she said, not unkindly. "Perhaps if you were to take the other side?"

"Yes, of course, but then how will I…" Will held his pistol ineffectually in the air, the pistol that had done its job too little, too late.

"Here," she said, relieving him of it. "Why don't I take the pistol for now, while you take my husband?"

And then, to Will's astonishment, Her Ladyship provided cover from behind, as they made their way back to the abbey, His Lordship leaning heavily on Will.

How can she keep so extraordinarily calm, Will thought, *when surely, she must know…?*

The duke heard the commotion and raced with the others to find the earl, Her Ladyship, and Will Harvey now back inside the house.

"Father!" Grace cried. "You've been hurt!"

"What happened?" Lizzy cried.

"It's just a tiny wound," the earl said, raising a finger.

The duke saw that it was tiny, but he also saw that the earl looked bad. Somehow, even Mr. Young hadn't looked this bad after his encounter with Dr. Webb, and that attack had been far more severe than just a tiny finger wound.

"It was the damnedest thing," the earl said wonderingly. "Jessamine Harvey bit—"

Kate whirled on Will. "Your aunt did this to my father?"

The duke noted the hurt mixed with guilt in Will's eyes at this accusation, followed by a deep sadness.

"Stop that this instant," Father commanded Kate with some of his old energy. "It's not Will's fault. It's not anyone's fault, least of all Jessamine Harvey's." He paused. "You could say that when we encountered her, the poor woman wasn't herself."

The duke marveled that he could still make what amounted to some sort of joke at a time like this.

"It's not even her fault what happened to my clothing," the earl said, looking down at his garments, which appeared to have grass and mud stains all over them. "I would like to change, and then perhaps I should have a bit of a lie-down. Wright, do you mind? I know it's not your duty, it's more properly Mr. Cox's job, but—"

"It would be my honor, Your Lordship," Mr. Wright said, and the duke could have sworn he saw a tear form in the butler's eye as he relieved Will Harvey of his place in carrying the burden, proceeding to help the earl up the grand staircase.

Fanny watched Mrs. Owen hustling and bustling all over the kitchen.

"I'm not sure what they'll be wanting," Mrs. Owen muttered to herself as she opened the refrigerator, went through cupboard after cupboard. "Perhaps some sorrel soup… Maybe some lamb… Oh, what did I feed them all for dinner last night?"

"I don't even know why you're bothering," Fanny said, feeling Henry Clay thread his way in and out between her feet.

"What does that mean?" Mrs. Owen demanded.

Fanny couldn't figure out what she'd done wrong this time. "Only, I can't imagine any of them will be hurrying to have their luncheon now, that they'd care what was served or even want it at all."

"Is that all this is to you?" Mrs. Owen said. "A chance to get away with a little less work?"

"I never said…!"

Now Mrs. Owen had burst into tears.

"Mrs. Owen? Why are you crying?"

"I'm crying for *him*!"

"Him, who?"

"The earl, you stupid ninny!"

"You're crying for…*the earl*?"

"Who else would I be crying for?"

"It's just that…he's just…"

"He's not *just* anything! And he's more than *just* the man who's employed me my whole working life. Fanny, the earl is *a person*!"

"You know," Father said to Kate, "you mustn't be too hard on Will. Jessamine Harvey was more than just a tenant farmer, more than just a worker on my land. Why, she and Ezra were at Porthampton Abbey their entire adult lives. Jessamine Harvey was a person."

Some person, Kate thought, while outwardly she agreed

brightly. "Of course, Father. Whatever you say."

"Whatever I say?" Father reared back against the fluffed pillows in mock horror. "I know things can never be too good when people start telling me, 'Whatever you say.'"

"Stop, Father." Kate laughed, but even to her own ears it rang false. "You know you've always been in charge of this house."

"Yes," he said softly. "Yes, I have."

After Mr. Wright had conveyed Father upstairs to his room and helped him change there, he'd returned to them.

"His Lordship has decided he needs a little rest," Mr. Wright had said, clearly striving to appear his usual officious self when anyone could see the tears in his eyes. "But first, he should like everyone to go up and see him," adding, "*just* the family," when the duke had moved to follow.

Grandmama had placed one foot on the grand staircase, but then turned. "Daniel, might you help an old woman out here?" and Daniel had hurried to her side, offering his arm.

Then they'd all gone up and found Father in his nightshirt, sheets pulled up, back against the headboard.

"I'm so sorry," he had said to Rowena Clarke. "You came for a nice weekend, but then you got a little more than what you bargained for, didn't you?" And to Benedict, seemingly out of nowhere, he added, "If I'd ever had a son, I imagine I could have done far worse than you."

Now Rowena Clarke and Cousin Benedict were gone; Daniel, too, but not before Father had told him, "Thank you, Daniel, for everything." Kate saw Daniel pause in the doorway and look back at Grace with concern, but Grace hadn't noticed. She was too busy looking at Father.

Now it was just the immediate family at his bedside, Kate and her two sisters on one side, Mother and Grandmama on the other.

"Right!" Father said brightly. "Well, I suppose we all know

what must happen next."

Happen next? What was he talking about?

But before Kate could ask, Mother was leaning over him, pressing her forehead to his and closing her eyes tight before laying a kiss on his forehead.

"If it's all the same to you," she said, "I think I'll go lie down myself for a bit."

"Of course, Fee," Father said. "We'll see each other again… shortly."

Mother was gone and now Grandmama was saying, "You've always had such a strong sense of duty, Martin. I don't know if he ever got a chance to tell you himself, but I know that your father was proud of you, as am I."

"Thank you, Mother," Father said, closing his eyes briefly as she, too, laid a kiss on his forehead before moving to leave.

"Do you need help?" Grace called after her as she tottered away on her cane.

"Not at all," Grandmama said, waving a hand in the air but not bothering to turn back. "I have always found that it is far easier going down again than it ever is going up. You girls stay."

And then it was just the four of them.

"We all know what must happen next," Father said again. What did he…

"Father," Kate said, realization dawning, "you can't possibly mean—"

"Someone must shoot me," he said, quite calmly, quite cheerfully even, as though he were simply saying, *Yes, some cherries for dessert would be lovely.*

"No!" Kate cried, and her sisters cried with her. They'd agreed on little in life, but at last they were in agreement on this.

"We saw what happened to poor Mr. Young," Father said.

Clearly, he would demand to be heard on this, no matter that what he was saying amounted to sheer madness. He was still living. He was still breathing. How could he expect any member of the household to just shoot him dead?

"We know what will happen here," Father went on, relentless. "I will die. Then I will come back, a threat to my own family. That cannot be allowed to happen. I cannot bear the thought that I might one day bring harm to that which I hold most dear."

There had been moments when Kate had taken what was happening to them seriously, and moments when she had not. Maybe that was because it hadn't always been entirely real to her before.

Well, it was real to her now.

Kate knew people didn't believe she had a heart. There were times she doubted it, too. But she'd always known that it was in there, somewhere, beating inside her.

And that heart was breaking now.

"Look," Father said, still calm, still reasonable, still so bloody cheerful. "I could ask Wright. He's never said no to me about anything in his life, not that one would expect him to. I'm sure he wouldn't pick today, of all days, to start. But it doesn't feel quite correct to do that, do you know what I mean?"

Lizzy found that she didn't want to know what he meant. And yet unwilling or not, she kind of did know.

"I can't do it, Father!" Kate cried, a trembling hand covering her mouth. "I want to help you, always, I want to do whatever you ask of me... But I love you! I love you too much!"

"Yes," Father said, a touch sadly now, "I suppose I knew that. But the duke or Daniel? That doesn't seem quite cricket, either, does it? The one is our guest and the other, well, I think we have all asked too much of Daniel already. Certainly, we have asked too much of Will." He paused, musing. "I suppose I could do it myself, but what if I made a cock-up of things, as I am sometimes wont to do. Think of how much worse *that* would be for everybody! Someone else would still need to come along, finish the job."

How? Lizzy wondered. *How can he be so bloody cheerful about it all?* In his own way, she supposed he'd been right: he really was more British than the king.

"But what about a cure?" Lizzy said, desperately seeking some small hope. "Surely a cure will be found!"

"You know," Father said thoughtfully, a hopeful gleam in his eyes, "I think you may be right! Just because Dr. Webb is gone, it doesn't mean that there aren't other doctors left in the world. And if this has been going on here, it might be going on elsewhere, too, and perhaps doctors in those places are already working at it. Eventually, there's always a cure discovered for everything, isn't there?"

Although it had originally been her idea, it occurred to Lizzy then that this might not be entirely true, that last part. Was there always a cure? For everything? Lizzy didn't think so.

"Or," Father said, more hopeful still, "that Daniel is so resourceful, knowing about tourniquets and all, and even our Fanny, when she was helping with poor Mr. Young, she seemed to know a thing or two about nursing. Perhaps the footman and the maid will come up with a cure!"

"Yes, Father," Kate said eagerly.

"You must hang on," Grace implored.

"I'm afraid I can't, my dears," Father said, sighing. "I'm afraid that any cure, if and when it comes, will be too late for me. You must be strong in this."

"But why?" Lizzy said. "Why must it be so soon? Why can we not just…wait?"

"Because," Father said, "just as those who attacked your mother and myself appeared to move more quickly than Dr. Webb or poor Mr. Young did—perhaps since it had been longer since they had been infected with the disease themselves and so it had longer to work on their bodies?— my wound, although small, appears to be affecting me more rapidly than Mr. Young's did him."

Lizzy could see the wisdom in what he was saying. She might not be a doctor, none of them were, but it did make medical sense. Still…

"You can kill me now, Lizzy," Father said, "or you can kill me later. And if given the choice, I vastly prefer that you do it now, before I have the opportunity to become a monster to you all. You're the only one who's shot and killed anyone before. Will you do it, Lizzy?"

Would she?

Could she?

Yes, she'd shot and killed before, twice: first, the valet Parker; and, later on, Dr. Webb. But the former had been about to attack Kate and then her when she did it, while the latter had been actually chewing on poor Mr. Young. Those had been life-or-death situations. There had been immediacy, urgency, someone had to act quickly. And those people, or whatever they were, hadn't been *Father*.

Lizzy wanted to be brave, and thought she was. She wanted to be smart, too, and she knew that what he said made sense.

But…

"I can't!" Lizzy cried, much as Kate had done before her, and then she threw herself, sobbing, against Father's chest.

"I know," he said softly, stroking her back. "It is a lot to ask of you girls."

Then: "That leaves you, Grace," Father said.

Daniel was in the library, alone, when Grace walked in, causing him to look up from his plans for the perimeter defense.

"Oh, hello!" he said, smiling at the simple sight of her as he rose up from his chair. Then, remembering what had happened that day, he felt the smile leave his face.

"It's all right," she said, approaching. "It's all right to smile sometimes. After all, what good does it do anyone for us to be miserable forever?"

As she spoke, she kept walking toward him until she was standing right in front of him, nearly as close as she'd been when they danced.

"If we get out of here alive," she said in a wondering voice, "what will you do?"

"Do?"

"Yes. I don't think you can be a footman anymore."

He considered. "I think I'd like to be an actor."

"An actor?" She laughed, and it was a beautiful sound to him.

"Yes," he said. "For the longest time now, I've been thinking I'd be a very good one."

"You do, do you?"

He nodded.

"That's funny," she said, "because right now, you seem like you would be a very bad one."

"And why do you say that?"

"Because you want to kiss me right now, don't you? I can see it in your eyes."

Did he?

And did it show so badly that she could see it?

Without allowing himself to think of all the reasons this might be a very bad idea, he lowered his head, his mouth, laid his lips gently against hers.

A part of him must have expected some kind of resistance, or to be told that this was some sort of joke at his expense. But then he felt her lips, pressing back against his—if anything, more fervently than his lips; felt her arms go around him as she pressed her body to his, opening her mouth to him.

He wrapped his arms around her, tight.

In five days of increasingly extraordinary events, this was, perhaps, the most extraordinary of all.

At last, she pulled away a bit, ending the kiss.

Daniel could see now that there were tears in her eyes, even though she was smiling at him.

She pressed her forehead to his briefly and closed her eyes, and so he closed his, too.

Let this moment, Daniel thought, feeling the softness of her within his arms, *go on forever*.

Then he experienced the sensation of being watched, and when he opened his eyes, he saw her looking back at him.

"Daniel," she said, "there's something I need you to help me with."

"Anything," he found himself promising.

"Merry died, so horribly. I need to be strong now, because no one else can do this. I can't let another person I love die in the same way."

• • •

Earlier, Grace had asked Kate and Lizzy if they could stay, sitting with Father, for just a little while.

Of course they'd said yes.

"Don't be too long, Grace," Father had cautioned. "If you can't—"

"I won't, Father," she'd said. "I promise."

Then she'd gone to find Daniel.

And had kissed Daniel, a sensation so wonderful, unlike anything she'd ever experienced, she would've given all she had if only she could have remained living in that moment forever.

But she knew such a luxury of time was impossible, so instead she had asked Daniel to get her a pistol and then show her how and where to fire it at a man to ensure he did not feel any pain nor would he survive.

Now Grace was back.

The object she'd brought with her was clasped between both hands, but she held those hands behind her back, concealing the object from their view.

"Grace?" Kate asked in a wavering voice. "Show me your hands. What are you hiding back there?"

But when Grace neither obeyed nor answered—she doubted she could speak to her sisters right then if her life depended on it—both her sisters cried harder. In five days of increasingly awful events, this was the most horrifying moment yet.

"That's enough of that now," Father said, one daughter in each arm, patting both their backs simultaneously. "Off you two go."

Kate and Lizzy each kissed one of his cheeks and then,

sobbing, with arms around each other's waists and without a glance at Grace, they fled the room.

Now it was just the two of them.

"It won't be so bad, Grace," he reassured her.

"Of course not," she said, forcing a smile, while inside she thought, *It will be awful. It will be so awful, I don't know how I can possibly bear it.* And: *What if I let you down?*

Then she felt the tears filling her eyes—she couldn't have held them back if she tried, no matter how dearly she wished she could be brave for him, just this once. Her eyes filled with tears until her vision swam with them.

"I love you, Father," she managed to say, "*so* very much."

She let her left hand fall away from the object so it was only her right hand holding it behind her back now, and she told herself it wasn't even there as she approached him.

"And I you, my dear," Father said. "Now, come on, get it over with! Why, it won't be so bad at all! One moment, I will be here, and the next"—here he turned away from her, onto his side, focusing his gaze on the far wall—"I will be in heaven, where one day, although I hope it won't come too soon, I shall be reunited with you all, and—"

Grace pulled the trigger.

CHAPTER
FIFTY–TWO

Kate had tried to get, along with Lizzy, as far away from Father's bedroom as possible. But there was nowhere in the house far enough to be safe from the sound of that gunshot ringing out. And as soon as she heard it, unthinking, she found herself racing back the way she had come.

They all came running.

Kate arrived first, just in time to see Grace step out of the room, the arm holding the gun now dormant at her side.

"It's finished, then?" Kate said, even though she needn't have.

Anyone looking at Grace, with the blood spatter on her clothes, her hair, some on her face even, couldn't have mistaken that it was finished.

What had they all expected? It was never going to be like it had been with *them*: a shot to the brain, a beheading with a blade, and little mess or fuss afterward to clean away, save for severed body parts. But no blood. Nothing like this.

But Father had still been a living, breathing human being when Grace shot him. So what could they have expected?

And what did Grace expect from them now?

For, without meeting anyone's eyes, Grace nodded curtly and, gaze cast downward, moved to slink past them.

What did Grace think? That they would revile her? That she would become a pariah now among them?

Kate stepped forward, unwilling to let Grace pass. Then, gently, she removed the pistol from Grace's hand and, more gently still, folded Grace in her arms.

"Thank you, Grace," Kate whispered in her ear. "Thank you for doing what I could never do."

Then Kate released Grace, and it was Lizzy's turn to embrace and thank their sister. And finally, Mother, laying her face against Grace's and whispering, "Thank you, my dear, dear girl."

And then when Mother was finished, when the whole family was finished with Grace, Kate watched in wonder as Daniel stepped forward with his arms outstretched and even greater wonder as Grace fell into his arms.

Kate would think about *that* later.

But for now: "So," Kate said to those assembled, feeling as though she might be addressing the whole world, "what do we need to do next?"

CHAPTER
FIFTY-THREE

A funeral was in order.

That's what had been decided.

Martin Clarke was not someone like the valet Parker, to be stepped over; or Dr. Webb, to be left where he fell; or poor Mr. Young, to be hastily disposed of. Martin Clarke was the Earl of Porthampton Abbey, and as such, he deserved a proper burial, no matter what it took to achieve one, no matter what the risks involved.

"It's such a shame," Mother said to her father, daughters, and mother-in-law, who were assembled with her in the library. "To have so few people. I'm sure, if they could, the entire village would want to turn out for Martin, to pay their respects."

None of them said what they were thinking: Who knew how many people were left in the village now, or what condition those remaining might be in?

"Well," Mother said with a shrug, "there's nothing to be done about it now. We have who we have, and that shall have to be enough. The whole household will be there, the servants, too, of course. I'm sure that Martin would appreciate that everyone who mattered most to him will be in attendance."

"Surely," Kate said, "you don't mean that *all* the servants are to be included."

"Who," Mother said, "are you suggesting we leave out?"

"Why, the stable boy, of course! It's his fault, by way of his aunt, that Father is—"

"It's not his fault," Grace said, "nor his aunt's, either. What happened to her could have happened to anybody. It would have eventually happened to Father if..."

She let the thought trail off, and no one bothered to finish it.

"It could still happen to any of us," Lizzy said. "And stop calling him that, Kate!"

"What?"

"'The stable boy!' 'The stable boy!'" Lizzy made a sound of disgust, something she rarely did. "Why must you keep calling him that? He has a name, that name is Will Harvey, and he's a person!"

"So-*rry*," Kate said.

"Your sisters are right, Kate," Mother said. "Further, we should have a service for Jessamine Harvey as well."

"Surely, Mother," Kate said, "you must be joking."

"Surely, Kate, I am not. Will Harvey is a member of this household now—everyone currently under this roof is—and as such, he is as much entitled to see his relative properly laid to rest as we are your father."

"Don't you think, Kate," Grace said, "that it was just as hard for Will Harvey to do what he did as it was for me to do what I did? What you couldn't bring yourself to do?"

"Perhaps—"

"Enough, Katherine!" Grandmama's voice rang out. "You must listen to your mother, who, I might add, is doing a fine job of managing things." She turned to Fidelia. "You know, my dear, Martin only ever wanted you to be beautiful and happy. I hope you will find a way to still be both."

"For once," Grandfather said, "Hortense is right, and I quite agree with her."

"Thank you," Mother said, briefly covering her mother-in-law's wrinkled hand with her own still pretty one before going on. "Now, then! What things need to be attended to? We'll have to find proper attire for Benedict and Rowena. I doubt our new cousins thought to bring mourning clothes when they came for a weekend…"

Daniel and Jonathan went to the barn, and there they worked together to create a box in which His Lordship might be laid. He should have had a proper coffin—the finest in the land!—perhaps a rich mahogany, elaborately carved, with gold fittings or, at the very least, brass. Instead, he would need to settle for a simple pine box, plain as could be, even a bit misshapen due to the need for haste.

Back at the house, the earl was wrapped in a shroud and laid in it, the top of the box then closed, for no one would want to look who didn't have to.

Daniel, Jonathan, the duke, Benedict, Mr. Wright, and Mr. Cox then bore the box down the grand staircase, and the others followed them out as His Lordship left the abbey for the last time.

It was a cruelly beautiful day for November as they stood on the lawn, the family, servants, and the duke ringing the rectangular hole that had been dug in the ground.

Surrounding that group stood a second line of people: the farmers and villagers who had come to live at the abbey for now, their backs to those lining the hole in the ground. The farmers and villagers all held weapons in their hands as they faced outward, on the lookout for any threats that might come to disturb the peace.

Benedict and Rowena Clarke stood in their borrowed mourning clothes.

Grandmama leaned stoically, both hands on the head of her cane, dry-eyed. Let the others cry. Indeed, most of them did. She had shed tears for her son when she left him earlier in the day and then later when the shot had rung out. She would not cry again.

The duke swallowed, several times, thinking someone should say something, but not knowing who that person might be or what could possibly be said.

Lizzy and Kate stood on either side of Mother.

The walk would have been too far for Grandfather, who had remained behind.

When Daniel stepped to Grace's side and she put her hand in his, no one said a word about it, not even Mr. Wright.

Will Harvey stood apart from everybody.

There was no vicar to say anything. Martin Clarke had performed that role in the little church on Sunday, but who was there now to perform that role for him? Who was there to hold everything together now that the earl—the head of the family, the spirit of the abbey, the heart of the entire community—was no longer with them? And who would these people be without him?

"Well, my dear," Fidelia said, "you always did your best to show me a good life, and no one can say that it hasn't been one."

• • •

Later, sometime after Her Ladyship spoke her one sentence and the earl had been covered with dirt, Will was surprised when, rather than leaving him to bury his aunt by himself, all of them—every single one—accompanied him to another part of the property.

Will was surprised, and pleased.

And he was beyond touched when Lady Kate put her gloved hand over his and gave it a sympathetic squeeze.

He was about to thank her for the kind gesture, when she leaned closer and, in a whisper no one else could hear, said, "*Horsey.*"

He drew back, looked at those startling blue eyes in wonder. "You remembered," he said.

"I never forgot."

Still later, in the kitchen, Fanny put her small hand on the shoulder of Mrs. Owen, who was still sobbing.

"Don't you worry about anything," Fanny told her. "I know the family and their guests will be needing their luncheon. But you just go on ahead and cry all you need to. I'll see to everything."

And then Fanny did just that, pausing from her labors just one time to take out some kippers and put them on a simple plate.

"There you go," she said to Rosencrantz and Guildenstern, as she set the plate on the floor. "His Lordship would want you to have these. You, too, Henry Clay."

. . .

At the funeral luncheon, they all spoke of the earl.

They talked about all the things he had been to them: kind, irascible, funny, charming, impulsive, difficult, generous, stubborn, childish, wise, *changeable*.

"As changeable as the weather," Mother said fondly. "If I didn't like one of his moods, it hardly mattered—wait, and a different mood would be along in a minute or two." She sighed. "He was my life."

After the food had been eaten and the wine drunk, and the conversation had died down, Mother took to her bed.

CHAPTER FIFTY-FOUR

"Mother," Kate said, sitting down on the edge of the high canopied bed, "you've been such a rock through all this, you can't let me down now."

"What else is there that you want me to do?"

"Why, take charge of things, of course! Keep doing what you have been doing so well. With Father gone—"

"All your father ever wanted me to do was look beautiful and be happy."

"And you can still do those things! But you can also—"

"And with your father gone, Cousin Benedict inherits the estate. You know, Kate, what your father hoped, once he discovered Benedict's existence, was that the two of you might marry."

"Yes," Kate said drily, "I had figured that part out. And is that what you want for me, too, Mother?"

"No," she said, surprising Kate. "Unless at some point you decide that you love Benedict, that's not what I want for you at all."

"Then what do you want?"

"I am content to be what I am, what I have always been." She paused. "But I want more for you, Kate."

Kate considered this, what this *more* might consist of.

Then she rose from her place, crossed the room, and yanked on the pull cord, causing a bell to ring far away from where she stood.

"You rang?" Mr. Wright said, entering a short time later.

"Mr. Wright," Kate said, "I wondered if you might do something for me?"

"For you, my lady, anything."

Mr. Wright would never be Father—no one could be— but he'd always been so devoted to her, and for this she was grateful. Indeed, she was devoted to him as well. In a way, he was her responsibility now.

"Good," she said, smiling. "Please summon the rest of the family, including our new cousins, and the duke, Daniel, and Will Harvey, too. Tell them all I'd like to see them in the library."

"What is it," Grandmama said, "that couldn't wait until morning?"

"Do we really need to have yet another meeting now?" Lizzy said.

"Daniel's already set up the perimeter defense," Grace said. "There are guards out there right now, protecting us even as we speak."

Yes, Daniel had been useful, and Kate was grateful to him for it. His ideas had been excellent, even if they'd been enacted too late to save Father, but ideas weren't everything. And while military knowledge was a fine thing—the world would always have need of great generals—it wasn't all that was needed or even the most important thing.

"Don't worry, Grandmama," Kate said, not bothering to

respond to either of her sisters' comments. "This shouldn't take long."

"But what exactly is this *this* of which you speak?" Grandmama said.

"I would never have dreamed such a thing possible," Grandfather said, "but now Hortense has been right twice in a single day—the world must be tilting farther on its axis! What is this *this*, Kate?"

"*This* is deciding who is to run Porthampton Abbey now that Father is gone."

"He's been dead less than a day!" Grace objected.

"Yes," Kate said coolly. "I am aware of that. But if we don't act quickly and smartly, we might all be dead before too much longer passes. Or worse."

"Who did you have in mind?" the duke asked.

Kate narrowed her eyes at him. Was he suggesting that he be the one? He had stepped forward, after all, taking the reins from Father once before. But then, Father had needed the reins taken away from him. She, however, wasn't Father. She found, though, no guile in the duke's eyes. He simply wanted to know.

"Why," Rowena Clarke spoke up, "I should think it would be obvious."

"Is it?" Kate said.

"Of course. With your father deceased, Benedict inherits the estate. He is in charge now. It is what the entail dictates."

"And who is there here to enforce that entail?"

"Pardon?"

"Do you see any lawyers here? Judges? Is the king, perhaps, hiding under your skirt?"

"I'm afraid I don't understand all of what you're saying," Rowena Clarke said huffily, "but what I am understanding, I do not like."

"Too bad."

"It's all right, Mother," Benedict said genially. Ever genial, was Cousin Benedict. "I think I see where Cousin Kate is going with this. And truth to tell, I don't want Porthampton Abbey."

"You don't?" Grandmama said, sounding grossly offended.

"No," Benedict said. "Naturally, when I came here on Friday, I was all set to claim it...*someday*. Although I never suspected someday would come so soon and certainly not like this, nor would I want it like this. It's not mine to lead."

That's good, Kate thought, *because I'd never have let you take it anyway, not now.*

"If not yours," Grandmama said to Benedict, "then whose?"

Kate glanced over at Will and saw him looking straight back at her. She hadn't told him what she planned to do. Why would she? And how could she, since she'd only just come up with the idea a few moments ago when she'd been upstairs with Mother? And yet somehow, instinctively, he knew, for he tilted his head toward her in a nod that could only be seen as approving agreement.

The others waited. And while they waited, Kate thought.

She thought about how lucky they'd been so far, if you could use the word "lucky" about a series of events and circumstances that had also included the death of Father. But yes, lucky. So far, they'd mostly only been attacked by stragglers. But three at once had attacked Father, and more would come. More would find them there. And soon. It was just a matter of time.

She thought about how, just a few days ago, her concerns in life had been the possibilities of love and marriage and the entail looming on the horizon. She almost laughed at the quaintness of it all: *the entail.*

"I wonder," she said thoughtfully, "if it will prove to be true, what they say: that uneasy lies the head that wears the crown."

The others looked at her.

"What does *that* mean?" Grandmama said.

Kate looked back at them.

She thought about the awesome duty and responsibility of it all: being responsible for all the people—and they were all people—living under her roof.

"It means that Porthampton Abbey is at war," Kate finally said. "It means that I am in charge now."

ACKNOWLEDGMENTS

Thanks are due to the following:

Stacy Abrams, for being a smart and delightful editor

Everyone at Entangled Publishing, for also being smart and delightful

Greg Logsted and Jackie Logsted, for being as amazing at being first readers as they are at being husband and daughter

Yoyo—*Mister* Yoyo Kitty to strangers—for being the purrfect inspiration for Henry Clay

Booksellers, librarians, teachers, reviewers, and readers everywhere, without whom none of this works

Grab the Entangled Teen releases readers are talking about!

Risen
by Cole Gibsen

My aunt has been kidnapped by vampires, and it's up to me to save her. Only…I had no idea vampires existed. None. Nada. I'm more of a reader than a fighter, and even though I'd been wishing to escape my boring existence in the middle of nowhere, I'd give anything to have it back now if it meant my aunt was safe.

Then there's the vampire Sebastian, who seems slightly nicer than most of the bloodsuckers I've run into so far. Yes, he's the hottest being I've ever come across, but there's no way I can trust him. He swears he's helping me get answers, but there's more to his story. Now I'm a key pawn in a raging vampire war, and I need to pick the right ally.

But my chances of surviving this war are slim at best, when the side I choose might be the one that wants me dead the most.

The November Girl
by Lydia Kang

I'm Anda, and the lake is my mother. I am the November storms that terrify sailors, and with their deaths, I keep the island alive.

Hector has come to Isle Royale to hide. My little island on Lake Superior is shut down for the winter, and there's no one here but me. And now him.

Hector is running from the violence in his life, but violence runs through my veins. I should send him away. But I'm half-human, too, and Hector makes me want to listen to my foolish, half-human heart. And if do, I can't protect him from the storms coming for us.

Black Bird of the Gallows
by Meg Kassel

A simple but forgotten truth: where harbingers of death appear, the morgues will soon be full.

Angie Dovage can tell there's more to Reece Fernandez than just the tall, brooding athlete who has her classmates swooning, but she can't imagine his presence signals a tragedy that will devastate her small town. When something supernatural tries to attack her, Angie is thrown into a battle between good and evil she never saw coming. Right in the center of it is Reece—and he's not human.

What's more, she knows something most don't. That the secrets her town holds could kill them all. But that's only half as dangerous as falling in love with a harbinger of death.

Assassin of Truths
by Brenda Drake

The gateways linking the great libraries of the world don't require a library card, but they do harbor incredible dangers.

And it's not your normal bump-in-the- night kind. The threats Gia Kearns faces are the kind with sharp teeth and knifelike claws. The kind that include an evil wizard hell-bent on taking her down.

Gia can end his devious plan, but only if she recovers seven keys hidden throughout the world's most beautiful libraries. And then figures out exactly what to do with them.

The last thing she needs is a distraction in the form of falling in love. But when an impossible evil is unleashed, love might be the only thing left to help Gia save the world.

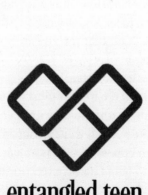

entangled teen

an imprint of Entangled Publishing LLC